Merie Vision Publishing, LLC
www.merievisionpublishing.com

ISBN: 978-1-961213-37-1

Library of Congress Control Number on record

Book Cover Design by Caci Wallace

Book Design and Editing by Merie Vision Publishing

First Print Edition March 2024

2 3 4 5 6

Under The Apex

B. A. Harris

To my two best readers, Caci and Samm.
You guys begged for more and kept me going and
believing in myself.
~B

Chapter 1

*M*oving to Germany was probably the best idea I have ever had. Sure, dropping everything at 30 years old and moving to a new country when you don't speak their native tongue is not everyone's idea of a good time. But for me, it was the best choice out of any of the remotely appealing options of change I'd come up with.

"Samantha, I don't see why you just don't join the pack."

I knew I was in trouble when my closest and only friend back home in the Midwestern Region of the United States, Luna, used my actual name instead of Sammy or Bob.

"You're moving off to the middle of nowhere Germany to do what? Hide in plain sight?!"

"Luna," I heaved out a sigh, "at the risk of sounding like every whiny teenager ever,
you just don't get it."

When I spoke as if no one understood me, it always made her roll her eyes, in which this case was no exception.

"You're *part* of the pack that you're trying to get me to join. The pack that, by the way, is full of nothing but canines."

I tried to keep the sound of annoyance out of my voice when I said "canines". Luna and the entire pack were different species of Canidae shifters. On the other hand, I was a Felidae, a Bobcat-type Lynx to be more specific. Typically, this would work out in my favor when out on "camping trips" as the Bobcat was native to my region, and I was quieter than most of their heavy-footed canine species.

Luna always tried to be sensitive to my plight of being one of the few feline shifters in the region; however, being a Coyote, she was a pack-oriented creature. I loved and craved solitude. Us felines always ended up living in the same region, exchanging niceties and helping each other when needed, but didn't seem to truly form packs.

"So, what you're trying to say is to avoid joining a pack of slobbering dogs, you're going to move 5,000 miles away from me." She wasn't trying to hide the hurt in her eyes or voice this time.

" I echnically... it's just over 4,700," I said, which was rather unhelpful apparently. I immediately knew I had made a grave mistake.

Luna had just about blown a gasket at my nonchalant attempt at a joke. Usually, she was incredibly tolerant of my inability to take anything seriously, and my need to lighten the mood using inappropriate humor. This was not one of those times. Her face had turned a funny shade of purple, and the strings of words she was barely forming were coming out so fast and with such heat that I could almost feel it on my face.

I interrupted her rant on her best friend leaving her to get away from her and her kind, "Luna! You're not listening!"

Being accused of being inattentive always got her attention as she really was one of the best, most kind, individuals I'd ever met in my life.

"I don't have any family left besides you. I don't have any friends besides you." Already an isolated creature by nature, I had isolated myself even further to avoid run-ins with the pack as they wouldn't't stop trying to collect me.

"As much as I love you, that can't be all for me."

After my mother had died in a car accident when I was 24, Luna was all I had left. I had never known my father. Even though our speaking of him was rare, my mother always spoke nicely of him. The only thing I knew was that his name was Ryk and they had a fleeting romance. Despite the fact that he didn't want to stick around, my mother had never seemed bitter about it.

"Look Luna, I'm not trying to guilt you or anything, because I'm happy as hell for you. But, you *ARE* a married woman now." I said with a look, which made her press her lips into a thin white line.

"You can't stretch yourself between me and Noah just to try to keep me here and happy."

She and her new husband Noah, who was the leader of the area pack, couldn't seem to do anything separately. They tried to include me in things, but I tried to avoid that for a couple of reasons.

One, they had absolutely nothing against a lot of good, old-fashioned P.D.A. It was highly uncomfortable to be around. One minute, you're eating your spaghetti and telling them about the new kitchen gadget you were getting yourself for your birthday, and the next, you look up to see the two practically in each other's laps at the dinner table making eyes at each other.

Two, when your best friend's new husband tried to make his case on reasons to join a pack every time he saw you, it got old very quickly. The intensity with which Noah tried to get me to join the pack always put me off.

After all, I was just a small Lynx. There wasn't anything special about me. I had always assumed that it was Luna. When Luna turned the charm on him, he could hardly resist. Otherwise, why else would a pack full of canines want a little Lynx? It just never made sense. So, I chalk it up to Luna.

"So, this is about me getting married and not having enough time for you? And don't tell me how to be married!" Now, it was my turn to roll my eyes.

"No, Luna. This is about me finally allowing myself to do something for *me* that makes *me* happy." I sighed and sat down next to her.

"Look," I began, "you know that I have always wanted to travel. You know how much I need to be away from these endless plains. I need the woods. I need to be somewhere where I can still feel the Spirits in the wind. Not in a suburban neighborhood in the middle of a concrete jungle." Something had been calling me for some time, I just wasn't sure what it was.

This seemed to calm her down and get her to at least start understanding. Her big blue eyes lost all the anger that had been in them previously and began to well up with tears. She turned them back to me, "Will you promise to come visit often, and never tell me no when I ask to come for a visit?"

This made me give her a big, cheesy grin. She really was a giant softy. Her disposition was that more of a loveable Golden Retriever than a Coyote.

"My dear, you could visit me every single day and I wouldn't't get tired of your company."

ೞ

Appeased, for the time being, she started helping me with planning the move. Luna was the most organized person I had ever met. While I kept a clean and organized home, Luna could have easily organized entire businesses, which she practically did because she was the pack's financial guru.

Within three months, Luna had helped me rewrite my resume, thus, mostly, securing a job, selling my house, finding a rental home, booking flights, and packing my 30 years of life into boxes. Moving an entire life overseas, we discovered, is no easy feat. Luckily, the rental home was fully furnished, so all I needed to pack were the smaller personal items and my clothing.

The plan was to rent for a year or two until I got my feet underneath me in Germany. Once I had my shit together again, I'd work on buying a home. Luckily, I didn't have to worry about citizenship and all that, given my dual citizenship status thanks to my mother having been born in Germany.

I had only been to Germany twice. Each time, I was so young that I could barely remember. My mother had taken me to get me acquainted with nature. She said I may need to be and I never doubted her. I knew, as a very small child, what I could possibly become. My mother had been human, but my father was a shifter.

I didn't know what species he shifted into, but I knew he was most definitely a shifter. She never hid the magical world from me. Sure enough, as a young girl, the changes began. So, it was a good thing she told me about all of the magical creatures she knew of. Then, Luna's grandmother taught me about the ones my mother didn't know about.

My mother had befriended some local shifters that she had met through Ryk to help me when the change began, so I would have friends in the community. This was how I met Luna and her grandmother. Through these very kind people, I learned all about myself, the shifter community, the magical community at large, and how to be a magical being in a largely non-magical world. Luna and her grandma were the only ones that I really cared to be around anymore though.

- 4 -

So, here we were, Luna and I, on the plane over the Atlantic Ocean. Luna, snoozing as if she had not a care in the world. Me, trying really hard not to think about the fact that I was, the gods could only know, how many feet up in the air, over a freaking ocean.

I nudged Luna awake. If I was going to be awake and anxious as hell, she was, at least, going to be awake with me. We had chosen a night flight, but in my excitement, I hadn't paid much heed to the moon phase.

It was one week until the Full Moon and I was beginning to feel it. I couldn't sleep. My Cat was restless. I couldn't get up and pace the plane to rid myself of excess energy. So, there it was, contributing to the nerves.

Luna scowled at me when I finally succeeded in waking her.

"Pray tell, what was the point of selecting a flight at a ridiculous time of night so that we could sleep during a large portion of it... if you're *not going to sleep?*"

I grinned at her and whispered, "The Cat is nocturnal. You tell her to go to sleep."

She looked me dead in the eye. What she saw wouldn't be noticeable just yet to a human eye, for another four days or so. However, her eyes were almost as good as my Cat eyes, so she could see the yellow streaks in my green eyes beginning to shimmer like liquid gold. A sign that the *Cat* was beginning to stir under the surface.

Groaning and sitting back up, she grabbed one of my hands and held onto it. She patted the top of it and told me to think soothing thoughts. She elaborated, "Like schools of tuna swimming in the ocean."

I glared at her and reminded her, "I'm a landlocked Lynx."

She grinned mischievously. "Bass then."

That did it. The nervous energy bubbles finally reached the top and I laughed until my eyes were streaming. She joined in, still holding my hand.

When the fits of giggles finally abated, we leaned back in our seats and stared up at the ceiling of the plane. *I would not think about it as a tin can flying over an ocean right now.*

"Do you think I'm making a mistake?" I tried to keep the nerves out of my voice and sound hypothetical.

"Hell of a time for second thoughts, Sammy," she said with a dry tone.

I turned to look at her, blowing the curtain of golden hair out of my eyes, "I'm not having second thoughts, really. I just don't have anyone else that I value their opinion quite as much as I value yours." *You're my only friend* being the underlying message of the statement.

She took a deep breath and looked back up to the top of the plane. She was silent for a minute at least.

Looking back to me, "No, I think you're making a mistake. Do I wish that you'd still be in town? Hell... in the country? Yes. But you haven't been happy at home. Not even when we were kids. You always needed something different. Something, oddly enough, less."

I could tell she was trying to keep it together.

"Maybe you'll find it where you're heading. Maybe it will take another couple of moves, but I know you're on the right path for you." Looking away from me again, "I'm sorry that I was being selfish and ever tried to make you feel differently."

I squeezed her hand firmly, "Thank you. You have no idea how much it helps to hear that."

Now, I could do nothing but smile. "If the roles had been reversed, I don't know if I could have accepted it with such... grace."

"Yeah," I paused dramatically, "We'll call it grace."

This made her laugh because she had been anything but graceful about it at first.

"Thanks for coming with me. Even if it's only for a week." I appreciated that more than she could ever know.

"You're welcome, Bob."

I rolled my eyes at her use of the nickname that she had graced me with when we started to change. I always had been relatively tomboyish. When I changed into a Bobcat, well, that left me open for a lifetime of being referred to as Bob.

"Now, let me go back to sleep before the plane actually lands." She let go of my hand and cozied into her seat.

We said our goodnights, I put my arm back behind my head and stared sightlessly ahead wondering what the morning would bring.

ଔ

The air was alive out here. I didn't know where exactly "here" was. It seemed so familiar even though I was fairly certain I'd never seen it in my lifetime. The colors were so sharp you could almost taste them. The sounds were so rich you could almost feel them in your bones. You didn't even have to look very closely to notice the golden particles floating on the gentle breeze. A breeze that smelled of pine and moss. Not an unpleasant mixture. Even though I was relatively certain I was dreaming, I closed my eyes and inhaled deeply the smells, tastes, *and feelings I was pulling out of the air. When I opened my eyes, I half expected it to be gone. No, I was still there, in the middle of a forest that just felt mystical. You could imagine that the old Gods would inhabit this space. Their presence was heavy. Even though I was completely alone, I had the eerie sensation of when you're standing too close to someone else, but not uncomfortable. No, it was like the feeling of a childhood friend. All I could feel was peace. I could hear water trickling not too far ahead, so I followed my ears. When I went to move, I noticed I was in my human form. This surprised me due to the vividness of this dream space. I moved but made no noise. The low-hanging branches of young pines reached out to cling to my clothing. Instead of feeling hard and bristled, it felt soft against the skin of my arms. I found the source of the trickle. The stream was small, but big enough that it would take me five, good-sized, paces to get across. There was a perfect rock ledge to sit a few feet above the water and observe. So, I did just that. As I was soaking up the ambiance, thinking how lucky I was to come here in an almost meditative dream during a stressful time, I unintentionally switched into my Cat. I had never changed at random before without it being intentional. Just as I was getting my bearings, I changed again, but this time, it was painful. When the pain subsided, I looked down into my reflection to see the face of a Coyote staring back. More than a little alarmed, I was a bit beyond on edge now. Then, the feeling of a change came over me again. It happened again and again and again. Each time into a different species. A raven, a wolf, a panther, a cheetah, even a snake. I finally exhausted myself back into human form. I lay on that stone for what felt like eons, staring up into the trees, trying to catch my breath, glad to be back in my own skin, wondering just what in the ever-living fuck had just happened to me, while simultaneously trying to remind myself that it was just a dream. "I'm only dreaming," I heard myself whisper out loud. But was I? I had never had a dream quite this vivid before. Nor, one where I was able to be this involved and articulate. I heard a voice just then. A deep baritone, soft, yet commanding, "Why have you come here?" My first instinct was to high-tail it out of there. But where? So, remembering that this was my dream, I replied in a disrespectful tone, that I hadn't a choice in coming here as I was pulled into this dream just like any other person gets pulled into their dreams. I felt a presence behind me that made my hairs stand up on end. I silently wondered if the superhuman strength would still be with me in this dream or if it would be one of those weird ones where you feel like you're fighting through water. When I sprung up in a defensive crouch and turned around, it was as if I was frozen in place by the sight of the person before me. Before I could open my mouth...*

"This is your captain speaking, the weather in Stuttgart is a balmy 22 degrees Celsius on this fine July morning. The local time is 8:46, and it looks to be the making of a beautiful day. Thank you for flying United and have a lovely day."

Dream completely forgotten. I shook Luna awake. "We're here!"

The excitement I was trying to conceal by whispering it to her was barely concealed. It was just bubbling under the surface of my words. Luna roused and rubbed the sleep out of her eyes.

She looked at me and said, "Now starts the fun part. Let's get to baggage claim and go get your keys to your new home. But first... I need breakfast."

I laughed. "Always thinking of your stomach!"

Chapter 2

*I*t took a scant 30 minutes to get to the small town from the airport. After spending so long grabbing our luggage and getting the rental car, that 30 minutes felt like an eternity. Luna insisted on driving. The control freak in her couldn't resist, nor could it handle the idea of balancing its very life in my hands in unknown territory.

I could tell her Coyote was ready to run through the fields. This was something I could sympathize with, but not yet. According to the weather app, sunset wasn't until 9:18 PM. Luckily, we had plenty to keep our minds occupied.

Luna was the first one to put together that *Bäckerei* was translated to Bakery. I'd never seen someone pull over so fast in my life. It smelled fabulous inside. Spicy meat, sweet pastries, and – thank all that was holy – coffee.

At this point, I had pretty much only learned how to tell someone I didn't speak much German, and to ask if they knew English. When we got to the counter, with a horrible American accent, I blundered through, *"Ich spreche ein bisschen Deutsch. Sprechen Sie Englisch?"* By the grace of the gods, the server did indeed speak English. *Note to self, work on your German.*

Luna, hardly able to contain herself, ordered three different types of breakfast sandwiches, and three different types of pastries. Her superhuman metabolism didn't even slow down while she slept. Just to be annoying, I ordered one less of each. "You know you're still going to be hungry after that," she said.

"Yeah, well who is going to be ready for new and different food sooner than you?" I retorted with a smile. It was going to take restraint to not overindulge on the German food, even knowing I now *lived* here and I could have it any time I wanted. Food has always been a rather large weakness of mine.

As the server came back with our food and a not-so-subtle incredulous look at our lean bodies and all we had ordered, she shook her head and set the plates on the table. In her thick and rather charming German accent, she asked if I was the American who was moving into the cottage on the edge of town.

I was no stranger to small towns and the way news traveled. I smiled politely and swallowed my food before answering with a bob of my head and a smile. She thought it was strange that a young woman would want to move to the very outskirts of the town, especially when living by herself.

I could see that the people of Deutschland were indeed direct and how it could be taken as rudeness. She asked what brought me to Germany. Beginning to become annoyed, I looked at her and simply said, "Peace and quiet." Luna paused her chewing, momentarily, to stare blankly at me.

The server, whose name had been established as Laurel, didn't seem to take offense. I guess in a country famed for its sense of being direct, people rarely became offended. Had I said something callous like that at home, the recipient wouldn't have taken off in a huff.

Not Laurel. She just smiled some more and said, "Peace is something you'll get out there! Nearly no one goes out that far. So, you'll enjoy yourself then! Let me know if there is anything else I can get for you two." She left it at that, humming as she flitted between tables.

Luna shook her head and resumed her eating. I was not far behind her. We ate the rest of our food in silence. I made a mental note that my new favorite food of any kind was *Mohnkuchen*. A delicious poppy seed cake.

I asked Laurel for another four pieces of *Mohnkuchen* and the check. She laughed and asked me where it all went. I shrugged and smiled, "I like to jog."

☙

Back in the car, I took a moment to be thankful that the Germans also drove on the right side of the road. After all that food, I should be a little more subdued. Especially, given the night of very little sleep in an uncomfortable airplane, but I wasn't.

I felt like my body was buzzing. We were on the way to the cottage to meet my landlord and get the keys! How could you be calm when, in approximately fifteen minutes, you were officially going to be living in Germany?! I wasn't sure if it would feel real even when he handed me the keys.

When we pulled up to the cute little circle drive of the cottage, it took all I had not to go all misty-eyed and press my nose up against the window. Mine. This was mine. Well, sort of. For all intents and purposes, signing the lease had made it mine for the next 15 months. I had gone ahead and signed the longer lease so that I wouldn't chicken out and move back home.

We were a few minutes early, so Luna and I decided to wander the yard a bit. The cobbled stone fence surrounded the front yard and opened at the driveway entrance and exit. You could see where the previous tenant, or maybe even the one before, had attempted to put a flower garden in the half-moon on the inside of the circle drive, but it was overgrown and weedy.

The cottage itself was white with dark brown trim and equally dark brown trim shutters and window boxes. It was a traditional German cottage, with aged timber throughout the exterior of the home. It was possibly the most beautiful little thing I'd ever seen.

Going around to the side of the home, you could see it went deeper than you thought. Giving it the appearance of being small from the front, but in reality, it was bigger. Advertised as three bedrooms and two bathrooms, I could now see how that was possible.

Here and there, flowers were blooming in vibrant colors. Even the weeds here were pretty! I could be seeing through rose-tinted lenses, but who could tell? I swear, even the little garbage bins on the side of the cottage just somehow fit into the picturesque image.

Once we got around to the back of the cottage, I stopped dead in my tracks so quickly that Luna bumped into me from behind. Mouth hanging open, I just stared. "I get to live here," I finally said. The yard in the back was quite sizable. Even if it hadn't been, the woods and mountain terrain they covered were just beyond it, which happened to be the main reason I had chosen this location in particular.

It would be nice to go through my first Full Moon with Luna here. Even though our inner animals weren't species that typically jibed well together, she was one of the few people whom I'd ever changed with. When you've known someone since before you could remember, I guess it's bound to happen that way.

As our mouths were hanging open, our enhanced hearing allowed us to hear the car coming up the street. Given that there wasn't much in the way of houses, besides this one, we made our way back up to the front to meet whom we could only assume would be the landlord.

The man was slowly, painfully so, exiting the car. He looked to be somewhere north of 70 years old. A little hunched in his old age, but even so, he still stood a good 6 inches over my own 5 feet 4-inch frame. He had a slight paunch that hung over his belted jeans, what appeared to be, strong arms, and a full head of thick silver hair.

He took a moment to manually lock his car, put his keys in his pocket, pat the pocket, and then look up at the sky. When his eyes finally landed on us, I could smell his attitude toward other people and having to be around them. Literally, shifters can smell the physical changes one gets with each different emotion. Not to mention the distinct look of displeasure on his face.

"I suppose you are Samantha Rush." It sounded more like an accusation than an inquiry. Without waiting for me to answer, he led us toward the front door, much faster than I'd have thought he would. "Keep up, I don't have all day." Luna snickered quietly and passed me up.

"You'll have one key, I'll have the other. The garbage bins stay on the side of the cottage when not waiting for the collection. Collection is on Sunday and Thursday. I don't want to see the grass getting any taller than it is now and don't do anything different to the landscaping besides maintaining or improving what is already there. Do you understand so far?"

He got us through the door and looked behind at us, "Yes, sir," Luna and I said together. He looked at Luna, "Who are you, the girlfriend?"

Always pleasant, Luna just smiled, "Sammy could only be so lucky. No, I'm just the best friend. I came over for the week to help get her settled in."

"Well… that's just fine." By the time we had done the official walk-through inspection of the cottage, I could forgive him for his crusty attitude just for allowing me to rent the place. It was absolutely beautiful. Everything was original, yet somehow it all looked new.

He told us his name was Herschel. Herschel Stürner. He left his card on the bar in the kitchen, with a reminder to call him – not text, call – the second something appeared to be wrong with the house. No matter how minor, he didn't want me trying to fix anything myself and making things worse.

I smiled and assured him that the chances were better of snowflakes in hell than me trying to fix something myself. The corner of his mouth twitched, and I thought perhaps there was a small twinkle in his eye, but much like a snowflake in hell, they were gone as fast as they had shown up.

"I live just a little farther up the road, so I'll see if anything isn't the way it should be."

I raised one brow at this statement. "I didn't think there were any other houses beyond this one." I had chosen to ignore the overbearing statement he made, as this was the first time I saw him smile.

"When you don't like people, you find the last house in town."

He didn't shake my hand or say goodbye. The only thing that indicated he was leaving us was a slight incline of his head, and him about-facing and heading for the door. Luna looked at me smiling like a lunatic. I, myself, couldn't help but grin.

I waved to him in case he decided to look after he got back in the car, but he didn't. "Well," Luna began matter-of-factly, "he was sweet." I snorted, "If he was any more of a curmudgeon, he'd be me."

I turned back toward the inside of the house, looking at all the plain yet somehow elegant furniture that spread out through the living room. "I cannot *WAIT* to sit with the fireplace on, watch some TV, and knit!" Luna shook her head.

"One, is that what they call cats playing with yarn these days?"

"You seriously couldn't help yourself with that one could you?" I reached out to swat at the back of her head, which she ducked.

"Two, you're gonna have a problem with that one Bob. You don't have a TV." Much to my horror, she was correct.

That old coot! "How could he call this fully furnished without a TV?!" I shouted, completely at a loss.

"You're in Germany now kid. Maybe TV isn't something they care so much about here. And *maybe* you'll just have to stop being such a damn hermit and go out and meet some people. Maybe," she made sure there was furniture between us, "even a guy."

Apparently ready for me to pounce over the couch as I did, she easily dodged me. Nonetheless, I was able to catch her foot with my own and trip her up so she landed flat on her face. "I think you broke my nose," she muttered through the carpet.

"Serves... you... right!" I managed between the gasping laughter that I fought to control. When I sobered, I reminded her, "It's not like it won't be healed in ten minutes anyway."

She sat up and I heard her crunch it back into its perfect placement on her face. "Make that five. Now, let's go see what we can do about getting you a TV."

☙

We had to drive to the next town over to find a TV. Since my boxes weren't arriving until tomorrow, we had nothing to get back for in a hurry. I got a really good deal on the TV and a Blu-ray player. I may have indulged a bit and spent more on a soundbar than I should have, but that's alright.

The neighboring town we were in was large enough to have some take-out restaurants. So, we grabbed some takeout and headed back to my village. I couldn't get over the fact that I was able to say my village. I hadn't stopped smiling since I got here.

When we had finished our food and the leftover *Mohnkuchen*, sitting cross-legged on the kitchen floor like heathens, we got to work getting the electronics we'd just purchased set up which had never been my strongest skill.

"Honestly Rush, it's just a few wires. You plug them into the holes that are shaped like them. I swear, babies do it." It wasn't the first time I'd heard this.

"Look, I'm more of a hiking, knitting, gardening type girl. Plugging things in is beyond me." It wasn't much of an exaggeration. Of course, I could plug things into the outlets, but when it came down to hooking Blu-ray players and sound bars up and actually making them function, I always took four times as long as the average person should. "Why in hell do they have to send so many damn cords with one device anyway?"

Once she had plugged in the final devil cord, she brushed her hands off, even though there wasn't a speck of dust in the place, and stood. "Are you ready to take that jog now?" She asked as her eyes glittered as if the sun was hitting the water, a sign that the Coyote wanted to get out of this human shape for a bit.

We still had a few hours until the sun went down. Even though my Lynx was ready to get out, I suggested maybe we should go to the market and fill the refrigerator and pantry before we do anything. That way if we didn't come across any unsuspecting rodents or hares, we would have food when we got back without having to go back into the village.

Luna, who didn't like to eat raw even in Coyote form, didn't disagree with this plan. Yet, I could tell she wanted to get out in those woods as much as I did. So, we made a quick shopping list and got to it.

On the way back home, I realized I was going to need to go to the next town and buy a car next week. Unless there was someone in this town that knew someone who knew someone who was selling a car, in the fashion of small towns. While walking home with grocery bags hanging from my arms wouldn't fatigue me, it would draw the attention of too many people, as it was eight miles to the market.

We put the groceries away and threw together some spaghetti silently and quickly. The smell of excitement was in the air and vibrating off of our bodies. I was also nervous. *What if there were late-night hikers in the woods?* I must have spoken out loud because Luna answered me, "If there are late-night hikers then we'll blend in easily enough. There are Coyotes and Lynx up here too."

The Lynx in this area looks different than I do, but I wasn't about to sound like a know-it-all. We chugged some water pretty quickly and went out the back door into the yard. I locked the door, put a piece of tape I'd brought with me on the key, and taped it on a dark piece of wood. No one would notice that in the black night.

There were no streetlights which made it perfect. We could see, but others would not. We undressed quickly, not bothering to fold our clothes. Twenty-five years of getting naked around other people, in order to not bust uncomfortably out of clothes when you shift, really takes the embarrassment out of nudity.

Luna had opened her mouth to speak, but I was already changing. She laughed at me and began to shift as well. We usually had a very minor adjustment period around each other in animal form. A few seconds and no more. Our animal halves took a few seconds to realize that it wasn't just any Bobcat or Coyote across from them and to see the human counterpart shining through.

Once this adjustment was over, I rubbed once against her and pounced off silently toward the back of the yard where the edge of the wood lay. I could hear soft padded paws hitting the ground behind me, which made instinct kick in and had me speeding up and hopping into the first tree that looked like it would support my weight.

I wasn't a large Bobcat by any means. Not by shifter standards anyway. We tended to be slightly larger than the natural version of the animals we changed into. I weighed in at roughly 40 pounds, but my legs were incredibly powerful. I leaped, and I rarely missed my mark.

Looking down the tree trunk at Luna, I stretched and shook, doing my best to look bored. She let out a soft growl from the bottom of the tree. I hopped into a neighboring tree and then down to slink off into the dark, with Luna not far behind.

Being a predator in a strange land, everything was on high alert in my body. I heard and scented a mouse rustling in the foliage at the base of the exposed tree roots of a downed tree. I felt the eyes of an owl peering at me from the top of one of the large evergreens. Luna was snuffling noisily about not too far off.

It was time to get to know my woods. To start marking. I started rubbing my face and back all along the trees and shrubbery. When a tree looked particularly gnarled, that called for the scratching post-treatment. Felines have scent glands in their paws, and the same is true for feline shifters when we are in our animal skins.

After what only felt like an hour, with what was definitely a few miles traveled, Luna and I started off at a lope to get back to the cottage. Before we broke the edge of the wood though, we quickly slowed to a stop. Ears pricked; we heard nothing but the rustling of other creatures of the night. Noses high in the air, but nothing was suspicious there either.

We silently crept up to the cottage, and when we were certain no one was about, we shifted and grabbed our clothes, and let ourselves back in. Once I had the door locked and our clothes were back on, I turned on the small light over the stove. All we had to do was look at each other.

When you spent so much time as an animal, words weren't always necessary. It was a fact that made me hard to seem close to when it came to human friends. Sometimes, I would forget that they were expecting me to say something back to them and I came off bitchy. Luna's face had to have been a mirror of mine because she looked about as blissful as I felt.

There's something about those woods," she said sometime later after she had - yet again - filled her stomach with a few chicken salad sandwiches and was working on a bag of potato chips.

"Yeah. They're the very definition of mystical."

She nodded and yawned. We had been out there longer than we'd realized, and it was now nearing 2 o'clock in the morning. After traveling, running errands, and "going jogging," it was no wonder we were pooped. I looked her over and she was definitely about 30 seconds from sleep.

We groggily made our way up the stairs. She took the room directly across from me. We got ourselves snuggled into our beds and heaved a collective sigh. We whispered good night to each other, and we were asleep before we could count three sheep.

Chapter 3

The next day my belongings were delivered without any mishaps unless you count a broken coffee mug and a missing earring. The fact that mostly everything survived a nearly 5,000-mile trip was cause for celebration.

Luna, always organized, began unpacking boxes before the guys delivering them had even finished unloading the truck. She had already unpacked half of my kitchen boxes before I'd finished tipping and coming back in the front door.

I thought this was great because where she would put things would have been where I'd eventually have figured out it should go in the first place. Most likely years later. Within an hour the kitchen was done.

We stopped to eat a few times. I even made a trip into town to grab some of the pastries Luna liked and more of the *Mohnkuchen* for me. Even with my supernaturally high metabolism, I was bound to either gain 100 pounds or become diabetic if I didn't cut this out.

Although we took pauses in work, we had everything unboxed and in an appropriate place before it was time for dinner. I made tacos, and Luna made her amazing Pico de gallo and guacamole to accompany them.

Sitting at the table, we ate in companionable silence for a period. The evening sun was shining through the windows through the tall trees in the backyard. I saw some dust floating in the sun dog that touched my table. Suddenly, the dream from the airplane came back to me.

I wondered how that dream had felt so real. It felt sharper than in real life. I told Luna what I could remember of the dream. How beautiful the woods were and how bright the colors were. I even managed to remember the spontaneous shifting from species to species until I was exhausted and panting.

I didn't tell her about the man before waking up. I wasn't even certain that the being was a part of the dream or if it was my subconscious hearing men speaking around me while I was sleeping and interjecting itself into my dream space.

"Have you ever experienced a dream so real, that you can still taste, smell, and *feel* the things you were in it?" I asked.

Luna was a practical person, so she shrugged her shoulders. "I've had great sex dreams that I wake up from the big finish if that's what you mean."

I shook my head and took my last bite. "I have had those, too, but this was different and the spontaneous, multi-species shifting?" I rolled my shoulders to relax the tension that was building in them. "What the hell was that shifting about?"

"Rush, you just made a crazy life change." She motioned to the rest of the room. "Don't you think that *maybe* that could have had something to do with it?" She did have a point. I'd read a lot of dream interpretation articles and whatnot. Obviously, I was no expert, but I couldn't shake the feeling that it was something more significant.

I voiced that very thought, and she nodded her head. "I understand that. I get *why* you would feel that way. You're bound to be having some big feelings like now." This was also true. "But," she continued, "maybe it is also symbolizing even more change to come."

"*More* change? What more change could I need?" My eyes are the size of dinner plates at this point.

"Well," she gave me a mischievous look and a smirk, "maybe you'll finally meet a guy that can tolerate you." I threw my napkin at her face.

"Easy, you broke my nose yesterday," she said, as I laughed.

When the moment passed, I sighed, "It would be just like me to meet a guy when I have absolutely no interest in one. Probably be a guy who doesn't even speak English!"

"That does sound like your luck, unfortunately." She grabbed our plates and took them to the sink. There was no dishwasher in the cottage. In America, this would have bothered me, but somehow it just added to the charm of the place.

"I didn't mean it you know," I heard Luna say over the sound of the plates clanking. "I think guys do more than tolerate you. I just think the ones you've aligned yourself with in the past couldn't handle how great you were, compared to how great they weren't."

"I'm far from great," I retorted. "I'm just a girl who likes to knit and watch reruns of old shows with a nice glass of Pinot." I stared blankly ahead for a moment. "Maybe I'll get a cat," I grinned, "or three."

Luna couldn't help but laugh at that. "You sound like my grandmother."

I nodded my head smiling, "I am seriously going to miss that woman. She taught me how to knit and got me addicted to Golden Girls." Maybe, I'd have to knit something today with her in mind.

"She did take a liking to you right from the start. As you know, she is a Mountain Lion. So, she is Felidae like you. Probably why she didn't force me into what I perceived as boring then." She laughed and shook her head, "She had a step-granddaughter sitting there ready to take the reins."

I'd never known my grandparents. My mom never talked about her parents. I'd always assumed they were dead. As time went on, I never wanted to ask for fear of upsetting Mom. Not that she would have been mad. I just didn't want to make her sad if it was something like that.

"Yeah, Grandma Katie is great. She really took me under her wing. She taught me what she called, *how to cat*."

Luna grinned, "Must be why you're so much like her." I took this as a compliment.

"Back to the conversation at hand, yeah... your dream was odd. But I don't think it's anything that should worry you. A dream is just a dream after all." I figured she was probably right. But wondered if she would still say the same if she had had the dream herself.

ᘓ

The next few days were spent cleaning and organizing. We got some gardening done. Nothing major. We just straightened up the landscaping bricks and pulled out some weeds. It reminded me that I needed to pick up a lawn mower or call Herschel and ask if there was a lawn mower designated for the cottage.

Everything was really coming together. On the morning of the Full Moon, Luna and I did our Full Moon ritual. This consisted of waking up early, the inner animal wouldn't allow otherwise, drinking coffee outside, meditating, watching a ton of silly rom-coms, and eating our weight in high-calorie foods.

Around midday, Herschel stopped by for no apparent reason. He said he wanted to check things out to make sure that everything was still in good enough shape. I hadn't put any effort into hiding the change in vibrancy in my eyes, so I was a little self-conscious. It wasn't something that was crazy enough to warrant speculation, I just didn't like being questioned.

I hoped the fact that I was wearing a fuzzy Bobcat print robe, that was really leopard print but Luna dubbed it the Bobcat print, with equally as fuzzy, big, goofy, unicorn slippers would deter him from actually wanting to come in, but it didn't. He strode into the cottage, and I couldn't stop the soft growl that escaped me.

Herschel cocked his head to the side as if he heard me, but didn't turn around to look at me. He just stood there with his hands on his hips, looking around and nodding. I took the nodding to mean he didn't see any new damage.

"You have good taste," he said. Luna had to motion for me to pick my jaw up off the ground.

"You'd better watch out, Herschel," I said, deciding to test the waters of his sudden nicer disposition. "That almost sounded like a compliment." I grinned idiotically.

"Well, it was." He didn't sound too pleased about that fact though. "Did you buy that TV brand new? I should have known to buy one considering a young American would be renting." Well, I could see the compliment session was over.

"Yeah, you know us Americans. We have to have pizza, watered-down beer, and smutty TV." I shrugged. It was rather sad that this comment wasn't the joke it was meant to sound like. He nodded his head and began to head back toward the door.

"Oh! Herschel! Do you have a lawn mower that is specifically designated for the cottage or should I go and pick one of those up? I wasn't sure if that was provided by you or if it was my responsibility." He looked at me for a long moment as if his mind was elsewhere. I had the strange feeling he was up to something.

"Did you look in the shed?" He asked me. I looked at him as if he had a screw loose. "As in... a shed at your house? Because I don't have a-..."

Herschel cut me off. "Look again, Girl." He cackled and walked out the door.

"Did he just... laugh?" Luna asked incredulously. "Did he also just insinuate that we somehow missed that there was a shed in the backyard?" We both walked over to the back door. Just to be safe, we took a peek.

Sure enough, there was a shed in the far-right corner of the yard. A pretty little thing that I'm sure I would have noticed. Especially, considering we had been here almost a full week. "What. The. Fuck." Luna and I said together.

Now don't get me wrong, as part of the magical community, we had been exposed to the Fae, Vampire, witches, and other supernatural beings. However, we'd never been around any being that could hide something away such as a shed in the backyard for six days without breaking a sweat and without us being able to smell the glamour.

It would be different had we seen some sign of the little building out there. Like, if the glamour was off somewhere, or if we had smelled the gasoline, oil, or other chemicals that typically get stored in a garden shed, but we didn't.

We'd even been back there in animal form each night. Our senses are always heightened. In our animal forms, they're equal to or better than that of our natural animal brethren. "Bob?"

"Huh?" was all I could manage to spit out.

"I think you have a Fae as a landlord." I just nodded. Still staring at the shed.

"I just might. I guess that's why he didn't shake our hands." If he had, he would have risked us feeling his magic strongly enough to notice. "Now that I'm thinking about something other than the big changes I just made, he doesn't quite smell human."

Luna agreed silently by nodding her head. "Well, there's nothing to do for it now." She was right of course. "Plus, if he was planning to burn the house down around our ears he would have by now." I just stared at her with a worried look.

"I'm only joking, Bob. I highly doubt he cares. He probably sniffed us out before he got out of the car." I was sure she was right. Now, all I had to do was play it cool around him. I didn't want to give him any reason to, you know... smite me or something.

We made our way back over to the couch ready to turn back on whatever show we had been watching. I couldn't quite focus on it just the same as I had before though. Life, it would seem, was about to get very interesting.

ॐ

As the colors in the sunset were about to fade away into the night, Luna and I were trying hard to not jump out of our skin. I didn't plan to shift when the sun was still up until I had lived here for much longer.

We were stripped down to our skins underneath our robes. I'm sure we would have looked strange to outsiders looking in. Two women pacing back and forth in their robes, barefoot, with their hair pulled back.

Luna stubbed her toe and a deep rumble came from her chest. "Alright, good doggy. Time to go outside for a run." We liked to try to give each other the impression that we were cool and not sweating bullets for putting off the change longer than we normally would have.

Still having to be cautious, we made sure no one was near before we pulled our robes off and slid effortlessly into our animals.

Changing was so much more mentally and physically satisfying on the Full Moon. The animal lay just beneath the surface for most of the day and you felt like you were going to burst. Almost as if you were being stretched far too thin. Then. when you finally shifted, it was like gliding into water that was the perfect temperature and just floating there.

Luna and I didn't stay too close to each other tonight. We didn't want to tempt fate. It was still quite warm. Somewhere around 75 degrees I'd imagine. The moon had cast a silver sheen over the landscape of the edging of the forest that we had stayed in. The deeper into the wood you went, the darker it got.

I tended to like the moon hitting me when enjoying the Full Moon change. Otherwise, I would have loved to explore further. Instead, I found myself sticking near the cottage and heading in the direction that I'd imagined Herschel's house was in.

I could tell I had gone in the right direction because I could smell that odd Fae magic scent was much stronger here. I couldn't believe I hadn't noticed it on him before, but then again, maybe when he dropped the glamour on the shed I had been made able to scent it stronger.

I remembered him saying that there weren't any houses beyond his, so I knew it was around here somewhere. Finally, I found it. A cute little cottage, much like my own. One light remained on in the kitchen above the stove.

I didn't dare get any closer to the house in case he had any Fae booby traps in place. Knowing the Fae and their trickery, he had. So, I stayed just at the edge of the tree line. I watched the house like a big fat house cat watching for a mouse to come out of a hole in the wall.

Eventually, I saw movement in a window on the second floor. I could see his face peering toward me as if he felt me there. I felt rather tense when I saw his gaze land on me. My tail stopped twitching and I scarcely breathed.

He looked as if someone had told him a joke that he was pretending to think was funny. Probably wondering what in the hell kind of Lynx that was. So, I decided to take my chances. I got up and stretched as if feeling lazy, just to let him know I wasn't worried. I rubbed my face and back along the tree nearest me and took off.

I ran through the woods into the thick of it. The moonlight fell through tiny sections where the trees didn't touch together, which were few and far between. It was incomparable to anything I'd ever experienced. Even photographs wouldn't have been able to do this justice. So, I took a few moments to be thankful that I could see it and took in all the beauty to save in a pocket of memory.

I heard an owl overhead let out a soft call as if speaking to its mate. My cat heaved a sigh and got up to wander back toward the direction of my new home. I turned to look one more time over my shoulder at the thickest section of the woods I had yet to be in. *I'll see you again,* I thought to myself.

I lazily walked back to the cottage yard. Before breaking the edge of the forest, I peered around while in a crouched position. I heard Luna coming up from behind me to my left and she did the same, waiting for my signal to go.

I didn't see anyone or anything of note, so I got up and trotted back to the cottage, and changed back into my human skin, sliding the robe over my shoulders. Luna had done the same and was lying in the grass watching the stars.

Since that seemed like a good idea, I went in and got two water bottles, and brought them outside. I also brought a bag of snacks. I lay back in the grass next to Luna, surprised at how warm the ground felt still.

"We can't stay out here long, or we'll fall asleep outside," I commented after I had drunk half of my water. Luna dropped the water bottle from her lips and laid back in the grass again.

"I know, but it's nice to do it while we can."

I decided I would wait until tomorrow to tell her that I had gone to check out Herschel's house. I didn't want to ruin the moment by making her worry about the fact that she had to leave in less than two days and couldn't keep me from doing anything she'd think of as risking my neck.

So, we laid there in silence. Luna had apparently fallen asleep because I heard a soft snore. Eventually, I gently woke her, and we went inside. I made her get in the shower before getting into my clean guest bed sheets, and I did the same before getting in my own.

Now that I felt clean, full, and not thirsty, I could fall asleep. "You will not have any weird crazy dreams tonight, Sammy. Don't even think about it!" I looked at the clock, 3:30 in the morning. Oh yeah. I was going to sleep well.

Chapter 4

he next day was bittersweet. I hadn't quite accepted that Luna had to go home the next morning. I don't think she had either. We drank our coffee and ate our breakfast reminiscing on childhood memories. Laughing, and just enjoying each other's presence.

"So, do you want to take a human hike up one of these mountains in the forest today?" Luna asked in earnest.

"Is that really what you want to do on your final day here this week?" She said that she'd really enjoy the human experience of hiking. At least, as human as we can get with our endurance and strength.

"Plus, I'll be coming back to visit a lot. It's not like we are short on money." I nodded in agreement.

"Also, it's cheap for one person to fly," I added helpfully. In agreement, we got dressed in what we deemed suitable hiking gear, which were yoga pants and tank tops. I was an avid hiker back in the US. So, I had some backpacks with water bladders in them. I filled them up and we slung them over our shoulders and hit the trails.

We thought about going to a place designated for hiking, which probably would have been smart, but we had our compasses. We knew which way we were heading and which direction we'd need to go to get back home. We also had flashlights, snacks, and, not to mention, our incredibly heightened sense of smell. If worse came to worse, one of us could shift to heighten our senses and lead us back home. We were hoping to do it strictly human though.

There was a small trail leading into the woods in the backyard. We decided to start with that and head back deeper into the thick of the forest. She had gone in quite far last night apparently because I smelled her on the trees.

"The deeper in the woods I got last night, I smelled more cats by the way," Luna said as she was thinking back on last night. "There are definitely more cats around here. I just didn't actually see any."

She said the scent had been strong though as if the cats had been around recently and frequently. I figured that I'd have to make sure I wasn't seen by any other cats in the area knowing that I looked as differently as I did. Even the natural Lynx in the area would know something was different and off about me. Natural animals tended to be very wary of shifters. At least the wild animals, because domestic animals loved us.

"As long as we're sharing, I snuck up on Herschel's house last night. Just to watch." I said it fast, and before she could scold me, "I stayed in the tree line though!" She furrowed her brows, but she didn't go off like I thought she might.

"Did you find anything out?" she asked as she walked on. It was more of a tromp now really.

"I didn't." I sighed, "I do think we are right about the Fae assumption." I told her about how much the house and the surrounding area smelled like Fae magic.

"He must be using a glamour to keep something under wraps there." I thought she was very correct about this.

"Considering what he is, he probably knows what we are." I was a bit nervous about that fact. In all my experiences with the Fae, not many of them had been pleasant.

Don't get me wrong, they were never horrible to me, but the Fae were known for their ego and vanity. They were the next most powerful being to a god in the magical community and they liked to cause mischief from time to time. Most of the Fae I had bumped into were not pure Fae.

There were many times when I had caught on to one of the Fae trying to seduce a human. Their populations had been decreasing for centuries, so they would mate with humans to increase their numbers. The half-Fae children were either just as powerful as their Fae parent or had no power at all. In the end, the child was either taken away to the Faerie realm if they exhibited power, thus leaving the mother childless, or the mother was left to raise a half-Fae child with no power on her own.

When one of the half-Fae children went on to have children of their own, the chances were just as good that they could have power. It just caused issues for everyone involved, especially the mothers. When the children they carried held Fae magic, it made the women go half mad. On top of the madness, they would begin to age. The human body was not meant to carry that type of energy inside it. Their aging slowed back down once the child was born, but the madness would linger.

Well, I had gotten in the way a few times. Sometimes it's hard to tell the Fae apart just by their scent, as some didn't stick to one look when it came to their human glamour. There was one in particular, who went by a different human name each time I had scented him. He was no fan of mine.

The pack back home kept telling me to leave it be. If I didn't have the backing of a pack, then I shouldn't be meddling in other creatures' affairs. It just gave me the creeps and really pissed me off. Luna gave me a look that told me *no*. "Don't go poking around trying to get in another creature's business again. You're going to get yourself hurt."

I put my hands up, "Hey, as far as I can tell, he's not doing anything stupid, so why should I?"

By all outward appearances, so far, he was a good citizen. Maybe a little cranky, but he kept up the cottage, people in town respected him, and he kept to himself. I wondered if maybe he was an outcast of his people. The inquisitive look must have been plastered all over my face because Luna said, "We all know what curiosity did to the cat right?" She raised one of her eyebrows high.

"....made it smarter and of more help to the world?" I retorted sarcastically. She sighed in an overly dramatic fashion trying to make her point that I was being dumb and simply said we should keep moving.

We got to a bit in the forest where the trees were so thick it almost appeared to be nighttime. It was very eerie but beautiful. If you've ever been outside during a full solar eclipse, that's kind of what it looked and felt like. The birds were silent. The breeze was still. There were a few rays of sun coming through a partially dead evergreen tree a few yards away. If there was any place to stop and snack, it would be here before we started having to go up inclines again.

We sat down and started snacking on jerky, trail mix, and some protein bars. I heard water coming from somewhere in the distance and I was taken back to the dream I had on the plane again. This felt very much like the scenery from the dream. It wasn't as sunny, but it had the right ambiance. I thought to myself that I would probably come back here once Luna was safely back home out of lecturing distance.

She thought the dream was just a dream, but I get the feeling that she would still not like me chasing after what I felt was more than a dream in the tangible world. It didn't look like people hiked through here very often. I didn't suppose most people wanted to get this far out into the woods. Not sane humans anyway. We got up and started to go farther up the small mountain that was in the belly of the forest.

We got to where I swore I could hear water extremely close, but couldn't see it. Every fiber of my being wanted me to turn tail and run back the way we came.

"Lu," I said in an urgent whisper. "Do you feel that?" Eyes the size of saucers, she gave me a slight nod.

Even if I wasn't, Luna was definitely ready to turn around and head back home. Me being the stubborn and pushy person that I was, wanted to push through that barricade of fight or flight responses and figure out what in the ever-living shit was going on in there.

Luna had already grabbed my hand and started taking long strides back toward the way we had come. Luckily for her, it was on the decline of the mountain. "I don't know what the hell is back there, but someone is trying to keep us away from it and that's good enough for me."

It was obvious that she was deeply unsettled by this. I probably wouldn't mention that I had smelled the Fae magic again. Once she had pulled me far enough back that the alarm bells stopped going off in my head, I had time to take a good long breath.

Sure enough, air tainted with Fae magic entered my nose and lungs. *What is that Wiley old Fae hiding in there?* I wondered to myself. I turned and looked over my shoulder again. I told myself I was definitely coming back here, but I'd probably give it a while. Maybe I'd become friendly with Hersch and do things to get on his good side. I could make excuses to drop in on him under the guise of a friendly neighbor girl just wanting to check in and see if my "elderly" landlord needed help with anything.

I'd just have to keep this little scheme on the down low while Luna was still with me. Even though she was my best friend, I was still capable of keeping a secret. It was just part of my nature. I would always argue that this point made me a really good friend. Not that I had many.

When we got back home, it was nearing 4 o'clock in the afternoon. We showered and then plopped down on the couch with a bottle of wine between us. Luna, looking as if she was ramping up for a lecture, and I was steadily trying to figure out how to distract her from it.

"Sammy, I don't think you should be messing around with whatever is out there." *I knew it.*

I looked at her blankly, "I don't recall saying that I was going to." I couldn't very well lie to her and tell her that I wouldn't. It wasn't in me to lie. Omit the truth maybe, but not to lie. She would smell a lie even if I'd tried. It was just best to answer with truthful statements.

"Oh please," she continued with an irritated scowl. "I felt you dragging your ass while I was trying to haul you down the mountain and back home."

Ok, she had me there. "Okay, damn it. I will *avoid* going back there if I can." She stared hard at me. "That's the best I can give you, Lu."

"Fine, but you will *call me* if you get into any trouble. Noah and I will be here in a heartbeat." Now, that I believed. Noah may not be able to get the whole pack behind me since I wasn't part of it. That just wasn't how it was done. However, he would do whatever Luna needed him to do for her friend.

I realized I had a dopey grin plastered on my face at the thought of Luna and Noah. That was real love. The kind of love that any person should want. I appreciated it from a distance. It made me happy that my best friend had found it, but... I was a loner. I kept my circle so small that it could hardly even pass as a circle. It was more like a few people huddled together. Maybe I should try to make a friend or two here. If one of them happened to be a cranky old Fae, so be it.

"I'll be on my best behavior," I finally said. "*And,*" I said with some emphasis, "I will call you if I get in any trouble. Who knows," I shrugged, "maybe I'll make a new friend or two. Go wild."

She laughed lightly. "Okay, ease up there. Let's not go overboard. We all know you'd rather be sitting here watching old TV shows in your underwear than going out and around people." She laughed and shook her head. "You're such a damn *cat* it's a bit ridiculous."

◈

At least, we were in agreement on that.

We decided to go out for dinner instead of spending our last night together for a while having to cook and clean up after ourselves. I tried to keep it light and not let the sadness push through, but it would seep around the edge of my blockade every so often.

She caught me at one of those moments as I was staring down at my plate and pushing around some of the potatoes. I had been thinking about how this was going to be one of our last girl's weekends in a while. I wanted to try to make it back home a few times a year, and I'd hoped that she would come back here at least that often.

"What are you thinking about so hard?" She asked me. I kept my eyes down on my plate and stabbed at a few more potatoes before stuffing them in my mouth.

"I was just wondering," I paused to swallow my food, "if you'd be able to make it back a few times a year?" I looked up at her and quickly went on. "I want to make it back at least three times a year and was hoping you could too."

Her eyes softened and she grabbed hold of my hand, prompting my tear ducts to start trying to leak. I blinked. "I will come as often as I can." She gave my hand a squeeze and released it to get back to her sandwich. "How could I not? It's too pretty here to stay away."

That made me laugh, "Yeah, not your best friend being here or anything." She just smiled and shrugged her shoulders. Now that I had successfully gotten my moping out of the way, we could eat our dessert and spend the rest of our night in peace.

CR

We decided not to shift that night. We sat in our pajamas out in the yard on blankets watching the moon glide across the sky. Just enjoying each other's company was enough for the night. I preferred this for her last night in Germany. When we shifted, there was always that little part of me that wanted to run from her, and that little piece of her that wanted to chase after me. This way, it was just us.

Our animal sides seemed to understand. We were still within the Full Moon energy, so had we shifted, our animals would have been overjoyed. Normally, with the waning moon still so close to being full, our animals would have been begging to get out, but not tonight.

Tonight, was about our human friendship, so we kept it human. Brownies, wine laughs, and memories. I checked the weather on my phone and seeing that it was going to be clear and warm all night, I ran inside after a quick, "Be right back!" I grabbed as many pillows and blankets as I could carry and made my way back outside. I dropped the pillow out of my mouth and into her lap. "You up for some camping under the stars?" I asked her.

In response, she grabbed the thickest of the blankets and spread it out on the ground. We made quick work of getting the rest laid out and the pillows set up. We had to go back for one more trip of blankets and pillows each though. I was a four-pillow sleeper and she was a blanket hog.

Once we had gotten ourselves tucked in under the stars, Luna under two comforters, and I under my weighted blanket surrounded my pillows with one under my head and one under my knees, we heaved a collective sigh. Bugs tended to leave the supernatural alone. So, we didn't have to worry about any of that.

It was just so pretty out. I didn't want to shut my eyes, but eventually, our conversations dropped off and our eyes drifted closed. I told myself that out of all nights, tonight, I didn't want to have any more creepy dreams... and I didn't.

CR

- 32 -

The next morning was short and sweet. I helped Luna double-check that nothing was forgotten, got all her stuff in the car, and drove her to the airport. *You're not going to cry; you're not going to cry.* My mantra for the day, and possibly for the next month.

Luna looked straight ahead and didn't say much either. Before hitting the airport though, we stopped at one of the restaurants we had previously enjoyed and had a nice meal. The silence had broken by then and it was just two friends having an early lunch.

She took care of the check and said it was payment for my taking her to the airport. Even though the car was a rental that she had paid for. I didn't argue since I hadn't started my new job and I just spent a ridiculous amount of money to move to a new country.

I turned in the car and took her to her gate. She looked at me and her eyes finally watered. "Don't you start now, or you'll get me going," I said as I wrapped my arms around her. "In your purple suitcase, there is a wrapped gift."

She looked at me suspiciously. "You're not going to have my luggage get searched, are you? I hate it when I get home and all my stuff has been rifled through."

I shook my head, "No, not this time. Though that would have been funny." I made a mental note to get her with that next time. "No, this is something you have to wait until you get home to open." She smiled the watery eyes away and hugged me tighter.

"Okay, well there is something for you in your master bathroom that I snuck in there before we left." *That sneaky little wench.*

"At least I know you're not trying to get *me* caught by security since I don't have to be on a plane for a stupid amount of time again." She laughed. Then, I laughed. We both got silent and gave each other one more big hug. Both of us broke apart sniffling as if we had dust in our noses.

"Alright, no more stalling." I kissed her cheek, turned her around, and gave her a gentle push to get her into the line for security. "I love you. Call me, or text me, or something me as soon as you get home, please! I don't care what time it is here."

"Okay. I love you too, Bob." I stood and waved as she got past the point where I could see her. Then, my face dropped. I no longer had to act uppity. I didn't get to completely fall apart for a few minutes until I sat down in the rental car, but it was a good healing cry.

When I composed myself and made sure I didn't look like I had been punched in the face, I returned the car and caught a ride to the nearest car dealership. I figured buying a car was two things, important and a good distraction. Nothing made you feel better quite like a new set of wheels.

Chapter 5

hen I arrived home, I was the proud owner of a cute, zippy little BMW 3 Series. I was beyond happy that the dealership had so many manual transmissions... I'm sorry, manual *gearboxes* to choose from. My new car was all I wanted. Manual transmission, a brilliant blue, leather interior, and it was fast. Not that it mattered because I didn't see myself zipping through the village, endangering all of the pedestrians any time soon. At least I knew I had the option to go fast if I needed or wanted to.

I had stopped at the market on the way back through town and grabbed some essentials. Meaning, I got an exorbitant amount of junk food because I knew I would need it. This would be my first night in Germany alone, without my best friend. I liked being alone, but not knowing the next time I'd get to see Luna made it hard.

I decided to try to be positive about it. I'd most likely see Luna several times a year. With there being a handful of *thousands* of miles between us, there would be plenty of time for us to miss each other. Plus, now I didn't have to deal with her husband trying to induct me into their pack every time I saw her, and by proxy, him.

I couldn't wait for her to open the little gift I put in her suitcase for her. She'd probably like to slap me silly for ruining her being able to tell me, but what can I say? I'm flawed. In the perfectly wrapped box, was a stuffed animal that had belonged to me as a baby, *I still had a bunch*, some super cute nightgowns, and some baby booties that I had knit at night while Luna had been sleeping.

I'm sure she already knew she was pregnant. After all, if I could hear the little heartbeat then I'm sure she could, considering it was *her* uterus that a baby had taken up root in. I was more than thrilled about it. As an only child, I wouldn't ever get to have any biological nieces or nephews, but what's blood really? I believe chosen family is just as strong of a bond, if not stronger than blood. Blood family, you are forced into the relationship. Chosen family is just that, the family you get to choose.

Sooner rather than later, I'd be Aunt Bob. That made me smile. I'm sure I wouldn't get Aunt Sammy or Aunt Rush, and that Lu would make the baby call me Aunt Bob. I was absolutely fine with that. All the more to confuse people with and I was always up for a laugh. Lu had been in the air for around four hours at this point, which meant she had another fifteen to go if all went smoothly and per the schedule.

"Ope!" I yelped once I had finished off this whole thought process in my head. I ran upstairs to my master bathroom to see what she had left for me. There was a wine bottle in one of those fancy wine bottle gift bags and at the bottom... "Yuuuuuck!"

The nasty ass had put her positive pregnancy test in a plastic baggy with the wine bottle in the gift bag. Good lord.

She also had a note, which I was hesitant to touch, but I wanted to see what she had to say for herself.

"Dear Aunty Bob, I miss you already! As you probably noticed by the urine sample I left you, I'm having a baby! You're the first person I wanted to tell, even before Noah. I can't wait to see what kind of cool things you'll knit him/her/they once we know what I'm having. I'll text or call once I land! Then, I get to tell Noah. EEK! So excited!" She signed it -Lu.

I knew it. Aunty Bob, it was! I thought it had a nice ring to it. I'd have to start knitting things in unisex colors ASAP. She sure was going to crap her pants when she saw my baby gift. I hadn't left her a note. I thought just the gift was enough to get my point across.

"Well," I said to myself, picking up the bottle of wine and throwing away the wine gift bag along with the pee stick. "I think it's time I cracked you open and ate some potato chips and chocolate for dinner. Golden girls sound good to you?" I asked for the bottle. "Yeah, it does to me, too."

So, I spent my first evening alone in Germany, eating crap, drinking wine, and knitting for my best friend's future child.

By the Friday of my first week alone, I was bored. Beyond bored. I didn't start my new job until the next week, since I had wanted to make sure that I had plenty of time to get everything situated and organized the way I wanted it. Also, to make sure I got my internet, computer, and everything else set up and figured out before having to do it on Day 1 of the new job.

Well, me being me and not able to sit still for too long, I got all those things done early that week. Because of this, I had nothing to do the rest of the week once I was finished with the yard work I wanted to get done. I was seriously contemplating just going out and mowing the yard again, even though it was nowhere near needing it just three days later.

"Fuck it." It was only five o'clock, but I didn't care. I got undressed and put my robe on and headed outside. I looked all around and used my other senses to ensure no one was around. I smelled especially carefully for the smell of Fae and their strange magical scent. Nothing. So, I dropped my robe and my human skin and high-tailed it for the trees.

Once I broke into the trees, I didn't stop running. I kept running for what felt like fifteen minutes. I finally slowed and climbed a small tree. I sprawled on the branch allowing my body to cool off from the exertion. I wasn't really sure what my plan was, only that I had to get out of the damn house and DO something.

I sat as still as I could for a while, panting to cool myself. When I was able to quit panting, I listened closely to the sounds of nature around me. I heard birds, squirrels, foxes, and even some little rodents rooting around in the vegetation at the forest floor. It may not be much, but instead of boredom, now I felt at peace. I closed my eyes and listened, breathing slowly. I quickly calculated how long it would take me to get back to where me and Lu had been hiking when we turned around and made a run for it back to my cottage.

Then, I thought better of it. I'd want to tell her I went back, but I didn't want to stress her out since she had a baby on board. I huffed and slid down out of the tree. The Lynx really wanted to go check that place out again. I was in an inner battle with myself. In the end, I decided to go snooping around Herschel's house again instead.

I headed in that direction to get started. Once I was a few miles out, I smelled something that gave me pause. I stopped and crouched down between a copse of bushes and swiveled my ears to see if this was a single animal or if there were multiple around. I hadn't expected to run into any for quite some time, considering the local Eurasian Lynx populations were being brought back from the brink of extinction.

I didn't hear any others. It appeared to be on its own., but it was probably best for me to not be seen by any of the local cat wildlife. They'd never seen anything like me before and who knows how they would react. I sat and waited, and the longer I waited, the more opportunity I had to figure out just why this seemed odd. I was downwind and getting good full breaths in which to scent the intruder.

This cat didn't smell like a natural Lynx. This cat was a shifter. A male shifter. *Shit*. Not exactly what I was hoping for. That explained why he was so much bigger than I was expecting a natural Eurasian Lynx to be.

I stayed hunched in the bushes for what seemed like forever. He finally moved out far enough that I could probably sneak off without making much noise. I did, and once I got far enough away that I was sure his ears couldn't hear me, I bolted. I was very fast, even as far as shifters went. I was back in the cottage in a matter of 10 minutes.

"*Son of a bitch*! Leave it to me to move away from my home to a tiny village to get *AWAY* from other shifters, and within two fucking weeks, I spot one!"

I was less than pleased. I grabbed a beer out of the fridge and paced back and forth. An onlooker could probably see the steam coming from my ears. I paused by the glass back door feeling as if I was being watched. I looked, and within a few seconds, spotted the movement in the tree line. If I felt like I was being watched, it was because I was.

There, in the low branches of one of the trees near the path into the woods, was the shifter I'd thought I'd evaded. I could see his foot dangling from the branch. I couldn't help but wonder a couple of things. One, how did he catch up to me? I was young for a shifter, shifters pretty much lived until they were killed thanks to our healing abilities, but speed was something at which I excelled at. Two, was this going to become a problem or would he and whomever else he was associated with leave me alone?

Maybe it wouldn't be so bad. Maybe it wasn't a whole damn pack of shifters for me to have to dodge again. Maybe it's just him, and he was curious about me. Maybe he was interested because he'd never seen a Bobcat before. "Maybe he didn't see anything at all and you're just being paranoid," I said aloud as I rolled my eyes and groaned.

I finished off the beer and grabbed another and headed upstairs for a shower. If I wasn't able to run through the forest anymore tonight, I'd have to go out for dinner and maybe hit the local Biergarten. I could use beer and fresh air tonight.

☙

I had been sitting at the Biergarten with a book for about thirty minutes, trying like hell to put aside the matter of the shifter in the forest. It was working for the most part. I had to read every other paragraph over two or three times, but if there was a will there was a way...or so I told myself.

When I had to read a paragraph over for the fourth time though, I snapped my book shut and tossed it down on the table. I picked up my beer glass and pulled my feet out of the seat adjacent to me and crossed my ankles, slouching down in my seat. I took a moment to look up at the sky.

It was a half-moon, and it was a bright one. I closed my eyes and soaked up the energy from the moon and decided I was going to try to use it for being positive and *not* for overthinking. Just as I had decided this, a chirpy voice with a thick German accent said, "Hallo Sammy!" I took a deep breath, lowered my head from its skyward glance, and opened my eyes back up.

There stood Laurel. *Okay, be positive*, I thought to myself. I smiled at Laurel and greeted her back, offering her the chair I had just recently taken my feet out of. She sat down with a smile. "I haven't seen you in the bakery lately for your Mohnkuchen." The tone wasn't accusatory, just a segway into a conversation.

"Yeah, I've been skulking about the cottage missing my friend," I forced out in a sheepish tone. "She just found out she's pregnant before leaving Germany, and while I'm incredibly happy for her and her husband, I'm a bit sad that I'm going to miss so much." I was a little shocked at myself for this, as I hadn't even admitted that internally just yet.

She gave me a caring smile. "That could explain it then. I came over because I thought you looked frustrated and like you could use a friend."

I hadn't thought too much yet about letting a new friend into my life. Hell, I hadn't ever really had any friends that weren't shifters. I was always too concerned with how I'd eventually have to tell them the truth about what I was.

A relationship that I had to hide a major part of my life never seemed to tickle my fancy, but, what the hell. "Truth be told, a friend probably couldn't hurt." I smiled. I hadn't had to make any new friends in too long. So, this could either be incredibly awkward, or I could let Laurel do all the talking for a while.

As it turned out, this was something she was more than happy to oblige. It's no wonder the woman was so good at her job at the bakery. She was Charm if it had been given a body. She could talk your ear off without making it seem like a chore to listen, or making herself seem self-absorbed. She always managed to remember to take a break to ask how I felt about a topic.

By the time I left, we had been talking for almost three hours. I now knew that Laurel was 32, single, never married, no children, her parents lived about twenty minutes north of here, she had a degree in business, but stayed on at the bakery because she liked the work and the people, and she had two cats. We had talked in depth about each of those things, and she knew all the same about me.

She called herself from my cell phone so that we'd have each other's phone numbers and promised to text or call me sometime. I hoped she would, in more ways than one. I had a great time with her, but I really hoped she would call or text before just popping into the cottage. I wasn't a fan of surprise company.

Laurel had asked me if I wanted a ride home since I had walked. I politely declined as it was too nice a night out to not enjoy the walk home. It was only five miles. Considering I was in yoga pants and a tank top, I figured I could jog off some of that beer that I just drank. I dug into my fanny pack and grabbed out my earbuds and turned on my favorite playlist for a good jog.

After my own jog through the woods earlier this afternoon as a Bobcat had been so rudely cut short, this little midnight jog was just what I needed. When I was most of the way home, I had the sensation of being watched. I made it look like I was scratching my ear and tapped the earbud in that ear once to get the music to pause so I could listen to anything going on around me.

I heard an owl nearby, and a dog barking in the distance, but other than that, nothing. I figured it was time to kick it into a higher gear. I sprinted the rest of the way home in what had to be a new record. I got in and locked the door behind me as fast as I could. Then, because I was a bit spooked, I took a lap around the house to lock all the doors and windows and make sure all the blinds were shut.

I didn't fancy the idea of my shifter friend being able to look in and see me. I was sure that was who it would have been that was watching me. If this person didn't have any ill intent, why did they hide and watch me like a creeper instead of coming out and showing themselves? Then I realized that I had done just that in the woods. Instead of approaching, I hid and watched. *Just like a damn creeper.*

"Ugghhhhhhh," I groaned as loud as I could. I stripped naked, got in the shower, and scrubbed off the sweat and dirt from the jog. My road wasn't paved, so from mid-calf down to my ankle was covered in dirt where my yoga pants didn't cover the skin.

First, my landlord is Fae. Then, the shifter in the woods. Then, being watched by whoever was watching me from the trees. I decided I was *definitely* making an excuse to stop in and see Herschel the next day. The crotchety old thing may just have some kind of idea who I was dealing with here. I could say I was offering to hit the store for him and then be a thorn in his side and not stop talking and see where the day took us.

Yes. Yes, that's exactly what I'd do. I turned off the shower and got ready for bed. I texted Luna a quick goodnight and promised to call tomorrow around 3 PM her time. Once I was finally situated with all my pillows, I closed my eyes. I ran through a visualization meditation that always helped me get to sleep and was out in no time.

Chapter 6

Saturday morning, I woke up around 8 AM. Usually, I would wake up between 6:30 to 7:30 AM. Since I had been up so late the night before at the Biergarten and stressed out from being followed home, I suffered from broken sleep. The last time I had woken up was around 4:30 in the morning. Because of this, those three and a half hours of solid sleep I got at the end were nice.

I scuffed slowly down the stairs in my slipper socks and pajamas and got my coffee brewing. Moments like these made me wish I was a witch who could snap their fingers or do some other kind of mumbo jumbo, I wasn't really sure how that worked, and just have my coffee ready and waiting.

I meandered back into the living room, tossed my meditation pillow unceremoniously down in the middle of the floor, and plopped down. After rubbing the sleep out of my eyes and scrolling through different guided meditation videos, I finally selected one and got a quick 15-minute meditation in to start my day. Even though I'd still be a bit tired, this always helped to pull me out of the groggy haze of sleep.

I mentally chastised myself for making coffee instead of drinking water and going on a run, but I was already behind schedule in my meddling for the day since I had slept in. There was always the option of a night run...I didn't necessarily want to be followed again either. *Screw it,* I thought to myself in a huff. *I'll just go tomorrow.*

While I drank my first cup of coffee, I got dressed and ready for the day in the usual weekend wear of yoga pants and a tank top. I had to wear a light jacket most mornings though. The temperature would start out below 45°F and then gradually climb to

70°F, or a bit higher if lucky. Looking at past weather patterns gave me hope though. It seemed to stay warmer through October and never got as cold as it did back home.

I grabbed my to-go mug and slid into my little car that I was really beginning to love. I shivered for a quick moment as the cold leather interior touched my warm body. As a shifter, I ran a little warmer and could generate heat easily enough. It wasn't long before I had the windows rolled halfway down to enjoy the crazy fresh air that I had yet to get used to.

It was time to start "Operation Get Herschel to Like Me." Not knowing what the cranky old Fae's favorite food would be, I decided to take a leap of faith and go with the fact that most creatures liked baked goods. Naturally, I found myself at the bakery.

Laurel was working. God knows what time she got here since the place opened at 6 in the morning. I have no idea how she looked so put together and chipper after a late night. I was *NOT* that person. She looked up from entering her table's order into the computer and saw me. She smiled and waved.

"Guten Morgen, Sammy!" she said cheerfully.

"Now *THAT* one I know. Guten Morgen, Laurel."

I needed to convince her to help me with my German. My mom had taught me some when I was a small child, but I didn't keep up with it. "Use it or lose it," as they say.

"The Mohnkuchen just came out about 20 minutes ago. It's still fresh.

"How much today?"

Clearly, I was becoming predictable. "Well, I think I'll just take a whole damn cake."

"*And whatever else you think a possibly ancient Fae would like,*" I thought in my head.

"Do you know if my landlord, Herschel, ever comes in here and what he likes to order?"

She gave me a curious look. "He does, and his order is usually similar to yours. Mohnkuchen, coffee, and a breakfast sandwich."

I was mildly surprised to find that I was beginning to like the old curmudgeon more and more every time I found something else out about him. You can never trust a Fae, so I wouldn't be owing him any favors any time soon.

"That's perfect, Laurel. Thanks."

I left the bakery with a cake-half of it was coming home with me-two coffees, and two breakfast sandwiches. It took some balance, but I made it to the car with no casualties. On the road back toward home, I pulled over on the side of the road where I had noticed I was being followed the night before.

I used my nose first and scented the Eurasian Lynx shifter I had seen in the woods. Looking around, I noticed his tracks in the trees lining the road. He had headed the same direction I had. I inhaled slowly and deeply. I wanted to sample the air to make sure I was currently alone. I was. I sighed in relief.

Getting back in the car, I pulled off and again wondering why the bastard was following me. I wasn't going to waste too much time and energy on it. I'm sure all would reveal itself in due time.

I planned to park on the street in front of Herschel's house in case he was one of those people who didn't like others parking in their driveways... but I realized as I pulled up why I had never seen the front of his house. His house was set so far back off the road that there was no way I was carrying all this that whole way without dropping something.

I pulled up the long circle drive and parked behind his car by about 5 feet. *You never know how picky someone will be about how close you park to their car.* I balanced everything, again, in my arms and closed my door with my hip. I locked it with a touch and headed up to the door.

Before I even got there, Herschel was there, and had the door already open waiting for me.

"Did you break something already?" he asked with his brows furrowed and his hands on his hips.

I smirked and told him that the cottage had burned down and I was bringing him consolation breakfast. It took him a moment to catch my sarcasm and smirk back, but he did.

He stepped aside, waved for me to come in, and shut the door behind me.

Step one, complete. I have gained access to the house.

I smiled to myself at my great success in winning people over with sarcasm and being generally annoying. If it could work on this guy, it could work on anyone.

"The cottage is fine. Still standing. Nothing is broken." I made sure to cover that so he wouldn't smite me from existence with a look. "I was just bringing you some breakfast goodies to say thanks."

He looked at everything I had sat down on the counter, then looked back to me. "Thanks for what?"

"For being such a good landlord to the weird little American girl who had never done anything even remotely this crazy in her entire life."

He looked at me as if he couldn't figure out what to say to me next. I had stumped him. Finally, he looked over at the cake. He grabbed one of the coffees and a sandwich and moved to the little two-person cafe table in the corner of the kitchen.

"Knives are in the second drawer on the left." He looked up at me, "For the cake." I took this as an invitation to sit with him. I grabbed a knife and the cake.

"Plates?" He directed me where to get them and I joined him at the table with two plates with very large pieces of cake on them

ੳ

I took my half of the Mohnkuchen home and waved as I drove off. I could feel him looking even though he had shut the door. I had a silly smile on my face. I felt like I had just jumped a major hurdle and cleared it by a mile. He was obviously warming up to me.

The conversation had been kept light. We spoke of the cottage, the forest, the town. Local things. I spoke a little about home and my best friend being pregnant. There wasn't any harm in talking about the things that he already knew about me. It's not like he couldn't just pull most of that information off of my rental application.

He did leave me a wide-open door to walk through if I had wanted to though.

"I saw the most exquisite creature the other day," he had said with a twinkle in his eye and a quirk of the corner of his mouth.

Not to be outdone, I had taken a sip of my coffee and looked inquisitive. "Oh? What was it?"

He went on to explain that it appeared to be a Lynx of some kind, but not like any he had ever seen here in Germany. He had seen one like it a long time ago while he was visiting a family member back in the States in Colorado. He said it was much smaller than any he'd seen around here. I told him it sounded like he was seeing the North American area's Bobcat or Red Lynx.

He continued on to ask me what I knew of them.

"Just that they are relatively solitary creatures. They can and do inhabit the same area as other Lynx, but they don't run in packs like wolves or wild dogs do." I also told him they try to avoid areas inhabited by humans, with a sly side smirk of my own. *Cat and mouse, Sammy. You're the cat.*

I pulled into my driveway and took a moment to appreciate the beauty of the place. It was picturesque in a way that I had not seen before in my life in America. I have never really remembered much of the trips my mother and I had taken to Germany when I was a child. Not the external stuff anyway. I just remembered being with her, hiking together, cooking together, camping, making tents indoors out of blankets, and whatever else we could find where we were staying.

I closed my eyes and inhaled deeply. If I concentrated hard enough, it was as if she was there with me for a moment. I could almost feel her hand covering mine on the gear shift. I sighed, opened my eyes, and looked at my hand. It was, of course, only mine.

I picked up my cake out of the passenger seat and got out of the car. I instantly scented the shifter.

"Quit following me, or I'll make you wish you never had," I said fiercely to the trees.

I locked my car and went inside. This time, since it was the middle of a beautiful day, I left the blinds wide open. I even opened the windows to let the forest air blow through.

I was trying to make a point in stupid little minimalistic ways. It helped me feel a bit braver about having a shifter stalker. A shifter, who in his animal form, was twice the size of me in mine. I was the smallest of the Lynx species, but I was the most common.

I had a brownish-red tinted coat with faded black spots, powerful back legs that were slightly longer than the front legs, and much to my dismay, tufts of hair that sprouted from the tips of my ears that tickled when a breeze would blow. The hair around my neck and jowls, called the Ruff, was pretty fluffy. All in all, I found Bobcats to be beautiful.

Natural Bobcats would run from me as I was larger than they were and probably smelled weird and unnatural to them. However, I loved watching them from afar. They were so graceful, and even playful when they thought no one was looking.

This guy appeared to be a Eurasian Lynx. After our first encounter, I had done my research on them. They were actually native to the area, though their numbers had dwindled, and they were recovering. He probably had intended to fit into the area. Maybe, he just wanted to be near another shifter. I supposed there was the potential that I was blowing everything way out of proportion.

Oh well, putting it out of my mind, I decided a midday run was called for. Maybe I'd run into town and back. I was hardly likely to be stalked during the middle of the day. I grabbed my fanny pack and a large, insulated water bottle, locked up, and hit the road.

ର

Over the course of the next couple of weeks, I managed to slip into a cautious friendship with Herschel. He'd stop in for coffee, or I would. I had started my job, which allowed me to work from home. So, in the mornings that he popped in, I would take a 30-minute break to sit and chat. He was even thoughtful enough to bring me my favorite cake and breakfast sandwiches from the bakery!

Most of the time, I would go to his home only on the weekends. He would stop in a couple of times a week to have coffee with me at my cottage in the morning. Very rarely did we go into town together. I think neither of us really wanted to admit to ourselves, or the town, that we had become friends. Laurel was very nice, but Hersch was more my speed.

I enjoyed friends that were game to get together for morning meetups so that we could have the rest of our days by ourselves to do our own thing. Friends who could just take a quiet stroll with some coffee through the yard to talk about plants, birds, and other things of nature.

Seriously, Laurel was great. She was so sweet, and always there if you needed her to lend an ear, but there was something about her mouth. I had a sneaking suspicion that anything those ears took in would fall right back out of it. I didn't mind people knowing me, but I didn't want all of my business to be all over this town. I was no stranger to small-town life. This is why, even back home, I kept to myself.

Luna thought that this was hilarious of course. So far, I had managed to make better friends with my Fae landlord than I had with the sweet girl who worked at the bakery. She was not as uptight about it as I thought she would be though. She was just happy that I was attempting to make friends. Even though, I was being sneaky about stuff.

Sometimes, Hersch and I would just talk about the cottage, and other times we would just enjoy each other's company. One morning, I told him about the Eurasian Lynx I had seen. Obviously, leaving out the fact that it had been a shifter. I described him as silver-grey with large, well-defined spots in his coat, and a long white ruff. The tufts from his ears were long and black. He had to have been around 75 or 80 pounds.

"Yeah, that sounds like you have seen one of our Eurasian Lynx. The species has made quite a comeback in the last 50 years or so. I did not see them so often before now."

I nodded at his confirmation. "I didn't think they were supposed to be that big though. Have you ever seen one so large?"

He looked me square in the eye, "You would be surprised at the amount of oddities you will find in this forest, my girl."

I couldn't tell if he had been trying to warn me about something, or if he was trying to elude to there being more than just the one Lynx shifter in the woods that I needed to look out for. Either way, it sounded ominous to me, but he could also be saying that there was more than a Fae disguised as a creaky old man. *You really need to stop this inner monolog Rush. You're freaking yourself out.*

One morning I sat down to work, and it wasn't long before I looked out the glass door and saw the shifter sitting directly in the center of my yard. I had been working at the kitchen table, so I could have a view of the outdoors.

"Screw it." I set myself as offline on my work computer and opened the door.

I took a cautious step outside and asked why he had been following me. Clearly, as he was in his animal form he didn't respond. All he did was twitch one of his ears back and turned and began to slowly walk away.

I turned my head towards the sky and heaved out a sigh. *When Luna finds out about this, she's either going to laugh her ass off, or kill me...if I'm still alive to tell the tale.* I stepped away from the cottage and began to follow him down the trail.

Chapter 7

I followed the shifter through the woods for what was about three miles. The whole time he nonchalantly walked in front of me without a care in the world for the fact that I was behind him. This said to me that he didn't think of me as a threat.

Typical male.

I huffed out a breath with my observation which finally made him flick a tufted ear back in my direction.

"I'm not going to follow you forever you know," I half shouted at him. This went unacknowledged. "Okay then, since I'm not actually going to get any answers out of you, I'm going back home. Nice *NOT* talking to you." I whirled around and started clomping off. I'm sure you could see steam coming from my ears.

I didn't get very far before I heard him say, "Wait."

There was Command in his voice. I turned around, but just kept going backwards.

"Why should I? So, you can drag me even further into the woods and do God knows what with me?"

After all, the only thing I knew was that he was a shifter. A relatively dominant one if his voice held that type of power. "I don't think so, Buddy. Not today."

"How else do you plan to get the answers that you seek?" I stopped. I had come out here with the intention of getting answers as to who the hell he was, why he was following me, and how many more of him there were. *I'm too damn curious for my own good.*

I narrowed my eyes on him. "Fine. I'm here. What do you want with me?"

He had shifted behind a little patch of bushes that stood about waist high. Low enough to see that he had a tattoo of a cat paw, about the size of what his own looked to be, on his left chest muscle. A chest that was dusted with blonde hair to match the dirty blonde hair that fell about his ears. Lu would have loved this guy.

This guy was a walking stereotype. Blonde hair, blue eyes, not too thick of a German accent, but it was there. This was Hitler's wet dream. I had blonde, wavy hair, but the green eyes that I sported were much different from the blue. I'd still fit in in a crowd though.

"Tell me," he began, "what brought you to Deutschland?"

Yup, he's a native alright. The way he pronounced the w's as v's, and saying Deutschland instead of Germany let me know that for sure. I'd say though, given the dialect, he wasn't from a small town. His accent sounded more refined.

I could hear the vibrato of Command in his voice. A less stubborn person would have submitted and averted their eyes. I clearly didn't know what was good for me though, as I looked directly into his.

"I came to get away from other shifters, and people in general." I furrowed my brows. "Who are you, and why haven't I ever seen you in town if you live around here?"

"I am Karl," he said simply, but didn't offer up a last name. He'd used a dismissive tone, so I wasn't sure if he was going to answer my second question.

He did though.

"I do not live in town."

Ok, so he didn't want to give me any more than I was going to give him.

"You obviously know where I live, yet you don't want to tell me where you live?"

He looked me over. He could tell I knew the game being played.

"I live in the forest."

True.

"What kind of Lynx are you?" He asked me curiously.

I should have moved to Mexico, at least there they have Bobcats.

I couldn't help the small eye roll that came with this question. I had always been one for animal conservation, but I felt like, as a Lynx shifter, you should know what other types of Lynx there are in the world. I could feel him bristle at my annoyance.

"I'm a Red Lynx, or more commonly known as, a Bobcat. Natural Bobcats are only found in North America."

I tried to keep the impatience out of my voice. "Why have you been following me?" I tried to sound as intimidating as he had been trying to sound. He smirked at my tone although, he clearly was not fazed by it.

He waved a hand as if this was a silly question. "I had never seen a Lynx like you before and I was curious."

Half-truth.

Yes, he may have been curious about me, but it didn't feel like that was all.

"Plus, I smelled the shifter blood in you."

Well, if that wasn't a creepy way to put it.

I didn't think that was the rest of the truth either. If I didn't end this conversation soon, I was going to start getting forehead wrinkles from the constant back and forth between lifting and furrowing my brows.

"Okay. Now that we've established the basics, are there more of you lurking about here in the forest?"

At this, he gave a belly laugh that I had not been expecting. "Why?" He said with a little lilt at the end. "Are you interested?" He grinned at me.

I put both hands up and told him quite plainly, no.

"I couldn't be less interested actually. Like I said earlier, I moved to this incredibly small town in Germany to get away from the plethora of shifters in my previous area." The truth rang in my voice so clearly, even a human couldn't argue that I was lying. "I just want to be left alone. That's it. I won't cause any trouble for you and however many others of you there are." I was beginning to babble. "I just want to live in peace and quiet. It was... interesting meeting you Karl."

I turned and started walking home. He softly said, "It was nice to finally meet you, Samantha." He said it loudly enough that he knew I would hear it, which made me more annoyed.

"Nice my spotted ass." I muttered as I tromped on. His laugh carried to me on the breeze.

☙

By the time I had gotten back home, I decided I was going to up the ante on my streak of rebellion. I'd spend even more time outdoors, and while I was spending all this time outdoors, I would completely, 100 percent, *ignore* any shifter to glance my way. Unless they were a threat, of course. Then, I'd obviously have to act.

I had also decided that today would be taken as a vacation day. I was really glad that the company that hired me gave employees their time off up front instead of only getting what you have accrued so far. I slammed the door shut behind me, swung through the cottage grabbed my purse and keys, locked up, and took off in my car toward the market. I was going plant shopping.

The market wasn't terribly busy, considering it was the middle of the workday, so I could fa-la-la my ass as slowly in each section as I wanted to. I grabbed some mostly full-grown tomato and pepper plants, small rosemary, and lavender plants. I also grabbed some basil, cilantro, parsley seeds, seed potatoes, and some cucumber plants. Then, I got a bunch of five-gallon buckets, huge tomato cages, soil, organic fertilizer, and gardening tools.

I wasn't going to, but I also grabbed pretty flowers. I'd ask Hersch, the next time I saw him, if I could get a couple of gooseberry bushes and where he'd like me to plant them if he said yes. I had fond memories of sitting under our neighbor's apple trees with Lu eating gooseberries fresh off the bush when I was a child. I wouldn't mind living that life right about now.

By the time I got all of this loaded in the car, which took an expert level of Tetris skill. I decided that I didn't care *HOW* far I had to look here in Germany, I was trading this car in for a Wrangler. I liked my BMW, but I really would like more space. Plus, they came with manual transmissions too.

I drove home slowly to not knock anything down in the car. I had my front windows down since it was just the dirt up front with me. I took this time to sing as loudly as I could to Alanis Morisette with the intent of it being a big fuck you to anyone who dared stalk me today. Before I knew it, I was already home.

As I was working on mixing soils and planting, my mind had time to wander back to the conversation I had with Karl. He had been friendly enough I suppose. Though he tried to use his dominance in his voice to get me to give him answers that I would have readily given without the bullying. A dominant shifter can get a submissive shifter to respond just by using the dominant pitch in their words. It almost made your bones shake.

Packs were made up of dominant and submissive shifters. The most dominant was the one who would lead. Then, the rankings went down in dominance from there. Another shifter could challenge the next higher-up's position as they grow more and more dominant with age and experience. This was more typical in your Canidae species than Felidae. We, cats, were usually more laid back. We didn't need the power struggle, but knowing there were powerful leaders at the top of the pack to protect the submissive animals was a comfort to them.

For some reason, the alpha thing never worked on me. I never understood why. Maybe I was dominant myself. I wasn't sure. I had never been part of a pack before. If I was being honest, there was a small sense of needing to belong somewhere. I had never felt the sense of belonging back home surrounded by the canine pack. Being as stubborn as I am, when they tried to get me to join them, I refused, and it made me dig my heels in even more.

Karl had not given me the full truth when I asked why he had been following me. I didn't feel like there was anything sinister going on. Because of this, I wasn't overly concerned, but if I had just completely upturned my life to move across the Atlantic to get away from all the shifters at home, only to find myself surrounded by more shifters here, I was going to scream. I had a very strong feeling that this was the case.

It took me somewhere around two hours to get all my planting done. I brushed the dirt off my hands and looked up at the sky. I enjoyed the view, but it was missing a little something. I made a mental note to ask Hersch if, maybe, we could add a pergola to the back of the cottage over the patio. I thought it would fit quite beautifully and then I could get some vining plants, hang pots from the sides, and, maybe, some bird feeders.

I decided to go inside and update Luna on everything that was going on. Plus, I needed an update on how she was feeling anyway. I looked at the time. It was about 8 AM back at home. Maybe, I'd give her another hour. It was about time I ate something anyway. I'd just run inside and make a couple of BLTs for lunch and then call Luna and give her an update.

ର

Karl mulled over the feisty little feline's attitude and responses on the way back to the village he and the other shifters inhabited in the woods near the peak of one of the more difficult-to-climb mountains. She didn't respond to Command when he'd used it, except with sarcasm and disdain. That was interesting. He had yet to meet a shifter who was able to brush off Command in his 75 years of life. So, either she was very old, which he doubted given her general attitude, or she was more dominant than him. He also doubted this since her attempt at sounding intimidating was laughable.

She hadn't given much away, but he knew now why she had come here. Well, she was in for a big surprise if she ever came this way again to hunt through the forest. They had all seen her and her friend hiking in human form. Her friend wisely made her turn around, but he hadn't missed the way she turned and looked over her shoulder with the fire of determination in her eyes.

What was humorous to Karl, was that her determination to know things was going to get her the knowledge that she *didn't* want. If she were to get through the glamour and barrier that Herschel had put in place several hundred years ago, then she would realize that there were, in fact, many more shifters than Karl in the area.

He did mentally applaud her for her courage and bravery, but she was lucky that this colony of shifters was of no threat to her. If she didn't manage to curb her inquisitive nature a bit, she would eventually find herself mixed up with the wrong crowd. If Herschel had been just about any other Fae, she would have found herself in trouble.

Karl had walked a bit in his human form but shifted into his Lynx to finish the journey up the mountain. It made the way up the several steep inclines easier to be in a lighter-weight body with four legs to distribute the weight on. The powerful hind legs of the

Lynx also enabled him to leap up some of the hills to just get them over with.

As he got to the barrier, he was filled with humor at the fact that, had she and her friend been in their animal forms, they would have been able to walk right through the barrier, and been able to see the borders of the glamour. The barrier was able to sense the human soul in an animal body and let shifters through. The glamour worked in the same way. She would have found herself surrounded by many cottages on the ground level, and just as many, if not more, tree houses above for those were-cats who preferred to live life off the ground.

As Karl went through the barrier and into *Dorf der Gestaltwandler*, he trotted his way to his own home, shifted once up the tree, and he was at the door. He didn't feel self-conscious, as nakedness in a shifter village was more common than being clothed. It was easier to walk around naked than to have to stop what you were doing to remove your clothing, place it away somewhere, and have to return to where you left your clothing when you were ready to shift back.

Karl put on a pair of shorts and grabbed a quick bite to eat. Being a shifter, you already burned more calories than a human, but when in animal form, your caloric needs surged. Otto would know that he was back by now. As the Alpha, he would be able to sense any of his "pack" as they crossed the barrier once the pack bonds were in place. They used the term pack loosely, to be inclusive to all shifter species. There were a few wolves, a handful of different bird species, there were even a few bears, but it was made up mostly of different species of Felidae.

Karl walked down the steep and winding staircase from his tree home and meandered down the road toward Otto's house. Wandering the streets of the village always made him feel at home and at peace. Passing by the different homes, the several community gardens -where enough light would pass through the trees either naturally or through intervention by the villagers - it was just an amazing thing they had created.

Dorf der Gestaltwandler, or Village of the Shapeshifter, was the first of its kind. The idea was beginning to take hold in other areas of Europe, but Karl's home was by far the most populated at around 200 pack members. Of those 200 pack members, roughly 90 percent of them lived in the village. The remainder lived in homes of their own nearby in the forest, but a handful wanted to remain in the towns nearby and traveled to the village to stay throughout full moons, or just to visit.

Karl made it to Otto's home. It began as a cottage on the ground level. Not dissimilar to Samantha's cottage, a traditional German cottage, but it wrapped up a tree from the back of the cottage via a winding wrought iron staircase with an intricately designed railing, into a tree house for the second story. The railing of the staircase had imagery of different forest spirits and deities every 6 steps or so. It was a beautiful piece of work that Karl had helped design and craft himself.

The second story was where Karl knew that Otto spent most of his time. As in the back of the tree home, there was a room where the walls and ceiling were all glass so he could feel the sense of being in the forest, but out of the elements if need be. There was an additional large platform above the tree home. This area was only reachable by climbing the tree in his Jaguar form, so that he could lay and be truly in the forest. Otto was the only one who ever had been on the platform, as this was his sanctuary.

Karl rang the rope bells outside of Otto's home and let himself in. The doors in the village were never locked. They had no need to lock doors.

"Hallo das Haus!" called Karl as he walked through the door.

He found Otto in his gym room on the ground cottage level of the home. He was stripped to the waist, wearing a pair of sweatpants, and sported a tattoo similar to Karl's, but the paw print was larger to match the size of his own Jaguar paw.

Otto stopped hitting the boxing bag and took off his gloves. He gestured to the door while he was drinking water, indicating to take this to another room. They landed in the kitchen area of the level and Karl sat at the table crossing a leg over and resting his elbows on it. Otto stayed standing, using a towel from the gym room to wipe the sweat from his body. He slung the towel over his shoulders and leaned up against the counter across from Karl.

"Well she's a feisty creature. Young. She is probably still the same age that would match her appearance if she were human." Karl paused, recalling the details of the conversation with Sammy. "She says she moved away from her home in order to get away from other shifters, and to live her life in peace and quiet."

At this Otto laughed, "Well she moved to the wrong town in Germany then, didn't she?" Karl nodded his head and agreed.

"She is intelligent. She didn't want to give up any more than I did, and when I gave her half-truths, her eyes narrowed." He mimicked her cranky little face with narrowed eyes and laughed. "I doubt she knew she was doing it because she was so riled up." Karl's face sobered and he looked his Alpha directly in the eye to show the intrigue behind the next statement. "She did not respond in the slightest to Command."

At this Otto, raised a brow, "*Wirklich?*" Otto exclaimed, slipping into German, his mother tongue.

In his 160 years of life, he had only had one creature who did not respond to Command, and this was the half god, half shifter hybrid named Alaryk who was probably three times his own age by this point. This man disappeared about 30 years ago and witches had been suspected in the disappearance. If they were able to contain the god and shifter hybrid, then they were far more powerful than the shifters suspected. After a couple of decades, the search had been called off and death was suspected.

He doubted that she was more dominant than his beta, Karl. That would be the only known way for her to not respond to Command.

I wonder, thought Otto.

"*Danke*, Karl, for looking into the girl. I'll take it from here." Karl nodded his head in acknowledgment and waved as he headed out the door. He knew there was something up the old cat's sleeve. Only time would tell what this was.

Chapter 8

I called Luna the evening after I had followed the shifter, Karl, into the woods at his silent request. I was nervous to tell her. I thought she was going to be upset about me following a stranger into the woods, but I should have known she was just going to laugh at me. She knew I could take care of myself against another shifter. I wasted a little time and cleaned the cottage up a bit. She must have known I was avoiding calling because she called me at the tail end of my cleaning, sounding suspicious.

I relayed the conversation word for word and she agreed with me. It did sound like there were more shifters than just him. The way he laughed and evaded the question could only mean we were correct. I would just keep my nose to the ground while I was in town and see if I bumped into anyone who smelled like a shifter. On the Full Moon this week, I'd avoid the direction we had walked so I wouldn't run into any of his buddies.

Luna had been more concerned with the fact that I was "cozying up" with Herschel. She thought a passing acquaintance was all it should be.

"Lu," I'd said, "please don't refer to it as 'cozying up.' I know he's not actually an 80-year-old man, but he currently looks like one."

That thought alone was enough to make me cringe. She conceded to finding it amusing that I was making friends with a cranky old Fae. She thought that since we were both cranky supernatural beings, we were a force to be reckoned with.

Luna was having morning sickness issues currently, but otherwise the pregnancy was going well. The pack doctor had done a sonogram and all the rest of the pregnancy stuff that I had no idea what she was talking about, but the baby was growing well, and Luna was still strong. She just didn't have as strong of a stomach. The only time she caught relief from the nausea was when she was in Coyote form. Apparently, this was her form of choice all the time right now. She'd rather spend most of her time as a Coyote than deal with morning sickness. Luckily, the pack doctor said there was nothing wrong with shifting while pregnant.

She told me to be careful, and asked me not to do anything stupid with any other Fae I might meet. "Even if they're trying to seduce a human?"

I could hear the stern look on her face over the phone which made me giggle. "Seriously, Sammy. You don't have me and Noah there anymore to help get you out of something if it winds up being more than one shifter can handle."

She did have a point there. "Okay, I'll be good, but those other Fae were asking for it...flaunting it like they were!" Of course, I had to defend my right to defend others.

On Friday, it was going to be the end of my first month in Germany. I had formed a nice routine in my time here, especially now with having the plants to take care of. Monday through Thursday I would wake up early, make coffee, get ready for the day, and log in on my work computer by seven in the morning. I'd work until about eleven or noon and then take a break.

By then, the temperature would be warm enough for me to water any of my plants that needed watering. So, I would drink my afternoon tea and water my plants over lunch. A couple times during the week Herschel would stop in to have tea if he hadn't stopped by for coffee in the mornings too recently. We would talk about the plants, his gardens, or any good town gossip. It was amazing to me that he was such a gossip.

After that, I'd eat some lunch and get back to work. I only worked thirty-two hours a week. Thanks to this, I was always done by four in the afternoon, and I always had three-day weekends. This was always a good time to call Lu or for her to call me if she was able. We made sure to talk at least three times a week on the phone. From there, I'd either go into town for dinner, or I would make dinner at home and eat it outside. If it rained, which it only had one time, I would eat inside with the windows open and smell the mossy earth scent that graced us with its presence in the humidity.

I was truly settling in here and I loved it. This was exactly what I was looking for. Lu had been right. I needed *less*. Less city, less suburbia, less people. Less all of it! This was the perfect life for me and I didn't intend to let it slip away. When I was further into my lease, I planned to ask Hersch if I could buy the cottage from him to make it my permanent home. The thought of it brought a big smile to my face. I wasn't sure if he would go for it or not, but it was worth a shot.

Tonight was one of the nights I was driving into town to grab a quick bite to eat with Laurel. Tomorrow was the Full Moon, so I'd put in some contacts that match my normal green eyes to hide the fluorescent shimmer a bit better. Now that I knew there were shifters and Fae about, I didn't want to chance the wrong person putting together what I was. Not that another shifter wouldn't be able to smell me anyway, I just didn't want to flaunt it.

I climbed into my new matte charcoal Wrangler and settled in. It made me do a happy dance in my seat. I had liked my BMW, but I was *so* much happier with my Jeep. It was definitely more my speed rather than a zippy little sports car was. Driving into town, I knew Laurel and I would have to keep things short and sweet. I was too antsy to be around too many people tonight. I could use the impending rain as an excuse to leave early if need be.

We met at the biergarten in town like we had the first night we sat and talked. The scent of rain not far off soothed me. Most cats may not like getting wet, but this was one were-cat who loved the rain. I almost wanted to go ahead and shift when I got home if it was raining by then and run around the forest, but then I remembered I was avoiding that particular area of the forest. The thought put a very slight damper on my mood.

I parked and looked over at the crowded patio to see if I could spot Laurel. She was pretty easy to find. She was about 5 feet and 8 inches tall, typically wore heels when out, and had beautiful strawberry blonde hair. It was straight as a pin and always looked like she had gotten it professionally blown out each morning. My wavy mass of hair usually had me looking like a blonde Hermione Granger.

I finally spotted her at a table in the center of the patio...*surrounded by people.*

Yikes! I put on a face that didn't look annoyed at being surrounded by people instead of sitting near the edge of the patio under the trees that lined the outside of the fence. Laurel had clearly already had a few of the Pilsners she usually ordered. Her smile was broad and she had been chatting with a table of men next to us. Most men couldn't resist a chance to flirt with Laurel. She wasn't just beautiful, but she had a great personality to top it off.

I sat and ordered a Kolche and took a moment to enjoy the scent of the air again. Rain, moss, and the nearby forest. Even here, in the center of the tiny town, you could smell it. The air was still. It felt as if it saturated and grounded me. I could deal with being human for a while just for a friend and the gift of the beautiful weather.

Coming back to the moment, I listened to how her week had been. I told her about my plants, how my friendship with Herschel was progressing, and how my job was going. It wasn't until then did I realize that I missed having a friend close to me who I could talk to about who I really was...at the core of my being.

I was a shifter without a pack. Even though Luna was just one person, she had always been my pack. Yes, we were able to talk several times a week and I could still tell her everything, but it was so much different being an ocean, and then some, away. I was pulled out of my depressing line of thought by the server bringing me another drink.

Even though I metabolized alcohol much faster than humans, I could still catch a slight buzz if I drank beer quickly enough. So, I drank at a leisurely pace, ate my beef döner, and listened to everything around us. The beautiful thing about Laurel was that you didn't have to do much talking because she had it covered.

A breeze blew in my face from the direction of the street, and I smelled it. A shifter was in town. I kept my face clear and leisurely lifted my head and looked around. All I saw were humans, no animals, but the nose doesn't lie. I spotted the side view of a man who looked eerily familiar. This was odd seeing as the only people I knew were the bakery and biergarten staff, the regulars at both of those places, and Hersch. This piqued my curiosity

I told Laurel that I didn't feel too hot. "The weather change must be giving me this headache." I tried my best to look as if I had a migraine coming on. My mom could attest to the fact that I was great at faking sickness. I had to do it a lot as a kid in school around the Full Moon. She looked at me with sympathy.

"Go tuck into your bed with some hot tea and ice on your neck. It is my turn to pay for dinner anyway." I thanked her, hugged her, and climbed into my car.

I had the top off, so I breathed deeply to make sure no shifter had been in my car. It didn't seem so, but I could still smell them on the breeze. The sky was darkening, just like my mood, so I drove toward home.

How have I been here a month, and I'm just now smelling shifters in town? It couldn't be coincidental that I had been approached and now I was smelling shifters in town. Maybe now that they knew I was aware of their presence, they were no longer hiding. It hadn't smelled like Karl either. Once I met someone, I'd never forget their scent.

Then, there was the man whose side profile looked familiar. The little hairs on the back of my neck had gone erect, like right before lightning strikes. That seemed to me like it was something significant. I would keep my feelers out for it to happen again and I would pay attention in town to see if I saw him in the future.

When I got home, I put the soft top on that I kept in the back of the car. All the while smelling the strong scent of a were-cat.

Someone has been here recently.

I walked around to the back of the cottage and, in one of the shady mud patches where the grass didn't grow, saw a paw print. Easily, three times the size of my own...possibly larger. It was most definitely larger than Karl's. My eyes went skyward as I shook my head.

I went inside and tossed my shit down and pouted on the couch for a few minutes. It took me until I was in the shower - trying to give myself an attitude adjustment with scalding hot water - to decide that tomorrow, under the Full Moon, I wasn't going to avoid the forest like I had originally intended. I wasn't going to avoid the shifters, either. I was going to shift during the daylight hours and find a decent hiding tree deeper in the forest in the direction Karl had been taking me, and wait them out.

There was obviously more than Karl, and I was pretty damn sure that my cantankerous Fae friend knew all about them and was keeping things from me. He and I were going to stop dancing around this topic *very* soon and get down to business. I got into my bed once I was dried and dressed. It was early, but I was too annoyed to do anything else anyway. So, I laid there planning my next move until I fell asleep.

❧

I had read somewhere once, that recurrent dreams could be trying to clue you in on something to come, or they could be you not dealing with underlying issues you have that you may not even allow yourself to admit to having. In this case, I was pretty sure it was something to come. It amazed me again how cognizant I was in this dream space.

I was back in the vivid dream-forest I'd had the night on the plane flying to Germany. I was on the same rock that I had simultaneously shifted several times into different species on, looking down at the crystal stream. I turned around, half expecting to see the man from the dream the first time, but thankfully, I appeared to be alone.

This forest was soothing. It felt like a weighted blanket when you were having a rough day with anxiety. I made my way down off the rock and started hiking downstream. I wasn't paying attention to my surroundings for the first little while. Just looking down at my feet and wallowing in my feelings. Thinking the whole way that, perhaps, this was a meditative dream my mind was taking me to so that I could deal with the emotions that had sprung up on me throughout dinner.

When I did look up, my surroundings suddenly began to look very familiar. I was at the spot where me and Luna had been warded off by the glamour. I pondered on whether my subconscious had worked this into my dream or if this area had been in my dream all along, I just happened to find it in waking life.

I narrowed my eyes and walked toward where the boundary lay in wait. I got within a foot of where we'd been stopped on our hike and stuck my hand out toward it. There was no sense of foreboding. It was just a slight apprehension that had nothing to do with the glamour. My hand touched nothing, but I could see a ripple effect as my hand, theoretically, went through the border of the glamour.

"Why have you come here?" I heard again. I jerked my hand back and turned around quickly and there was the same man.

Before I could respond or explore any further, I was woken up by the sound of a loud clap of thunder. *Fuck.* I had been so close. I knew now that these weren't just dreams. There was something more to them. This weekend, after my shift, I was going back to the glamour wall. I wasn't sure why I was being pushed in this direction, but there was no point in waiting around to be forced to figure it out. I may as well get to it myself.

With the revelation of a plan of action, I felt much better. I was able to shut my eyes and be lulled back to sleep by the sound of thunder and the slap of rain on the ground.

Chapter 9

I woke up the next morning and could immediately feel the look of stubborn determination on my face. As much as I wanted to stick to me and Luna's Full Moon routine, today was going to have to be different. I needed to prepare myself. I couldn't go in guns blazing. I needed to be diplomatic. Calm. Centered. All of which were not the strongest areas of my personality.

I made a single cup of coffee this morning, so I wouldn't be too amped. At this point in the month, the coffee was more a ritual and comfort than necessary for waking. I didn't have to try very hard to wake up when the Full Moon was near. I decided to take a shower although I had taken one the night before. I felt like a cleansing shower meditation was just what I needed. Plus, the humidity would help soothe my dry eyes since I had forgotten to take the contacts out last night.

There was something extra today. Something I couldn't settle. I wrote it off as being anticipation for my plans to hunt the shifters in order to learn more about them and their numbers. Why the hell I was smelling shifters in town near my car now while, simultaneously, seeing a man who made my hair stand up as if I'd been electrocuted. Something in me today just couldn't settle.

I put on clothing suitable for a jog, and a light jacket. I was going to jog into town to eat some breakfast. It was only 8:30 AM. I could make it in time for the bakery to still have some of their great breakfast sandwiches. I'd need all the protein I could today. Today, I was going to be in my animal form for a lot longer than I normally was, so I'd need the energy. I didn't mind eating raw while I was Lynx, but there was something in my human brain that hated killing another being, even though it was pure instinct to do so at the time.

Fanny pack, check.

Earbuds, double check.

Key to lock up, another check.

I hit the gravel and set off at a quick pace. The bakery was on the end of town closest to me, so it was about five miles out. I could be there in thirty minutes, easily.

The sun was shining, and it had already begun to warm up and burn off some of the rain from the night before. It was a bit foggy in some areas, but it just added to the lovely quality that Germany possessed. I still held firm that even though I appeared to be surrounded by shifters again, and other supernatural beings, that this was the right move for me. That wasn't just me trying to convince myself. My gut told me the same.

About half a mile before I made it to the bakery, I slowed to a walk to cool down and even out my breath. I was pretty sure that Laurel was off work today. It would be the young boy in his late teens working the counter today. This usually meant I had a silent breakfast., but when I walked in, I saw none other than Laurel, sitting at a table with Karl.

I kept a straight face and decided the ball would be in his court. I was interested to see if he behaved as if he knew me when Laurel would finally notice I was here. I ordered my two breakfast sandwiches with some tea and a lemon poppyseed muffin. Then, I went to sit down. When Laurel saw me, she blushed and waved sheepishly at me. It wasn't like her to blush, even when in the company of a man she may or may not have spent the night with. Judging by her body language, she either wanted to spend the night with him, or she already had.

"Guten Morgen meine Freundin," I said to Laurel from the next table.

She smiled, "You've been practicing!" I nodded and finished off the mouthful of sausage and eggy goodness before I responded that Herschel had been teaching me little bits here and there when we weren't talking about old people stuff. At the mention of Herschel, I could swear I saw the slightest tick in Karl's jaw.

Laurel noticed my eyes shift to him at that moment. "Sammy, this is Karl. A dear friend."

I turned to face Karl and he smirked knowingly at me. "Yes, I believe I have seen Sammy somewhere. Perhaps, on the hiking trails?"

I nodded my head with pursed lips. "Perhaps. I have not been on the trails since my friend from back home left."

Keeping it as the truth with omission was probably the best tactic. I pushed a little further, on instinct, "We hiked until we literally *couldn't* hike anymore and *had* to turn back around."

His smile broadened. *What was it with this guy and the smiles?*

"Yes. Well, many newcomers make that mistake. Lucky for you, it is mostly downhill from there." This confirmed my suspicion that there were shifters behind that glamour. They probably had seen us out there that day and heard every word.

"Yes," I parroted. "Lucky for me." I polished off the rest of my breakfast and said my goodbyes.

I walked for a bit longer to let the food settle, but I still made it home before 10:45 AM. I made a cup of tea and sat amongst my plants on the patio while listening to music I could sing to. Today, was more of a ballad day than an angsty day because it was more soothing to me. I knew I had a good voice. I wasn't superstar good, or I'd hardly be working in a QA department reading over documents to ensure they were filled out appropriately, but it felt good. I sound nice too, if you ask me. I sang to all my plants and then, sat in silence for a while.

I decided that I would shift around two. This would give me plenty of time for lunch and to let it settle. Then, it was game on.

ʘʘ

Since it was still daylight outside when I intended to shift, I walked to the woods as if going on a hike in case anyone happened to be about. I was incredibly aware of my surroundings as I went off the trail to find a hiding spot for my clothes. I left them in a hollow of a tree near the roots and looked around once more. Smelling my surroundings and noting the lack of humans or supernatural creatures alike, I began to shift.

I was caught completely off guard by the sudden onslaught of agony. My skin was on fire. I felt all the bones shift, pop, and remold into animal form. The hair pushing through the moving and molding skin felt like flaming hot needles going through and it was taking a very long time.

I had shifted so many times since it first began when I was a child, that going into my Lynx was second nature. It would always flow and would be over in under a minute. The pain would be there, but it was minimal. This was like being burned alive. It felt like the first few shifts of your life, and it took five, long, *excruciating* minutes.

When it was over and the pain finally subsided, I realized I was lying on my side on the ground, panting. I gave myself a minute to lay there and wonder what the fuck that was all about. My animalistic instincts felt different as well.

Sharper...more confident.

I began to stand, and everything was wrong. My paws were larger. My back legs felt longer and I felt a lot heavier than I should.

I noticed, too, that my coat that I could see on my legs was no longer the brownish-red color. I was pure silver, with light black speckling going over my legs. I ran to my cottage to look in the window at my reflection. Sure enough, I was about twice the size of my Bobcat, my coat was shimmering silver with black speckles dusting throughout it, and my Ruff was twice as thick. Not to mention, the long black hairs sprouting from my ears.

I was completely frozen with shock. Shifters didn't just suddenly start shifting into other creatures. At least I was still in the Lynx family, but that was still completely unheard of. I wasn't sure what to do. If I should shift back and run inside to call Lu, who probably wouldn't even be awake yet, or if I should go through with my plan. I guess, at least now, they wouldn't recognize me as Sammy if they happened to see me.

Maybe I could pass as a local natural Lynx. I doubted it highly unless I managed to be upwind of them. I had a sudden wave of determination wash over me. My animal was telling me to hunt... and most every fiber of my being wanted to go along with that. I trotted back out to the forest. This body moved differently. The back legs were even longer than the front legs on the Bobcat. It just felt extremely unnatural for me.

I realized I was thinking too much with my human brain. I toned down the human and listened to my instincts. I looked ahead and picked up every small movement. My ears swiveled and twitched to hear as much as I possibly could and my nose was scenting the air with every inhale I took.

Ahead, I noticed a small hare which was probably 30 yards away. I looked up the tree nearest me to see if I could make it up and over to the hare to attack from above. The Lynx thought I could.

Time to test out these new legs, I thought to myself.

Then, I reminded myself to shut down the human. I squatted down and jumped up to the low limbs of the tree with amazing ease. I'd analyze all of this later when back in my human form.

I leapt silently from tree to tree, but the hare still sensed danger. Its eyes were huge and round like dinner plates. Its nose twitched as fast as it was breathing. I saw a paw lift and made my move. I had it down and no longer of this earth in a matter of seconds. Quick. Painless. I moved the remains I didn't consume myself and hid them in a tree to not attract any other ground predators.

This was where human me reminded animal me of the job to be done. I decided to really try this new body out and ran for it. It was glorious being bigger and stronger while in this form. I was an Apex predator now in this area, and my body knew it. The Bobcat had predators that would take it out from time to time. Therefore, it was more cautious with its approach in the world, but this Lynx had no natural predator.

I had to remind myself that we did know of a predator that could take us out. The inner beast did not want to agree, but I reminded her that we were heading to where we were going to stalk the other predators now...other shifters.

The Lynx was satisfied with the spot we had found. There was a water source, pines, silver birch, and other large trees. Most importantly, was the faded scent of shifter. The area was, obviously, frequented by them.

I quenched my thirst in the stream and climbed a leaning pine until I felt well hidden.

Now we wait.

At this point, I had been in this new body for a little over an hour. It would be nearing 4 o'clock since I had gotten a later start than I'd intended to. I reached out with all my senses and determined that I was safe enough for a moment. I decided to get a little cat nap in while we waited for my people.

Huh? My people?

My human side wondered when we had started thinking of shifters as our people and not people to avoid. Just another thing for me to reflect upon when I was able to tone down the animal and turn up the human. I crossed one paw over the other and began to doze, head still erect. It didn't feel like long before the smell of a were-cat reached me in my tree. My eyes popped open and I looked down through the thick needled pine branches. I saw Karl and another Lynx I hadn't yet seen drinking from the stream. I let my senses completely take over at this point to reach out to see if there were more somewhere near.

There was a plethora of scents, but none were other shifters. I hadn't thought far enough ahead as to what I would do if I did see another shifter out and about while I was stalking them. I hadn't thought if I would confront them or if I would wait to see if more passed through the area. The animal wanted to confront Karl. I let myself break through the animal more so I could make an "educated" opinion. I didn't think I should confront Karl.

Much to the chagrin of my Lynx, I decided to stay up in the tree. Completely still and completely silent. Breathing slowly, so I wouldn't be heard. Karl and his friend trotted off to the west where the forest got even thicker. Probably going to hunt. So, I sat, and I waited.

And waited.

And waited.

A couple of hours had passed, and I was about to give up the hunt, but then the hairs all down my spine stood on end and I got that feeling I had back at the Biergarten.

A beautiful black jaguar, of all creatures, was walking toward the stream. The only word to express the feelings was...

dazed. Before I knew it, my breath was coming shorter, so I had to remind myself to calm the hell down or I was going to get us caught. I lay my head down on my paws and watched him. I got a good look at his paws and began to believe I had found who had been in my yard to leave me the big paw print.

He was obviously a shifter. Jaguars weren't exactly native to German forests.

So, why has he been in my area?

It was too coincidental that I had spoken with Karl, and shortly after I found a jaguar print in my yard. I would bet my life on it that he knew he'd left a print for me to find. Not surprisingly, my animal side wanted me to stay hidden this time. This cat was easily six times my current size. She didn't want me to get her hurt.

Just like a cat to think of oneself.

At this point, I agreed with her. I was staying up in this tree to see which way he was going to go. I smelled blood on him. I was downwind so I was able to pick up little scents. He too, must have made a kill. He lay down near the water and began to clean himself. There was a patch in the trees that let some sun through that he was basking in. That had to feel so nice.

Yet, here I am, stuck in a tree.

My cat wanted to be laying in the sun just as much as I did. There should only be a couple hours of daylight left. The moon would be at its apex soon as well. I had at least another four hours with my animal. If this was *my* animal, I had time to think about it, as the jag didn't appear to be moving any time soon. He had sprawled out on his side. Back legs kicked out in complete relaxation. He knew there was a slim to none chance that there was anything out there bigger than him.

I decided to use this time to think. I had absolutely no idea why I would suddenly change forms. For 25 years, I had been a Bobcat and now, suddenly, I was turning into a Eurasian Lynx?

I wondered if it had something to do with me moving and my animal needing to blend in, but I had never heard of this before. To my knowledge, you were what you were.

I pondered over it for a good solid hour and the jag wasn't budging. I wondered if he knew I was up here and was taunting me...daring me to come from my safe spot. I hadn't bothered to clean the blood off of my face from my kill. This meant there was a definite chance that he knew something was up here. The breeze had been steadily blowing in my face though so the wind was on my side today.

Eventually, he shut his eyes. When he actually appeared to be in such a deep sleep that he lay his head down instead of holding it erect, I quietly moved through the branches to the lower level of the tree. I looked for a solid spot on the ground that was covered in plenty of pine needles to cushion my landing. I would rather jump directly to the ground than make the additional noise clinging to the side of the tree with my claws.

I found a sufficiently padded spot and bunched my shoulders, preparing to make the leap. I looked over where the jaguar slept one last time, and... *shit.* He was no longer sleeping, but looking me directly in the eye. Instincts kicked into hyperdrive, I jumped as far as I could and took off upon landing. I heard him pursuing me and my Lynx was less than confident in our ability to outrun him. I shifted direction so I could get a glimpse at how close behind he was.

The answer to that was way closer than I'd have liked him to be.

He was only about ten feet behind me.

I got to a thicker wooded area and began weaving in and out of the trees. I started bouncing off some trees to slingshot me into another direction. The hairs along my spine were 100% on end at this point. It wasn't because of being dazed by a glorious creature in front of me that seemed to be doing something to my body chemistry, it was because that very same creature was now within swiping distance of me.

Damn! That was exactly what he did.

He swiped my back legs out from under me. I rolled, leaped, and managed to cling to a branch within my jump range. I had to claw myself the rest of the way up. I looked down at this creature, who I knew was also a cat that was capable of climbing trees, but was not as strong a climber as I. I, however, was able to jump directly into a tree or scale trees that were completely straight with little to no problem.

This guy was too heavy for that.

He paced under the tree, never taking his eyes off of me. The worst thing I could have done was run. Running away had pushed his predator's instinct to hunt into overdrive and here we were. Cat and mouse. The moon was at a point in its travels across the sky, that it still would have been too painful to shift. Too close to the apex. That was not something I was not putting myself through again tonight until I had to.

It would appear that we were at an impasse.

Chapter 10

*I*t took quite a while for the beast below me to calm down. My inner turmoil probably wasn't helping him to calm down. I'm sure every shifter within a 10-mile radius could feel my anxiety. As if to prove this, another jaguar, this one had a beautiful burnt orange base coat, covered in rosettes of different sizes and patterns, slunk out of the bushes. The black jaguar did *not* appreciate another big cat creeping in on his prey.

He very forcefully let the other predator know to back off. He lunged forward and growled while reaching a paw out to swipe. The other jaguar took the hint and backed away slowly, careful not to turn his back on the other predator. When at a safe distance, he turned and ran off to hunt somewhere else.

I looked up and felt for the Moon's energy. We were at the apex now. The beast below me continued to pace and pant. Occasionally, a small growl would come from him. I wanted to slink off through the trees, but my Lynx did not. According to her, this was a bad idea just like running had been. So, we waited.

The moon slid out of the zone that would most affect us shifters, and he began to visibly calm down. His pacing became slower and slower until he stopped and just watched me. I stared directly back at him, despite the feeling that I was doing something wrong. I felt oddly calm in this situation, I had been scared, but I never felt truly that my life had been in danger. You would think having been chased by an animal six times your size, you would have the rationality to feel fear for your life.

No, not me. The anxiety hadn't been a worry for my own person, either. I felt a change coming. Despite what I had just done with my life, I didn't like change. I was a person who revolved around routine. One could say it was ingrained into my very DNA, considering what I was and how we revolved around the moon.

I let out a long breath and a little Lynx mew. He locked eyes with me and lay down, letting out a long chuff. As the moon slid further out of the Apex, and the world around us was cast into darkness, we sat. Me in my tree, him about 8 feet from the tree, where he could look without craning his neck. We did not lose eye contact.

The liquid gold sheen that made a shifter's eyes so unique during the three days before and after a Full Moon danced through the darkness. Finally, he sat up, and he began to shift. He did not take very long to complete the process...maybe twenty seconds. This indicated that this was a powerful shifter, likely much older than me.

Great - you've been looking this guy in the eye for the last hour of your life. Way to go.

It could be seen as a challenge to look, a more, dominant shifter in the eye for longer periods of time. Most shifters would cast their glance down every few seconds just out of respect. Others physically could not stand to look a more dominant shifter in the eye. Then, there was me. I lacked the general sense of self preservation. The alarm bells never went off in my chemistry like it did the others.

When he had completed his shift and looked up at me to meet my eye again, those alarm bells that I was missing about dominance, were ringing at full blast in my head. I hissed due to the shock. Standing before me, was the man from my dreams in the forest. He had a lean, muscled body, and stood at probably 6'1" or 6'2". His eyes were a striking green with yellow streaks, just like his cat's. His face was well put together, with a strong nose, wide, full mouth, and a strong jawline.

His hair was a dark chocolate shade, almost black, and it hung down around his chin in soft waves. He had a quiet beauty. When he moved, it was just as graceful as one would imagine a cat to move with. When he spoke, his voice was deep, but soft and soothing. I could imagine it was intentional. He was attempting to calm me and get me to come out of my cat body into the human one. I was freaked out, to say the least.

Why have I had two dreams, with this man involved?

Dreaming of the forest with the glamour wall was one thing, but to dream of a man I had never once seen or heard in my entire life was another, entirely.

He crooned to me in German. "Es wird okay sein." Repeatedly.

I didn't know what he was saying, but the tone with which he spoke soothed the human and the cat. He stayed back when I stood on my branch. I put my paws on the thick trunk of the tree as if to climb down, while I looked him directly in the eye. He gave me a slight nod and said, "Fürchte dich nicht, ich will dir nicht schaden."

Whatever he was saying, my cat understood. I broke eye contact for a moment to complete my journey down the tree. I quickly hunched and looked back to him to be sure it wasn't a trick and that there wasn't suddenly a massive black cat coming after me. There wasn't. He was just still standing there.

I crept into some bushes, as nakedness wasn't something I was as comfortable with as other shifters seemed to be. Luna was the only one it didn't bother me with. Other people's nakedness didn't bother me per se, but with my own, I was just not on their level. I was raised by a human.

I began my shift. The human side didn't want to, I thought it was a trick and that he was going to try to get to me while I was shifting. However, my cat understood the sentiment behind his words. She tried to soothe my human side as we went through this newly painful change together. I growled and shouted as my body went through the painful twists and contortions to bring me back to my human body.

It took less time than it did to shift into this new Lynx body, but I was still on the verge of 3 minutes of suffering when I finally came out of it, hunched, feet and fingertips on the ground, but curled into a ball. I was covered in sweat from the exertion. I swiped a shaky hand through my hair to remove the sweat-dampened mass of waves from my eyes. I calmed my breathing and opened my eyes back up, to look instantly into the eyes of the man before me.

Again, I had the sensation of the hairs on my neck standing up and being in a daze.

Who is this man, that he can do this to me? What IS he?

I slowly stood, as my legs felt like they had all the muscle tone of mashed potatoes. Once on my feet, still looking into the eyes of the stranger, I stepped forward out of the bushes toward him. No longer ashamed of my nakedness. It was like he'd put me in a damn trance. If he wasn't nervous, then I shouldn't be either.

I stopped a good six feet away from him, as he had backed up quite a bit while I was still in my fight or flight mode.

I lifted my chin and asked, "Who, and what, are you?"

A small smile played across his mouth, exposing a dimple on the left side. "Karl was not wrong about you. You are feisty." He took a moment to observe my body language. Shoulders back, feet firmly planted where I stood, hands clenched and hanging at my sides.

"I am Otto. Alpha of the group that lives in the forest." He looked as if he was concerned about something as we stood in silence for a few moments. "I was informed that you were not one who shifted into a natural Lynx of this area."

It wasn't said with any form of rudeness, but since I knew absolutely nothing about what happened, it made me feel defensive to have someone bring it up before I was ready or had even spoken to my best friend about it.

"Apparently, Karl was wrong." It was an evasive statement, and I absolutely despised being that person to use those tools, but I wasn't ready to talk to anyone about it. Especially, not the Alpha of the area pack.

My animal inside wanted me to divulge everything to this man. She was acting as if she was a purring kitten who wanted to rub herself up against his calves, which left me blushing and averting my eyes to the ground.

This was clearly the wrong thing to do. The cat, I would blame it on her, managed to make it a slow transition to the ground in order to look at every bit of naked male glory that stood before me. I kept my breathing slow and even, but I could feel the uptick in heart rate, and knew he'd be able to hear it. So, I placed a determined look on my face and returned my gaze, quickly this time, to his.

My face softened, "I've dreamed of you."

My lips parted as I caught myself about to drop my jaw. I had not intended to bring that up. Not until I knew more about this clan of shifters. Maybe not even then. I wonder if he felt the same odd tugging sensation toward me by his animal as mine did for him. I managed to cram my lips back together in order to avoid saying anything else unintended.

His left brow shot upward. "That is..." he seemed stuck on his words for a moment, but continued. "That is another interesting piece of this puzzle." He took in a controlled breath and eased it back out of his body. "I felt when a new shifter had moved into the area," he began slowly. "I will typically send Karl out to keep an eye on any lone shifters. To be sure they're not bringing a threat to the area."

I was surprised he was giving me this information, but as strong as I sensed he was, what harm could come from him telling me these seemingly mundane procedures of the pack.

"But, when he said you did not respond to Command, and that you seemed young in demeanor, I knew I needed to come to you myself."

Great. Yup. That's me. The new freak in town.

"Look, Otto. I left my home, to get away from a pack that wanted me to join them." I tried very hard to feign disinterest. "I've never been one to belong to a group. I like being by myself." *Do you though?* I heard my animal say.

"You are going to have to work harder to convince yourself of that if you want to convince me," he said, with a look of confidence.

"Okay then, I *prefer* to be without a pack." I put my hands on my hips, "That better?"

His shoulders shook with his laughter. "A bit, though I must say... you would be entertaining to have around."

Here we go again, I thought. I didn't want to leave this place and I wasn't going to let them make me. I started turning to walk away, much to my animal's dismay.

"Call off your stalkers, and please, let me be."

I began to walk toward home, but I didn't realize exactly how far into the forest I had come.

"Long way back?" I could hear the smirk in his voice, and him walking up beside me. I turned my head to look up at him, as he was just beside me now. Shoulders almost touching.

"Why don't you come back to *Dorf der Gestaltwandler* for the night, and you can stomp your way back to your cottage in the morning?"

"*Dorf der Gestaltwandler?*" I parroted. "What in hell does that mean?"

He shook his head smiling. "Village of the Shapeshifters, in your tongue."

I didn't think it would be so hard to say no to this. I didn't want to be part of a pack, right? I didn't want to be with all these people, or did I?

My inner monologue and turmoil must have been evident on my face for he followed up with, "Then you can say, with conviction, that you do not wish to be part of a pack."

He had a point there I supposed. I gave a slight nod, afraid to say anything more.

"We are very close to the barrier that you and your friend found while hiking in your human form." He turned and began to walk in the direction of his home.

I began to really wish I had my clothes with me. I didn't even have my phone, which made me feel even more naked than I already was. I walked behind Otto, trying to keep my eyes up, but the view from behind was just as good as the view from the front. I... purred.

Stupid fucking cat, stop breaking into my human time! I shouted in my head.

I blushed and looked straight ahead at his back or at the general surroundings, and swear I heard a low chuckle. He was too quiet to be for sure.

"Tell me," he said, "who is your father?"

I walked a bit faster to catch up and be beside him instead of behind him so I could focus on the conversation and not embarrass myself even further. I shrugged a shoulder. "Some shifter, that's all I know."

Otto must have heard the half-truth in my voice as I did, he cocked a brow again and looked down at me. I wasn't sure how much to tell him, as the human side of me wasn't sure I should be trusting of these people. Though, the animal was all but screaming at me to trust them, trust him, be with them!

It was difficult though, considering he had been chasing me through the forest all of two hours ago. To be fair, I had started the evening off by stalking them. I was starving and exhausted from the painful shifting and the chase, and ready to go to sleep. My judgment was impaired.

"His name was Ryk. And *that* is all I know."

It never bothered me, until I was having to explain it to someone, that I didn't know my father. Otto was silent for a while, but I smelled the shift from mild curiosity to intense interest.

"Was tonight the first time you had shifted into a different form, or have you always been able to do this?"

I hated being questioned, but he was being kind about his questioning and not making a huge deal out of anything, which made me feel more cooperative.

"Tonight was the first time. If you couldn't tell, by the slow and painful shift." I shivered at the memory of the pain.

"I am sorry," Otto began, voice containing sympathy. "You will have to shift again in order to get beyond the barrier."

I groaned and stopped moving. "Maybe I'll just hike back home, it's not too terribly late."

He looked at me and held my eyes, "You do not look like you would even make it halfway home."

I *was* incredibly tired, but having to shift again might just make me pass out. Unless I could manage to shift into my Bobcat, but even that would drain what little energy I had left. He reached out his hand to me as if to help as we were going up a rather steep incline. I reached out tentatively, but drew back momentarily. Something about this man unsettled me to my core, but this had been a very rough night, so it could all be compounded. I took his hand and felt suddenly as if I had been struck by lightning.

My animal roared in triumph. While the human half wanted to shrink away. Otto's pupils dilated and then constricted and his grip tightened on my hand. Every muscle in his body was tensed, standing out. I could smell his need but need of what, I wasn't sure. It wasn't necessarily a physical need that had struck the two of us that night. Though, at that point, I'm not sure either of us would mind. A soul-deep connection had been forged with just a touch.

"Well... *fuck.*" I ground out to myself.

I had always heard stories of the Mate Bond, but never had I seen it. Most shifters I knew weren't even sure it had actually existed anymore, or if it was just a story or a long-term memory from a different time. I was so annoyed. He helped me up the rest of the hill and grabbed my other hand, backing up toward a downed tree, and sitting us down on it. Still holding both of my hands, as if not wanting to lose contact.

He took a deep breath and shook himself as if to stabilize himself. He released my hands and made a face as if he were pained, while I — *embarrassingly enough* – whined like someone had kicked me.

What the fuck Sammy, pull yourself together.

I waited for Otto to say something, but he just looked at me. We sat there like this, just breathing, until I no longer could.

"As much as I'm... enjoying this naked hike through the woods business, I can't sit bare-assed on a log for much longer."

He tried to keep the smile from coming, but he couldn't. He stood and quickly grabbed my hand again.

"We will be there very soon. I promise." We moved on, and as promised, we were there within a few minutes.

ଔ

Otto had been entirely blindsided by the Mate Bond. At least, this is what he assumed had just happened to them. His Oma and Opa were a mated pair, but he had never seen or heard of it happening to anyone in his lifetime...which, in fact, was a long one. He felt as if he had been caught in the middle of a lightning storm. Every part of him had wanted to gather her up and never put her down.

He very nearly had. It had taken everything in him not to grab her, but while her animal he was sure felt the same, he probably would have scared the human side of her. On the night of the Full Moon though, when the animal is so prominent, instincts are hard to deny.

They knew next to nothing about each other, and their human sides did not trust each other. She held back when she spoke to him, just as he did to her.

All in good time, Otto. He told himself that he had lived without this for 160 years. He could be patient enough for them to come around to each other, but when he released her hands, his breath almost gushed out of him from the feeling of absence.

She had clearly felt it too, since she emitted a soft whine. She quickly flushed and reminded him of her nakedness and sitting on a tree being uncomfortable, but all his mind got from it was her nudity. He had been trying very hard to ignore up to this point. A body is just a body. Anyone living in a village of shifters knew this. It didn't matter how physically attractive you were, it took intent in order to arouse.

She had no intention of attracting him, yet she had. Now, he knew why. Otto kept his eyes on hers, or directly ahead, and led her to his home. She was so tired she could barely walk straight. She didn't need to worry about him looking her over like he wanted to.

When they reached the barrier, he looked at her with sympathy. "Do you think you can manage to shift into your original form?"

She looked up at him with exhaustion dulled eyes, pale face, while trying not to sway, and it broke his heart.

"If what I think just happened, did indeed happen, you should be able to pull some energy from me while you're shifting. That is, if you can't manage your original form."

She shook her head in defiance and started to shift. She was definitely young, and stubborn, as well as fiercely independent. This could actually pose a problem for the new, and not consummated Mate Bond. He saw a future of wooing someone who didn't want to be wooed. It's a good thing that he, too, was stubborn.

Her shift looked terrible. As soon as she began, she fell to her knees. Otto wanted to reach down to help her, but knew in those moments of pain, the last thing you wanted was someone's touch. He opened up their Mate Bond instead and pushed what he could at her. There was not a guidebook on any of this, so he did what felt was right. It seemed to help. Her breaths came easier, and the form of the Eurasian Lynx began to take shape.

When she was laying on her side catching her breath, Otto did a quick shift and rested his head on her shoulder, chuffing on his exhales, periodically. When she rolled to her feet, shook, and looked to him with her eyes shining, he knew he had helped, at least somewhat. He bumped her lightly with his shoulder, insinuating for her to follow him through.

Chapter 11

*T*followed Otto through the barrier. While in my Lynx form, I could see through it as if I were wearing sunglasses. Once through, the shade lifted, and all I saw was a beautiful little village. There were little cottages, tree houses, and gardens. He led me through the village and finally came to a stop at a cottage, tree house combination. It was connected by a staircase from the second floor of the cottage up into the tree level.

It was amazing.

If I were in my human form, my mouth would have been gaping. As it was, I was still somewhat breathless from exhaustion and the third shift of the day. For that reason alone, I was able to get away with my mouth being open. I felt him pushing his energy at me, which I gratefully accepted. I had, indeed, felt like I was going to pass out during that shift. I was leery of taking much more energy from him, as I wasn't sure if it would somehow link our minds. I was not ready for that.

The jaguar became the man so quickly. I was jealous. In a matter of probably 10 or 15 seconds, he was a bipedal creature again and opened the door with human hands. He stood to the side, allowing me access. I stood in the center of the room, unsure of where to go. It seemed to be laid out similarly to my own cottage, but I felt like an intruder, and I didn't want to do anything that would offend.

"This is my home," he said simply. "You are welcome to sleep down here, or in a guest room, or... elsewhere if you choose."

I wasn't sure if the *elsewhere* was him insinuating that his own bedroom was open, or that I could choose to stay somewhere else in the village. I was sure that his human side wasn't ready to just jump through the hoops the Mate Bond had placed in front of us either. Then again,,...he was a man, so I could have been wrong.

He walked and spoke at the same time, which was something I was not confident I'd be capable of doing at the moment if I were in my human form.

"The staircase up to the tree home, where the majority of the living space that I use, is in the gym room on the second floor of the ground home." We walked up the stairs toward it. Well, he walked. I hobbled. I could sense his distress at my slow, pained movements. The mere thought of this made me feel the need to toughen up and walk with less of an impairment.

"There are bedrooms in this level if you prefer to be down here." He looked at me as if searching for an answer in my eyes.

All I could show him was conflict. A large part of me wanted to throw all caution to the wind and just go with him. Another significant part of who I was didn't want any of this. Instead of shifting to answer him, I just started walking again. He caught up and took the lead in a matter of two strides.

We got to the room with the staircase and I made the feline equivalent of a groan. The stairs wound up the tree a good 50 feet. No way was I going to make it up *that*, but before I could figure out how to communicate this, Otto lifted me and started walking up the steps as if I was nothing more than a sack of potatoes. I didn't have the energy to fight for my dignity so, I took it. My joints began to throb as if the sudden loss of weight on my limbs allowed them to suddenly feel the pain.

He sat me down on my feet at the treehouse level, but quickly picked me up again as I swayed where I stood. I had slept in my feline form before, but not because of current reasoning. Unless Otto wanted to expend more of his own energy by pushing it at me again, it looked like I'd be sleeping as a Lynx tonight. He carried me to a bedroom that I could only assume was his own.

It was minimally decorated. A few paintings of forest and mountain lake views, a long dresser and a tall dresser, a king bed, and an end table on either side of the bed. There was a master bathroom, which was the door he sat me down outside of again.

"If you'd like to try to shift in private you may use this bathroom. From what I know of this situation, distance doesn't matter when pulling energy from your... mate."

It sounded as if the word was hard for him to get out. That, paired with the term situation, hurt the feline's feelings. The human side of me was glad because I wasn't the only one uncomfortable and floundering. I stalked into the bathroom and he shut the door. I tried some deep breathing exercises to mentally prepare myself for this shift. If this had been a different day from my previous shifts, it would be less painful and maybe a bit quicker, but since it would be my fourth shift of the night, I wasn't so sure about that would apply.

I felt Otto open up the Mate Bond and let it flow over me like a warm blanket. I began to shift and concentrated only on the feeling of the Bond and the energy Otto pushed through it. The pain was still present, but it was much less, and it took much less time for me to complete the shift. When the shift was complete, I sat cross-legged on his bathroom floor, observing my surroundings for a moment. The bathroom may be my favorite thing ever...besides the whole tree house thing.

He had a beautiful clawfoot tub in one corner by a large window that took up most of the wall. There was, what looked like, a wooden wine rack, the ones that were shaped like stacked diamonds, that had been repurposed to hold towels next to it. That made me smile. The toilet was in a recessed area of the room, as if it was in its own cubby. Between the tub and the toilet was a walk-in closet. In front of me, was the large vanity space. It held two sinks, which concerned the cat. She didn't seem to like the possibility that there had been someone before her. Behind me, was a massive walk-in shower with several shower heads.

I could have, and quite possibly did, purr at the sight of that shower. I stood up slowly, once again with mashed potato legs, and opened the door enough to just peep out without much of me being seen.

"Thank you," I said simply.

He had been standing there looking concerned, and he let out a slow breath. "You are more than welcome. If you so desire, you can take a shower or a bath before you go to sleep."

I mulled it over for a moment. Had I been at home, I would have just fallen asleep and washed the sheets tomorrow, but I was in someone else's home at present. That just went against the grain to dirty up someone's sheets that way.

"I'll shower, thanks." I shut the door and opened it again almost immediately. "You don't have, like... fancy towels that I shouldn't use, do you?" I doubted it, but it would be my luck that I wouldn't ask and would use some decorative towel.

He chuckled at this and shook his head. "*Nein*. You can use any of the things you see in there."

Good, that answered my next questions about washcloths and soap. I turned on the shower and went about my business collecting towels and finding a washcloth. When I stepped into the shower, under the four shower heads, I could have wept.

I washed quickly, using his soap that smelled of patchouli and brown sugar. This scent suited him. It smelled like the earth, with a hint of sweetness from the brown sugar. I washed my hair and, immediately, sat down under the jets letting the steaming water soothe the aching muscles and joints. Four shifts was not normally this taxing, but when your body is learning a new, larger form, it's excruciating...or so I learned.

I heard him knock and lifted my head. I'd almost fallen asleep here in the shower.

"Come in." I was careful to keep in my current position, as I was sure it was about as modest as I could be while naked in the shower.

He strode in, still not dressed himself, and asked if I needed help. The cynic in me thought she knew exactly why he would ask me if I needed help. I quieted that shameful voice in my head. He looked incredibly sincere, and I could sense the unease he was feeling about my discomfort.

"I might actually need some assistance standing." I was a bit embarrassed about it, but it was what it was. I was quick to add, "But you shouldn't need to carry me again. I just need help getting up."

He laughed and held out a hand for me. He pulled me up and smiled down at me. His eyes still held concern, but his smile lightened it some. Handing me my towels, he got into the shower as I dried myself and my hair ... I definitely struggled not to watch him.

He really was quite beautiful. Even if he wasn't, the grace with which he carried himself, and the calm demeanor he had shown me so far, with the exception of when I'd triggered his predator's instincts, would have made him so. I put my towels in the hamper and moved out into the bedroom. Again, so I wouldn't stare.

I wouldn't be making it very far, or up or down another set of stairs tonight. So, I sat on the edge of the bed and waited. He didn't take very long to come out. When he did, he had a t-shirt and two pairs of boxer briefs. I could only guess that two of those items were for me. He silently rolled the shirt to more easily put it over my head for me. This surprised me, as I hadn't been expecting any of this, but I wasn't going to fight his kindness at present...maybe another day when I was feeling more myself.

I put my arms through and lifted them while he pulled the shirt down over me. He crouched in front of me and put my feet through the borrowed underwear. I placed a hand on his shoulder and stood again, just long enough for him to pull them up. He had his thumbs hooked to the inside of the underwear as he pulled them up my legs. That same lightning that struck us when we first touched hands, left an electric trail up my legs and to my hips, following his thumbs.

If I was any less physically incapable of anything more than curling up into a ball in the bed, then I might think more on the physical reaction, but it was more than that. I had been through my share of physical attractions. I've even been through my share of bed partners that I couldn't stand on an intellectual level, but I had such a strong physical attraction to them that I couldn't help myself. This was almost a spiritual experience and I'd think more about it in the morning on my long hike home.

I sat back down and he backed away from me. Dressing himself in only his underwear, but dressed, nonetheless. This made me feel less like I needed to avert my eyes. He went back into the bathroom; I wasn't sure what for. So, I took it upon myself to pull back the covers and get comfortable. I couldn't help it at this point. I had intended to stay awake long enough to thank him, since my manners seemed as tired as I was, but as soon as my head hit the pillow, I was lost to sleep.

CR

When Otto came back out from the bathroom, he saw that she had wrapped herself around not one, but two pillows, and fallen right to sleep. She had one between her legs and the other she was hugging as if her life depended on it. Her face was buried in the pillow, so all he could see was her eyes. He knew when he picked her up while she was still Lynx to carry her up the stairs, and she didn't put up a struggle, that she was going to pass out.

He quietly moved over to the side of the bed she had laid herself down on, and pulled the covers up around her. She had persevered with a little help from him and managed to take a shower. He had begun to grow worried when there was radio silence coming from the bathroom. Only the sound of the shower streaming onto the tile. When he had seen her sitting up curled into a ball, the sight instilled a level of tender feelings inside that he had never felt in his life.

Otto was not quite sure at the moment how he felt about the fact that his animal had chosen this young woman and her animal as his mate, or even why it had chosen someone at all. He had made it this long in his life without feeling more than a casual spark with someone, but for some reason, his cat had chosen this woman. This woman, who seemed so fierce in her determination to be independent. He thought he would just have to figure it out as he went.

She would probably regret her choice of bed in the morning when she woke up to see him on the other side of it. He chuckled at the thought. He had thought it once and he'd think it again. Karl was one hundred percent accurate about her being feisty. Sure, he could go sleep in one of the other four bedrooms that were available, if his cat would allow it. However, the old feline did not want to leave his new Mate while she was so bone-deep weary. She would keep him entertained that was for sure... as long as she didn't ignore the Mate Bond between the two of them.

He wasn't sure how much of the old stories were true. So, he couldn't be sure if she could truly reject the Mate Bond or not. Of course, he didn't want to force her into anything. *Well*, he thought, *I*

- 90 -

suppose I have my answer as to how I feel about this. He leaned up against the door jamb of the bathroom and just looked at her for a few minutes. She slept quietly and peacefully.

He tentatively put feelers out with their Mate Bond to see if he could sense any feelings her dreams may be stirring, but she was out so hard, it was just peace. He crawled into bed sure to give her plenty of space. He was a tall man, but it was a king-sized bed, so there was enough room for two more people between them. He knew, at some point, he would wind up deviating to the center of the bed, as that's where he usually slept. Thus, he'd just have to deal with that when it happened.

For the time being, he would just let his animal, and himself if he was being perfectly honest, enjoy the feeling of having her near. He closed his eyes, and he too, was quickly asleep.

☙

I woke to the smell of earthy patchouli and brown sugar surrounding me, with my hand and face pressed up against a well-muscled chest. The springy hairs course against my forehead and between my fingers. I took a deep breath, enjoying the earthy scent of soap and man, and... *wait. Man?!*

The memories slammed into me, and I went stiff as a board.

I remembered trying to wait to stay awake until Otto had come from the bathroom, so I could tell him thank you again, but then nothing. I must have really crashed. I lay facing into his chest, with a leg thrown over his hip as if it was my pillow that I usually hugged all night. My head was tucked up under his chin. I wasn't sure if I should move and risk waking him up, or wait for him to wake up as well, and maybe he would roll away first.

This was where my animal and human sides were at war with one another. The animal wanted to stay. She wanted more than simply a morning snuggle. She wanted to complete the Mate Bond and never leave here again. I was not so easily convinced. The only thing I knew about the man was that he was Alpha, he shifted into a Jaguar, and he was as beautiful to look at as it was to listen to him speak.

I slowly lifted my leg off of his hip to lay it down on my other leg...*Keeping those puppies closed.* As I began to slowly pull back

– 91 –

as if I was trying to sneak away from a one-night stand to do the walk of shame home, his arms tightened around me and brought me closer up to him as he slept on. Well, most of him slept. There was evidence of another part of him being awake and it was pressed against my stomach.

Not ready for any of this, I forgot all the pretenses of trying to sneak out of the bed and pushed back to sit up. I couldn't very well go anywhere in my current state of dress, but I could, at least, get away from the semi-human embodiment of temptation that had me snuggled up against him as if he was never going to let go.

He woke up as I was pushing off of his chest and leapt up himself. We had both moved at the same time, and now were standing on opposite sides of the bed. Staring at each other.

"I'm sorry." He said quickly. "I'm not accustomed to sharing my bed with anyone other than my pillows. I did not intend to presume anything."

I smiled and waved a hand, trying to appear as if it didn't bother me.

I didn't use words, so he wouldn't know the lie from the truth. Honestly, I didn't know what was a lie and what was true at this point.

"That makes two of us." I opened my mouth to speak again, and my stomach interrupted.

Even without our supernatural hearing, he would have been able to hear that outside the bedroom door...*with it shut.*

I pressed my lips together and looked up as his smile slowly grew across his face until it was a full-blown grin. "I have, on good authority, that you favor the breakfast sandwich and Mohnkuchen with your morning coffee." I wasn't going to correct him and say that it was usually two or three breakfast sandwiches.

"You have good spies." I smiled for the lack of anything better to do with my face.

"While I make you food, you can tell me about these dreams of yours." I swallowed hard, then nodded and followed him out the door.

Chapter 12

*O*tto led Samantha out of the bedroom and around the back portion of the tree house where the kitchen, in this section of the home, was. The kitchen on the ground level of the home was not a full kitchen. It was more of a *Kaffee und Kuchen* sitting area. He held small meetings there with some of the higher-ranking members of the pack from time to time.

He went about getting coffee brewing and pulled out the supplies for breakfast sandwiches for each of them. After the night she had had, he was sure she would need plenty of calories this morning to get rid of what must feel like a horrible hangover. He took out his phone and sent a text message to Karl.

> *Go to Glenda's and see if she made any Mohnkuchen for her display this morning. If she did, bring it by and drop it in the downstairs dining area. Don't come up to the upper levels. Bitte und Danke.*

Hopefully, Glenda, the village baker, would have made some this morning with the rest of her creations and he could offer that to Sammy. He had an uncontrollable urge to make her feel better after that night. He filled two mugs with coffee and took them over to stand at the bar across from Sammy.

"*Milch oder nein?*" He asked her. When she stared up blankly at him, he shook his head. "You need to work on your *Deutsch*." She scowled but said nothing.

He got to work making the breakfast sandwiches, since clearly he wouldn't be getting anything out of her while she went unfed. He had woken up with her flat up against him, as she was pulling her leg off of his hip and she was stiff as a board. Her blonde hair tickled the lower half of his face since her head had been tucked up under his chin. The palm of her hand flat against his chest. He couldn't resist feigning sleep and pulling her back against him.

His body had reacted how you would expect when a woman wearing, naught but your own underpants and t-shirt, was against you in such a way. He had woken up a few hours previous to this, and they had both migrated to the center of the bed. They had been facing each other and only a couple inches apart. He had been only half awake and didn't think, he'd just pulled her the rest of the way over and tucked her up against him, wrapping his arm around her waist.

Lost in his reverie of the feeling of her, and how she just fit there, he'd almost burned the sausage for the sandwiches. He received a response from Karl at this point. Just a photo of the cake sitting on his counter downstairs.

"*Entschuldigung*. I will be right back." He ran down all of the stairs to grab it and back up in just a couple of minutes.

"Where did that come from?" She asked, with an edge of hunger.

"We have many different people with many different trades in this village." He sat a double piece in front of her with a fork. "Glenda is our resident baker. She begins early each morning."

She didn't seem to care too much where it came from, as before, he could finish his answer., she had begun to shovel it into her mouth, only pausing to take sips of coffee.

He smiled as he watched her. She sat cross-legged on his barstool, one arm resting in her lap as the other worked to feed her. She was slender and had gentle curves, but she was well-muscled. He could hardly expect her to be otherwise given the fact of what she was. Though, she was rumored to eat a lot, even for a shifter. Her hair fell to mid-back in blonde waves. Her eyes were as dark a green as the forest, with yellow streaking through them. The beast inside the man knew he had chosen well for them.

Otto had a suspicion that this woman was more than she appeared. More than a suspicion really, since she had shifted into a new form for the first time the night before. That, and the fact that she did not respond to Command, made it quite clear to him there was more to her than your run-of-the-mill shifter like him.

He had heard rumors, many years ago at this point, that Alaryk had gotten a woman with child. This young woman was about the right age for this story. If Alaryk had really fathered a child, she could very well be it. Alaryk, himself, was said to be fathered by a god, though. Though, which particular god was never disclosed to anyone. The only people who knew were him, and his parents.

The similarities were too specific to be a coincidence. Samantha did not respond to Command. Alaryk was unrestrained by typical shifter physiology and did not respond. Sammy shifted into a new form tonight for the first time. Alaryk could shift into any mammalian class species, maybe even more. Everyone had their secrets after all.

"Okay," Otto's head snapped up from the sandwiches he was assembling at the sound of her voice, which pulled him out of his thoughts by the tentative sound. "Here goes nothin'."

She relayed the story of her dream that took place as she was over the ocean in a plane to start her new life. She got to the point of her dream where she was spontaneously shifting into different species. Otto held up a hand to interrupt.

"Do you recall exactly how many different animals you shifted into in this dream?"

She shook her head and named off the ones she remembered.

"I remember seven animals in particular, but by the time I woke up, the others were a distant memory." He nodded his head for her to continue with her dream. She spoke of seeing him at the end. She also spoke of her being frozen at the sight of him, and him asking why she had come here.

"Well, I think we know what you being frozen at the sight of me was about, but why dream of the forest in the first place? A forest that you, theoretically, haven't seen before."

She held up a finger. "That's not necessarily true. My mom brought me here a couple of times when I was really little." She seemed saddened by the thought of her mother. "I was too young to remember much of anything specific. I just remember her being with me." This seemed like an appropriate time to give her the breakfast sandwiches.

He lay them down in front of her, and that seemed to distract her brain from sadness.

"What about the second dream?" Otto asked as he gentled his tone at the sound of her sadness.

She relayed her second dream to him. This dream was shorter, but he was there. Again, asking her why she had come here. Should he be suspicious or wary of this girl? In her own dreams, he was being defensive of this land when she came to them. He could just be a messenger from her own subconscious asking her to look at why she had uprooted her entire life to come here.

He said as much to her and she nodded her head. "Yes, I understand that. I've been over all those possibilities in my head."

She frowned down at her last breakfast sandwich on her plate. Otto was surprised she had been able to eat two already while telling a story. "But," she continued, "why were you in my dreams in the first place? I *know* I've never seen you before."

"I understand, but I think we already have a likely answer to that question."

ؒ

Otto looked at me fiercely with his last statement. I couldn't tell if he wanted to finish off the process of the Mate Bond, or if he wanted to eat me. It was as if his animal was just under the surface, and I was looking into the eyes of the jaguar and not the eyes of the man. As close to the Full Moon as it still may be, my animal was getting a firm "NO" about finishing the Mate Bond off. I was, under no circumstances, sleeping with this man today.

"Do you know of any shifters who have been... Mated?"

It was so strange to say the word in reference to myself. While I had only been exposed to Otto for a few waking hours since I had officially met him, he didn't seem to be too horrible of a person to be tied to, There still remained the issue that I was an independent person. I literally moved here to avoid becoming part of a pack. I grew irritable again.

"I do, actually." Otto said, which had me looking him directly in the eyes. Which was something I had been avoiding. Not out of submission, but for fear of what I'd see there.

"Who?" I asked incredulously.

It was so rare to hear of that happening and I didn't think it had happened any time in the last century.

"*Oma und Opa.*" He said simply. This one I knew. I recalled my mother speaking of her grandparents and calling them Oma and Opa.

"Are your grandparents still with us?" My social skills weren't up to par, so I hoped this was an acceptable way to ask this question.

He nodded his head. "Yes, but they moved away from *Deutschland* several decades ago." He looked as if he was contemplating something. "I will have to call *meine Oma* sooner than I normally would."

Satisfied with this answer, I watched him take my plate and place it in the sink. He went about his business putting the cake away in the pantry.

By the time he came out of the pantry, I was washing the dish in the sink. He was next to me with a towel in hand waiting to dry it before I knew it. I flushed and handed him the plate and fork. "So, where can I find some women's clothing that I can hike back home in?"

I didn't want to think about shifting again today, so soon after last night. He must have understood, because he didn't question me.

"Do you wish to walk around the village dressed as you are, nude, or in your animal form?" *Whatever that may be today...* he may not have said it, but I could hear it plain as day all the same.

I didn't want to seem like I was intimidated to be naked in public around strangers, even though I was I just really didn't feel like being naked around people I didn't know today. "I'll go as I am, thank you." I said primly.

He laughed at my tone, "Not every person in town has a cell phone. The particular woman we will be going to visit does not."

I looked at him wondering why this mattered. My thoughts must have shown on my face, for he further explained to me that if she had a cell phone he would have just messaged the woman, to have her bring clothing here instead of traipsing me through the village in his under garments.

"I managed through the unmanicured landscape of the deep forest last night. I am sure I can handle the dirt streets of the village." He nodded and put the plate and fork away, while I grabbed the cookware that he had used to make the sandwiches.

We washed and dried them in the same fashion, and then prepared to leave. He had an extra toothbrush for me to use, which I was very grateful for. I felt like the whole forest had grown on my teeth.

I had forgotten that we were not in a ground level home when we stepped out the front door and onto the staircase to go down. Again, I thought about how cool the design was. While in the kitchen, I had noticed that there was a huge balcony built into the tree outside of the door. It was a complicated design of boards being laid around existing branches. He had to have looked for a very specific tree to bring this concept to life.

Once out through the front door of the ground level home, he continued walking. I turned to look at the door and back at him, "Aren't you going to lock it?"

He chuckled, "To protect from whom? Who do you think would steal from the Alpha?"

I raised an eyebrow, "I don't know about stealing from the Alpha, but maybe one of your dominants decides they don't like the way you lead, come in to wait for you to get home, and kill you before you notice them. What then?" He laughed again as if it were impossible and waved me on.

The village was very well put together and organized. I noticed some people worked in the gardens, while others carted things to and from them. Some people worked from their homes like Glenda, who had made the cake this morning. Otto stopped to speak with her. She was a sturdy little German woman, broad shouldered, and a wide hip with a pleasant face and smile. She seemed stern, but the feeling about her was warm. I told her that her *Mohnkuchen* was better than what I got in the village. As I spoke, a twinkle formed in her eye as she looked me over, then returned her twinkling gaze to Otto.

He thanked her, I told her it was nice to meet her, and we moved on. We came to an area where there were several small shops. Otto took me inside one that had clothing on racks made of what looked like fallen tree branches that had been debarked, polished, and connected. It was an adorably sustainable idea. There was a lot of New Age type clothing available, baggy-legged, high-waisted pants that had a nice flow, braided sandals, bags to match, and flowy cotton shirts. It didn't take long before I knew what I'd get.

I didn't remember what I was wearing until the woman came down the stairs. I was assuming she was the woman who ran the shop.

"Lena," Otto said by way of greeting.

His demeanor had become different as we entered the store. He wasn't warm with this Lena, as he had been with Glenda. Glenda he had treated with a motherly regard. Lena seemed to bring out a different aspect that I had yet to see.

"*Hallo, Otto.*"

She was beautiful. Her black hair fell in loose curls down just past her chin, but not quite to her shoulders. Her dark amber eyes were rimmed with thick lashes that were as dark as the hair on her head. She had an exotic look about her that instantly made me jealous of the woman. The animal inside bristled immediately at this woman being in the same room as Otto. She had looked him in the eye as long as she could before averting her gaze down.

Then, she noticed me. Her nostrils flared as if she smelled something foul. Her eyes narrowed and her lips pursed for a split second before she plastered on a smile and spoke to me. "*Hallo! Ich heiße Lena. Und du?*" Otto began to answer for me, and I cut him off with a look, which seemed to shock Lena.

"*Ich spreche nur ein bisschen Deutch. Englisch, bitte.*" I had been getting very good at telling people I only spoke a little German, and asking for English.

"Oh! I am Lena, this is my shop." She said as she waved a hand, as if she had expected me to marvel at her greatness.

"It's a beautiful shop. I hope you'll take my word that I will come back to pay you. What form of currency do you use?"

I wouldn't be surprised if this place ran on a bartering system. This village seemed to be self-sustaining, which made me unsure if anyone would actually take money or not.

"I do take money, but, if you would like, I could just send you a list of items I was going to have to go into the next town to get. You could bring it back to me by next weekend."

Since I didn't have my money, and I was trying to save back up again so I could bribe Hersch to let me buy his cottage, I settled for the barter. I didn't want to have to come back here again that soon, but if it saved me fifty bucks, that's what I'd do.

I used a room in the back and changed. I heard radio silence coming from the shop front. It would seem that Otto didn't like Lena as much as Lena smelled like she liked Otto. This shouldn't have irritated me like it did. I didn't even know the man, and here I was, because of some stupid physiological Mate Bond, getting all these possessive feelings. I did not appreciate this.

As we left, Lena gave me a list containing fewer items than I thought there would be, and some cash. I thanked her and promised to come back with it by the same time next weekend to repay her for the clothing. I'd gotten a pair of flowy harem pants, a pair of thick-soled hiking sandals, and a black cotton tank out of there. As comfortable as it was, and depending on how the hike home went, I may just make this my new hiking outfit. Except, I'd definitely be adding a bra.

"Allow me to walk you at least halfway home?" He looked at me with tentative hope in his eyes.

I wasn't sure just yet. I'd intended to use this hike to think about the situation I'd gotten myself into. If he was going to be with me for half of the way, that would obviously cut my thinking time in half. I suppose I didn't have anything else to do today. I could over-analyze everything even more at home.

"That's fine, I just have to hurry, or my best friend might freak out that I haven't called or texted her yet."

Chapter 13

The walk back home, which would not normally have exhausted me, had done just that. I was completely wiped out. Otto walked back with me halfway, though he looked as if he would have joined me for the rest of the trip home if I'd asked. I'm sure he needed the time to mull over the happenings of the night before as well. Possibly, would call his grandparents to get the word about the whole Mate Bond thing.

As we parted ways, he caught me off guard. He took my hand and asked if I would have a meal with him when I came back to the village with Lena's supplies. I told him I would think about it, but we both knew I'd probably say yes. If for nothing else, than to get some more answers about our circumstances. He leaned down and kissed my hand, keeping eye contact the whole time. I swear my hand tingled for a solid half hour.

I didn't like the idea of being told who I was going to be with by my animal and some supernatural connection. Though, I supposed, there were women who would kill for this. To have the complete loyalty and devotion of one man, and one that was easy on the eyes, was a bonus. However, I had always been by myself, and I liked it. Sure, lately, I'd been questioning if I wanted to get out there and dip my toe in the waters. I wasn't terribly lonely, but occasionally, I felt like it would be nice to have someone to watch movies with or drink coffee in the garden with.

My life was great. Why did it have to change? Or maybe it's not as great as you have convinced yourself it is. Or then, there's that. I told myself to shut up and shook it off.

When I got near my clothing stash I could have cried. I was finally home. I grabbed my clothes and went into the house. I took my cell phone and plopped down on the couch, with complete and total dedication to not moving for the rest of the day. I decided that I may even take a nap.

I looked at the time, and it was coming up to 11 AM. I took a look at my text messages and saw only one from Luna.

Going hiking. ;) Will call you in the morning when I've woken up! Love you!

I smiled. I'm glad she hadn't been trying to contact me. I couldn't stand the thought of worrying anyone. Since she was going to be sleeping probably for the next 5 hours or so, I decided to commit to closing my eyes and taking a nice nap.

ભ

Where, the hell, was I now? It was another hyper-realistic dream. Just like the first two forest dreams, where everything had a golden sheen, and all your senses kind of merged into one. Instead of the forest, I was at the top of a less wooded, rockier, mountain range. Instead of a golden sheen, it was silver. I turned in a slow circle, looking for any other surprising new men to come into my life, but much to my relief, I was alone. I didn't think I could handle any more of that.

I wandered around as best as I could. The portion of the peak of this mountain that I could walk around was relatively small in the grand scheme of things. The footing was loose. Though the weather-beaten rocks and pathways appeared to have been untouched through the ages, so you would assume they would have been stuck in place strictly from age, but no. Each stone was loose as the day it was planted as if never stepped on before.

"Why am I here?" I murmured out loud.

There was quite literally nothing I could see that would lead me to any great discovery. Unlike the last couple of dreams I'd had. Dreaming about a man who was by all appearances, destined to be your Mate, was obvious in hindsight, but what was I to do on this mountain?

I pushed the boundaries of my comfort a bit and looked over the drop on the North side of the mountain. I crept close to it and eventually decided that since I'd established that the ground was loose, it would be best to spread out my weight on it so close to the edge. So, I came to all fours and peeped over. There was just more mountain. Very steep mountain, but when you looked out, there were many smaller mountains around this one.

Those that sat in the protection of this one were shrouded in mist and covered in deep green evergreen trees. The type that their branches seemed to hang and droop in quiet beauty. I backed up, stood, and checked the remaining sides. The South side of the mountain had sparse coverage of the same trees. Most were leaning or broken as if recently beaten by a storm. I started my descent amongst the trees.

More than a few times, I had to slide on my butt from one tree to another because of how steep it was. I knew I could have just shifted, but even in a dream, I didn't want to shift again. Not for a while. So, slow and steady it would be. By the time I made it down toward the base of this monstrosity, I had several cuts, scrapes, and bruises that were healing or healed. Which was interesting, considering this was theoretically just somewhere in my subconscious mind.

At the base of the mountain was a great basin of a lake, held captive between the one I had mostly slid down, and three others. I walked up to the water and looked in at my reflection. It was me. I never knew what to expect when I fell asleep anymore so I had to check. I began to walk around the lake looking for anything that could have brought me here, but after several minutes of fruitless searching, I decided to sit and meditate on it.

I sat with my back against a large tree trunk. I sat cross-legged, but placed my palms flat on the earth. Closing my eyes, I opened my mind and senses. Listening, scenting, watching from my mind's eye. I put out feelers into the area, and it wasn't long after that I heard a deep rumble. My eyes snapped open. What they saw took my breath away - partially out of fear.

Not six feet in front of me was the largest Brown Bear I think I'd ever seen. Not that I had seen many, but he was the biggest. I froze and said nothing. Scarcely breathing, but when I did take in a shallow breath, I noticed this wasn't a natural Brown Bear. My nostrils flared and I bent to stand. The bear groaned and took a step forward. Hoping I could get to his human side, I continued my upward path to standing.

As I reached my full, unimpressive height of 5'4", the bear pulled out all the stoppers and also stood. Easily twice as tall as me. My mouth dropped open. *I knew you should never run from a bear. Shifter or not. I had run from a black panther recently and look how that had turned out.*

"Where am I?" I said out loud, hoping to get the bear to realize that I knew it was no true bear. He let out an impressive roar.

And that scared me awake.

There was definitely not going to be any avoidance of this one while I mulled it over trying to figure out what I thought of it. I looked at the time and noticed I had slept for two and a half hours. Now, I had woken up starving. I took my cell phone into the kitchen, dialed Lu, and put her on speakerphone while I rummaged through the fridge, pulling out the makings of what would be a few really big sandwiches.

She wasn't happy that I had woken her up at 6 in the morning, but she took her phone down to the living room and posted up on the couch and listened while I rambled about the entire night, my entire morning, and then, the dream I'd just had. She didn't interrupt except to interject a well-timed sigh, laugh, or gasp. At the end of my story, when she remained silent, but for the noise of her chewing on her lip I said, "Well?!"

"I honestly have no words, Sammy."

What an ill-timed moment for me to have finally rendered her speechless. When I said as much, it seemed to get her brain flowing a bit better.

"I think the shift into a different Lynx form *could* be coincidental because of you moving to a different country and climate and all that. But it's paired with too many other weird happenings to be sure."

I waved my sandwich around in the air as I spoke next, "When have you EVER heard of someone moving and starting to shift into the local creatures?! I've never heard of a grizzly shifter suddenly start shifting into a fucking panda when they move to China!"

As I was obviously working myself up and becoming upset, Lu didn't take my tone personally. "No, but that's exactly the point. If that doesn't explain it, what in hell else would? I can't think of any other reason."

She had a good point, so I calmed down a bit.

"As for this Otto character," her tone immediately went strict, "I could kick your animal's ass for doing this when I wasn't there to meet and approve of the guy first."

She got quiet for a moment.

"What are you going to do about it?" I groaned and flopped back on my couch.

"I have no fucking clue. Half of me wanted to finish it last night and accept what had been pushed into my lap."

She giggled at that terminology. She could find humor in the most annoying times.

"Easy turbo. The other part of me wants to avoid him out of sheer, stubborn, willfulness to be by myself." I sighed heavily, "I have already made too many big changes."

I could just see the look on her face as she said, "You got that right. But, if your animal half thinks so highly of him that a Mate Bond came of it, *after* you'd dreamed of him even having never met him by the way, then maybe it's worth getting to know him a bit to see what you think then?"

"I don't know. I've got bigger fish to fry." I even annoyed myself sometimes with my childlike stubborn behavior. "What about the dream during my nap today?"

I heard her blow out a big breath. Which was Lu for "hell if I know". I quite understood the feeling.

"I think it may be time for you to pay the Fae a visit." I hadn't thought of that yet. "One where you're actually honest with each other and you're not tiptoeing around the fact that you each know what the other is."

"Now you're just asking too much, Lu," I said in jest. I chuckled, imagining the look on Herschel's face if I were to show up on his lawn and shift. Which, I decided, was exactly the way I was going to handle it. I told Luna as much and she thought that was clever.

"I don't know if he'll be able to help me though. This seemed awfully specific, and shifter related." I was hesitant to hope any information would come of it. "I'm not sure what a Fae would know about it."

I sighed and brushed it off. "Enough about me. Tell me about you. How is the pregnancy going? You sound like you feel better."

She went on to tell me all about it. Her second Full Moon being pregnant seemed different to her. The only word she could use to describe it was "more". Oddly enough, after experiencing the Mate Bond, I understood what she meant. I just didn't want to admit it to myself or anyone else yet. Not even Luna.

We ended our call, and I felt much better after having a freak out on the phone with her. Maybe I'd take a trip home soon to visit her and Noah. Mostly her, but I did enjoy Noah's company. I'd plan that another day. Even though I had just taken a pretty long nap, I was still tired. The level of tiredness, paired with the nerves of the push from something trying to get through to me from god knows where, left me cranky. So, I decided to knit and watch some TV. It had been a while since I'd done just that.

◌

I slept for 13 hours that night. Completely exhausted. I woke up feeling pretty good though, after a night with no dreams. I'm not sure I knew what a normal dream felt like anymore. One of these days, I was going to be doing some serious catching up on my self-care. Certainly, a long, hot bath. The thought of a bath made my thoughts flow to the massive tub in Otto's bathroom that then, led to thinking about that particular issue again, which I was not doing.

Having thought about self-care that morning, led to two long days of it, but I was also working on my plan to go and talk to Hersch. So, while I was cleaning, gardening, and eating good foods, what I *wasn't* doing was going to Herschel's house. I figured if I didn't go over there like usual, he'd come to me sooner than he normally would.

The plan was to be in animal form when he showed up and walked around to the patio like he normally did with coffee. I was fairly certain today would be the day that he'd show up. I was sitting in my living room naked as a newborn baby, with the back door cracked so I could get out easily in my animal form, mentally preparing myself to shift.

My animal had been rather cranky since I left the shifter village in the forest. She didn't see why we weren't there instead of

- 106 -

here. Now that I was about to shed my human form, she was happier. I felt more like a chicken today than a Lynx. Feeling like a coward wasn't something that I enjoyed very much so I sucked it up and began the shift. It was rough to start, but then I felt Otto push energy out at me.

Even from the probably 15 to 20 miles between us right now he knew when I was shifting, and was nice enough to lend a helping hand. I must have been doing a very good job of ignoring anything Otto up to this point, because if he was able to feel me shifting, then I should be able to feel him and his whereabouts as well. Once his energy washed over me, the shift was normal. No pain beyond what I would usually feel, and it took the same amount of time as it had pre-form change.

I shook myself and padded up to the bathroom to look in the dressing mirror I had posted up in the corner. I was half expecting to see a bear looking back at me with my luck, but I was still the silver, speckled Eurasian Lynx. This form was really pretty. I felt even stronger and more capable in this form. I jumped down the stairs, walked through the kitchen, and pushed the back door open.

Once outside, I laid down on the patio in the sun, enjoying the warmth. I was outside like this long enough to want to give up and go back inside, but then I heard Herschel's old Volkswagen pulling up in the driveway.

Showtime, I thought to myself.

I stayed where I was, laying down, but looked toward the side of the house he'd be walking around at any minute. I casually wondered if when no one was around, if he still played the part of the old man, or if he allowed himself to get around better.

When we saw each other our eyes locked. He didn't move for a moment. His nostrils flared as if he too, was scenting the air. I didn't know enough about Fae to know if their senses were also heightened, but he wouldn't be too far of a stretch considering how powerful they were. He continued to the patio, sat down in one of the chairs, and put the two travel mugs of coffee down.

"Well, I suppose the jig is up eh?" He said with a smirk.

I gave a little mew and stood. Slowly meandering back inside. I looked behind me to make sure he wasn't following before I shifted and got dressed again. I sent out a little thank you nudge for the assist to Otto – just out of sheer politeness I told myself. When I sat down across from Hersch he smiled and folded his hands across his belly.

"Well, what do you want to know?" He asked me.

"First off, I've known since you took the glamour down from the shed. Like you probably intended."

He nodded and rocked in his chair and kept his eyes on mine. "Second off, how much do you know about shifters and shifter communities?"

He eyed me speculatively, as if trying to figure out how much to divulge. I had figured out that he had put the glamour up around the shifter village. It smelled of his magic. So, I knew he knew about them, he just maybe didn't know I did.

"I know enough to know that you're an oddity, my girl." He took a leisurely sip of his coffee as if I had all the patience in the world. "When I first saw you through my window, you did not look as you did this morning. *That* shouldn't't happen."

I took my own leisurely sip of coffee just to level the playing field.

"You're correct. It shouldn't't. Any idea why it would?"

I could tell he knew something. He just didn't want to give up any precious nuggets of information. "Considering this is my life here, I'd really like to know whatever it is you do."

He looked conflicted still. "Tell me what has been going on and I will tell you what I can of your situation."

A knot in my stomach that I didn't know was there released when he agreed to tell me what he knew. I knew then that I would have been hurt and felt betrayed by him if he had tried to dance around it. Apparently, I felt that he was truly my friend. He may be Fae, but I enjoyed our relationship. So, I told him about the dreams I'd had about the forest and Otto, about the shift into the new form, the Mate Bond, and then the dream I'd had a few nights ago involving the bear.

It took a while to get through it all. I wasn't speaking as erratically as when I had called Luna and told her everything, so I was able to go into more detail. We had to go inside at some point to make more coffee and eat, but he listened intently and even lent a hand periodically. When I was at the end of my story he asked, "What do you know of your father?"

I whipped my head around to look at him. We'd never spoken about my father before, so there was no reason for him to believe that I didn't still have a father.

Once I got over that, I told him that all I knew was he was a shifter, and his name was Ryk. That he and my mother had met here in Germany. His lips pressed into a firm line and he shook his head. "Ryk, or Alaryk as his full name is, was not just a shifter." He finished drying the dishes and moved to the refrigerator. "Would you like *Bier oder Wein* for this?"

I went to sit at the table, "Beer me."

He grabbed two of the Kolche beers that I enjoyed so much from the fridge and brought them over to the table. He then looked for beer mugs and when I told him I didn't have any, said something about ridiculous Americans and their lack of manners, and came over with two open bottles of beer. It was kind of funny, because I'd never seen him drink anything other than coffee.

"I'm not sure where the best place to start would be." He took a rather long drink and set the bottle back gently on his coaster. "I believe your father was Alaryk König. He was half shifter." He looked me in the eye. "And he was half god."

I choked on my beer and it had my nose and eyes streaming.

Chapter 14

After Herschel had left from giving me the startling information about who my father probably was, I had to call to relay it all to Luna.

"So, you're telling me, that your father was some kind of shifter-god hybrid, who could shift into any species of mammal?"

I stared up at my ceiling as I had plopped myself down onto my bed and put Luna on speaker phone next to my head. "Yup," was all I could manage.

"Not only that, but also that he disappeared somewhere around the time you were born and there hasn't been a trace of him since?"

I nodded my head, but remembered she couldn't see me. "Yup," was once again all I could manage.

I could hear the wheels in her head turning. "So, there is a possibility that you will go through changes in form again?"

That was a possibility I hadn't yet thought of, nor did I want to.

"Yeah, I hadn't thought about that yet. But I'm kind of hoping not. It's not like there is anyone around to teach me how to shift back into other forms instead of it being at random." Herschel had said that the witches had always felt threatened by Alaryk, and were suspected in his disappearance. Shifters and witches had never been on good terms. It was said that the shifter "curse" had been placed on our kind long ago, by groups of witches who feared the shifters. The shifters were very different then. Very primitive. So, they very likely deserved it, but the bad blood between the two had carried on through the generations.

I'd asked him if that meant my father was dead. He shrugged one shoulder. "No one knows. They either succeeded in killing him - which would have taken much strength on their part to do - or they trapped him somewhere," he had said.

That was where the dream of mine had come in. Apparently, one of my father's favorite forms to assume had been a massive Brown Bear much like the one I had seen in the dream.

This made Luna almost giddy. "Your father could still be alive?!"

She started talking about how we'd have to figure out how to find him, get him out, and then I'd get to know him.

"You're forgetting one thing, Lu. The witches probably killed him. Even if they hadn't, how in the hell would two young shifter women, one of whom is pregnant, get some shifter-god hybrid out of a witch prison?"

I wasn't known to be as optimistic as her, but this time it felt like she was really reaching.

"The next time you have the dream, you need to purposefully hurt yourself." At my protest, she went on. "Not *bad*. Just enough that it wouldn't fully heal by the time you're able to scare yourself awake. I want to test a theory."

I was picking up what she was putting down. If I still had the wound when I woke up, it could indicate that it wasn't just a prophetic dream. I could be walking worlds in my sleep, and the witches could have put Alaryk in another realm just beyond reach.

"But what if he was put away for *good* reasons, Lu? What if he was a horrible person who was killing people and magicals alike?"

I didn't realize it, but this had been my fear since speaking with Hersch. He didn't say much about Alaryk's personality, but the Fae rarely grew attached or even cared to, so that wasn't atypical.

Luna scoffed. "Knowing *them*," meaning the witches I assumed, "the most he did was exist and have power."

She was right. They had always hated us, even though modern-day shifters kept to themselves and didn't harm anyone. Well, most of us anyway. There were shifters who went mad just like there were humans who went mad. The problem with a mad shifter was that they could potentially out the whole supernatural world, and they could become murderous and harm humans in the process. Luna laughed into the silence.

"What?" I asked.

"Well," she began with a sly tone. "You now have a bigger issue than your Mate Bond to *not* think about." She laughed again and I hung up the phone and tossed it down on the bed.

I swear I could still hear her laughing when she texted me. *Don't be a poop. That was funny and you know it. Keep me posted. Love you!*

I sighed and texted back that I would and I loved her too.

Then, tossed my phone back down. I guess it was time to go get Lena's supplies and take them back a couple days early. My animal growled at the thought of Lena. So, I screamed into my pillow and proceeded to lay there the rest of the evening, eventually falling into a dreamless sleep.

03

I could ring her beautiful little neck. By the time I had picked up everything on Lena's seemingly short list, my Jeep was full up. I even had the rear seats folded down to maximize my cargo space. When I pulled back into my driveway and got out of the car I was muttering something about bitches, when I smelled Karl. "*Hallo, Sammy!*"

He always sounded so bright and chipper, he must be a real douche canoe under it all. No one was that happy all the time.

Or you're just being cranky, stop it Sammy!

I rolled my shoulders to shake off the annoyance. "Hi Karl." I turned to look at him. I looked him in the eye and he immediately looked down and away, but then returned his gaze to mine.

Well, that was interesting. I decided to add that to my growing list of questions for Otto. He looked in the back of my Jeep. "Long day of shopping to cure what ails you?" His voice was full of mischievous sarcasm.

I gritted my teeth and ground out, "This is what I told Lena I would bring back in payment for the clothes I left in."

He nodded understandingly. "Do you know the mountain road that can lead you close to the village for things like this?"

I'm pretty sure I growled, which surprised him. "No, I do *not* know the mountain road that leads you closer to the village. Though it would have been stupendous for someone to have mentioned it to me before now."

He smiled and shrugged, "This is why Otto sent me here today. To show you the road." That relieved some of the tension in my shoulders at least.

I was starving, so the road would have to wait, but I didn't want to leave Karl outside just standing there and waiting for me. So, I awkwardly invited him to come inside and asked if he wanted a sandwich. He declined and watched me from the living room while I ate standing up.

"So, how do you know Laurel?" His constant smile remained in place.

"The witch and I have been... friendly... for years now." This was the second time in as many days that I almost died from food or drink.

When I stopped coughing from choking on the bite of sandwich I looked up at him, eyes blazing.

"Witch?!"

His smile faded. "I thought you knew already. How do you sit so near her, but you don't smell the witch magic on her?"

I thought back and most times when we were seated outside, the smell of the forest did seem to be very near. I had just thought it was the moisture content of the air on the days we would meet.

Witches constantly smelled of the earth. At least, their magic did, and the scent followed them everywhere. The only other times I had really seen her were in the bakery, where she didn't stand still for very long. The scent of her magic would be well covered up inside the bakery as well with the plethora of smells from all the different baked goods and coffee.

I was floored.

I was going to have to create a list of things to tell Luna. At the rate these bombs were being dropped on me, I'd never remember them all by the next time I got to speak with her.

I wolfed down the rest of my sandwich and grabbed my keys. "Let's hit the road, Jack."

When we got in the car, he looked a bit nervous to have me drive him anywhere. This brightened my mood. "Hold on tight. And remember, you're a shifter. You heal fast." I grinned and started the car when he told me to head toward Herschel's.

"Why? That's a dead-end road." He shook his head and kept his smile off his face. His right hand was up on the "oh-shit bar." I wasn't even going 45 mph yet and he was white-knuckling it. I rolled my eyes.

"You *think* it's a dead-end road. Herschel glamoured it to look that way a couple of hundred years ago much like he glamoured the village." *What a sneaky little shit.* "This is why he lives at the end of the road. So, he can keep watch."

So, obviously, Herschel and the shifters were on good terms. I couldn't fathom why though. Most Fae stuck to themselves. I know they didn't even really enjoy the company of their own kind, but they would still congregate in the same areas. The Fae were too busy, subtly, fighting amongst themselves using trickery to try to gain power over each other to ever truly be friendly with each other.

"How exactly did Hersch and the shifters get to be on such good terms?"

It was beyond any normal reasoning that he would aid the shifters as much as creating a safe haven for them by putting up glamours and deterrents and who knew what else.

"I am not sure. This is before my time that Herschel did all this."

I'd have to ask Herschel.

"How old are you exactly?"

You never could tell with a shifter, except sometimes by the way they spoke. The really old ones never would fully adapt to the lingual changes through the centuries.

"Exactly? I am 75 years old."

He smiled at me then. "And how old are you, exactly?"

I was just a kitten to these people. "I'll be 31 in June."

He laughed and voiced my previous thought, "You are just a small kitten." He sobered and looked at me. "Odd though that Otto's cat would have partnered him with one so young."

I didn't know if Otto had been telling the higher-ranking members of the pack, or if they were able to feel it when their Alpha had Mated with someone. Then, I just happened to be the one who walked out of his home the next day wearing his underwear and t-shirt.

I grumbled a bit about something to do with age not meaning anything about anything, but then it hit me.

"Wait a minute. How old is Otto?"

I wasn't sure I wanted to hear the answer to this question. Karl grinned his grin that I was beginning to take as his signature look.

"I think you and Otto can talk about those things together, don't you?" I glared at him. Apparently, too long for his liking because he adjusted his grip on the handle and told me to watch the road.

Once we had found the mountain "road", I saw why Otto had sent Karl to show me where it was. The damn thing could barely pass as a hiking trail. I was really glad I had traded in the BMW about now. I slowed it down and dropped gears. Now, Karl had his hand pressed up against the roof of the car. I couldn't help but to laugh. So naturally, I accentuated all of the bumps and made sure I drove over rocks and other debris that I didn't actually have to drive over.

By the time we came to a clearing that appeared to be a dead-end, but had enough room that I'd be able to turn my car around, Karl was ready to jump out from the car. Not surprisingly, that's exactly what he did. I was surprised he didn't scream "LAND" and kiss the ground. He came to the back of the car after he'd paced for a moment to get out his jitters, and grabbed a few of the large boxes, and had some bags on his arms. I, not being as lengthy as he, was not able to get as many boxes. So, I grabbed the rest of the bags and one big box, which was an awkward enough haul.

When we got to the barrier, Karl said something in German, and we were able to walk through in our human forms. I'd have to figure out what that phrase was that he said, but not just yet. The night I met Otto, he must not have trusted me enough, regardless of the Mate Bond, to speak the phrase in front of me. This would have shown me how to get into the village without shifting. That clarified some things for me.

I hadn't been to this part of the village when I was here. This must have been the strictly residential section. The homes looked like something out of a fairy tale. Even the ones high in the trees. Some had plain ladders to get up. Others had more intricate ladders or staircases, like the one connecting the ground floor of Otto's home to the tree level.

"*Hallo*, Sammy."

I jumped, almost dropping the box. Speak of the devil and he shall appear. Otto was suddenly walking on the right side of me and as I had been looking to the left, he had sufficiently scared me.

"Um... hi."

I didn't intend to be bashful and weird, but I just felt so damn awkward about everything! Karl had gotten ahead of me by quite a bit. So, I quickened my pace. Otto pulled the box from my arms and put a handout to stop me so he could take some bags. To which I firmly held onto.

"Thank you but I can handle the bags." *I'm as strong as any other shifter, damn it.* I thought to myself.

We walked on in the awkward silence until we made it to Lena's little shop. I still loved it, even though I didn't love her so much. She came down the stairs in her slow and sexy manner and I hoped she would trip and land on her face. Any woman would be jealous of her purely just because of how she looked. Not just me. It was my turn for my nostrils to flare, as she thanked the men, but then acted as if I didn't exist. One day... one day she'd trip on her face, I told myself.

❧

Otto felt when Karl opened the walkway through the barrier and let himself and Samantha come through. His pulse jumped momentarily until he reminded himself, he wasn't a schoolboy. He was the 160-year-old Alpha of the Baden-Württemberg area pack. He hadn't taken on the responsibilities of leading the pack all those years ago, to be brought to heel by this woman, but then, he saw her and his animal had other plans.

He grabbed the box from her, careful not to touch her, and attempted to take some of the bags from her, but she was definitely a woman of the 21st century. She didn't want to be pampered. His animal felt pride at the person he had chosen for them. When Samantha's nostrils flared as if she was taking in a deep breath in order to remind Lena of her existence and what she had done for her, he had expected a brawl. When she said nothing and composed her face, he lifted a brow.

"Lena, you are thanking the wrong people."

Otto didn't want Lena to think she could behave that way toward Samantha in his presence. It would make her think she had some kind of upper hand. She, most certainly, did not. His face must have belied the frustration he was feeling because Lena looked down and away quickly. When she looked up and tried to hold Samantha's eyes, she didn't manage for long. Once again she was forced to look down and away.

"Forgive me and my manners. Thank you for gathering this and bringing it here for me."

He watched Samantha and felt her irritation beneath the cool demeanor. He had felt a lot of emotions coming from her in the last few days. He'd even felt her shifting because he knew it would still likely be a lot for her. So, he had pushed some energy through the Bond.

"You're quite welcome, Lena."

Otto took Samantha's keys from her and gave them to Karl so he could escort Lena to the car to grab the last of the boxes. Karl would keep an eye on her to make sure she did nothing underhanded. Now, he and Samantha needed to go back to his home and have a conversation. Several, actually.

Once there, he led her through the ground-level home, up the staircase into the upper level, and onto the balcony off the kitchen. It spanned the whole back side of the house. This was where he'd shift and head up to the platform at the tops of the trees so he could really see the stars. There was no light pollution this deep into the forest, and it never failed to take his breath away.

"Would you like anything to eat or drink?"

Samantha shook her head and thanked him anyway.

"Did you get the chance to speak with your Oma?"

Otto nodded his head. He had, and she had been quite excited about the ordeal. She wanted to fly home and make a big fuss over it, but he told her not to. He didn't expect her to listen though.

"There are a few significant factors about the Mate Bond. I can lend energy to you, as you can lend energy to me, which we already learned. What we didn't know was that we are connected through emotions as well. I could tell you have been restless and going through something the last few days, but as it does not connect our minds, I couldn't tell what."

That made him restless in turn because he did not know why she had been angry, then anxious, then back again. Subsequently, to feel her shift, he had almost shifted himself and ran to see what was happening. Instead, he'd sent Karl to watch over her out of sight and scent distance.

"Another interesting thing is that, since you are Mated to the Alpha, you automatically hold equal power in the pack as me."

Samantha's eyes widened at that. "But I... but."

She was so flustered she couldn't speak. So, he tested the waters, opened up the Bond, and tried to send what he thought felt like soothing energy.

"Thanks. I didn't want to be part of a pack. Let alone be the equivalent of a damn Alpha."

Her face was pinking up in her annoyance. It was charming.

"I know. So, you have said. But that is what your animal chose for you."

Eyes narrowed at Otto, Sammy asked, "What else?"

"Well, it doesn't have to be accepted."

She perked up a bit at that. "What do you mean it doesn't have to be accepted? We can make it go away?"

His animal was gnashing its teeth inside at him for telling her that it was optional, but he didn't want to be "stuck on" with someone who didn't want to be "stuck on" him.

"Yes, if we do not... consummate the bond after a time... it will die."

"Yes... we can." He repeated with a sigh. Then, he looked at her with his vibrant green eyes, animal dying to get out. "But I'd like it if we didn't."

Chapter 15

The animal inside was raging as I was perking up at the idea of being able to make this Mate Bond go away. I didn't know who I was supposed to listen to, the animal, or the human. I also wasn't sure why I was clinging so hard to being a solitary creature. Sitting alone, or with my Fae friend, or my apparent witch friend. There was just too much going on in my life right now that I couldn't think straight. I decided to table this thought and soothed my animal by telling myself that I wasn't sure what to do about the Otto situation, insinuating that there was a chance.

"I'd like to table that conversation for now." I tried to keep my tone as soothing and gentle as possible so he wouldn't think I was flat-out rejecting him. "I had another dream, which led to a long conversation with Hersch."

He gave me a look that made me want to laugh. If he had been in his Jaguar form, his head would have swung in my direction and his ears would have perked up. It was very amusing to see how animalistic those who lived here truly were. I felt like an imposter when I was here because I had led such a human life.

I told him of the dream with the bear, and then I told him about my conversation with Herschel.

"What do you know of Alaryk?"

I wanted to know about him. My mom never spoke of my father, and I got the feeling she was trying to protect me from something. I just wasn't sure if she had been trying to protect me from *him* or from something else. Otto's face transformed to a look of concentration.

"Well, Alaryk is – or was – an old creature. Like Herschel said, he could shift into any mammalian species." He looked me over, observing all my features, and smiled gently. "You do favor him a bit. He also had your blonde hair. And your eyes are his."

So, he had known him? I needed more out of him. "Yes. But what was he like? Was he a good man? Was he a bad man? Why would the witches want him gone?!" The level of my voice raised with each question, and I didn't realize I'd had all that in me.

"He was a good man. As far as I'm aware, he never harmed anyone." Otto stood and walked across to the door. "I am in the mood now for some wine, and I'm sure you are too. I will be back momentarily."

He walked inside and I could see him go into the pantry. If my dad was indeed Alaryk, which the odds were looking increasingly good for that, then what else could I do? And that meant... I was a descendant of a fucking *god*?! My brain didn't know how to compute this information.

Otto came back out with two wine glasses held between his fingers by the stems, and a bottle of red wine. He sat back down next to me, as calm and cool as a cucumber. Everything he did seemed to be done in that manner. Though I knew better now because I could feel the emotions rolling through him if I paid attention to what was going through the Bond. He poured the wine as he began to speak again.

"As I was saying, Alaryk was a good man. I believe the witches wanted him gone because they thought he may be on the way to removing the shifter curse that makes us *have* to change during the apex of the Full Moon."

My eyes widened and it took all I had not to let my mouth drop open. "So, my most likely father, who is half god, could have known the key to unlocking this centuries-old shifter curse placed on our species by the witches?"

He nodded slowly.

"He was also much like you. He enjoyed the solitary life, but he was still around frequently. As if he wanted to enjoy the feeling of being around a group, without actually being part of the group." He looked at me with a raised eyebrow and a smile.

"Yeah... that sounds familiar I guess," I muttered into my wine glass.

The wine was exceptional, but the bottle was unmarked. "Where did this come from?" I raised my glass to indicate what I was talking about.

"Just another of our pack professionals doing what they do best." He had a twinkle in his eye and I could tell there was a secret there.

"You make it, don't you?"

He freaking would. Instead of answering my question, he asked me how I enjoyed it.

"I would *enjoy* it more if you'd just answer my question." I said grumpily. *Shifters, ugh.* "But yes, I like it very much. Which is why I was asking where it came from."

"Well then, as the maker of the wine, I am glad you enjoy it and I will make sure there is some put in your car before you leave, if that's what you wish to do."

There it was again. The not-so-subtle invitation to stay.

"Is there anything else about my father I should know?"

Avoidance had worked well for me so far, or so I told myself. If I really looked at all the compounding events, I'd likely change my mind on that.

"Not that I can think of at present. The only thing is that no one truly knows *which* god is your grandfather. But everyone has their own idea, and there is a general consensus."

I narrowed my eyes. I'd have to research the gods rumored to be local to this region. My mom had taught me a lot of Norse mythology as a small child, but growing up in a modern world, it wasn't something I'd paid much mind to.

"As for the Mate Bond thing," I abruptly changed subjects because they were equally as bothersome to me at this point. "I'm not saying we should throw it aside. But I don't know you."

I was trying to figure out what I wanted to say as I was saying it, and it was making me sound like an indecisive child. "I am open to getting to know you," *I think*. "If you help me figure out this situation with my dreams and my father."

I hadn't meant for it to sound like a bargain. But that's how it came out.

"Are you propositioning me?" There was a playful tone in his voice that made me hold back a smile by pursing my lips. Though I knew I wasn't fully successful at it.

"I only meant, that it could be time for us to work together and learn about each other and see if it's something we, the human sides, actually want to do."

He poured us another glass as we'd been through them already, Shifters tended to drink more quickly to catch a sense of relaxation.

"That is very logical of you."

I could feel he was holding back a question.

"What? What are you not saying?" The chiding tone I used reminded me of my mother. I guess we all turn into our mothers at some point.

"Well. I was only going to say that after being alive a bit longer, you'll learn that the best decisions aren't always made using logic." He took a pause to lock eyes with me. "Sometimes, the best decisions are based on instinct. Especially when it's something as rare as a Mate Bond."

I could feel the need to connect building. In both of us. It took all I had to just keep my hand resting on the arm of the chair I was sitting in and not to reach out and touch him. So, I broke eye contact.

"Will you stay for dinner tonight?"

I had been doing well thus far at not being awkward. Well, *as* awkward. So, I was probably at my limit. "I would like to." I'm sure he could catch the scent of honesty. "But, I think I'm about at my awkward socialization cap for the day."

Apparently I was amusing because he let out a deep belly laugh that I could feel all the way down through my toes. "Well, I will walk you to your car if you are ready to go."

I nodded and stood. Finishing off my glass of wine. It just seemed even better with the second glass I'd had.

"The wine is a bit stronger than what you would find normally. So, if you feel like you need a bit before you go, that is also fine."

He was definitely correct about that. As I'd stood my body felt very... floppy. No wonder humans drank so much. "I think by the time we get to my car I'll have burned it off."

Between the stairs and the probable mile and a half walk, I would be fine. He nodded his head and led the way down the stairs and out the door. As we made our way closer to the boundary of the village where the glamour wall was, his hand suddenly slid into mine. Just like each other time we had touched, it zapped me and the hairs on the back of my neck stood on end. Practically, just like any other time he'd been around before the Mate Bond took hold.

"Was it you who I saw walking near my car in town the day I was on the patio at the biergarten with Laurel?"

He looked down at me and pursed his own lips. "Yes." He said simply, but as we continued to walk he also continued to speak. "I had to get a picture of who you were myself, and not just through Karl's eyes. I knew there was something special about you."

I felt the blush cross over my cheeks as I looked down.

We got to the glamour wall and stopped walking. Before I knew it, his other hand wound itself around my waist and pulled me against him in one smooth motion. I swear, everything the man did was like silk gliding across your skin. I was sure my eyes were the size of dinner plates. I didn't know what to do with my hands so they wound up trapped between us as he just looked down at me. As if he just needed the contact. He touched his forehead to mine and inhaled deeply.

I closed my eyes at the contact and relaxed against him. *Do. Not. Purr.*

It was too late. It happened, as much as it could for my human form.

His shoulders shook with a small chuckle and he rubbed his face down mine as if his animal was closer to the surface than mine ever thought of being. It was such a feline thing to do. Before I knew it, his lips had gently pressed themselves against mine. There was nothing I could do but enjoy the moment and kiss him back. It was soft, and innocent. When he pulled away, he rested his forehead against mine again.

I don't know how long we stayed like that, but it was growing dark and I wanted to call Luna. I put my hand against his chest and pushed back just enough to say it was time to go. He got the gist of it and pulled back. His hands slid off my waist and my body could have wept from the loss of contact. It was as if everything in me wanted to complete the Mate Bond except that pesky human side of me and all her logic.

He spoke the words to open the barrier. "*Ohne die Dunkelheit kann es kein Licht geben.*"

I repeated it in my head. I knew "the dark" was in there, but that's all my mind could wrap itself around. He pulled my keys out of his pocket that Karl must have left on the table next to the door of the ground level of his home.

I walked through the barrier and looked back at him one more time. I flicked my fingers out in a small wave, and he did the same. I climbed in my car and sat there for a moment before pulling away. All I knew at this point in time was that he was the most quietly intense man I had ever met in my life, and I would think about that parting of ways the whole drive home, and possibly the rest of the night.

◌◌

Otto stood at the barrier long after he had watched Samantha pull out of the clearing and the barrier closed back up. He felt as if he moved from the spot where they'd had that connection that he'd lose the feeling. He hadn't meant to kiss her. He'd told himself he wasn't going to push or coerce her in any way, but he couldn't help himself anymore and he'd had to hold onto her for just a moment.

It was dark outside, but his feline eyesight was just as good as a human using night vision goggles. As old as he was, it had only grown stronger. He was growing very hungry, so he finally pulled himself away from the spot they had stood and began the walk home. He was wrong. He didn't lose the feeling. He still felt as if he was gliding through space and time. He had to snap himself out of it. She had said she would like to use the time spent on figuring out the dreams to get to know one another... that wasn't a no.

Not to mention the instant response she'd had of relaxing into him once their foreheads touched. Not many people realized the significance of touching foreheads. It was an old belief he had. A belief that the spirit was expressed from the mind's eye, and the

- 124 -

energy point of the forehead would reach out and connect when touched with another's. This had been the most powerful example of this belief.

Before he knew it, he was home. He made himself a quick meal of Jägerschnitzel and fried potatoes and went through the motions of eating and cleaning up. He had finished off his bottle of wine through dinner, and now that his stomach was satisfied, he could think. He showered and lay down on his bed without dressing.

So, she is our Alaryk's daughter, he thought to himself.

He had known Alaryk had been spending a lot of time with a woman somewhere around 34 years ago, but Samantha was only 30. That could explain why they had seen less and less of him there at the end. Alaryk's own forest home was located about five miles west of here in the forest. It still had its glamour around it to keep it hidden from any intruders, but he wondered if anything inside of it could give them a clue as to what had happened to him.

From the digging he had done on her, he knew Samantha's mother had died in an accident. She was an adult orphan with no family to call her own. Having been raised by a single mother with no living grandparents, she was all alone except for her friend Luna, but now Herschel and Laurel. He was glad for her that Herschel had taken a liking to her. For a Fae, Herschel was a decent man. He was someone you wanted on your side in a fight. He was a very, very old creature. One whose power could only be imagined.

He decided to table any other thoughts on the subject until morning. He closed his eyes and again, was taken back to the barrier and the feeling of the moment. Then, he fell asleep.

ᏆᏒ

By the time I had arrived home, I heard bottles jiggle in the back of the Jeep and knew Otto had asked Karl to put a case of wine back there for me. I smiled and opened the hatch to see that I had been correct. Thank goodness, because I might need a glass of shower wine tonight. Once inside, I sat it down on the counter in the kitchen. I really should ask how to store it, since I've never kept wine long enough for it to be an area of concern.

I stripped as I walked up the stairs and into my bedroom, dumping all my clothes on the floor by the bathroom. The hamper was so full at this point that it wouldn't matter. There hadn't been any time between major life events to do laundry. It still felt as if I were floating on air after that connection. My animal was content, except for the part of leaving and not consummating the Mate Bond. Had I continued to drink that strong, but still delicious wine, I may have done just that.

As I walked back down the stairs to get a glass of shower wine, the thought crossed my mind that I couldn't drink this with him again until I'd made my decision on what to do. Otherwise, next time, it wouldn't be a soft and gentle kiss. As gentle as it may have been, it had turned my bones to liquid and my head into an over-inflated balloon. I lost myself in thinking about that and managed to almost overflow the wine glass.

Whoever came up with the concept of showering while drinking wine, overpoured or not, was a genius. Once I'd finished it off, I started a load of laundry. I flopped down in bed and realized I hadn't eaten, which was probably why I felt so floaty from the wine. I didn't feel like making anything or going down the stairs again. So, I stayed plopped down on my bed, looking up at the ceiling, thinking about that last moment at the barrier.

This reminded me to try to look up the phrase that Otto had spoken to open up the barrier. I tried talk-to-text on my phone just to see if autocorrect would help me out with the spelling. Several minutes went by before I got something that sounded right.

Without the dark, there can be no light.

Oddly optimistic for a group of a species with an ancient curse put on them. Regardless, it made me smile.

At least now I knew that this Alaryk, my probable father, was a good and decent man. So, if he was indeed trapped in some alternate realm, and if I managed to free him, I wouldn't be setting some horrible creature back on the world. Thus, I was able to sit in silence, with the windows open, listening to the night bugs. All I could feel was the peace and contentment of that moment at the barrier with Otto. Calling Luna was completely forgotten, and I fell peacefully into sleep.

Chapter 16

The next few days went by as normal. I worked, had coffee with Hersch some mornings, gardened, and took care of my home. It felt good to have everything spotlessly clean and organized again. Having it as messy as it had gotten while everything was going on drove me up the wall. I wasn't as big of a neat freak as Lu, but when life gets messy, and your house is messy on top of that... It can be a bit much.

Friday morning, I told Herschel about the non-Mate Bond business that Otto and I had discussed. I asked him if there was anything further he could elaborate on that Otto may not have touched on. He told me he didn't believe so, "But if the witches who put your father away are still around, this means you need to be very careful with whom you trust and even more careful not to expose who you are." He'd said it in an almost fatherly manner, with more care than I'd ever heard from any Fae.

"So what you're saying is, I shouldn't't tell Laurel what I am?"

He gave me a pointed look, as if I'd just asked the dumbest question ever. "That, my girl, is exactly what I mean."

He told me that Laurel came from a family of witches who had been local until the last couple of decades. Laurel had moved back as an adult because she was somewhat of a black sheep in the family. They loved her, and she loved them, but she wasn't as powerful as the rest of them, because she didn't care to be. So, to make things less stressful on herself, she'd come back home. That was kind of sad, and it made me feel like I wanted to trust her with my secret even more.

"Do you think it was her family that put Alaryk away?"

Herschel had been here for hundreds of years. Everyone in town thought that the cottages just kept getting passed down to the next person in the family once the present one would pass away. Really, it was just Herschel changing form every 60-100 years based on how he was feeling and if he was ready to change his current form or not.

"I think the chances are more likely than not. Which means, do not do anything stupid." He sounded so much like Luna at that moment I had to laugh.

"Now I see why you have held up the old man glamour for so long! It fits your grumpy ass so well!"

He pursed his lips and looked me directly in the eye. "When I look like the grumpy old creature that I really am, *most* people leave me alone...If they have any sense." He raised a brow, indicating that he was speaking of me pushing my way into his life.

"Exactly how old are you?" I narrowed my eyes on him. I knew I would likely get the runaround, but I had to ask.

"I have seen centuries go by, and watched the world of men grow in technology, but not in sense."

Well, that's more of an answer than I thought I would get. "How old is, or was, Alaryk?"

He hummed in his throat while he thought. "He would be somewhere in the ballpark of 500 years old I believe."

My eyes were going to fall out of my head, I was sure of it. I mean, obviously, I knew we shifters pretty much lived until we were killed by something or someone stronger than us, but somehow, I had a hard time picturing my mother with someone who was that old. Even given the fact that he didn't look like it. Perhaps, she found the way the old ones spoke and behaved to be charming. Something like a living time capsule that could tell you firsthand of times long in the past.

"Pick your jaw up off the ground, girl. The bugs will get in."

Something about the German accent made things meant in jest seem so dry, but to me it made it even funnier.

"Now," he started, "What are you planning to do about your young man?"

I snorted out a very unladylike sound. "What young man?" I buried my face into my coffee cup to hide my blush.

"I may not be able to smell your bluff like you shifters can, but I can still tell when you're trying to pull the hood over my eyes."

I groaned and slouched down in my chair, crossing my ankles and folding my arms.

"I don't know, damn it. I'm going to work with him on this crap and just go from there."

I also thought of how my animal would take my rejecting the Mate Bond and how it would play, at least, some role in the decision-making process. "What do you know about him?" I gave him the side-eye.

He laughed at me. I could tell it was *at* me because of the way his eyes lit up when he looked back to me again. "I think that you need to talk to *him* about those things and figure out how you feel about it for yourself." He gave me a toothy grin. "I'm not going to do your dirty work for you."

We parted ways that morning with him cautioning me again not to trust the witches. "*Any* of them," he specified.

"Much like I probably shouldn't't trust a grumpy old Fae?" I retorted sweetly.

"Especially like you shouldn't't trust the grumpy old Fae. Wherever *they* are." He smiled and left, walking down the road toward his own home.

❦

When I was done with work for the day, I went to have dinner with Laurel, as was our usual Friday night routine. I was fairly certain I could pretend I didn't know what she was. It wasn't too hard to avoid the truth with someone who couldn't smell that you were doing it. I arrived and smelled Karl on the breeze. I looked to the patio where Laurel and I usually sat, and sure enough, there he was sitting with Laurel.

It's not that I *disliked* him. I just didn't *like* him that well. He was arrogant and he always acted as if he knew something I didn't. I'm sure he did, but it creeped me out all the same. Not to mention, he got under my skin in an irritating fashion. I hated being out of the loop with anything. I took a big deep breath and enjoyed the scent of the air. Being surrounded by forests had its perks. It made grounding yourself way easier when you didn't have to imagine the smells you chose.

I saw him lift his head slightly as if he smelled me coming. I greeted Laurel first, hugged her, and sat down. Eventually, I turned my eyes to Karl and said hello to him. I was really enjoying this looking him in the eye thing these days. He could only hold mine for a few seconds at best before he'd look away. I smiled and ordered my drink and the usual Döner for dinner.

"So," I finally decided to break some ice with the three of us. "How do you two know each other?"

Laurel shrugged. "I grew up here."

This wouldn't explain how a young girl, who I was not supposed to trust according to Hersch, would have known Karl back then. Considering he was well into his adult years at the time.

"I did not meet Laurel until she moved back to this town." She smiled fondly at him. "We have been close friends ever since."

Oh no. I recognized that look. I looked between the two of them to make sure I wasn't just seeing things. *Oh, for fuck sake.* There was some unrequited love story at play here and I hated that more than anything. So, Karl was allowed to trust Laurel but I wasn't? Or maybe he didn't trust her enough to tell her what he truly was, and it was just a physical relationship for him. Nonetheless, I saw the look of love and devotion in Laurel's eyes. It had been unmistakable.

"Sooo, you're just *close friends*?" I knew she wouldn't answer me honestly in front of him, but I did see the faint blush rise to her cheeks.

"Yes, that is all."

Karl stayed silent during the exchange. Just smiling. *Okay, guess I'll have to get both of them alone for this one.* I let it slide and listened to funny stories from the ten plus years that they'd known each other. I decided to push my luck with a drastic subject change.

"So, are there any local urban legends?"

Karl's eyes snapped to me, and I felt his foot press down on mine under the table in silent warning. Laurel was trying to flag down the server, so I pulled my foot from under his and kicked him in the shin, which made him jump. This caught Laurel's attention, and she asked me to repeat my question. Her eyes lit up and she went on to tell me about a local "legend" of abnormally large creatures in the woods and creatures that you wouldn't usually see in these parts.

She laughed, "But we all know these are just stories parents tell their children to keep them out of the woods." She looked at Karl. "Right, Karl?"

His face didn't betray anything, but I could feel the irritation coming off of him in waves. This led me to believe that Laurel had no idea what her beloved "close friend" was or that she suspected, but had no confirmation...Well good, I was glad he was irritated with me. Poor Laurel.

When it was time for us to go our separate ways, I noticed Karl got in the car with Laurel. I shook my head after them. That was a disaster waiting to happen. If I wasn't allowed to trust her, then Karl shouldn't't be allowed to... well...sleep with her. Looks like I'd have to add that to my list of topics to chat about with Otto. If I was supposedly going to hold as high of a rank as Otto in the pack, then that shit wasn't going to fly. If I looked at the true reason of why it irritated me so badly, it wouldn't be anything about shifter secrets, and it would be about Laurel and hurt feelings.

I pulled into my driveway, feeling just as annoyed as when I had left the Biergarten. I pulled out my phone to check the time. It was 9:30 on a Friday night. I felt jittery. I didn't want to go to sleep, nor did I want to watch TV. Instead, I grabbed some extra blankets and pillows and took them outside like I had when Luna and I slept outside. Finally situated in my fuzzy superhero pajama pants, tank top, and slipper socks underneath my weighted blanket, I took in all that surrounded me.

My plants, the cottage behind me, the forest in front of me, and the sky above me - with each of those things I felt my irritation waning. I was grateful for this place, and for Hersch and Laurel. To an extent, even the shifters in the village. They could help me find out what happened to my father and maybe, just maybe, I'd get to have one if everything went according to plan.

The breeze shifted, and my mood dampened slightly. Karl was close, and I'm sure I was about to have company after what I pulled at dinner.

"You can come out Karl, I know you're there." Come out he did. He had obviously run here in his Lynx form, for he was naked. He didn't look happy, but he'd have to deal. "To what do I owe this pleasure?" It just wasn't in me not to be sarcastic.

"Why did you do that?"

I lifted an eyebrow at him, "Sleep outside? I don't know. I guess I like being outside where any annoying old shifter could come and interrupt my peaceful night."

He scowled at me and said, "You know exactly what I mean. Laurel may have her suspicions, but she does not know what I am."

I glared at him and put all my feeling into this one. "Then it seems like *you* need to stop toying with her!" I was getting really mad now. "Even if you were human, you'd have to be an idiot not to see the way she looked at you! You know *exactly* how she feels!" He blew out a breath and I thought I saw a look of sadness pass over his face.

"Had you been paying close enough attention, you who must have much more life under her belt than I if you are to berate me so, you may have noticed the scent of feelings did not just come off of her."

I thought back to dinner and couldn't decide if he was telling the truth or not. I steeled my spine and glared at him. "Do you love Laurel as she loves you?" I could hear it in my voice. I'd finally succeeded at creating that special vibrato to get what I wanted out of people.

Karl looked me in the eye for as long as he could and then away. "Yes," he said simply.

"Does Otto know?" I had to be missing something, but I doubted he would tell me what unless I made him.

"Yes, Otto knows. The problem is my own." He shifted back then, and headed into the forest.

What the hell is it with these people? I shook my head and got comfortable again and focused my attention on listening to the night bugs and looking for any shooting stars. I could use a free wish or two at this moment in time. I fell asleep before I could get one though.

I woke up in the morning with the sun. It wasn't bad since I'd had an early-ish night. I made my coffee and went back outside. It was somewhat brisk. Probably around 45 degrees, but I wrapped myself up in my fluffy blanket I'd made myself and sat in my chair with my hands wrapped around my mug. I smiled into my coffee. Last night's drama was long forgotten.

☙

That's how Otto saw her. Wrapped in a large fluffy blanket, hands wrapped around her cup of coffee, and a smile on her lips. The wind was blowing toward him, so he could smell her and her coffee clearly. He knew he could enjoy the moment of seeing her like this for a few minutes more if he so wished, unless the wind changed. He noted the pile of blankets and pillows on the ground just off the patio and grinned.

She had slept outside. It would appear she'd do well in *das Dorf* if she chose him in the end. As high up in his tree as he could safely put one, he had built a large platform to see the sky better for those restless moments when you wanted the open sky instead of the woods. It wasn't *very* large., but it was large enough for several people. Maybe he would make a point to show this to her next time she was at his home.

He watched her roll her shoulders as if stiff from sleeping on the ground. Even shifters could get stiff muscles. Otto decided that if he watched her from the woods for any longer, it would just be odd. Even as enjoyable as it was to see her with her guard down. His Mate was a beautiful, complex creature. He'd decided that he was going to take the time they had while researching her father's disappearance to let her get to know him, as he wanted to get to know her.

He heard her let out a soft yawn and decided there was no time like the present to begin. He began walking again, no longer trying to be quiet. When her eyes flashed to his, he saw a momentary spark of annoyance, but that quickly dissipated as she caught the scent of what he had in his hand. Of course, he'd brought *Mohnkuchen*. Would he risk showing up here this early without it? No. No, he would not. She left her coffee mug on the little cafe-sized table and walked inside while he was still half the distance of the yard away.

When she reappeared, she had two plates and forks, and another mug of coffee. She had obviously been paying attention when he'd made his own cup of coffee that morning. He smelled the honey and cream before she handed it to him and gestured for him to

- 133 -

sit. She was still wearing the blanket as if it was an article of clothing, which made him feel as warm inside as she must be being bundled up the way she was.

ᴄᴙ

"Guten Morgen, Samantha."

I cleared my throat and repeated the phrase.

"I hear you and Karl had a bit of a disagreement last night."

My eyes went skyward while I finished chewing and then took another sip of coffee. "Are you here to chastise me then? It's not my fault that he seems to have been stringing my friend along for who knows how long now." He must have been able to tell I was about to go on a long tangent, so he picked up my fork and stuffed another bite in my mouth before I could start in again. I glared at him while I chewed.

"I did not come here to berate you for your experience with Karl and Laurel last night." My gaze narrowed further on him; I highly doubted it. "Honestly. I also believe he needs to just tell her. She already suspects it of him at any rate."

Well, that was news and it confused me even more as to why Karl would leave them both hanging that way if they both felt that way for each other. *Hypocrite*, I heard myself say in my head. *Not the time for an internal debate.*

"If you think she's trustworthy enough for Karl to be with, then why does Herschel think that I shouldn't tell her what I am?"

I relayed the rest of the conversation about it, without giving him the details of Hersch asking me about *my young man*.

"Herschel has seen many things in his time, and it has made him overly cautious." He crossed his arms over his chest, which I greatly appreciated... on the inside of course... and looked thoughtful. "Though, if she *is* of the family of witches who are responsible for your father's disappearance, it would be prudent to keep your true identity from her until we know for sure if she can be trusted."

He stood and took hold of our dirty dishes and took them inside. It was a simple gesture of familiarity, but it felt like one of those big, giant leaps for mankind type of gesture. He came back out with the coffee carafe and poured us both another cup. I rolled my

– 134 –

shoulders, as they were tight from sleeping outside. I'd managed to push my pillow away from me in the night so, I hadn't slept on one. Otto remained standing and came behind me, where his big hands found exactly the point in my neck that needed to be massaged.

He had a gentle, but effective touch. It wouldn't have taken me much longer on my own to work out the knots, but I had to admit, this was much nicer.

"I came here this morning because I had an idea on where to start our research into your father's disappearance." All I could manage was a *hmm?*

He chuckled and removed his hands from my neck to return to his seat. He sat back in his chair and took his mug back up again. "He had his own cottage, not too terribly far from *Dorf der Gestaltwandler.*"

Instantly, I perked up at this. "Really? When can we go?"

Otto smiled at me. "Now."

Chapter 17

I got ready as quickly as I possibly could. Once I'd dressed, I realized I should ask him if he was planning on driving or shifting. I asked from where I was, not needing to yell. Having supernatural hearing was convenient as hell sometimes.

"We will drive to the clearing where you parked your car last time and then hike the rest of the way."

I wore the pants and hiking sandals I had acquired from Lena's shop with a simple tank top and pulled my hair over in a braid. I topped it with a baseball cap just because.

I walked down the stairs and found Otto looking at photos I had hung on the wall of me and Luna, Luna's grandmother, and my mother. He looked up to me as I finished the trip down the stairs.

"Is this *deine Mutter*?" He pointed to a picture of Mom.

I nodded my head. "She died in a car accident a little over six years ago."

He inclined his head, "I am sorry to hear that." He looked back at her again as if he recognized her. I suppose maybe he could have, considering this is where she had been born, and where she'd lived until she became pregnant with me and my father disappeared.

I grabbed my fanny pack off the hook by the front door and put my phone in it. I grabbed the keys and jingled them, "Let's hit the road, Jack." He held the door open and shut it for me. "I am from America and I lock my doors," I said as he started walking to the car. He laughed and shrugged.

"It is probably a good idea for you to lock your doors for now anyway." I drew my brows together and he realized his mistake.

"I did not mean to cause you concern. I only meant that until we know more, I'd rather you be safer than not safe enough."

I could tell he was frustrated with himself for the mistake when things had been going well and I wasn't being awkward. I'm sure he felt badly for scaring me. Shaking off the nerves it had brought up, I climbed into the driver's seat. I hadn't gotten the running boards put on the car yet, and it was a bit on the tall side for me. Otto was biting the inside of his cheek to prevent laughter as I was buckling my seatbelt.

"Not a word." His humor was catching, for while I was pretending to be tough about it, I was also trying to not giggle, and I freaking hate giggling.

He had to point out the road to the clearing again, that's how well hidden it was. Once on the road, I was fine. In fact, it reminded me to ask him how I should store the wine. That provided an easy topic of conversation for as long as that would last. I parked my car where I had last time and slid out. I locked the door and put the keys in my fanny pack, patting it slightly.

Being here at the barrier again made me think about the night here with Otto. I chanced a look at him, and if the heat in his eyes while looking at me was any indication, it took him back to then as well. I cleared my throat and asked him which way we needed to go. He drug himself out of it and simply pointed and began walking. I sighed and caught up with him. Words had never been my forté, so I placed my hand in his and continued to look forward while walking. All I knew at the time was that I couldn't stand the thought of him feeling rejected.

ભ

Otto had enjoyed her company so far this morning. Her spunk made him feel more playful than he had in years. Not that he knew how to show a playful side, but he wanted to try. When he had seen her have to jump into her car, he wanted to laugh out loud. Instead, he had held it in. He'd been the Alpha for going on six decades. He didn't have anyone around to be able to express that side of himself with. Therefore, that side of him had shriveled. He was going to need to learn to loosen up again if he wanted to keep Samantha.

They had some casual conversation on the ride to the clearing, but nothing of significance. What irritated him the most was he didn't know how to get to know someone anymore. He knew how he felt, but words were not his strongest area.

When they had arrived at the clearing, he was immediately taken back to the night they stood there and she allowed him to hold her. He caught her when she had shyly looked over at him and was sure everything he was thinking about was shown on his face in the moment. Her face had softened for a few scant seconds and then shut down. When that had happened, it felt like someone had clamped down on his throat with a vice.

When he'd started walking and she had grabbed his hand, it had soothed the animal inside. They had been walking for over four miles now, and she hadn't let go of his hand once. "Tell me about yourself, Samantha." He'd blurted it. He felt awkward doing this basic conversational skill. He looked straight ahead, embarrassed by how silly he felt.

She looked down, then back up at him. Her green eyes were unsure. *She must feel awkward as well*, Otto thought. In an odd way, that comforted him a bit.

"Well, what the hell. I'll be 31 in June. I like to be at home or out in nature. If you turn on some cheesy TV show or movie, I'm happy as a lark. While I'm watching TV I like to knit. Yes," she quickly continued, "I said knit. I have never known my father. My mother raised me herself. I've really only ever had one good friend I could be honest with, and that's Luna. Luna's grandmother taught me how to cat. I suppose that's me in a nutshell."

He smiled as she spoke. He could hear her nerves. "What about you? How about you start with your age."

His mouth pressed into a thin line. He decided to skip the age for now and see if she noticed later. "My birthday is October 31st. I prefer the woods to anywhere else on the planet, clearly. I enjoy making wine, and walking in nature. TV is okay, but if I must watch it, I would rather watch a movie because I do not like having to wait so long to see how a story ends. I prefer to read. My parents and grandparents are still alive, though they relocated from Deutschland. I don't believe I've truly had a friend. The closest has been Karl, but I have always had Pack."

There, that wasn't so hard. He could feel the persistent question coming, so he was about to answer her about his age, "And I'm..."

Then, the need to turn around washed over both of them. He gripped Samantha's hand tighter to keep her from turning. "Easy. He had the same type of barrier put in place around his cottage as what is around the village." He released her hand and backed up a step or two. He began to undress and noticed as she did the same, though she was a bit more bashful about it and kept her body angled away.

He shifted and bumped her leg as she was bending to complete the undressing, and she nearly fell face first into the dirt. She swatted at him and he'd bounced to the side. Giving her the equivalent of a cat grin. *There, that wasn't so hard,* he thought. He felt her open up the Bond and she shifted. This time quicker than when he had last seen her shift, and she had drawn less energy from him than she had previously. So, this new form was quickly becoming easier for her. He could feel the excitement, yet some apprehension, about seeing her father's home. Otto then felt her push her emotions aside, and watched her puff herself up and walk through the barrier.

☙

I didn't know what I had pictured, but it wasn't that there would be this much land in the barrier. Apparently, my father was indeed a loner like myself. I went back out of the barrier and picked up my clothes, transferred them inside the barrier, and saw that Otto was doing the same. Once back inside the barrier, I shifted. I wanted to see all of this with human eyes, and to be able to ask questions in the moment as I thought of them instead of having to remember them all later.

Dressing quickly, I barely had the time to notice if Otto was following my lead. Before I could verify if he was, I had taken off at a brisk walk down the overgrown trail. It wasn't much of one, but I could tell it had previously been used frequently. There were spotty patches of sunshine coming through the trees. I wondered if he had chosen this portion of the forest because the trees were thinner and they let more sunshine in. It was certainly a picturesque piece of land.

I felt Otto come up behind me and stay close, as if he was on guard and ready just in case something had managed to get through the barrier. I supposed there was always the chance of a rogue shifter having walked through here and squatting. The thought of that made me feel angry. I picked up the pace a bit and finally came up on the cottage. It looked a lot like mine, except older. The timbers were more weather worn and the windows were dingy with all the years' worth of dust on the inside and dirt on the outside kicked up by the wind.

I reached out and touched the door handle. Otto stopped me by grabbing my other hand and slightly tugging on it. The look he gave me said he wanted to go through first. I reluctantly stepped back in order for him to move through the door. His nose in the air, he walked in. There didn't seem to be anything amiss, or so my nose told me. Determining that it was safe, Otto waved me in. He slowly walked through while taking everything in.

I flipped a switch to see if the old solar power system was still working. Quite surprisingly, it was. Under all the dust of age, I could see my mother's influence in furniture. Upon further investigation, there were photos of her around. I even found one of the two of them above the fireplace in the living room. When I picked up the frame, I used my pants to wipe the dust off so I could see more clearly. With my other hand, I gently touched my mom's face. *God, I miss you.*

Otto had been right. I did have my dad's eyes and hair color. His hair was a smooth, about ear length, wavy mop just like mine. The eyes that looked back at me were shaped just like mine, though they were a lighter shade of green. His specific shade was more like a mossy grey than my green and yellow.

Otto suddenly stood behind me and put his hand on the frame as well, tilting it toward him. "I remember your mother now, and if I remember correctly, she is where you get your spunky behavior, correct?"

I smiled, as I could feel my tear ducts trying to leak on me. I nodded my head and simply handed him the frame.

I went through the kitchen. It definitely appeared as if he wasn't expecting to be gone. There were essentially petrified remains of what had been food in the pantry. Either he, or my mother, must have been into canning because there were rows and rows of canned vegetables and fruits. It was an oddly old-fashioned domestic task that I couldn't see my mother doing. I meandered up the stairs and came across a room with a crib in it. *Had they meant for this to be my room?* My eyes were trying to do the leaking thing again, so I quickly walked out of that room and into what had been theirs.

I started rifling through drawers and such to look for any kind of clues. In the large walk-in closet, I found a large box of journals. I perked up at this. My mom had journaled. I still had them in boxes in the guest bedroom of my cottage. I hadn't wanted to throw out her handwritten words, so I kept them. Maybe these were more of hers. Previously, it had felt like an invasion of her privacy to read them, but now I was beginning to think I should for nothing more than information.

Otto had seemingly been trying to give me space, but he must have felt my excitement pick up for he was in the door shortly after my discovery of the journals. This box was about a three-foot cube. I turned and grinned at him. "I found a bunch of Mom's old journals." I looked back and opened one. "At least I think they're Mom's."

When I flipped to the first page, I saw her handwriting, but the third journal I opened was not hers. Now, I was even more excited.

Skimming the page, I saw that our handwriting was similar, too. While mom's was long and flowing, mine was small and cramped like this. Our *R's* and *E's* were especially similar. I put it back or I'd wind up here all day just reading journals from before my time. As it was, it had taken us over an hour to walk here. It felt like we had been here just as long already, and it was going to take us an hour just to walk back. I was starving.

As if he knew where my thoughts were taking me, Otto held out a hand to help pull me up. I went to lift the box, but he stopped me and did it himself. I wasn't about to argue, just because that would be an awkward carry for my short limbs all the way back to my car.

"Thanks," I said simply. "Maybe there are cloth bags somewhere around here that would be less awkward to carry?" Otto shrugged a shoulder, unphased by the task at hand. "Ok, I just want one more thing before we leave.

I went to the closet space again and found a sweater that had Mom written all over it. It was definitely something she would have worn in the late 80's. Big, soft, and brightly colored. I took something that must have belonged to my father as well. It felt so strange to think or to say, *"my father"*. They were words I hadn't said with much frequency throughout the course of my life, but they were becoming more commonplace over the last few days.

I tied my mom's sweater around my waist and tucked my dad's into it so my hands would be free. "Okay, I'm ready to go."

Though I didn't feel ready. Looking around one last time, it felt wrong to leave here. This was where I should have been born, but because of some witches, I'd been denied my birthright. Anyone's birthright really. Having two parents, I shrugged it off and followed Otto back down the stairs and out the front door.

I decided I was going to come back here, not only to do some more searching once I was done going through all these journals, but to clean the place up. Make it shine in all its glory. I gave it one last look, a little nod, and we were on our way.

ʘ

Otto made his way through the woods with Samantha while carrying the box on his shoulder. He had broad shoulders and a strong upper body - even for a shifter - that made him a good candidate for a pack mule. He did not mind it either. Samantha walked on the side of him that he did not have the box, and occasionally, her arm would brush against his. She had started to get sad just before they left, so it was a good time to get moving toward home.

Despite knowing that she was a strong woman, she had looked so fragile in the cottage in the woods, and so unsure. He thought for certain if he kept feeling her emotions swing all over the place the way they had been, he was going to have to just pick her up and carry her out of there whether she liked it or not. When she had found the room with the crib in it, which had shocked Otto a bit if he must say, the strong flow of sadness that had moved over him was stifling. He had almost closed off the Bond between them a bit just to stop the feeling, but that would have left Samantha to deal with the emotions on her own.

He was certainly going to have to speak with her when they arrived back to her car. He would need to feed her before she would leave - or stay if he had his way about it - as he could hear her stomach growling as they tramped through the vegetation of the forest floor that hadn't been moved through by humans in quite a long time. While he cooked, he would talk to her about what shocking revelation he had learned while in the cottage.

They were about halfway back to her car in the clearing when she had finally thought long enough about whatever had her face screwed up in concentration. "I just don't understand why the witches would want to get rid of him." Her brows were drawn together and her hands were fidgeting with one of the sweaters she had taken from the closet. Seeing her take those had made his heart ache for her. "Even if he had been on the way to breaking the shifter curse, what skin is it off their asses? We haven't done anything to any of them in how long?"

He shrugged his free shoulder, "I do not know. Perhaps..." he blew out a breath. Since she was of course asking this now, if he didn't want to be accused of withholding the truth, he would need to answer this now. "Perhaps, it is because your mother was one of the more powerful witches in the region."

Chapter 18

My mother? You're sure you are talking about *my* mother?"

He nodded his head across the table from me. I still couldn't get over it. An hour ago, Otto had said he had recognized my mother as a witch. Not just any witch, but one of the more powerful witches of the region. I didn't understand.

How could I have lived most of my life around the woman and not known?

How could I not have smelled it on her?

So many questions were going through my mind all at once.

"There is magic that can make things undetectable even to us." Otto adjusted his shoulders as he said it. Clearly, that fact bothered him. He shook it off though. "I'm sure you must have many questions and feelings right now, but you still should eat." He nodded down to my untouched food.

He was right of course. With our metabolisms so high, it could leave us weak if we didn't eat when we were hungry, which I had been before he'd spilled the beans that my mom was a fucking witch. I ate just to satisfy my base needs and then plopped my head down on the table to pout.

How could my mom keep that from me?

Why hadn't I found out?

Who else knew?

Why did the witches do whatever they did to my dad if my mom was one of them?

Did she help? I was so confused!

"I'm sure Sabine had her reasons."

WHAT?!

"Who the fuck is Sabine?!" Otto looked at me carefully. He could see the animal lingering just below the surface and heard the growl of her in my voice.

"Sabine Schulz was your mother's name... at least it was while she was living here."

I was floored. Absolutely floored. I felt it coming on before I could respond to that asinine statement. I burst uncomfortably into my new Lynx form in a matter of seconds. I shook off the pants as I sat there panting in my rage, hurt feelings, and also, somehow, wonder. I was angry, but I was learning so much in such a short amount of time.

Otto helped me pull the shirt, which was still in one piece, off of my animal form. He folded it, picked up the pants, and gave them the same treatment. If I were a larger creature, my clothes would have been toast, and that shift would have felt awful, but I was lucky.

For now, at least. Who knew if I would still be this Lynx at the next Full Moon.

Otto had a hand on my withers and could feel me vibrating. He took me down the stairs into the ground level and opened the front door for me, where I shot off like a bullet. I could feel him completely open up the Mate Bond. I assumed so that he could keep track of where I was and make sure I didn't hurt myself or others in this fit of rage. Through the Bond, I felt him begin to shift. Before I knew it, he was hot on my trail. He wisely hung back. It was as if he was there, but not there.

I bounded up a tree, and began jumping from tree to tree. I stopped for breath and flopped down on a low hanging branch with my back foot hanging off lazily. I felt the tail of a rather large feline brush against my foot and looked down. There he was, in all his big glory.

Was there anything about that man that could be ugly? Just one little thing? That's all I ask.

I snorted and as my breathing evened out, I scented a hare. In one fluid motion, the animal inside me perked up and slid down from the tree with barely a sound.

I followed my nose and kept low to the ground. Otto hung back. Interfering with another animal's hunt, especially one as riled up as mine, was a good way to start a fight. Not that he had to worry much about that, seeing as he was so much bigger than me. One swipe of his huge front paw could have me in a coma. I saw the hare and stopped. My body tensed, ready to make a move. The hare's nose was twitching, but then I saw its eyes go even wider and it took off as another Lynx burst through the underbrush and chased it off.

At the moment, I was highly upset at the mere fact that Lynx didn't have the capability to roar. Instead, an annoying high-pitched, growling meow came out of my throat. I was going to take off after the other Lynx, thinking it had been Karl, when I realized it didn't smell like Karl. In fact, it didn't smell like a shifter at all. This had been a natural Lynx. An awfully stupid natural Lynx if it had no qualms about stealing a larger cat's prey.

We were near where I had first spotted Otto in his Jaguar form, so I plodded the rest of the way there to drink from the stream and lay down in the sun. Otto's cat was a water cat. So naturally, he walked into the stream and began splashing around. My cat gave him a look that would have told him exactly how stupid she thought this activity was, but he didn't care. He laid down in the water and drank from it that way. I curled a lip and huffed out a breath.

My brain was still overloaded with questions and emotions, but after expending some of the energy, it was more manageable. Otto stayed in the water for a few minutes and then got out of the other side. This was where he had been when I had gotten brave enough to come down out of the tree that first night. We locked eyes and my cat immediately thought, *mine*. At least I would say it was my cat. I had way too much going on right now to think about that on top of everything else. *Or it could be just what you need to help you through.*

Ignoring that thought and scenting the air for any humans, I began to shift back into human form. It didn't take long. Possibly because of heightened emotions, because I'd shifted into this form more frequently now, or possibly because I had the new knowledge that I was part god, part shifter, part witch, and, clearly, rules didn't have to apply to me. Knowledge is indeed power. I walked to a decent sized rock in the sunshine and sat. I don't care how many times you've done it, sitting naked on dirt or pine needles wasn't a good time.

I didn't feel self-conscious anymore. I think I was too emotionally exhausted at this point to care. I looked him in the eye again as he just sat there in cat form. "Tell me about *Sabine*."

I couldn't hide the bitter undertones in my words. The child inside me was not happy with her, to say the least, that she had not been truthful with me my whole life. The adult in me, who knew her as a woman who would do what she had to do to protect those who were hers, knew if that's what she thought she had to do, it's what she would have done. Definitely, without a doubt.

Otto chuffed out a breath at me and flopped down his head as if he was going to *ignore* me. Um, no. I picked up a small stone next to me and threw it right into his stomach. He jerked upright, growled in his throat, and narrowed his eyes. He padded across the water and acted as if he was going to rub on me. Then, he jumped onto my back from behind and pushed me into the water. The *very, very cold* water. I landed on all fours and gasped while he let out a hoarse, guttural vocalization that almost sounded like a laughing pig and not a big cat.

Was he playing with me?

I stood up out of the cold water and sashayed myself over to him. He froze in his tracks with his eyes round. I ran my hand down his spine and felt him shiver, but then I grabbed his tail and yanked, which had him jumping away from my touch. I laughed and shifted back into my Lynx. It only took a matter of a few seconds. I was really getting the hang of this. I headed back toward the shifter village at a run.

Ɇ

Oddly enough, Otto couldn't remember the last time he had played like that. It made his heart happy that she had allowed him to. When she had gotten that glint in her eye, began her sashay over to him, and touched her hand to his spine, it had frozen him on the spot. He should have known it was just a devious act to get him back for the water incident. Happily loping back toward *das Dorf*, he felt lighter than he had in gods knew how long.

She was quite glorious. Going through all that she was and to still have it in her to be able to play the way she had left him in awe of her. He watched her running ahead of him and it made his heart happy. *Mine*, his animal would blurt when he looked at her, and the human side of him agreed. There was an extra pep in his step. She was definitely unique. Part shifter, god, and now witch. Not to mention the heavy dose of sass that he hoped she would keep as she aged. It made him smile when he was in human shape.

As they crossed through the barrier, he continued to let her lead him to his home. Her currently fluffy backside and short tail lead the way. He shifted when she stopped at his door and looked at him. He felt her discomfort at being unclothed out here where just anyone could see her. Being raised in a human world would do that. Once inside, she shifted back and got dressed. Even though she was uncomfortable at being unclothed outside, she didn't seem to mind it as much when it was just him.

He was still getting dressed as she said, "Okay. *Now* tell me about Sabine."

She sat down on the couch in the living room and folded her arms across her chest. He moved to follow her. Once there, he lifted her legs, sat close to her, and lowered her legs back down to cover his lap. *That was more like it*, he thought. He folded his hands over her legs and sighed. Having contact with her soothed his animal.

"I do not know very much to be honest." The look she gave him screamed of murderous intent and he laughed. "Honestly! I know she was a witch, a natural witch. Not one to mess with the Dark, but she was more powerful than any witch who drew only on nature." He thought for a moment. "I wonder if this is why the other witches wanted your father out of the picture. A hybrid childlike yourself would scream trouble for them if you chose the shifter life over the witch life."

This now made him wonder if her mother had indeed been in an accident. "What kind of accident did you say took your mother from you?"

She pursed her lips up a moment before answering, "A car accident." Her facial expression quickly changed to one of realization as she figured out what he was insinuating. "You don't think it was an accident, do you." It was more of a statement than a question. She must have understood the fierce look of protection that he took on that was probably flowing strong through the Bond. Her eyes were round, but he didn't feel any strong emotions coming off of her, beyond the anxiety he felt slithering around her from so much change.

"I don't, and I think you must be especially careful now to keep your true origins to yourself... Even from the pack." She breathed a deep, grounding breath and reached her hands out to take his. He readily accepted them. "Karl knows some, but only what he observed of you. Nothing more. I am... private, with my musings."

He watched as Samantha laid her head back on the arm of the couch, still holding his hands. Her slender neck lengthened, with her pulse beating strong in her distress. He had already decided he was going to keep her, just like he had already decided that he was going to help her with this search for her father; but how is he to be there for her while she was now dealing with the possibility of her mother being murdered and not taken by a simple car accident? He would have to go just based on instinct.

He let go of her hands, put his arms around her waist, and pulled her to his lap where he just held her. He felt like this was a good start. He rested his head on hers as she began to relax into him. Her breathing began to calm, as well as her heart rate. She smelled of the forest during a spring rain, which made sense now knowing who her mother was. He idly wondered if she would smell the same when winter hit the forest.

All he knew was that he was going to make damn sure that she was still around here to figure it out. Their story was not going to end with her leaving the country and going into hiding as her mother had. They would figure this out.

Together.

"Your mother was also a good woman. I am sure that if she felt it was safe for *you* to know who *she* truly was, then you would have known."

He didn't say if whomever was possibly responsible for her "accident" had known about Samantha. She very likely may not be here anymore herself, which made him tighten his hold around her waist. He felt her begin to stiffen, but he pressed his face into the crook of her neck and just stayed this way.

ⲅ

This felt so natural.

This felt so right.

The human side of me was beginning to soften toward the idea of Otto and I being mated, but there was still that stubborn side of me that wanted to cling to my independence. For the moment, it felt right. I wished it was just something I could get out of my system and be done with. If I did try to just "get it out of my system", then the Bond would be consummated and there would be no going back.

At that point, I didn't know if I *wanted* to be tied to someone forever.

If something happened to him after a Bond that soaks into your physical being was forged, where would that leave me and my animal? Devastated for the rest of my life? *No. Fuck that.*

My mom had managed, but I saw the toll it would take on her, especially when I was old enough that she let me go to sleepovers with Lu. She would first be relieved to have some time to take care of stuff, but when we would say goodbye for the night, her hugs were just a *bit* longer.

I began to stiffen in his hold, as much as I liked it. A significant part of me didn't want to like it. Then, he buried his face in my neck and I had that liquid bone sensation again. The light stubble on his face left tingling sensations where it touched. One thing I knew for sure was that this Bond turned the simplest touch from him, even those without any sexual intent, into lightning dancing from his skin into mine. *Every... damn... time.* I shivered, just as he had when I ran my hand along him while he was in his Jaguar form.

He must have sensed my hesitation and conflict through the bond, because he let my waist go and rested one of his hands on my hip. It only made the internal conflict worse. I was going to have to dedicate some time to this conundrum and working my way through it because I wasn't sure how many more of those moments I could handle without bursting, or just making my move in the most unladylike of manners.

"Samantha..."

I cut him off. "Sammy. You can call me Sammy." He smirked a bit and I felt his hand tighten on my hip a bit.

"Sammy," he started again, saying it as if he was testing the way it sounded coming from his mouth. "Would you prefer for me not to touch you, while you go through your decision-making process?" *Germans and their blunt personalities.* I sighed, there was the conflict again.

"I don't know, Otto. I'm just playing it by ear right now." I explained to him a bit about what I was feeling and why I felt so conflicted. He listened intently. I had just unpacked quite a bit on him. "But, I don't *not* want you to touch me."

"Well, they say that slow and steady wins the race." He smiled gently. "And it isn't as though we don't have plenty of time to get there. You know, seeing as we are shifters."

He had a point there. He was so damn... logical and mature. Once again, my gaze narrowed on him. "How old are you?" I could hear the timber of Command in my voice. I really was a badass today.

He laughed loudly and grabbed me around the waist again. Somehow, I wound up underneath him, unable to move.

This can't be good.

"I am..." he paused to look me in the eye before he finished his sentence, "one hundred and sixty years old."

My own eyes had to be bugging out of my head, while his eyes quietly took me and my reaction in.

I am MATED to someone over five times my age?!

Had I not been raised in such a mundane, human fashion it wouldn't have been such a shock. After all, I'd live just as long as he would... Or would I? Would I have a *witch's* lifespan, only slightly longer than a human? Or would I live as long as a shifter?

In the instances of shifter and human children, if the child could shift, it had the lifetime of a shifter. If it did not shift, then it was an average human lifespan. I'd never heard of a shifter, witch hybrid before. So, I had nothing to compare myself to.

I cleared my throat and wiggled under him. "Well, that's uh... nice." I paused and looked up at him sweetly, "Grandpa."

He growled in his chest. "You are quite lucky that this *grandpa* is wanting to try taking things slowly for you." As if to drive the point kissed me on the forehead and stood up, holding out a hand to help me up.

I let him pull me up, and between the lingering scent of patchouli and brown sugar of his body wash on him, and the exact way he'd pulled me to my feet, I had a deja vu moment of the night I'd first met him.

Shake it off, Sammy.

"Well... I need to get home and call Lu."

It was about dinner time here. I would probably stop by Herschel's and make him feed me since I didn't feel like cooking after the day I'd had. "Oh! And I need to get started on reading those journals!"

He nodded and asked if I'd like to leave some here for him to start going through, but as much as we, my cat and I, trusted him... I felt this was something personal for the moment. Something I needed to look through before any other eyes read those pages and I said as much. He understood.

Much like last time, he walked me to the clearing. This time he held out a pinky to me, and we walked back to my car holding pinkies. It was insanely sweet. There was an odd fluttering sensation in my chest and a goofy smile on my face.

Next time, I told myself, *I will start asking questions to get to know the man beneath the Alpha.*

Once at the barrier, I turned to him and didn't just throw caution to the wind. I flung that bitch as far as I could. I leapt into his unexpecting arms and kissed him for all I was worth. He caught me easily enough and weathered the storm I'd unleashed on his mouth. I was slow and thorough. By the time I had planned to be driving away, I was being pulled deeper into the raging sea. His hands on my back had found their way up the back of my shirt. One locked around my waist and the other moved up toward the back of my head.

I could have stayed like this forever. Knowing that, I ended the kiss and did what he had done the first time we stood here... I rested my forehead on his. His heart was pounding against mine. The hair over my entire body stood on end. My hands that were locked behind his neck felt that the hairs on the back of his neck were also standing. When the shock to our systems had faded a bit, I slid down out of his arms and looked up at him, grinning. Until this moment, I hadn't realized quite how tall he was.

"Thank you for helping me today."

It was a blanket statement. He had helped me by taking me to my dad's cottage, by carrying back the giant box of journals to my car, by being there - even from a distance - while I had a meltdown or two. He'd just been there for me all day... and I greatly appreciated it.

"I'll make it a habit to help you more often if this is the form of payment." I laughed and so did he. "You're welcome. Sammy."

Chapter 19

*O*tto hadn't done very much in the way of sleeping the night before. Cold shower? Yes. Drinking some of his shifter-strength wine? Yes. But nothing dulled the ache that was in him after that goodbye with Sammy. He had been ready to bury himself in her on the spot if she wouldn't have ended the kiss. He wasn't very sure how much more of this he could handle. His new daily mantra was," *I will give Sammy the time and space she needs."*

It was clearly working. She was coming around faster than he had imagined she would. But what would happen when she did?

Would she still want to live in town, or could he possibly convince her that this was the place to be? She clearly loved the forest just as much as any of them did. *Slow down, Otto. You are thinking too far ahead.*

Except, he couldn't help but think of the future. He felt with his whole being that he had waited his entire 160 years for this woman to come into his life, and he didn't want to wait anymore.

He was coming back from a run in his animal form. Running through the forest when the sun was coming up was an eerily beautiful thing to witness. To see the complete dark switch to muted tones of blue and grey, to a dark orange overlaying the natural tones of the forest... it was something to behold. He loved it out here. His good mood faded a bit as he approached his home and smelled Lena was there. He shifted at his door and saw her sitting on his stairs.

He sighed and shut the door behind him, putting on the pair of gym shorts he kept by the door for situations like this one. Most shifters wouldn't pay attention to another's nakedness, but considering he had a physical past with this one, he liked to remain clothed. She had never forgiven him for ending the short, non-romantic relationship they had and he never stopped sensing her arousal when she would come around him.

"Lena," he said shortly. "What is it?"

"Why haven't you consummated your Mate Bond yet?" She asked in a sly tone, as if she knew something he did not.

"Not that it is *any* of your concern, I am only telling you this because I want you to *finally* realize that what was between us - which was purely physical - is long over and will not happen ever again. Considering Sammy and I have only just recently met, we are giving each other time to get to know each other." She hissed out a breath.

"*Sammy* now, is it?" She stood and walked toward him. "What does that child have that I do not?"

He raised his eyebrow at her and kept his tone calm and detached, though he was sure she could smell his growing irritation with her being in his home.

"That *child* has more maturity in her pinky toe than you have in your entire being." He said in a chilled tone. "Now, leave my home. Do not come back unless it is for something I should know or revolving around the pack or Sammy's safety."

Since he's used Command with his last words to her, he had needed to be very specific. If he hadn't and just told her to leave his home, she could then use it as an excuse to not come back if she had any information he'd need, or if she discovered any dangers to any of them. Her eyes flashed, but when he looked her directly in the eye, she quickly looked away. Even though she growled in her throat as she did, she walked out quickly after this and slammed the door.

Otto shook his head and went about his morning, eating a second breakfast, and beginning a new batch of wine. He wanted to play around with adding some currants in this next batch. He made a mental note to speak with one of the many gardeners they had in the village about getting some. At this time, he heard his cell phone vibrate in the next room. He walked out to look. It wasn't a number he had saved, but when he read it, he knew who it was.

"Guten Morgen, Otto! The first journal entry was somewhat of a success. Though, it left me with more questions than answers." He saved the contact info as "Sammy" and responded.

She must have asked Herschel for his phone number. He highly doubted anyone in the pack would have come across her this morning, nor would she have known any except for Karl and Lena. His eyes went skyward at the thought of Lena. She had been becoming more and more of a problem lately. Their short fling had been somewhere around fifty years ago, yet she still hated him and tried to defy him at each turn. Since Samantha had walked into her shop, and Lena had likely smelled the pheromones emitted by mostly Mated pairs, she had been more intolerable than usual.

Since Mated pairs were so rare, he didn't realize that another shifter could scent if you had been fully Mated or if you were still in the non-consummated phase of the Bond. He didn't like that at all. Not because he felt it insulted his manhood by any means, but because that meant any others around could tell that she was still technically on the market. His mood was fouled for the second time this morning by that thought.

She would come around. He knew she would. He just wished she would hurry up already.

⚭

The morning after my impulsive goodbye kiss, if you could call that full on assault to all the senses a kiss, I woke and attempted to meditate before even getting out of bed. My mind had so much information and questions to go through that it began in on me as soon as I was awake enough to realize I was no longer dreaming. The longest I could quiet my mind was just south of five minutes. So, I made my coffee and watered my plants. That, in itself, was a meditation to me.

I scented the air when I was done with the plants and knew I was alone. I sat at my table and decided to really put my mind to the me and Otto thing. It seemed to me that if I were to take the Mate Bond out of the equation, he still would have caught my attention. He was caring, smart, responsible, sexy as fuck, and could kiss so well that you couldn't form a rational thought. I don't think I would have been able to make it a one-night stand with this guy. However, the thought of forever, especially a shifter's forever, was terrifying. Yet, I couldn't do what my body wanted to do so badly without completing the Mate Bond.

I knew where this was going. So, I might as well just give my entire being what it wanted, but something was telling me it just wasn't the right time. I'd, at least, worked through the fact that more of me wanted it than didn't. The only reason I didn't was fear of loss. Losing my mother had been the worst thing to happen to me. It had crippled me for a long time. I'm not sure what would happen to me if I lost a Mate. I'd talk to Lu about it some more.

I hadn't called her last night when I got home. I'd been too preoccupied with organizing the journals. There were so many. Most of them were leather-bound and more of them were my mother's than my father's. I separated them out by who they belonged to first and then put them in chronological order. It was a bit on the OCD spectrum, but I liked order. Going back inside, I refilled my coffee, ate a pastry, and stared at my work so far, which was spread out on the living room floor.

Well, time to get to work. I pulled my hair up in a messy bun with the scrunchie I usually kept around my wrist. Forever a 90s girl. Normally, I would play music when faced with such a large task, but not today. I didn't need the distraction. I couldn't decide where to start. So, I decided to read them chronologically together. Day by day. This seemed logical enough. Two birds, one stone. *I can do this.* I blew out a breath. *Or can I?*

Putting it off just a little longer, I went upstairs and got a notebook and a pencil. I usually kept several on hand for work. I decided to designate one for my parents 'journals and any notes I could take. I decided to grab my sticky tabs too, so I could quickly flag any page of interest that I could ask Otto or Hersch about next time I saw them. I grabbed the first journal from both of their groups and went to the couch.

It started with my father.

29 Dec 1985

It is snowing again today. Instead of switching to rain as it did yesterday, it has continued to snow. Sabine loves it. Therefore, I must love it too. The way her eyes light up when it begins is more magical than any forest snowfall I have ever laid my eyes upon. She is out there just now. Wandering around the gardens that are waiting for Spring to come.

Sabine's kind were looking for us again. Herschel, the Fae elder, assisted us by putting a barrier around our cottage that is very similar to the barrier around Dorf der Gestaltwandler. The witches may be strong, but they will never get through a barrier created by that old creature. Sabine had wanted to trust them so badly, but when she told them I was not just any shifter, that I was the shifter with many forms, whose father was a god, they quickly broke that trust.

It would seem that there is something about me that the witches know that I do not. Sabine thinks they believe I can break the shifter curse causing the rest of them to shift at the apex of the Full Moon. I am lucky that I am not encumbered by this curse. I will need to speak more with Herschel about what he may know of the witches' assumptions about me.

In the meantime, I am going to go out to cheer up my Mate by tossing a loosely packed snowball at the back of her head.

I hoped all of these journals would be as informative as this entry had been. First one and I felt as though I'd struck gold. I jotted down a few notes revolving around my checking into my mother's family origins and to ask Herschel what he knew that he wasn't telling me, especially if I couldn't find anything else in the next entry.

It looked as if they both journaled each day. I took a moment to picture Mom out in the giant yard of the cottage in the woods with the snow falling around her. She had been so beautiful. Her hair had been auburn, her eyes dark green. She had that darker European skin tone that never really changed throughout the year. In the summer, she always got a smattering of freckles across the bridge of her nose and on her shoulders. I pictured her in the sweater I took from their cottage, imagined her taking a snowball to the back of her head, and I smiled.

I put my mother's journal down, not quite sure if I was as ready to dive into it as I thought I had been. It had been nearly 7 years, and still seeing her big loopy handwriting crawling across the page hit me right in the tear ducts. So, I decided to text Luna a quick update.

Hey Lu. I've been meaning to call you. Have a ton to update you on. So much actually that I have a freaking notepad full of things to tell you about. Give me a call when you're awake. Love you!

I stopped out the back door, still in my pajama shorts and tank top. All I smelled was the forest and my morning glories that were growing well on the trellis I'd put up against the back of the cottage. I realized in the middle of the fifteen different trains of thought I had going on in my head at the moment, that I didn't have my usual morning visit with Herschel. That was curious. Just to annoy him, I sent him a text asking if something was up. I had seen him text before, so I knew he could. He just didn't like to.

He responded quickly and told me that everything was fine, but he had been informed that I would likely be busy and feeling a bit emotional this morning, and that he had decided to avoid getting caught up in any waterworks. I rolled my eyes... Otto. I asked him to give me Otto's number, so he sent me a screenshot of it. I texted him. Being social had never been my forte. I typically let everyone else do all the talking, but Otto was a creature of few words.

Reading over my message one last time before sending it, I nodded. That sounded good. I hit send and went back inside after stopping to smell my flowers one last time and popping a little tomato off the plant and into my mouth. My phone dinged relatively quickly once I was back inside. I smiled at his response.

You will get your answers. You are intelligent and persistent, and you have me on your side. Oh, and Guten Morgen!"

I could all but hear the smile in his voice.

I may have been a little overzealous in saying I wanted to do this alone. You can come help with the journals if you're still willing and able.

I quickly texted and sent before I lost my nerve, but the nerve wasn't lost, it was resting in my stomach until my phone dinged again with his response.

I will be there soon.

My smile reappeared and broadened. If I knew how to whistle, I would have been whistling on my peppy walk upstairs to make sure I brushed my teeth to rid myself of the coffee breath I was sure to have.

ᐯ

When Otto showed up at my back door he knocked and let himself in. I waved and smiled, feeling a little bashful after our parting of ways the night before. As if he knew I was going to be awkward, he strode quickly to me and gave me a strong, possessive kiss. He knew how to make a girl feel less bashful alright. I was most definitely glad I'd given my teeth a good scrubbing again before he got here.

"Wait," I started. "How did you get here so fast?" I looked him over, "You're dressed...already?"

A broad smile covered his beautiful face, making his dimple flash. "I have little deposits of clothing all over this forest, but I'd be happy to remove them if they bother you."

I was picking up what he was putting down. I cleared my throat and spread my hands out before me to the floor. "As much as a morning romp through the sheets sounds appealing, I have other things to focus on currently."

He looked down at my hyper-organized stacks of journals and cocked a brow.

"You have been busy."

I shrugged. "I couldn't sleep."

I swear the man looked into my soul when he simply said, "Me either."

No time for games. I had him dive into my father's journals since his would flow back and forth between German and English, with his own notebook and pen, as I did the same with my mother's. It took several hours before I felt like I was getting anywhere. I kept getting lost in the love between my parents.

Learning who my mother was before me and was learning who she was as a partner was fascinating. A *real* woman, with *real* feelings, and *real* woman's needs. Not just a single mother.

I had known my mother as Veronica Rush. Now, I was getting to know her as Sabine Shulz. Mom had always been a bit quirky, but the stories she'd tell about her and my dad made me laugh out loud. Some of them were so good that I had to share them with Otto. He would smile and once even said, "I see where you get your sass." I took that as a major compliment.

Mom had been a force to be reckoned with. I had lost most of my animosity toward her for lying to me my whole life. I finally read something that made a thought come into my mind. When she was pregnant with me things were getting too heated with the other witches. They couldn't leave their cottage because they were always being trailed by someone. The risk of being seen going in and out of the barrier and giving up their location was far too great. After a magical run-in and struggle with a small group of the witches, near the *Dorf*, she knew that their time here was coming to an end, but she knew that no matter where Alaryk went, they would find him. He was too prominent a figure in the shifter community.

She had said in the last entry I read, that she would do whatever it took to protect him and their child. It was like a lightbulb went off in my head.

"Otto!" I blurted out excitedly.

"What? What did you find?"

I was trying to figure out how to say this without sounding like an insane person. After all, who would come up with such a crazy plan? Possibly someone who parented me.

"What if..." I looked back to the journal entry and that specific line. "What does this make you think?" I read the line off to him. He mulled it over for a minute and then his eyes widened.

"You don't think..."

I nodded. "I think!"

I put a big red flag on the page so I wouldn't lose my spot and shut the journal. I stood and went to the kitchen to drink some cold water. When I turned around and leaned up against the counter, he was behind me.

I looked up to him. "I think my mother hid my father somewhere."

And I think that the bear from my dream was him reaching out to his only blood relative he could reach.

Chapter 20

We continued through the journals together for several days. I would get up earlier than usual, work the required amount of time, and by the time I was finishing up my workday, Otto would be walking through the backdoor. Usually, with one baked good or another. If I still had a meeting left or needed to get some reports out, he would start going through the journals, sprawled lazily and cat-like across my couch. This made focusing difficult for wanting to just watch him.

One afternoon while I was finishing my final meeting, I felt like I was being watched. I looked up to see it wasn't Otto. He was flipping a page, clearly engrossed in his own work with the journals. I looked out of the corner of my eye to see if I could see anyone that way. I saw a flick of movement of a light color near the treeline. I put on a hefty sigh and put my hand on my chin, feigning disinterest in my job, and looked out the window. Luckily this wasn't a meeting I generally had to pay attention to.

I first looked at my plants, then scanned the tree line where I thought I had seen the movement. I saw it there but pretended I didn't. A Snow Leopard. A milky, honey-colored body, covered in many rosettes, and a long fluffy tail. The eyes had been trained on me as it hunched down to the ground as flat as it could be. Not to brag, but my eyesight was better than even most shifters, especially for one so young as me. I looked back to my computer and sighed again. This time, signing off from the meeting and closing my computer. I went about putting the computer back in its case along with my headphones and mouse.

I very quietly said, "Otto, what Snow Leopards do we know that would be watching me from the tree line?"

I didn't want them to hear me if they were trying to. He perked up a bit at that, catching that I was trying to be stealthy. He put the journal down without even marking his place and came up to stand behind me.

He slowly spun me around with heat in his eyes and kissed me until I was breathless. He pressed his lips against my ear and whispered. "Lena."

That was all he said as he then went to look out the door and scan the tree line himself without any particular look of searching on his face. He too was a good actor. When I was able to breathe again and my heart rate was back to somewhat normal, I narrowed my eyes at his back.

"What about Lena watching me made you think you had to kiss me senseless?"

What was this burning sensation in my chest? Was that jealousy? *Oh, lord*. He turned back to me and crossed his arms across his chest, causing his muscle to flex. After that kiss, seeing him in this stance made my mouth go dry. I redirected my stare back to his face and gave him a no funny business look. He sighed and moved into the living room.

"She is no longer out there, but come in here where we won't be watched if she comes back."

I followed him, my own arms crossed under my chest. I knew I was being huffy, but at present, I didn't care.

"Lena and I were..." he paused as if trying to figure out how to word it, "intermittent lovers, a long time ago."

My eyes narrowed again. "Just how long is a long time ago?" I realized I was still standing while he had sat down on the couch. So, I sat down on the coffee table diagonal from him not wanting to be within touching distance. *If he felt he had to put on some big show for her while she was watching me like he had, did he still harbor any feelings toward her? Or was it the other way around and she still held the torch for him?* "While you're at it, explain your intermittent lovers terminology to me." I did not enjoy this feeling.

He was clearly trying to keep a smirk from his lips by biting the inside of his cheek as if he thought my jealousy was amusing.

"A long time ago, meaning somewhere in the realm of 50 years ago." He had raised his left brow and his dimple on the same side was beginning to peak at me. "And intermittent lovers would mean, occasionally we…" When he didn't finish, I glared at him.

"I may be young to you, but it would serve you to know that I have had many *intermittent lovers* myself, as you so eloquently put it. So, I can handle the terminology, 'had casual sex, 'if that's how you wanted to end your statement."

He laughed, the dimple flashing and melting some of the ice that was building up in me toward him. As my shoulders lost some of their rigid posture, he lifted me from the coffee table and pulled me to the couch as if I weighed next to nothing. Before I knew it, I was a little spoon and he was snuggling his face into the back of my neck and a low hum came from him.

I took a big breath and let it out. "What I need from you, is a list of names and where I can find them to bring about their most painful death," he joked.

I didn't enjoy being mocked, and I let him know by pinching his forearm hard enough for a bruise to start forming. He yelped and I laughed. Annoyance forgotten. Something about this interaction reminded me of Luna, and I suddenly bolted upright.

"Fuck! Luna is coming tomorrow."

I looked around at the state of disarray and knew she'd have a meltdown if she saw all the journals, notebooks, and random bits of crumbled and discarded paper strewn about as they were. She had decided to come visit and to help me go through the journals, and "sort out the rest of my life", she'd said. This meant she was going to spend 50 percent of the time helping with the journals, and the other 50 percent of the time convincing me to complete the Mate Bond with Otto. She'd take one look at him and be convinced that it was exactly what I needed to do. She was a romantic at heart. She wore it right on her sleeve. I suppose I was too, but I didn't want anyone to know it.

Today was Thursday and my last workday of the week. "I have to clean. She has OCD during her best of days, let alone when she's three months pregnant."

He watched me start picking up with a contemplative look on his face. I stopped, looked at him, and knew immediately what he was thinking. "Yes, she knows about the Bond, so naturally, she will force herself into a situation where she will stumble across you," I said dryly. This seemed to appease him. So, he got up and helped put the books back in their neat stacks, but we kept the ones we hadn't yet gone through separate from the others.

As he was leaving through the back door, I saw him scan the treeline again before turning back and leaning his forearm up on the door jamb and smiling charmingly at me. "Would you happen to like for me to cook for you and have some wine?"

I pursed my lips and all but pushed him the rest of the way off my step and onto the patio. I informed him that I would not be drinking any more of that strong stuff in the general vicinity of him for quite some time. He laughed and grabbed the hand that I was using to push him from his back and spun me around to pull me into an embrace.

He held me like this for a few minutes. Smiling into my hair. I was completely enveloped by him and engrossed in the moment. I stood up on my tippy toes to try to move in for a kiss, and instead he gently took my face in his hands, and gave me a very chaste kiss on the forehead. He lingered there for a moment before pulling back. He had a bright twinkle in his eyes. "I will see you tomorrow."

I nodded, seeing the game he was playing here. It would appear he was trying to withhold anything more than innocence now to drive me crazy. The look in his eyes is what gave him away.

"See you tomorrow." I folded my hands behind my back and smiled as he backed away and headed toward the village.

જ

Two can play at that game.

Once Otto broke through the trees, he switched over from enjoying "Sammy mode," to predator mode. He had meant to walk home and enjoy the forest with human eyes today - as human as they could be anyway. The colors and textures were so beautiful.

Even at his age, he hadn't gotten tired of the forest. He sighed and undressed to shift. Tucking his clothes into the hollow of the tree he used to hide them in. Then, he shifted, effortlessly, into his Jaguar.

The faint smell of Lena he'd picked up before he shifted, was much stronger now in his animal form and he could pinpoint exactly where she had been. He quietly moved to where she had been crouched down and looked to see what she would have seen. He knew he would have to convince Sammy to get some blinds, window frosting, or something. He didn't like the thought of her being able to be seen by anyone who held any ill will toward her, which Lena obviously did.

He moved through the area surrounding Sammy's house, careful not to be seen by any unsuspecting humans. That would make headlines throughout the town and the neighboring villages. He found fainter scents of Lena around different vantage points. All which would allow you to see into different parts of Sammy's cottage if she had her blinds open. This led him to believe she had been here several days in a row, looking through different areas of the cottage. He growled deep from his chest and took off back through the forest to the village.

When he stopped sprinting to drink at the stream, he wondered whether he should let it play out or not. Obviously, he would keep Sammy in the know. He did not want her to be caught off guard by anything if Lena did intend anything nefarious. He could not see her doing anything truly bad beyond spying in her jealousy. Though, this did not mean that Otto would underestimate her. He thought about it all the way back to the village.

As he stalked through the streets, probably looking quite dangerous with his mood being as it was at current, he looked through his periphery toward Lena's shop/home. Her lights were on as if she were there, but that did not necessarily mean anything. He may have to speak to Karl about keeping an eye on her for him while he was with Sammy and could not keep watch over her himself. Once shifted and inside his house, he found his phone where he had left it and messaged Sammy to keep her blinds shut if she didn't want to be looked upon. He was sure she wouldn't listen, but he could only do so much.

The unlikeliest of friends we were. She was a Coyote, and I was a Lynx...*so far*. She was the most affectionate person I knew, and I would always hold back. She didn't mind people staring, and I fucking *hated* it. I was quietly waiting for Luna in the terminal. As soon as she saw me, she was squealing like a pig and running to me with her arms open. I smiled and shook my head. Even though it was not my thing, the fact that someone was that excited to see me didn't hurt anything.

"Lu," I finally said, obviously struggling to breathe. I tapped her back, "Lu I can't breathe!"

She laughed and pulled back. Her eyes were wet and she was all sniffly. Good lord. "Someone have a little hormonal imbalance going on?" She pinched my arm, "Ouch!" I growled at her.

"Well then don't mention a pregnant lady's hormones to her face." I flattened my lips and stared her directly in the eye. "Okay, the food on the plane sucked. Let's go get some Schnitzel!"

"I swear you have three stomachs." I took her bag that wasn't on wheels for her and held my arm out for her.

"Hey, I'm eating for two."

She took my arm and we made our way to my car. She liked the Jeep a lot. The four-door model was a big step up from the crappy old two door, soft-top I'd had back at home. I had the top off, so I tossed her bags into the back and we were on the way back to my little town. Stuttgart was all fine and dandy, but I was done with the majorly populated areas.

"So, Noah doesn't mind you flying while you're pregnant?" I looked over and she had the tiniest little bump showing. She had to wear the tightest shirt she owned to get it to show. That made me smile, she would be the one to *want* to show her swelling belly off.

"I'm only 12 weeks along. If I have any weird complications further into it or when I'm around 6 or 7 months, he probably won't like it."

I shrugged a shoulder. "I'll just come to you when you're that far into it."

I knew it was highly unlikely for her to be able to give me enough warning for me to come and be there for the birth if she went early, but I'd still be able to make it back in plenty of time for her to be done screaming and squeezing the circulation out of the hands of those in the room with her. "I want to come visit when the baby is born, but if you won't want anyone underfoot during that time I'll just get a hotel room."

She gave me a dry look as if I'd said something stupid and looked back out her window. I heard her take a long, slow inhale and let it out just as slowly. "Have you gotten tired of it yet?"

A half-laugh escaped me. "As if I ever could. The moss here is so thick in some areas, you sink a few inches when you step on it." The tone of my voice would have answered the question even if my words didn't.

"Speaking of wistfulness," she turned in her seat and wiggled her eyebrows at me. "When do I get to meet Otto?"

I rolled my shoulders back and kept my eyes straight. "When I feel like having your scheming ass in the room with him."

She burst out laughing at this and I was silent the rest of the short ride back to town. I loved Luna with all my heart, but she was - pun intended - like a dog with a damn bone when she had an idea in her head. When we pulled into the driveway I took a cautious sniff of the air. No shifters - good. I released a breath I didn't realize I was holding and got out to grab Luna's bags. When we walked in, she took quick stock of the piles of journals and the notebooks we had been using to take notes in. The reason she decided to come was to help with these and to be there for me during all this crap. I'm sure she also wanted to get an eye full of Otto and the village.

I knew Otto would be by at some point today. He didn't seem like the kind of man to let work sit around waiting to be done, but Luna didn't need to know that. I would let her wallow in her impatience until he decided to grace us with his presence. I carted her stuff upstairs while she began raiding my pantry and the refrigerator. She packed enough stuff for three weeks instead of the one week she was planning on staying. I said as much to her when I went back downstairs.

"Well," she started around a mouthful of sandwich, "I want to help you figure out as much as possible. So, I packed extra just in case."

As much as I appreciated that, I also didn't necessarily want her in any kind of possibly dangerous situation. Not for the first time, I questioned if it had been wise to let her come to visit. When she was done eating, she wanted to dig right into the journals.

"Can we just hold off on the work portion of your trip until tomorrow?" I was tired of looking through my parents' lives. It was mentally exhausting. "We could just watch movies and eat shitty food tonight, while I drink really strong wine," I said hopefully.

Looking back at the stacks of journals, Luna sighed and then nodded her head. "Well, you just bought yourself an extra day with me."

I grinned at her, "Oh no. Whatever shall I do?" I'd raised my voice by an octave and put the back of my hand to my forehead in simulated drama.

She laughed at this and we got into some pajamas and slippers and got the movie day started. During the scene in *The Proposal*, while Luna and I were having a fangirl moment over Ryan Reyonld's naked behind, I heard the back door open.

Luna paused the movie right as he was wrapping himself in a towel, got up with the remote, and walked into the kitchen. I glared at her. *I guess turning the TV completely off would have been too much to ask.* I'd forgotten to text Otto that we were pushing the journals off until tomorrow. I heard him grumbling something in German that I didn't understand. *Uh-oh.* Luna was the first to round the corner into the kitchen, "I'm really hoping you're Otto." There was no threat in her voice, just mild awe.

It wasn't hard to understand why. Even in the simple black t-shirt and blue jeans, he looked like a fucking god. I watched her take all of him in as she leaned up against the wall, crossing her arms across her chest, and one ankle over the other. She had no shame whatsoever. He held her eyes and smiled softly, inclining his head. "I am. You would be *the* Luna." He held out a hand as if to shake hers, but instead he bent low over her hand and kissed it before standing and giving her back her hand.

She looked to me, eyes round. "Oh, I like him."

I pressed my lips into a thin line.

"At least one of you does," he said with a laugh.

Taking in our attire he moved around Luna and I to the living room. He raised an eyebrow at the TV and turned to me with a smirk, "Taking a break?" I know his intent wasn't to make me feel bad, but it did.

"I decided to take the day off of peeking into my parents' lives before me. It's emotionally draining."

He held up a hand, "You don't have to explain anything. I understand. I will leave you two alone to enjoy your night."

"No!" I jumped when Luna yelled it out.

"Jesus, Lu!" I rubbed my ear.

"I mean... no you don't have to." *I knew it. Schemer.*" I'm assuming you like chick flicks?" She asked him. "Here, pretty soon, Sammy is making tacos and I'm making pico de gallo." He smiled broadly, looking from Luna to me.

"What's not to love about a chick flick? - and I happen to love tacos."

Something about hearing him say *chick flick* was just weird. His accent and the proper way he spoke did not mesh well with it. I laughed, naturally.

Chapter 21

The night had gone by without a hitch. Luna even taught Otto how to make her pico de gallo, which is something she didn't even do for me. *Schemer*, I thought again. She thoroughly enjoyed riling up my animal. She would touch his arm or shoulder bump him, just to get me going. It took all I had not to growl at her several times, and she knew it. Even though I logically knew that she was married, and she was just trying to annoy me. The animal inside did not enjoy the teasing.

The goodbye was a bit awkward while knowing that Luna was sitting inside listening. I offered to house him for the night in the guest bedroom.

"I do not believe I would be able to *stay* in the guest bedroom for long."

My mouth lost all its moisture as I attempted to outwardly appear unaffected. I'd rolled and readjusted my shoulders, clearing my throat, and looked away.

Smooth, Sammy. Very smooth.

I didn't really know what to do at this point. So, I began to back away and wave, but apparently, he needed some physical contact.

He grabbed me around the waist and touched his forehead to mine again and just breathed. If he was trying to woo me with quiet romance, he was slowly chipping away at my ability to resist. I had my hands on his chest this time which reminded me of the tattoo I had seen there, similar to the one I had seen on Karl's during both of my first interactions with them.

Why couldn't anyone ever be clothed when I met them?

"Do all the members of the pack have this?" I tapped a finger on where I remembered it to be.

"Hmm?" He opened his eyes and pulled his head back to look down at me.

"The tattoo... Do you all have it?"

He rubbed it idly. "Oh, *ja*. It is something we all have upon entering the pack. It is somewhat of an initiation, I suppose." He thought a moment longer. "Or we just wanted to feel cool, I don't know."

I laughed and poked it harder. I pushed back and really intended to go inside this time.

"*Guten nacht, schöne Sammy.*" I thought I could deduce the majority of that.

"Goodnight, Otto." He inclined his head and went on his way.

When he had broken the tree line, I sat down in one of my patio chairs and slouched down, leaning my head back and rubbing my hands down my face. I opened my eyes to look up at the sky. I heard Luna open the door and come out to sit in the other chair. I smelled it before I heard her set the glass of Otto's wine down beside me. She could tease me all she wanted, but she knew this wasn't the easiest thing for me to have to go through. So, it was all just to try to lift my spirits a bit.

"Sammy, he's great."

I grunted, "I *knoooooooow*!"

She touched a hand to my knee and I popped my head back up to look at her. "It doesn't make it any easier knowing that he's great." I threw my head back again, except this time a groan of frustration came out.

"It probably doesn't help either that he walks in looking like a German version of Adonis." I brought my head back up again to glare at her.

"That too." Not to mention the fact that my animal had chosen his and would leave me heartbroken if I chose not to.

"There's nothing wrong with taking things slowly, Bob."

I knew this, but I also couldn't imagine figuring out how to date someone that you had a freaking Mate Bond with, and *not* sleeping with them and sealing the damn bond if you weren't ready for it. I said as much and she looked as if she hadn't thought of that.

"Well, I'm here to be your sounding board. Even if I think you'd be crazy to reject the bond, I'll support you in the end. I may yell at you a little bit first, but in the end, I'll support you."

I knew she would. Just like deep inside, I knew there was no way I was going to reject that bond. I just had to figure out how to accept it and be okay with it first. I felt like there was just something I was missing. On a fundamental level, I wasn't going to be any good to anyone without whatever this missing piece was. I had a sneaking suspicion it had to do with my parents and this whole god/witch/shifter hybrid business. Hopefully I could get it all figured out with the help of Luna and Otto.

I could tell Luna was losing steam pretty quickly. Between the time change, not napping, cooking and cleaning, and not to mention the pregnancy, I was surprised she was still speaking. I finished my wine relatively quickly, gave it a moment to settle in, and released the tension in my shoulders. I took a few deep breaths and slowly sat up.

"Well, it's 8:30. If you're ready for bed, let's get inside and you can take a bath or a shower and hit the sheets. I won't be far behind you."

I stood and helped her stand. We went to our separate rooms, showered, and only poked our heads out to say goodnight. It really had been a nice night. A good break before we really dug in and got to work. No offense to Otto, but I thought that adding Luna to the team would really up our firepower. She was smart as hell and had a tendency to see things before other people realized they were even there to be seen. So, while me and Otto were making notes, she could go through those notes and really start piecing stuff together.

Tomorrow we would give her the details of what we had figured out so far, as well as some of our theories. Including the theory of my mom possibly having put my dad... wherever she put him. Nonetheless, for now, I was going to tune out the world, get a little pre-sleep meditation going, and drift to sleep.

ര

I was back on the peak of the mountain that I had last dreamed of. Instead of feeling the nerves this time, I felt ready. Maybe I could get some answers. I showed up in this dream world perched on a large rock. Luckily, not close to the edge of the drop-off. I looked around and scented the air to see if, perhaps, the shifter I was looking for was here and not in the valley this time. He wasn't up here, that much I knew. It crossed my mind for me to go into my meditation zone to see if he would show up again as he had the last time, but I didn't enjoy the thought of being pushed off of a mountain by an angry bear.

So much to my dismay, I started down the steep decline once more. I kept my eyes peeled for signs of any other form of life, but there weren't none. It was as if the bear shifter, hopefully my father, was the only living thing here. This led to many thoughts about how it was unrealistic, but then I remembered the world I was part of. When I finally reached the valley with the lake, I looked around for a bit before I found the spot I had settled in last time. I looked in the water, just to look for life, but saw none.

This time when I sat, it didn't take as long for him to arrive. I felt him coming. It was almost as if the air parted ways for him. Each paw hitting the ground was a contradiction to itself. They were soft footfalls, but they brought with them such momentous presence, you may as well have been in Jurassic Park. I opened my eyes and watched him round the trees to look at me and grunt. It felt right to stay seated, so I did. If our theory was correct, potentially, this was my father, and if this dream world didn't have any other living creatures in it, he could have let his animal completely take over at this point.

He padded slowly up to me, stopping maybe four feet away. He breathed heavily and let out a deep grunt. I wasn't really sure what to do at this point. We appeared to be at an impasse. At least this time he wasn't roaring at me. If I never saw a huge Brown Bear roaring at me again it would be too soon. Growing impatient, I slowly stood up. I didn't want to move too quickly and ruin his calm.

"My name is Sammy."

I felt silly talking to a bear who may or may not be my father who had no idea who I was. "Are you Alaryk?"

His eyes showed recognition as if something deep in there knew the name, or I was reaching. I wouldn't know until this was all said and done with.

"Ryk?"

I said it softly, but his reaction to it was as if I'd shouted it. His eyes dilated and he roared as if in pain. He stamped a foot down in my direction and it hit me to try something. I was the equivalent of an Alpha in Otto's pack right? Well, maybe I could use Command on him.

"Stop!"

I hadn't expected it to work, but I felt the power of it as the word was forced out of my mouth. He stopped and shook his head rapidly. If that had worked, I may as well up the ante.

"Change."

His eyes constricted to pin pricks. He hunched and roared again, head hanging so low his forehead was almost pressed into the dirt of the forest floor. I could see the change beginning, slow and tortuous. I had no idea how long he'd been in animal form, but this was just as painful to watch as the first time someone shifts.

Watching bear paws stretch and elongate into human hands, weight melt away from the body, and fur sucking its way back into skin in slow motion is almost as unpleasant to watch as it is to go through. He was letting out a final roar in his bear/human limbo, as the final pieces of the human puzzle fell into place. Until it was no longer a bear's roar, but a human's scream. He was still hunched on all fours, with his head hung low.

I could see his hair was indeed my color, or mine was his. We even had the same skin tone. I hadn't seen his face yet to know for sure, but this had to be him. I could hardly breathe through the feelings pressing down on my chest. My hands were balled into fists.

"A-... Alaryk?"

I had never stammered in my life, but I wasn't sure if insinuating right off the bat that I was his child was the best thing for his mental stability right now. He looked up to me, flashing his light, mossy-colored eyes at me. They were streaked through with silver.

"Danke." It came out raspy, as if he hadn't used his voice in as long as I thought he hadn't used it. "Ich heiße Alaryk."

I went through my speech of not speaking much German and asking him to speak in English. He appeared to search his thoughts for a few moments before he nodded. He began to stand, and it was slow and pained.

"I have been in animal form for far too long." He limped over to a tree to lean up against it.

"Do you... do you know who I am?" I was cautious as I still wasn't sure if I wanted to go there with him yet.

He took in all the features of my face. I wanted him to come to the conclusion himself. After all, if it were possible that my mother hid him away here to protect him, he may not feel too happy toward her or me at present. Finally, his eyes widened. "You cannot be."

I almost wanted to laugh. "I can. I am Samantha. Daughter of Ver-," I'd habitually been about to call her Veronica, "Sabine." I gave it a moment.

His mouth opened slightly; his eyes were huge. "That could explain why you were able to Command me, and it worked."

He asked me how old I was and when I told him he nodded his head slightly.

"Who put you here? - And where exactly is here?" He inhaled deeply and let it out slowly through flared nostrils.

"I am here because the witches, their prophecy, and their inability to keep their noses in their own business." Each word that was spoken held a grave rumble to it as if he were in animal form and growling still. "But, it was your mother who finally put me here, against my will, to protect me from them."

So, I had been right. "Yes, but where is here?" I wasn't sure how much longer until I'd wake up so I needed to get as much out of him as possible.

"Your mother is exceedingly powerful for a witch. She is special and pure of blood." Not something I'd ever be able to say that's for sure. "She put me in a trance, performed a ritual of some kind, and before I knew it I was here. If I am accurate in the pieces I was able to decipher, my body is still somewhere in the real world, but I am in this illusion world. I have been lost to my animal for quite some time it would appear."

"Do you know where she would have hidden your body? Otto and I went to your home and didn't see you, but we weren't looking closely if you were hidden with magic." He shrugged a shoulder.

"If she didn't keep me in our home, then I'm unsure of where she would have moved me." It suddenly dawned on him. "Why can she not tell you herself where she has me hidden?"

I looked down at my hands, which I'd been wringing in front of me for I don't know how long.

"WHY can she not tell you where to find me, Samantha?"

I sighed. "Mom died in a car accident six years ago."

Now he did roar. I could literally feel his pain as if it were my own. In a way, it was my own, but I had lost a mother, he had lost a partner. Both hard, but different.

"I don't know how much time I have left before I wake up again. Is there anything else you think I should know?" I thought back to what he'd said. "You mentioned a prophecy. Can you tell me about that?"

He looked at me through his grimace of pain. I could see him fighting the spontaneous, emotion-driven shift off with everything he had. "You... you were prophesized my child. The child of the god and shifter hybrid, and the Black Forest Witch. The one Alpha to rule them all." My mouth dropped open and I could feel myself starting to be pulled away.

"I'll figure out how to find you." I said as quickly as I could, before I woke up.

❦

I woke up sweating and panting. I could feel that the Bond was wide open and Otto was frantic. He was also getting closer and closer. I'd never noticed being able to feel how close of proximity he was before now. I rolled over and checked the time on my phone. It was only four in the morning. Otto had called me five times in the last 20 minutes. I got up and wrapped myself in my robe and put on my slippers. I may as well get coffee started because I wouldn't be going back to sleep.

I took out three mugs in case Luna were to wake up. I filled two and went outside. Before I knew it there was a freaked-out black Jaguar getting closer and closer, shifting quickly into the freaked-out man who was in front of me. He took in the scene of me in my robe with coffee.

"What happened?" I told him to go get some clothes and I'd tell him all about it. "You are fine?"

I nodded my head. "Yes, I'm fine."

I could see some of the tension drain from his body as he went inside and put on the pants and t-shirt he had there. I really just wanted him clothed. I didn't intend to tell him anything until Luna woke up. I didn't want to have to repeat everything twice. I said as much and he half-growled at me.

"It was another bear dream. The bear is who we think he is and I have information. Happy?"

He huffed out a breath in his best teenage girl impersonation and sat back down. He reached for the coffee and nodded his head toward me in thanks.

"Guess you should have taken the guest bedroom after all, huh?"

"Can we wake Luna?"

I shook my head. "I am not waking the pregnant woman, who just flew across an entire ocean for me. Let her sleep. There's nothing we can do about anything this second anyway."

He wasn't pleased about it, but he appeared to understand the logic behind the idea. "What did you feel that freaked you out so bad?" My curiosity was piqued. I don't recall ever being truly scared while I was there.

"It felt like you were gone." I drew my brows together.

"Gone... like, I'd left town gone?"

He ran his hands through his hair. "No, meaning you were just *gone*. No longer in existence. Mate Bond closed."

I could hear his emotion building with each statement. He shivered momentarily and closed his eyes, taking a slow breath. When he opened them, I could see the shimmering gold flowing in his eyes. That was two men within the last hour of my life that were on the verge of a spontaneous change. This one didn't intimidate me in the slightest though. I reached out and grabbed his hand, which he pulled on. Before I knew it, I was standing in front of him with his arms around my waist and his face buried in my diaphragm.

"I was right here, but maybe not on some level."

I realized I had been stroking a hand through his hair. He was *mostly* calm again.

"Maybe I should wake up Luna." I heard the door open and Luna shuffled out in her slippers and robe.

"No need. Luna's right here." She took stock of the moment she'd walked into and smiled. "Glad to see no one else has been sleeping either."

She promptly stole my seat, which left me either Otto's lap to sit on, or just to stand. With this story, I was going to need to pace, so standing it was. I pushed back from Otto, hearing him roughly exhale as we lost contact, and began to tell my tale.

Chapter 22

I realized partway through that I should have called Herschel to hear the story as well. He may have had something to add here or there, which made me remember a term my father had used in the first journal entry I had read. He'd called him the Fae "elder". Once I was done regaling my story to the others, I went inside to grab the notes journal we were keeping and added that tidbit to it. I also documented the highlights of the dream so I wouldn't forget anything, as if I could. I quickly was back to pacing.

"I don't want to leave him like this much longer."

I was beginning to feel anxious about this. How are we going to find where my mother hid him?

"Getting your dad out is second priority, Bob... at least it should be." She looked toward Otto, who still looked like he was struggling for control. "Wouldn't you agree, Otto?"

He gave a short, sharp nod. "If Sammy is the child of the Witch's prophecy, learning more about it should be our main focus... and keeping her safe."

He probably didn't mean to come off as intimidating, but the power of the Alpha was rolling off of him in waves. I could feel Luna's discomfort. It was harder for her to be around him like this because she was of a different pack. If he flew off the handle for any reason, her safety wouldn't be a main concern of his. Pack bonds would keep him from doing any real harm to anyone in his pack, unless they were challenging him for his position. For an outsider, if his animal was in the driver's seat, then who knows where it could go.

Realizing that it likely wasn't helping matters much, I stopped my pacing, went to stand back beside Otto, and rested my hand on his shoulder, trying to push soothing energy through the Bond. He shivered under my hand, but over time began to calm down.

"I am glad to know I have not one, but two white knights here... but no one needs to worry too much. There's not much of a chance of them realizing I'm here, or who I am for that matter." At least I didn't think there was. "I hate that I'm even asking this, but Hershell is 100 percent trustworthy right?"

Otto nodded his head. "He has helped to keep us hidden for longer than even I have been alive, and likely longer than even your father." He shifted the direction of his gaze up to mine. The animal wasn't so near the surface. His breathing had evened out and he wasn't shivering anymore. "Herschel is somewhat of a voluntary outcast amongst his own people. He hated the politics among the Faery. He hated the lying, scheming, and the underhanded way of the rest of his species. So... he made this place his home, and has been our strongest ally."

"What did my father mean when he called him the Fae elder? Just that he is an elder among his own people?"

Otto nodded, so I moved on. "We'll need to bring him in on this too then. I also..." I paused, because I knew I was going to get pushback on this. "I also want to test the limits with Laurel a little bit."

Otto's back went straight. "*No.*"

His voice held the strongest dose of Command I'd ever heard. So much so, that Luna kept her gaze averted and tilted her head to the side in a show of submission before she caught herself and shook it off, then looked at me, eyes wide.

"You know that doesn't work on me." I said haughtily. "If she's *also* an outcast in her family, then she could hardly care if I'm some random shifter girl. I'm not intending to tell her exactly who I am."

Luna scoffed. "I don't think you should plan to tell her anything. She could figure out who you are, and then use you to get back in good standing with her family." Her voice was full of annoyance as if I was just being thick. Otto clearly agreed with her because his back was still stiff as a two-by-four.

I removed myself from Otto's immediate vicinity and said that I would think about not telling her, but the final decision was my own. I went in, made more coffee, and waited for the pot to finish brewing. Luna came in and stood across the bar from me.

"You have him entirely freaked out now, you know."

I sighed. I did know, but if he weren't so blinded by the emotions he felt because of the Bond, he would see I actually had a good point. When I repeated this thought to Luna, she snorted.

"You do? Because he's not the only one who thinks it's dumb."

"You, my dear best friend, are blinded by the love from a lifetime of friendship and chosen sisterhood." I smiled a little to try to soften her up a bit.

"So, because we care about you, we're wrong in our thought that telling Laurel is the last thing you should do? I say let Herschel have a vote."

I gave her a dry look and whipped out my phone. I texted Herschel and asked if he'd come over as soon as he could.

When the pot of coffee was done, I carried it out to the porch with honey, and had Luna bring the cream and sugar. However, Otto didn't look like he needed any more caffeine for the next month.

"I asked Herschel to come over so he can weigh in on some things."

He ignored me and looked to Luna as if trying to decide something, but shook his head and looked back at me.

"I think you need to come stay in the village until we figure more out." I opened my mouth to protest but he lifted a hand. "Just until more is known about your father, this prophecy... you."

"I don't think it's necessary." I attempted to keep all emotion out of my voice, but I'm sure there was an underlying sense of annoyance.

He actually growled at me. "I *do*."

I was a bit taken aback by this, but realized I hadn't really given him much room for an opinion in anything. I had shot down most things either he or Luna had said this morning.

"I am sorry, but you can even stay in one of our empty homes if you prefer that to staying with me. I would feel much better with you behind the barrier since witches can't get through." He'd gentled his tone.

I sighed heavily and looked to Luna to see what she thought. The look she gave me told me she thought this was a good idea.

I exhaled through flared nostrils. "Fine, but you get to go inside and cook breakfast then Luna... since you're on his side."

This got her to give a little laugh. The sun was just breaking the horizon, but we had been out here for quite a while at this point. I plopped down in the chair she'd been sitting in, slouched, and folded my arms under my chest.

"Thank you." I heard Otto all but whisper it.

"Yeah, yeah, yeah." I muttered and kept my eyes on my feet.

Super Alpha my ass.

ᘓ

Two days later, I was packing up some essentials to load into the back of the Jeep. The journals were already loaded up in a bunch of different cloth bags. Luna and I would be staying in one of the empty homes within the protective barrier of the village in the forest. Herschel had agreed with *them* on this course of action, and that I should probably keep my secret from Laurel for a while longer. He said he would do some digging of his own on Laurel and her family because he "was less likely to mess it up."

We were also informed that the reason Otto had felt me disappear, thus leading him into his full-blown panic mode, was that while I was physically in my bed, the essence of who I am was wandering around in these other realities. So, while my soul was in these other planes, Otto couldn't feel me. I had essentially cut off the Bond while I was there, at least for him. I hadn't felt any different. I still felt him, but now that I was thinking about it, the details were omitted. I should have felt his anxiety the moment it hit him, but I hadn't.

Even with all this stuff going on, I was in a good mood today. Luna was here, and I had gotten them to agree to go and search my mom and dad's cottage and the surrounding property today. I made my case by stating that it was a safe activity because we wouldn't be around anyone besides each other, and for the majority of the time, we'd be behind the barrier that only a shifter could get through anyway.

So, here we were, at 6:30 in the morning. All loading up the car and preparing to drive to the shifter village. Herschel said he'd keep an eye on my plants for me, and that he would keep me posted on the Laurel situation. I felt bad having Herschel do this. It felt sneaky. I didn't feel like she was a witch to worry about. I felt even worse because I was being made to cancel our usual Friday night plans together for the second week in a row. Maybe someday I would have a normal life again, but apparently this was not that day.

I went in to holler at Lu to hurry up. She was pouring the both of us travel mugs of coffee with a grumpy look on her face.

"I still don't see why we have to get there so damn early," she complained. "It's not like the place is going anywhere."

Armed with a fake pout I pinched her cheek. "You'll be fine. The Full Moon is in a few days. You should be ramping up in the energy department by now. Baby." She swatted my hand away.

"Exactly. Baby. I'm growing another person! Of course, I'm tired."

"Get to drinking that coffee then. It's about a five- or six-mile hike to the cottage from the clearing we will be parking in."

She groaned and grabbed my computer bag for me to take to the car so I could continue to work. I knew she would feel much better when we got on the road. I hadn't taken the top off since I'd be parked in the forest for who knew how long. I did have the windows rolled down already, and as soon as we'd break through that barrier past Herschel's house, and got into the forest road the smells and feeling of the trees would hit her. That energy would do her a world of good.

❧

Otto was waiting in the clearing for Sammy and Luna to arrive. The only outward sign of his nervousness was his occasional move from one side of the area to the other. What made him nervous was not the fact that she was essentially unprotected at this moment - that contributed - but was not the root cause. No, what made Otto nervous was that she was going to be staying in the village.

What if she hates being here?

What if she truly hates being part of a pack?

What if, knowing she is here, I cannot give her the space she needs right now?

These questions, and more, were circulating in his mind when he saw her Jeep pulling into the clearing. He had been so wrapped up in his thoughts he had not even heard her coming. He needed to snap out of it and deal with the current tasks at hand, help them get settled, and go to Alaryk and Sabine's cabin. Luna waved to him from the passenger seat, and Sammy smiled. Waving back to Luna, he went to her side of the car first and opened her door for her, giving her a dramatic bow and sweeping his arm out before him. "Madam."

"He likes me more." She said with a grin to Sammy, who promptly rolled her eyes and jumped out of the car and went to grab their suitcases.

Otto loaded his arms with the bags of the journals. Though there seemed to be more than he remembered. He asked about it and Sammy said she had loaded the journals she had of her mother's from when she was growing up until she had died. This earned her a look of approval. "Great idea. Who knows what we could find to help us in those."

Luna seemed to be enthralled by what had been created here. She didn't seem to be able to look around at everything fast enough. He'd watched her get excited and make Sammy look at something at least ten times on the way to the cottage they'd be staying in, which was subsequently just on the back side of his own. He didn't want them too far with Lena being the way she was. He needed to make it a point to remind Sammy and Luna to keep a close eye on her. He had already told Karl to discreetly trail her, and to not delegate the task to anyone below him in rank.

"I think I need to ask Herschel if I can borrow him to do the same type of barrier situation that he has done here for your pack. I love this."

Sammy laughed at Luna. "Please put it to him just like that. I bet he will really take a liking to being asked if you can borrow him."

Otto chuckled and began the climb up the staircase toward the tree house they would be staying in. "There is no harm in asking him. Herschel used to visit America quite a bit. So, he may say yes."

He pushed open the door and led them through the sparsely furnished home to put their bags into what would be their bedrooms.

&#x06;

I followed Luna and Otto through the village and watched Luna the majority of the way. It was enjoyable, watching her facial expressions. I was sure this is what I would have looked like if I wasn't in my animal form the first time I had walked through that barrier. It was pretty glorious. I wouldn't mind living in a place like this, but I still liked human things too. I liked having a car, taking road trips, going to the market, and sitting on the patio at a restaurant. I wasn't sure I could give all that up in the near future just yet. Give me a few more years to get completely sick of humanity, and then we'd talk.

When Luna said she wanted to ask Hersch if she could borrow him, I pictured his face and laughed. According to Otto, he may actually be open to it. We'd just have to see.

"You are just behind my own home," Otto told us.

I nodded and threw my stuff down. "Can we go now?" I asked excitedly. Luna gave me a look that told me she thought I was being rude. I sighed dramatically. "Thank you, Otto." I gave her a pointed look. "*Now* can we go?"

They conceded and we made the most out of our early morning hike so that Luna could enjoy the scenery. I showed her some of my favorite areas I had noticed on the trip out here last time. When I showed her one of the really thick moss areas, her eyes went wide.

"I'm moving in. I'm calling Noah as soon as we get back and I'm leaving him and transferring to this pack and there is nothing anyone can do about it."

I laughed, knowing she would never leave Noah, but the idea was quite appealing for her to be here.

We made it in good time, even stopping periodically to take in nature. Once we shifted and made it through the barrier to shift back, I hurried down the path toward the cottage to begin my investigation. The problem was, I didn't know where to look. I quickly grew frustrated. No matter how much soothing energy Otto tried to push through the Bond, I didn't want to be soothed right now damn it. I wanted my frustration to be vented, not suppressed. It didn't help matters that we were so close to the full moon.

I left Luna and Otto inside to take a breather. The weather was still nice even though it was early September. Yet, the deciduous trees were starting to put off the scent that let you know Fall weather was quickly approaching. There was a large fallen tree around the back of the cottage. Hopping up onto it, I used this natural progression of forest life as a seat. I lay back onto it, as it was wider than I was, and closed my eyes. I focused on my breathing and began to find my meditative state. In my mind's eye, I saw my father as I had seen him in my dream.

Focusing on him and my breathing, I could sense him. I knew he was here in the forest somewhere, I just couldn't pinpoint where, but at least I knew he was here somewhere. Opening my eyes, I stayed there a few minutes longer just looking up at the trees. Calm was feasible now. Rolling off the tree, I walked back inside the cottage to see Otto and Luna knocking on the walls. I assumed to see if there were any trick walls that he could have been hidden behind.

"Any luck?"

Luna looked at me and shook her head. "No, the only thing I have found is more of an aversion to dust."

I sighed and went back up the stairs to the bedroom. Otto had found a bag and put a few journals that weren't in the box of them we had pilfered last time. As he walked in with the bag slung over his shoulder he asked, "Are you ready to begin the trek home?"

Am I? I looked back around the room and my heart grew heavy. Had things happened differently, *this* would have been my home. I would have had both of my parents, at the same time, throughout my life. The room across from this one that had been expecting to grow and change with me from baby to toddler, from child to teenager, until it was time to leave the nest.

Home, I thought. I looked back at Otto, who sat patiently waiting. "Yeah. Yeah, let's go home."

He reached out and his hand found the small of my back as we walked down the stairs together. That felt like home. The Bond that had been forged between us against both our wills, mine more specifically. *Would I have chosen this for myself?* I would never know, but there was no denying it now that it had happened. We found

Luna in the kitchen, dust smeared on her left cheekbone and streaking her hair.

"What did you do, roll around in it?" I couldn't help but to smirk. She looked so annoyed at the fact that the dust and dirt had the audacity to be here.

"Let's get moving. I need a shower, and quite possibly a nap."

Chapter 23

That night after Luna had gone to bed, I found myself wandering to Otto's. The temperature was lower as deep in the forest as we were, compared to my own cottage that I rented from Hersch. Not in an extreme sense, but just enough for me to feel chilled at first when exiting my temporary living quarters. I warmed quickly enough, as I was wearing my fluffy pajama pants with a long-sleeved t-shirt, on top of being naturally adaptable with temperatures. I didn't knock. I just made my way up all the stairs to get to the tree level. Once there, I went straight to the deck.

I curled up in a chair and rested my chin on my knees. My mind wouldn't stop racing. So, I found myself here. Feeling the gentle thump of his distant footsteps coming from inside and without removing my chin from my knees, I moved my gaze to the door where he was coming into view. He must have also been trying to sleep because all he wore were his boxer briefs. It made me feel a bit bad that I'd woken him up, but I wanted to be in the trees while being outside. The cottage me and Lu were staying in didn't have a deck. I hadn't paused to think that he would be in bed too.

We just stared at each other for a moment.

Mine.

My animal was becoming louder and more adamant about that affirmation. I thought back to something Otto had said before, *"Sometimes the best decisions are based on instinct."* I was feeling very instinctual right now and I didn't want to fight it off anymore. The shift in decision must have been shown through my eyes, for it was mirrored in his. His hand reached out to the door handle and he made his way out to me. I could see the goosebumps covering his torso, though I knew there was no way he was cold. He put off heat to make the stars envious.

His hand reached out, and I took it. I stood as he lightly pulled to help me up.

"Shift," was all he said.

His voice so low a human would have a hard time hearing it. I started to open my mouth to protest. Shifting was not what I'd had in mind, but he shushed me and repeated his request. He helped me out of my clothes. If he took his time about it and drug his fingers across my skin while doing so, I was not arguing. Before long, I had goosebumps too, but most definitely not from the cold. He kissed me slowly, but thoroughly...that ended too soon. He smiled at me with his dimple flashing. "Shift." He said again, and shifted himself.

Before long, I was in my Lynx form and following him up the remainder of a tree with a little lean to it, which made it easier for his bulkier cat form to climb. He walked out onto a branch and leapt onto a platform that matched his deck, so I followed. The trees opened up just above where the platform was built for you to see into the completely clear sky. The almost Full Moon was just about to hide behind the trees that were to the left of us, but the stars were putting on a show. They were twinkling as brightly as I had ever seen them, and pretty frequently, meteors would fly through the sky.

I shifted back and pulled my knees up to my chest and watched the sky while Otto shifted back as well. He sat next to me, put his arm around my back, and watched with me for a while. After some time, I chanced a glance at him, but he was already watching me.

"Thank you."

This was just what I was needing tonight on a Spirit level. He smiled again and slightly nodded his head as if he had no words. He may not have because the intense presence he put off drained me of any words I had left to say. He reached over and held my face in his hands for just a moment before kissing me slow and sweet.

When I wasn't fighting the natural attraction and need to be with him, everything the man did left me breathless. This was no exception. We came to our knees without losing touch as we learned each other's bodies. What a touch here would do, a kiss there. Though none of it seemed to matter. There was nowhere either of us could touch on the other that wouldn't have made our hearts race and our breaths come shorter. I didn't realize I was being laid back until I was already down. He searched my face for a moment. "Are you sure?"

The fact that he was a good man who would stop, no questions asked if I said no, was a modern-day marvel to me. Oddly enough, it evaporated any residual doubt I may have been holding onto. I nodded my head, and he let out a breath I hadn't realized he'd been holding. He lowered his forehead to mine and closed his eyes. He found his way inside and both our eyes snapped open, completely dilated. I swear our hearts stopped beating for a few seconds. It got very bright and the air around us pulsated. When it passed, our breath rushed back into us and our hearts beat again.

It could have been coincidence that our hearts beat in perfect rhythm, but I didn't think it was. I let out a quick laugh of solid joy and we sealed our Bond. When I stopped seeing metaphorical stars, I lay tucked up against his side with my head on his shoulder while I looked up at the real stars. A meteor shower was reaching its peak. It was like the sky was mirroring my own life right now. Tomorrow, I would take stock of all the small differences I was beginning to feel inside of me, but for now, I would enjoy the moment.

ଓଃ

Otto could sing while skipping through the forest right now if he wasn't completely tone-deaf because he was so blissfully content. So instead, he held *his Mate* a little closer and enjoyed the feeling of her small hand on his chest. When he'd heard the door to the deck open and close again, he'd lifted his head in bed to scent the air and found that Sammy was there. He'd felt her melancholy feelings since they'd parted ways upon returning to the village. Otto knew pushing his concern on her in the moment would have fractured any progress they had made in their cautious relationship. He hadn't thought she would have wound up in his arms tonight, or any other night so soon. Knowing what she had needed tonight, just looking at her as she had been, tucked up into a ball in his chair, he had brought her up to his haven.

In the longest two weeks of his entire existence, his life had drastically changed. Yes, he was still Alpha and all that went with it, but now, he didn't need to do any of it alone. If she chose to come here to the village and live with him, that is. Since this was still up in the air, and they hadn't even begun to talk about anything of the sort, he did not want to raise his hopes in case that wasn't what she wanted to do just yet. Regardless, now he had something to look forward to. He closed his eyes and inhaled deeply the scent of her. He could feel her own contentment rolling off of her in waves. He kissed her head and got up to move.

She looked confused as he moved to the weather-proof chest built into the corner of the platform. "I sleep up here sometimes when I am in one of my moods." He pulled out a large pillow, a bedroll, and some blankets. Sammy's smile broadened and she stood to help him set everything up.

"Usually, I sleep with somewhere around four pillows," she told him as they got situated into the bedroll. "I suppose you will have to do your best impression of a body pillow tonight." She wrapped around him as she had the pillows the first night she'd slept in his bed after their Mate Bond struck them.

Otto laughed and adjusted himself to be more comfortable with her and said he would do his best. He felt like a savage for taking her on a wooden surface and not having laid this all out beforehand, but he had been completely enthralled by her and the need to console her. She didn't seem to mind. Yes, he was a shifter. Their ways were not the ways of the human, but they still took part in humanity, and he had been born in 1861. Sometimes, that aspect of himself manifested as being a little old-fashioned. It didn't take much for him to shut down that voice in his head that wanted to shame him. For now, he was happy.

☙

Lena felt it the moment it happened. Their Alpha had sealed his Mate Bond with the little trollop. This meant the child's place was solidified in the pack, and as a ranking member. Not just any ranking member, but an Alpha herself. Lena couldn't have that. She growled low in her throat, her body vibrating. The change came on her so fast she hadn't even had enough time to fully comprehend that the spontaneous shift was about to happen.

Her attachment to Otto was purely human. Her inner beast didn't have feelings toward him beyond recognizing him as their Alpha. So, once she'd shifted and the rage had calmed, her human voice inside the head of the beast had an opportunity to think. She couldn't have the bitch who ensnared Otto in her trap ranking in the pack. She couldn't even have her *in the pack*. This would take cunning, which she knew she had. She would figure out something. She just had to figure out how to get Otto's guard off of her tail without him realizing she knew he was following her.

᥯

The next morning when I had made it back to the cottage Luna and I were staying in, I sat down with some coffee at the kitchen table. There was something innately different about me. Not just the Bond being stronger than ever, but perhaps side effects of the Bond being sealed. I felt stronger, physically and as a shifter. It was as if my body emitted the frequency of Command without me even using it. I could sense Otto's whereabouts more easily and in more detail than I had before, as well as his emotions. What he was putting off now had a big dumb smile plastered across my face. Another change I noticed, was that I felt more in sync with my animal than I ever had in my life.

Just on the short walk home, I had felt more of my instincts coming to the surface than I ever had before, and my senses were sharper. I felt very protective over myself and... as annoying as it was to say this...my pack. Something in me also knew that finding where my Dad was being hidden would help keep everyone safe. My intuition was stronger. Something was coming. I didn't know what, but it didn't seem too good.

I sipped my coffee and waited for Luna to wake up and come out. I had wanted to be here when she woke up so she wouldn't come to the wrong conclusion and think I'd gone rogue or something. With me, that was always a good possibility. I didn't have to wait long. I heard her slippers shuffling along the floor and got up to make her a cup of coffee. When I turned around, she was standing directly behind me, her eyes wide. I gave her a signature, what the hell look.

"What happened?"

My face must have gone from what the hell, to what the fuck are you talking about. "Umm, well... the Mate Bond was sealed?" She closed her eyes at the sound of my voice and her pupils constricted. "What's wrong with you, Luna?" She closed her eyes and took a deep breath. "Calm down." I told her. I didn't even have to try to use Command, my presence was enough it would seem. The effect was almost immediate.

She calmed after a couple seconds, took her coffee from me, and sat. "The Bond did something to you. I felt completely pulled to you at first." She paused and thought for a moment. "As if I would lay myself at your feet and kiss them...and you know I hate feet."

Beginning to be a bit weirded out, first I texted Otto to come and discuss some things with me and Luna. I also texted Herschel and asked him to come weigh in. There were too many things I'd noticed, and now with Luna's strange reaction to me, that I didn't think were all because of the Mate Bond...at least not in its entirety. Something was shifting in me. I could feel it growing even as we sat with our coffee. Aside from the frequency of Command coursing through my body, I also felt a strange warming sensation. Nothing painful, but more noticeable than your average body heat. It felt pleasant and calming. Like sliding into warm water.

When Otto arrived, he flashed me his dimple and I was wrapped in a strong, solid embrace. Luna cleared her throat and when we looked over to her she was grinning like an idiot. "I knew all I needed to do was come for a visit." She smugly sipped her coffee, and I threw a cinnamon roll Otto had brought at her head.

Unfortunately, her reflexes were as good as any cat I'd seen and she ducked and caught it, with her *left* hand even. Otto laughed at our shenanigans. This is what Herschel walked into. I knew he would be able to get through the barrier with no problem, seeing as he was the one who created it for us.

Us... there was that word again. I was accepting my Fate better than I'd thought I would.

"*Guten Morgen*, children." He had his cranky face on. "You summoned?"

I made him a cup of coffee and started another pot. Once everyone was sufficiently caffeinated and fed, I explained everything to exact details. Except, obviously, what had happened between me and Otto last night. When I'd had to explain that as the starting point, even just saying "the Mate Bond was sealed" had me blushing like a schoolgirl. Otto held my hand under the table through the story. I could feel him shift to confusion and questioning as I went deeper into it all, especially once I'd gotten to Luna's reaction.

She described it again for them and added that I was able to get her to calm just by telling her to calm down.

"Well then, it would appear you are indeed the prophesized child of The One of Many Forms and the Black Forest Witch." Herschel observed me for a few moments before continuing. "As you already learned, your mother was more than she appeared to be, but she was not just any Witch. She was the Black Forest Witch."

I raised a brow in *major* confusion. "What does that even mean?"

He looked me directly in the eye, which I took no offense to. "Your mother's family is historically a family of Elemental Witches."

I'd admit I was a little rusty when it came down to witches and their abilities. I was more informed on Fae, Vampires, and other creatures that would "go bump in the night." My Witch lessons, now that I thought of it, were probably intentionally skipped over, but I, for one, did not think that ignorance was bliss...especially not now.

"Okay. I'm going to need you to dumb that down for me later. For now, just explain what the Black Forest Witch is please."

He shook his head. Clearly, unimpressed with the fact that I had been so left in the dark my whole life.

Well, I know just how you feel about that Hersch.

"The Black Forest Witch is unlike any other. She is an Elemental Witch for all appearances, but her Element is the forest itself. She draws power from the forest. As the forest is healthy and she is in it, so is she." I struggled to comprehend all of this new information. "She was much older than she appeared, as well. The Black Forest Witch lives and heals with the forest. Much like a shifter heals."

I leaned back in my chair and dropped Otto's hand to cross my arms. He placed his hand on my leg, sensing I needed moral support. "So, do you know exactly how old she was?"

"Sabine was not the first of her kind, but there can only be one Black Forest Witch alive at one time. I first met your mother around 150 years ago." My jaw went slack and I looked to Luna, who this information had affected the same way. Otto chimed in here.

"I have lived in this forest most of my life. How had I not met Sabine earlier than I did?" That was a very good question.

"She had her own home here in the forest. One she had hidden herself. I know where this is, but I'm unable to see it. She shrouded it long ago."

Things were beginning to make more sense. Why my mother had brought me back here as a child. Why she wanted me to get to know the forest. Why I had never known my grandparents, because she had probably outlived them. My phone dinged, snapping me back to reality. It was Laurel.

We need to talk.

My instincts told me the cat was out of the bag. Tomorrow was the Full Moon. I would sneak away today, as best as I could with Otto being able to tell how close I was, to go and speak with her.

Late lunch around 2:30?

I asked, and she confirmed. That would give me enough time to come up with an excuse to dip out of the village for a bit.

"Okay, back to this prophecy. What does this mean for me?" Otto and Luna looked at Herschel with as much intent as I did.

"No one quite knows. The prophecy is unclear. The only thing that was clear, is that you are the true Alpha of the entire community of Shifters...maybe even other species." He said this last part with caution, as if he wasn't sure he wanted me to know this part. "The one Alpha to lead them all, so it was said."

As a Fae, especially one who had willingly cast himself out from his own people, he was not keen on the thought of anyone being able to control him. I didn't want to be able to control him, so I guess we were even with our level of discomfort.

Luna's look of awe deepened as she looked over toward me from Herschel. "Bob?" She waited for me to respond, but I just looked at her. I didn't know what to say. "Remember the little people when you're Queen of the Forest and Shifters." Her eyes were wide, and she wasn't really mocking me, but trying to help me find some humor to snap out of this.

I shook my head and looked down. "I really don't know what to say or do about any of this." All the wind had been taken from my sails. Otto squeezed my leg, reminding me that his hand was there. I put my hand on his and looked up to him.

"We will figure it out. I think now we should increase our attempts to find your father."

That reminded me. I looked back to Herschel. "You said that my mother had her own home here in the forest that she shrouded." He nodded. "You know where it is. I'd like to see if I can get through, and if perhaps... this is where she hid my father."

Herschel agreed to take us, but not today. That was fine with me, as I had a date with a Witch.

Chapter 24

*O*tto contemplated his Mate, and how she was quickly becoming more and more interesting. It would seem that her effect on Luna did not hold weight with him, being her Mate. He was sure that if she wanted to, she could use this power on him, but he hoped it never came to that for any reason. He could feel the shift in her and some unknown power growing. While Herschel was still here to question, Otto asked him if the warming and growing Sammy was experiencing could be Elemental Power growing inside of her. Herschel didn't know, but told them all to monitor if there were any indications that Elemental Witch, or any Witch Power, was growing in her.

Otto could feel that she was overwhelmed, but he could also sense that she was up to something. He decided to let it play out. She was trying to keep him in the dark, as well as Luna, but there wasn't any hiding from the Mate Bond unless you shut it down. That within itself would have been a dead giveaway to mischief. Her plan was beginning to come to light, when Sammy suggested that Luna stay and watch Otto with his wine, while she went to her cottage in town to get more of her things. Luna's eyes had narrowed on her, and when she looked to him, he just lifted a shoulder.

"Okay, I'll stay and enjoy the smell of wine while I can't drink any." Luna grumbled, but was compliant.

They went about their afternoons. Sammy and Luna went through more of the journals together, while Otto went out to show himself to the pack and speak to any who had questions. He knew they all would have felt the Mate Bond solidifying last night. Thinking of it gave him a very physical response, so he had to change the trajectory of his thoughts. They had a new Alpha to partner with him. They would all meet her officially in due time, but Alaryk needed to be found first. He could help with his daughter just from his knowledge alone, if things were to get out of hand.

When I pulled myself away from the journals with Luna at 1:30 so I could go and meet Laurel, she didn't argue or ask why she couldn't come. She just went with Otto. I figured it was something to do with this whole super Alpha business and didn't give it another thought. I peeled myself out of my pajamas and put on some sweats, a light hoodie, and rubber boots. It had decided to rain today. I didn't want to be caught without rubber boots in the forest while it rained. When I walked Luna to Otto's, he gave me a hungry look, and a soft kiss that felt like a tiger on a leash. Restrained, but you could tell there was much more behind it.

I left, barely. I'd wanted to stay and explore him more, physically, emotionally, who he was, what he liked. Everything. I was single-minded. I needed to figure out this situation with my father, and I felt like Laurel was going to give me some insight.

When I got to the restaurant, we had to sit inside due to the rain. This was probably better in the long run. Prying eyes wouldn't see us unless we saw them. She hugged me and sat down across from me at the corner table we chose. It was farthest away from other tables, and we had a good vantage point of the door and the rest of the people inside.

"What's going on?" I asked her. I had no idea what she wanted to talk to me about, so I didn't want to give anything away initially.

"You're being plotted against." She said it in a hushed tone, so low that humans wouldn't hear, but I could. "I know what you are. I've suspected, but I know." I opened my mouth to speak. She cut me off. "I'm not upset."

I relaxed a little and reached for her hand. She smiled and squeezed mine slightly before letting go and picking up her menu.

"Who?" Was all I asked.

"Lena. She wants you gone. She came to me in the middle of the night and asked me if I would help her."

"She knows you are a Witch?" Laurel nodded her head.

"Yes, I think everyone knows I am a Witch at this point."

The server came to ask what we'd be having so we took a break to order food. Once it was just the two of us again, she looked back at me. "I told her I am not very powerful, and that I am estranged from my family, but she wants my help still." She paused briefly. "I said yes." At my look of astonishment, she clarified. "I only said yes so that she would leave, and so that she would consider me an ally and I could pass along information to you if need be."

I relaxed again. "Thank you, Laurel."

She smiled at me. "Of course, what are friends for? She also knows that Karl has been trailing her." She switched to a look of sadness.

"So, you *do* know what Karl is." She sighed heavily and nodded. Her demeanor a bit subdued.

"Yes, I've known what he is for some time. I keep waiting for him to tell me himself, but he must not trust me for what I am."

I felt sad for her. "I'm sorry Laurel. I'll work on him. I know he cares for you."

I didn't want to tell her of the talk he and I had the night after we'd all sat on the patio at the biergarten. If he had a stick up his ass about her being a witch and that's why he wouldn't be with her, then I wasn't about to give her the hope of knowing he did in fact love her.

We ate in silence for the most part. I didn't divulge too much information. Just that I was staying with Otto. Giving her too much information that could be used against me, or even her in the future, wouldn't be wise. My biggest concern was that Lena would find Laurel's family to help her, or that Lena would find out exactly who I was and up the ante on her plotting. For that reason, I wanted to stay out of the public eye in the shifter village. When it was time to go, she hugged me again and told me to stay safe and watch my back. I assured her that I would be very safe and hoped she would do the same.

ନ

When Sammy got home, she had a small bag of clothes and her precious coffee bar. Otto had felt her drawing nearer the village and went to meet her at the clearing. He urged her to bring her car inside the barrier this time. Occasionally to have a parked car outside was one thing, but to have one constantly there led to the risk of them being stumbled upon. She parked it just inside the barrier and hopped out. Otto took her coffee machine and let her carry her bag.

"So," he began. "What did you find out?" She looked up at him, surprise in her eyes.

"I'll tell you once we are safely inside and I'll be leaving Luna out of this one or she will never go home to her husband."

His face grew serious and he picked up the pace, which she matched even though her legs were so much smaller than his. She kept walking past the cottage she was staying in to go to his own, he assumed, in order to keep Luna from hearing. She set the coffee machine down on his counter and went up into the tree level. She turned to look at him with what appeared to be annoyance in her eyes, but what she was putting off was a combination of jealousy and anger.

"Lena is trying to get rid of me."

Otto's face hardened. "Explain."

So, explain she did. By the end of her tale, she was pacing and talking with her hands and looked as if she was going to take it out on him for ever having been involved with Lena in the first place. She turned on him and stopped, huffing out a big breath. "The bitch has got to go." With that, she plopped down onto the couch and crossed her arms. The power was rolling off of her in waves. He sat down next to her and pulled her against him to soothe them both.

"We will figure it out, but I don't know about getting rid of Lena."

She pulled her head back to get a good look at him. "And why not?" She was like a hissing and spitting kitten in his arms. He bit the inside of his cheek to control himself.

"Because *meine Liebe*. If we exile her, then we cannot keep watch on her."

Sammy stilled and relaxed somewhat. "I am not, what you would say, carrying a torch for this woman." She growled softly at him.

"I *know*." She sat quietly for a moment. "I am going to go back to see Luna now, but don't tell her any of this."

Otto nodded in agreement, but held her tighter. "Are you sure you have to leave now?" He buried his face in her neck and felt her go momentarily limp. She stiffened and pushed back off of him. For a moment he thought she was back to playing cat and mouse, but she said she would come back tonight when Luna went to sleep again.

"She goes to sleep early these days. She's growing a person."

Otto accepted this and let go of her waist. She gave him a quick peck on the cheek before taking off with her coffee machine and bag. Now, he needed to figure out what to do about Lena.

☙

The next day, I woke up full of nerves. Even though I was wrapped up in a warm body that made me want to just cozy back down and not move again for a while, I couldn't fall back asleep. Today was the Full Moon. It would reach its apex in the evening, around 7 o'clock. I had no idea what I would be turning into tonight. Would it be one of the Lynx, or something entirely different? Who knew? "You are shaking your foot so hard, you are going to scoot the bed across the room."

I hadn't realized I'd been doing anything. "I'm jittery."

Otto rolled over to look at the time on his phone. "It is not even 7 in the morning yet and already you have the jitters."

I rolled over to my stomach and enjoyed the view of his unclothed upper body while he had his forearm resting across his eyes. "I can feel you staring."

I smiled into the pillow. "I'm nervous. I don't know if I'll shift into something familiar tonight or not."

He removed his arm from his face and swung it out and up, offering for me to come closer. *Oh, what the hell, just a few more minutes.* I could tell my nerves were getting to him too. His heart rate was a bit higher than usual, but so was mine.

"Even if you do not shift into either of the forms you have before, I will be there to lend a paw." He was smiling dopily with his eyes still closed. He opened one to a slit and looked down at me. What he saw was a facial expression showing off exactly how unimpressed I was. That finished it and he laughed.

I pushed off of his chest with the hand I'd had rested there and sat on the edge of the bed. I prepared to stand, but Otto had

- 203 -

other ideas. I was pulled back under the covers so suddenly the breath was forced from my body.

℞

A little while later I was walking back to the other cottage, significantly more relaxed than when I'd woken up. I had been with Otto more time in the last 36 hours than I had been with anyone in the last few years. Sad, but true. We seemed to be on track for me to make up for lost time though.

Luna was still sleeping when I returned. I didn't want to wake her. So, I picked up my current knitting project while I drank some coffee. She came shuffling out around 9 o'clock, grunting for coffee. Being the good friend that I was, I put down my knitting and got it for her.

When she was sufficiently caffeinated, she finally spoke. "You ready for tonight?" I should have known this would be her first topic of the day. I knew she was concerned, but I was an avoider.

"Not really. I'm trying to decide right now if I want to just get it over with and shift, or if I should wait until I have to."

She scoffed at me. "You'll wait until you have to." When I gave her a dry look she said, "You forget, I've known you since we were toddlers." She looked me over. "So, how was your night?"

"You know, you may be the most prying person I have ever met."

She poked me in the ribs. "You love me. Now spill the beans."

A smile slowly spread across my face. "Fine."

She rolled her eyes and sighed impatiently at me. "Fine? I'm telling him you said it was just fine."

I shrugged. "Go for it, he's older than us. So, I'm sure he'll be glad I don't kiss and tell."

She grumbled in her coffee. I sighed and gave her just enough to make her happy. "I could stay here with him forever, but I would miss the town and my own cottage."

"But it's not your own. It's Herschel's. It was a stepping stone, and I believe you have stepped already my dear." Leave it to her to drop a truth bomb on me before 9:30 AM. I decided an abrupt subject change was called for.

"I want to go back out to my dad's house today to sniff around a bit more."

Luna didn't appear too enthused about this piece of information, but she'd do it. She definitely was lacking her usual energy that she would get from the Full Moon. I said as much, and she said it was to be expected. "The pack doctor told me I'd likely not have energy back for another month or so with the rate I'll be growing."

I felt bad for her. "You can stay behind if you prefer not to make that trip. You're going to be shifting tonight, so I don't want you using up all your energy on this." I thought about it a few seconds more. "You could look through more journals and notes that we've taken to see if there is anything we may have missed."

She made a face at that too. "I don't know what I'll do just yet, but I will let you know when I know."

It probably would be better for her to come with me just in case the trip took longer than anticipated. I didn't want her having to shift among all these strange - to us - shifters without me. If it came to it, I'd make that argument, but not until then.

I texted Otto and told him what I wanted to do. He sent me a thumbs up emoji and that was it. I wasn't sure if that meant go for it, or if he was saying he'd be here soon. I didn't have long to wait for the answer, because I heard him coming through the door shortly after he'd responded to me.

"*Guten Morgen*, Luna. How are you feeling today?"

She grunted. "I could sleep for another five hours."

He looked at her with sympathy. "I would say you should, but in case Sammy and I aren't back in time for the shift, I don't want you to be here alone with no one else that you know present." I'm glad he said it and not me.

"Plus," I said. "It could be kind of fun to just shift out at my dad's. Right?" At least I thought it could be. There was more room where the trees opened up to the sky. I loved the thick forest, but I also loved seeing the sky through it.

She agreed, and we hit the road shortly after we finished eating. We didn't stop on the way to sightsee like we had the last time with Luna. There seemed to be a level of determination to get there and find whatever it was I thought we would find today that we hadn't before. If I was being honest, I didn't think there was anything else out there to find. Knowing that my mom had her own home hidden out here in the forest, made me think anything worth finding was going to be there. We didn't have the time to find Mom's place today, with the moon rising earlier in the evening.

After searching through the home for a few more hours, as well as the property that was included behind the barrier, I decided to start cleaning inside. There weren't any cleaning supplies that hadn't long expired, but there was water and rags. I could get a good portion of the dust and such from the surfaces. I was determined to find my father. So, I could get a head start on the cleaning for him. I made it to the living room and noticed the photo from the fireplace was missing. I asked Otto and Luna if they had moved it.

"I took it home for you. I was going to clean up the frame or put it in a new one before giving it to you." He was so damn sweet to me I almost couldn't stand it. I didn't know how to express myself. I heard Luna make an annoyed sound. She must have seen the struggle.

"This is where you kiss him and tell him thank you, Jackass." I glared at her, but did as she suggested, even though I tried to avoid physical contact during the day. Otherwise, nothing would ever get done.

I looked at the time on my phone. It was nearly 5 o'clock. We could make it back in time to shift if we pushed it or if we jogged it back, but I didn't want to push Lu too hard. "Do you two want to shift here and we can head back after or in the morning?" They looked at each other and their own phones to check the time.

Luna shrugged. "Whatever lets me sleep after shifting. So, probably shifting and sleeping here." Otto nodded his head, agreeing with whatever the pregnant lady said.

"Alright, well..." the nerves were apparent in my voice. "I'm going to go outside and get to it."

Huffing out a breath, I turned and headed outside.
We'll see what I turn into today.

Chapter 25

O
tto followed Sammy out of the cottage with Luna close behind. He could not help but to be a bit curious as to what she would shift into tonight. She did not seem very worried about it outwardly, but he could feel her nerves through their Bond as if they were his own. She was a brave person. She didn't let fear stop her from anything...at least in the few short weeks she had been in his life. That kind of courage took more than a few weeks to perfect. He gathered it must have been a lifelong trait.

The three of them undressed and put their clothes in neat little piles on the back patio. Out of his periphery, he watched Luna go to Sammy and touch her shoulder gently. Sammy looked at her with love and touched the hand on her shoulder and nodded. He felt the wave of love and appreciation come over Sammy and he smiled. Otto had never had this himself. Not with anyone outside the realm of his blood family. He enjoyed watching Sammy and Luna's relationship.

Sammy looked at him now. A sort of contentedness came to him through the Bond. It may not be love as yet, but he knew they would get there. He watched her take several slow, deep breaths with her eyes closed as she opened up the Bond completely in case an assist was needed on his part.

Sammy began her shift, but this time, instead of pain and physical stress, her change flowed over her like a silk sheet. He watched, mesmerized as her body contorted and visibly shimmered. You could smell magic in the air. A kind of magic she could only get from her father.

Otto's eyes were wide with awe when she had completed her change. She was absolutely stunning. He had never met a Clouded Leopard before, but now, he was seeing one and he was speechless.

"Wow," he heard Luna say, but barely as he was so engrossed in his Mate's new form.

Sammy's vivid green eyes looked at them. Stoic. Her eyes were rimmed in black, which made it appear as if she were wearing eyeliner. Her muzzle was a lighter color than the rest of her face, and her nose was pink.

"*Ja*, wow indeed."

He looked directly into the eyes of the creature before him, and began to shift. Luna began her shift shortly after.

◌

My shift into a new creature had felt fluid. No pain. Not even the minor pain I'd get prior to the crazy things happening in my life. It felt natural. My whole body had tingled. It felt as calm and fluid as watching the moon glide across the sky. Luna and Otto had said wow. I peered down at my legs and saw this was an accurate appraisal of the new form. My legs were covered in large black ovals. My body felt sleek and powerful. It felt safe to assume that my flavor of the month was a Leopard of some sort.

As awesome as that was, I was just happy that it hadn't hurt. I wasn't sure if it was another side effect of sealing the Mate Bond, or if it belonged to the cascade of oddities about me the Mate Bond had initiated.

For the time being, having a painless shift was enough for me. I lifted my head to the sky, watching the Moon peek through the foliage at us while I waited for Luna to finish her shift. Otto was quick with his shifts, and he had started not long after I had finished mine.

I felt Luna come up beside me in her small Coyote form, and I felt the awe and love from her. I looked toward Otto, and I realized I felt the same emotions pumping off of him. I gave him a slight headbutt. Luna got the same treatment. This made my animal so happy she could take flight. Two creatures with me who cared deeply for me. Luna let out a little Coyote yip and took off trotting toward the back of my father's property. I followed her at a slow trot, it not taking much to keep up with her, and felt Otto close on my tail. It felt great to have these two people with me tonight.

The interesting thing about the different animals I now had under my belt, was that with each animal I changed into, the overall feeling and voice of my animal remained the same. She knew when she had moved higher up on the food chain, and her sense of assuredness in herself would increase from there. However, she always felt like the same creature. I wondered if that would hold true if and when I shifted into anything other than a species of Felidae.

I hadn't yet been this far back in my father's barrier property. When I heard rushing water, I was intrigued. I had heard there were a lot of beautiful waterfalls in the forests around here, but I hadn't seen any yet beyond the small ones that were more of a ledge than anything else. I veered off toward the sound and found what I was looking for. A double waterfall. Even more intriguing was that I was fairly certain the ledge that the first waterfall emptied into was a pool of water. From there, it flowed down the cascade of rocks into the stream below.

We moved out of the barrier and into the forest. This was as deep as I had ever been. Almost no light got through the trees for quite a bit of our journey after we left the barrier. The trees were so thick. We finally got to a break in the trees after a mile or so of our animal's scouting. Enjoying the Moon's beams, I wandered aimlessly through this clearing. It looked as if someone had intentionally carved out this section of the forest. The edges were just that clean in some areas. As I was exploring, I suddenly hit what felt like a brick wall. There was a physical blockade... that I couldn't see.

I sniffed at the air for any hints of Fae magic, but the air moving through my lungs was clean. Shifting quickly back into my human form, I reached a handout and felt it again. Except this time, I could see shimmery sparks of energy surrounding my hand where I touched the wall. I called out to Otto and Luna only to find that Otto was already there and beginning to shift, having felt my confusion. Luna quickly showed up at my side and started her shift as well. When she was finished, I showed them my newest discovery. Otto reached a hand out and touched the wall, but no sparks. Luna did the same, also with no sparks. I touched it again just to be sure I hadn't been seeing things.

Sparks.

"My life is getting weirder and weirder."

Luna shrugged a shoulder. "I think you could very well have just found the home of the Black Forest Witch."

I was mildly shocked for a moment, then realized she was probably correct. "I suppose the only way to know for sure is to ask Hersch tomorrow morning."

In the meantime, I mapped out the circumference of the wall. It was more than just the clearing. It reached back into the woods quite a way before wrapping back around into the clearing.

Luna and Otto started becoming agitated as the apex of the Full Moon was on us. Odd, I thought. I should be feeling the same, unless this is another handy dandy hat trick from my father. Deciding to push it further, I didn't shift.

Otto and Luna shifted back into their animals and watched me with expectant eyes. I just shrugged. "I don't feel like I *have* to shift." I would have tested it further, but I didn't want to make the hike back to my father's cottage in my human form, naked and barefoot. So, I went ahead and made the shift.

As this was becoming normal for me, I looked at my legs to verify which form I had shifted into. Seeing I was still the Leopard, I led us back the way we had come.

౪

When we arrived at my dad's home, I shifted back once through the barrier. The Apex of the moon had come and gone, and with it, the need for Otto and Luna to be in animal form. Luna's shift was slower than it used to be. Possibly due to the earlier shift back into human form, paired with the pregnancy.

I instinctually touched my hand to her shoulder, which normally I would never touch a shifter mid-change. It could hurt. Yet, something had come over me and I did it anyway.

I could feel a passage of energy shift from me into Luna. Much like how Otto and I could pass energy from one to the other. Luna's shift came easier and faster. When she stood before me, her face said it all, but that didn't stop her from speaking.

"What the hell was that?"

Otto watched the exchange with avid interest. "I didn't know I could do it, but something made me reach out to touch you."

I told her how it felt similar to when Otto and I could sense each other or shift energy between the two of us.

"How is that possible?" She asked, and I shrugged.

"How are any of the last couple of months possible?"

We turned and looked at Otto as we heard him murmur, "The one Alpha to lead them all." Luna slowly looked back to me, eyes round.

I grumbled something about finding food and stalked off into the trees, pausing only to shift before the barrier. It didn't take long for me to find a boar. I took it down easily enough, even though I was incredibly careful of it. Boars were quite dangerous. I dragged it back to the cottage and Otto got to work doing what needed to be done in order to not have to eat raw. I could hunt, but I knew nothing about cleaning a kill. Luna and I sat inside while he took care of it outside.

"So...I guess this means you really are the one Alpha to rule us all?" Her tone was inquisitive.

"Lead... to lead us all, were my dad and Herschel's actual words. I have no interest in ruling *or* leading anything though."

She sighed heavily. I could tell she was exhausted. "I hope we find your dad soon. You need guidance, and to be protected. Not having information could really hurt you."

I'd had that thought myself. I just hadn't voiced it because it seemed obvious.

"I want to try something." I scooted away from her on the counter we were sitting on to make sure we weren't touching. I looked her in the eye and mimicked what it felt like to push energy at Otto through our Bond.

"I definitely felt that!" She had perked up a bit. "You don't have to touch me to do it?"

Otto walked in at this moment with a lot of trays of meat.

"Apparently not." I sighed, for the first time thinking perhaps I shouldn't have come to Germany. It had set so much in motion that I just wasn't mentally prepared for, but then I looked at Otto going about his business and felt an immediate pang of guilt for thinking that. Almost as if my thoughts were audible, he turned to look at me with such intensity. I felt ashamed. He had to have felt my guilt, and then drew his own conclusion.

At that moment, I hated myself. Not only was my pregnant best friend worried about my well-being, but now I had very likely offended Otto. I felt him shut the Bond down quite a bit. Not all the way, but enough that I was only getting a trickle of his emotion.

I gave Luna a look indicating I needed a moment with Otto. She nodded and walked up the stairs to rummage around for blankets. "I think I need to explain what you felt," I started.

His eyes were dark. "The intense wave of regret, then guilt, then shame?" He paused a beat, never removing his eyes from mine. "Is this what you mean?"

Instead of letting his sarcasm bother me, I held steady under his scrutiny. "Are you going to continue being a smartass or are you going to let me tell you what those feelings were about?"

He didn't say anything, just lifted an eyebrow at me, as if saying *well go on then*. I explained to him what I had just done with Luna before he had walked back in from outside. "I was thinking about all of the changes my life has gone through, and how dangerous it could be for myself, and for people I care about." Explaining myself was the worst. I always felt like I was making excuses. "That was the regret you felt. I thought for the first time that maybe I shouldn't have come because my move to come to Germany could hurt people."

He opened his mouth to speak, but I raised a hand to stop him. "Then, I looked over and saw you at the sink." Shaking my head I continued. "That's where you felt guilt because how could I wish that I hadn't come here, I love it here, and you're amazing." I looked down for the first time in my story. Feeling the shame all over again. "The guilt led to shame. At my cowardice and lack of adaptability."

He was suddenly right in between my legs as I was still sitting on the counter. He wrapped his arms around my waist, and his face was pressed into the side of my neck. His heart was beating in tune with mine, which was usual since the Mate Bond had been sealed. "You are no coward." My face was in his hands now, and it felt like he was looking straight into my soul. "The last month, I have been in complete awe of you." I tried looking away, touching moments never really being my strong suit, but he didn't allow it. "You are the bravest woman I have met in my life." He thought for a moment and smirked, showing me one of my favorite things, his dimple. "And I am an old man."

That got me to smile and sniff back the moment of self-pity I was having. "I didn't think Germans could make jokes."

He laughed and stood back. "We can make them, we just can't take them."

Luna, impeccable timing as always, came back at this moment. "So, are we going to talk about the elephant in the room?"

Otto and I exchanged a look. "I haven't turned into an elephant yet."

She let out a snarky, sarcastic *hardy har har* and rolled her eyes. "No, I'm talking about the fact that we probably found your mom's place tonight *and* that it's probably where your dad is."

᪥

We talked about it. I knew I'd have to talk about it without Luna, so I could talk to Otto about asking Laurel to help us get into it if Herschel wasn't able to. Not because I needed his permission, but because I wanted his opinion. I may have always done what I wanted to do regardless, but I liked getting viewpoints of others prior to jumping off the ledge. I had a tendency to make questionable choices otherwise.

We ate our completely unseasoned boar and made quick work of laying pillows and blankets out on the floor to sleep on, after shaking as much of the dust off as we could. All in all, it wasn't too terrible. A bit weird sleeping next to Otto in the same room as Luna, but sleeping was *all* I would be doing tonight...if I could even do that.

I wondered if maybe I'd visit my dad's dream world again, and I could question him a bit more. Sleep didn't come easy for me that night.

᪥

Lena stalked the outside of the witch's home. She knew she wasn't there. Her car was gone, the lights were off, and her scent was faded. The apex of the moon was well in the past. So, it was time to do a little investigating in the house. She *knew* the witch had run to the little girl and told her everything about their exchange. She had seen the intent in her eyes the moment she'd decided. Witches thought they were so fucking crafty. Maybe if they had a lifespan of barely longer than that of a human, they'd develop more cunning, but they didn't. She could have made a good ally, but oh well. She would find others.

Lena knew that the witch's family would probably kill for some information and killing was exactly what she hoped they'd do. Sure, Otto would be wrecked for a time. Though at the moment, she was sure he would get over it with time and with comfort from her. Once he was free of *Sammy*, Lena was sure he would see things more clearly.

She checked all the doors and windows on Laurel's home and finally found a window that was unlocked. Naturally, it was an awkward window to climb through, since it was directly above the kitchen sink. Well worth the prize she hoped... a dead shifter girl, and a broken heart for her to heal.

She could almost see it now, and it nearly distracted her from her task. Her heart raced at the thought of her plan coming to fruition, but she couldn't get there if she didn't do the work. She rummaged through drawers for what felt like forever, looking for an address book, photos, or something. She never found an address book. Kids these days...

She did, eventually, find a shoebox full of holiday and birthday cards under Laurel's bed with return addresses on them. She pilfered a few that were most prominent and had sent the most. They were likely where she would start her search and manipulation plan.

She knew Laurel had been mostly estranged from her family. If the amount of cards from these people under her bed were any indication, they would want their family safe if worse came to worse and they didn't want to help her without some... encouragement. Satisfied with her bounty, she made sure everything was back in place and went out the way she came, closing the window back down firmly. In a perfect time too, as Laurel pulled in her driveway as Lena had hit the trees. She would have to make the trip back home in her human skin. She didn't think carrying cards all the way back to *Dorf der Gestaltwandler* in her mouth was an intelligent or feasible idea. *Oh well*. She made the trip back home, smiling the whole way.

Chapter 26

Two days after the Full Moon, we were outside the invisible wall that we all assumed contained my mother's home. We had Hershel with us for confirmation, and confirm it he did.

"This is definitely where *deine Mutters* home is. I will not be able to help you beyond telling you this though."

This was not what I wanted to hear. We had been here yesterday as well, without Herschel. We had walked the entire circumference of the wall, looking for any kind of break, a weak spot. Anything. There was nothing to be found. Mom had been thorough, and she had been strong. So much stronger than I thought possible.

I was beginning to get discouraged. If Herschel didn't think that he could get through, then how was I supposed to get through? I knew my dad had to be in there though. I *had* to try.

"There were sparks around my hand." I looked at Herschel, determination coming out of my very pores. "When I touched the wall, there were sparks around my hand."

Touching the wall again, I was able to show him what I meant. I noticed too, that a heat began deep in my belly when I was in contact with it as if something in me was trying to rise to the occasion. I wondered if I was going to have some weird, watered down version of my mother's magic or maybe even watered down powers from the god grandfather that no one could seem tell me who it was.

Pulling my hand away before my body wound up spontaneously combusting on me or something, I heard Herschel start speaking. "You are the daughter of the creator. You are also the granddaughter of a god. Your abilities are only beginning to come to the surface. Maybe you will have the power to tear down, or get through, the wall."

I sure as shit hope so.

I reached out and trailed a finger down the wall one more time, watching the line of sparks follow it. Grunting in frustration, I turned around and began to start the walk back to the car. When no one else moved, I turned back around and watched.

Herschel was obviously intrigued. He let out a low humming noise as he mulled it over. He stepped close to the wall and I could feel the energy from it reaching out. It was as if the wall was trying to connect, positively or negatively I couldn't know.

Herschel reached out a tentative hand, pausing just before he reached the wall. He ran a finger down the wall. I couldn't quite determine what happened next. I gasped loudly. So did Herschel. This made Otto look up from his daydreaming. "*Scheiße!*" Otto yelled.

Herschel yelled, "Sohn einer Hündin, Sabine!"

Luna reached her hand out for mine and held it tightly.

I could only imagine that those were some pretty colorful words they shouted out because what I had seen would warrant that. When Herschel's finger had made contact with the wall, it was as if he began to glitch. Almost as if you were watching TV on an old school antenna, and someone moved to the other side of the room. There was static, waves, all of what you would see on a TV if the channel was fading out.

In between glitches, I got what I believed to be my first look at Herschel without his glamour. He shimmered. Not just gold or silver, but with a myriad of colors I hadn't seen in this realm before. *Exotic* was the only way to describe the rest of him. Elongated features, broad of shoulder, long slender torso, with what looked like colorful, physically swirling tattoos marking his arms.

As soon as he removed his finger from the barrier he was back as the, now extremely, grumpy old man I had grown used to and cared for. In that moment, I felt an intense wave of power wash over all of us. It made me shiver as if I was cold. Though, if anything, I had been warm.

I looked at Otto, Luna, and back to Herschel. Otto's face showed just as much bewilderment as I'm sure my own had. Herschel adjusted his belt line in the way any other mundane old man would and cleared his throat. He looked at us with an expression that we understood to mean we would never be talking about this moment again. I could only assume that my mother's magic in the wall had caused his glamour to misfire and show us a momentary glimpse of his true self. He nodded his head at our silence, and we all moved on together.

Herschel had shown us a road that got us within a couple of miles of her house. To save the pregnant lady who had shifted four times the night before, we had taken my Jeep. While driving back to the real roads - you know, paved ones that weren't imaginary roads going through the forest - I was very clearly distracted. It was an unnecessarily bumpy ride for a while. Luna made me stop the car so she could jump out and get sick.

Feeling guilty for activating her pregnancy stomach, I let Otto take over the drive. Somewhere on the remainder of the drive home, I realized I had never seen him drive. I didn't even know if he could drive. Being 160 years old, I guess I just assumed he could. Luckily, my assumption had been correct. He drove lazily and well.

I realized I only cared so much about Otto's driving abilities because it was a good distraction from the rage that threatened to boil over at nothing being easy anymore. It may sound spoiled and entitled, but I wanted inside that wall and I wanted in there yesterday. I knew my dad would be able to help me navigate all these changes. He would at least be more of a help here than wherever the hell he was now. Growling a little in my throat, I put my feet up on the dash, crossed my arms over my chest, and looked out the window.

I felt Otto reach out to me mentally. Instinctually, I almost closed up the Bond, not wanting anyone to witness the utter bitchiness I was feeling at everything right now. I knew that would hurt his feelings, so I let him see it all.

All I really wanted to do, at this point, was shed my human skin and climb some trees. I wished I knew how to shift into my Bobcat. In all reality, I hadn't really tried to turn into a familiar form. I was scared to. If I was being entirely honest with myself, I felt like I would screw something up and wind up this half-human, half-animal... thing. Then, I'd probably get stuck like that because I wouldn't know how to shift back from there. I knew I was pouting, and over analyzing everything as usual, but it had been rough. I felt like I needed a giant temper tantrum just to make me feel better.

When we arrived back at the village and my car was safely inside the barrier, Luna went inside to take a cat nap, while Otto led me by the hand to his gym room. I thought for sure he was just going to take me upstairs and let me work off my anger in some other way. Though, I wasn't sure if I was ready for a good old fashioned anger bang with him, but the idea of it was appealing.

Instead, he put my keys down on the weight bench and pulled some hand wraps out from the cabinet in the corner. He walked back to me and started putting them on for me, wrapping my hands fairly snug.

He was always so damn quiet. You had to either guess what he was doing, or just roll with it. This time it was fairly obvious that he wanted me to use his punching bag, but I'd never punched something that... hefty. I gave him a leery look with my hands down at my sides.

"What am I supposed to be doing?"

His light chuckle nearly always made my insides warm, like melted butter. Now was no different. "You are supposed to hit the bag."

I rolled my eyes as dramatically as I could. "I gathered as much, but I have never hit something that wasn't living."

He feigned a scandalous look, but couldn't hold it for long without chuckling again. "You hit it much the same. Just don't follow through quite so much. It is more of a jab instead of a full-throttle punch."

Feeling a little self-conscious, I hit the bag once like he described. He went to stand behind the bag and hold it in place for me. Not being able to see his face made it easier for me. I hit the bag a few times, and felt the frustration I'd been holding in start to bubble as if someone had shaken up a soda bottle. I started hitting harder and faster. Using every ounce of speed and strength I could come up with. I didn't notice I was yelling as I beat the living shit out of my stuffed opponent until I was finally out of breath and sweating. I stopped and rested my forehead on the bag.

Otto didn't come around yet, but he reached around and found my hand on the side of the bag. He placed his on top of mine, and he stayed like that on his side of the bag until I was ready to collect myself and be seen again.

I was beginning to lose count of how many times he had known exactly what I needed, before even I knew what it was, and delivered. Letting go of his hand, I walked around to him and hugged him tightly for a moment. Once I let him go, grinning, I pushed him backward toward his weight bench. He sat down and inadvertently pushed my keys off onto the floor, looking up at me now. I was sure he knew what I was about, the Mate Bond was wide open. I spent the next little while, thanking him in my own special way for knowing just what I needed.

♋

A week later, I had convinced Luna that she could go home to her husband. He was beginning to get antsy with her having been gone for so long, and I was getting antsy for another reason. I could feel that something was coming, and I didn't want her here for it. I was able to keep the growing anxiety manageable around her so that she wouldn't worry too much about leaving. She still fought me for a couple of days, but I had always been far more stubborn than she could ever dream of being. So, we put her butt on a plane back to the States and went on our way.

"Is there anything you would like to get from your house before going back to *das Dorf*?"

Otto was driving, because I'd discovered I liked watching him do it. I don't know why I found it so damn sexy, but I did. I'd seen plenty of men drive a car, obviously, but Otto was different with everything. I was beginning to dig the older man thing, because what else could it be?

Checking out his facial expression, I wasn't sure how to answer him. I wanted to go back to my own house and stop hiding behind the barrier. I liked my life there. The forest village was awesome, but I felt confined at the time...claustrophobic. That's not what I wanted.

"Sure, go ahead and stop there." I decided to table it for today. It didn't seem like the right time to bring that up. He felt content, happy even. I didn't want to rain on his parade.

"Even if I was unable to feel you thinking so hard, I'm sure I would be able to hear the gears turning in that pretty head of yours. What is the problem?"

I really hate this stupid Bond right about now.

I groaned grumpily. "I miss my cottage." I felt the sting of my words as I said them. "I don't mean being away from you or anything. That is something I have thoroughly been enjoying." The good thing about this was that he could hear, feel, and smell the sincerity of my words as truth. "I just miss my place. The village makes me feel claustrophobic."

I'm sure it wouldn't feel that way if I didn't feel like I was being forced to be there hiding from witches who likely didn't even know that I existed. That was the current case.

Otto sighed lightly. "I know. I have felt it." He drove on in silence for a couple minutes. "If you go back to your own cottage, would you permit me to stay with you so I can help keep you safe?"

When he said that, it felt like a 100-pound weight had been removed off my chest. Instantly perking up, I reached across the car and gave him as hard of a hug as I could the driver, and a loud, smacking kiss on the cheek. "YES!!"

Of course, I'd let him stay with me. Not even just my animal would be upset with me if I tried to sleep without him next to me anymore. I would be too. *Interesting new development, Sammy.*

When we got to my house, I'd told him I had been thinking of buying it. He smiled and nodded, but I could tell he was holding something back from me. This made me curious and mildly uncomfortable, but I'd ask him about it later. We were obviously still testing the boundaries of this relationship or I would have confronted him about it here.

I went through my room and found everything just as I had left it. The sun caught a necklace that had been my mother's. A locket. It contained a piece of wood from a birch tree. That's it. Just bark. She said she always wanted to keep home close to her, which made sense now seeing as she had drawn strength from the forest. I picked it up and put it on. I wore it mainly when I wanted to feel closer to her.

"Otto?" He answered from downstairs. "Are we starting to stay here now or do we need to go back to the village for anything?"

He came around the corner and the sun struck his face. His eyes were the prettiest green I had ever seen, and rimmed with lashes as dark as his hair. My breath caught for a moment and I didn't hear what he said. "I'm sorry - what did you say?"

He smiled gently at me before answering. "I'd like to go back there tonight, talk with Karl, and collect some of my own things before coming back here tomorrow."

I pressed my lips together and nodded. "That would make sense. I'm just excited."

His eyes honed in on the locket around my neck and he came up the stairs to me and lifted it to inspect it. "This is pretty, and far older than you, so I would guess this was your mother's?"

I nodded. "Your guess would be correct. She always wore it. All it has in it is a piece of bark from a birch tree. She said it helped her feel closer to home, which makes sense."

His eyes narrowed on it. He said nothing, but I felt his suspicion. I wasn't sure what would be suspicious about it. I would let him tell me when he'd worked it out. I figured he was probably thinking that she was somehow able to continue drawing some power from the bark. Maybe, she had endowed it with some form of power and it acted as an amulet of sorts.

Heading back down the stairs, I turned the light on over the stove, and locked up. I felt eyes on us as we got back into the car. The barely audible deep, slow inhale from Otto let me know that he felt it too, and he was scenting the surrounding area to see if it was Lena again or anyone else we may know.

"Sammy," his voice was barely audible even to my ears, "get through that glamour by Herschel's and through the barrier. Quickly."

Putting the car in gear, I took off from the driveway like a bat out of hell. When we got to the "road" in the forest, I slowed, but only enough so that I wouldn't burst a tire or lose a wheel or something. I would ask him what was going on as soon as we got through the barrier and it was closed again.

Karl was waiting for us inside the barrier. "Lena is gone."

Otto's face turned to stone. A very angry stone. I felt the vibration coming from his chest before I heard the growl of anger coming from his throat. He had me tucked up against his side. I wasn't even sure he knew he had done it.

"Was meinst du weg?"

I cleared my throat. He must be upset. I had only heard him speak German if he was surprised, grumbling about something, or angry, which was rare. Otto usually tried to stick to English so he wouldn't have to explain over again what he'd said. Karl looked at me and then back to Otto.

"I mean, she hasn't been here all day. The last I had seen of her was when she appeared to be going to sleep for the night yesterday."

I looked up at Otto now. I could tell the leash he had on his control was pulled taut, but he didn't react further.

"Get Max and Ella. I need her tracked down." Karl nodded and took off at a brisk pace to do just what his Alpha had asked of him.

This can't be good, was all I could think. "Who are Max and Ella?"

ଔ

Otto kept walking without looking down at Sammy. "Max and Ella are the best trackers we have in the pack. Wolves. They do the majority of the meat hunting."

As a man who had been in charge for the last 60 years of his life, and had spent the remaining portion of it more dominant than most other shifters, not having control and not having eyes on someone who was potentially dangerous to his Mate was infuriating. His rage stemmed from the growing anxiety in his chest.

What has she done? Was all he could think.

First, smelling the Witches at Sammy's cottage, now Lena was gone? She had to have gone to the Witches. The question was, how did she find them?

Otto pulled out his phone and quickly dialed Karl. "Karl," was his greeting through the line. "I want you to go into Lena's home and search it. Look for anything that could indicate involvement with witches."

Otto heard Karl inhale sharply. "Okay."

Once the phone was back in his pocket, they were approaching his own home. Never letting go of Sammy's hand, he pulled her through the doors and headed up the stairs.

"What's going on, Otto?"

He felt her own nerves over his and realized that he wasn't doing very well at keeping her calm. He took a deep breath, closing his eyes. *Calm down, Old Man. Max and Ella will find her, Karl is searching her home. You are doing everything you can be doing at the moment.* "To begin, there were witches near your home. Several, in fact, as far as I could smell."

Sammy's mouth dropped and he took her by the shoulders, soothingly rubbing her arms. "So, you think Lena is responsible."

He nodded his head slowly, trying to keep the calm energy flowing. As difficult as that may be for him right now. "I do, but what I do not know is how she found them, or they her."

A look of realization came over Sammy's face. "I need to call Laurel."

Before she could, Otto's cell phone started ringing. It was Karl. "What did you find?" He nodded and asked Karl to come to his cottage in the trees. "*Vielen Dank.*"

ରେ

After hearing Otto's most recent conversation with Karl, I called Laurel. I wanted to make sure she was okay. When she picked up, I let out a breath I didn't realize I was holding. "Laurel, are you okay?" I could just picture her pinching her face up and waving her hand dismissively by her tone of voice when she answered.

"Yes, yes. I am fine. Karl already called me. His cat is finally out of the bag." I laughed, resting my forehead in my hand. The relief that had washed over me left my body feeling loose. This was a bloody nightmare.

"Good, I'm glad something good has come of this. It sounds like Lena must have broken into your home." The noise that came out of Laurel's throat would have given any of our shifters a run for their money.

"*Ja*, the bitch has some serious karma coming her way, that is a sure thing." I had never heard Laurel call someone a bitch before, and it pulled a small giggle out of me.

Ugh, stop giggling! "I'm glad you're okay, but stay safe, be around other people today please."

It was her turn to laugh. "Apparently your own cat-man gave Karl the okay to bring me to wherever you have been hiding these days."

My eyes popped open and I looked over at Otto, who was pretending not to listen to me. "Are you serious?" I was having a hard time with this piece of information.

"As a heart attack. Karl is coming to get me now." There must be somewhere these people store their cars that I haven't seen yet.

"Okay good. I will see you in a little bit then."

We hung up and I swung back around in my bar stool to look at Otto. Who was still pretending not to pay any attention to me from his armchair in the living room off of the kitchen. I walked over to him and gave him the biggest hug I could manage. He pulled me down into his lap.

"I didn't think you would ever let an outsider in here. Especially not a witch."

He sighed and his breath tickled my neck, since his face was buried there. "She is not just any witch. She is you and Karl's witch." I smiled and rested my cheek on his head.

If there weren't 20 million other things to be on the lookout for just now, I would have liked to stay like this for much longer. Apparently, Otto thought we could afford a few minutes, because his arms were like a vice around my waist. I couldn't have stood up even if I wanted to.

I was glad we had sent Luna home. I didn't want her around here for all this. She'd be pissed when I told her what all had happened so far, but she'd get over it when we came out the other side. I felt Otto's heart beating against my shoulder. It was beating relatively hard still. Paying more attention to the feelings flowing through the Bond, I felt bad. He had so much anxiety and fear for me.

This realization made me a bit sad. I shared my calm with him, and decided it was distraction time. I wiggled lower into his lap, nudged his head up with my own and caught his ear lobe between my teeth. I felt his surprise at this and he let out a deep chuckle. He stood, keeping me in his arms, and carried me back to the bedroom, shutting the door with his foot.

Chapter 27

Days had gone by with no traction. We were spinning our tires in the mud. That's what it felt like anyway. Laurel was staying where Luna and I had. Karl would "stealthily" join her in the evenings. Max and Ella had lost track of Lena on the outskirts of town. Her tracks disappeared as if she'd gotten into a car. We assumed the Witches had picked her up.

Otto had given Laurel back the items of hers Lena had taken from her home. "It makes sense that she was able to get in touch with the Witches after Karl found these." She had been upset, angry really, that Lena had broken into her home, and that her family would have anything to do with this. "This. This is why I haven't spoken to them in years."

I felt a bit of pity for her. Had my mother still been alive, I probably would have been upset with her for hiding all of this from me my entire life. I was fairly sure that the only reason I was able to forgive her for it was *because* she was dead. I understood completely.

It reminded me that I needed to be out there trying to get inside my mother's wall surrounding her home. Calling me cranky would have been an understatement. I was pretty damn upset that this had derailed my plans. Reaching up around my neck, I held onto my mother's locket. I hadn't taken it off since I picked it up from my own cottage.

"Otto?" He was always nearby, so I didn't need to raise my voice. He *hmm*'d at me from the living room. I had been sitting at the kitchen table, trying to get in some work. I was still in my probationary period at work and didn't want to get fired. I had been essentially working split shifts for the last bit through all the crazy. I worked when I could. Even on days I would normally not have. "I want to try to go out to my mother's again."

I heard him sigh, and felt his first instinct to protect, but he surprised me again and just said okay. My human heart was beginning to get just as involved as my animal's.

This still gave me pause, because I didn't want to lose another person I was close to. He was very difficult *not* to love though.

"Sammy? Come here, please."

I locked my computer and stood to go in the other room. He had the old photo frame from my parent's photo in one hand, and the photo in the other. The photo side was facing me and he was staring at the back. I quickly stood beside him on my tippy toes to see what he was looking at. He lowered the photo and I could see my mom's flowing handwriting on the back.

Nicht in meinen wildesten Träumen.

I looked up to Otto, "What does it mean?"

He sat the image in the new frame and closed it up. "It means, never in my wildest dreams."

That was something she had always said to me. When she'd talk of how much she loved me. How she could never have imagined loving someone the way she'd loved me. I wondered if she had said it to my father. It flattened my mood just a touch, to see her handwriting and have that memory of her. I knew that everyone would die eventually. Even shifters and super powerful witches like my mother, but the physical presence of the ones you missed could never be replaced. No matter how much junk food you ate, or crappy movies you watched.

Otto handed me the new frame. I looked down at the old frame and saw that it had a chip missing from it. Roughly the same size as the one in the locket. Opening the locket, I crouched down in front of the coffee table that Otto had sat the frame on. It matched. The frame was birch, and so was the chip in the locket. I put the chip up against the frame and it fit almost perfectly. Time had worn some edges, but it was a pretty close match.

"I could really use a dream right about now." I explained these things to Otto and he listened intently.

"I think there are too many little pieces that fit into the whole to ignore them," he told me carefully. Nodding my head in agreement I said that I wanted to go there today. I felt his nerves about it, but he agreed on the condition that we had to bring Herschel.

Herschel agreed to go with us, and so the three of us made our way there. I didn't want Laurel out with us in case we were being tracked by any of her family. Since my nose couldn't be trusted to scent witches while being in or near the forest, Otto was on witch-scent duty. So far, the air was clean.

I was a bit leery because I didn't have a cell phone signal this far in the woods. That didn't make me feel very comfortable in the event that we needed to call in for reinforcements. Otto had given Karl the general location of where we could be found, but who could know if we could *actually* be found that way.

I could tell we were getting closer. My spidey-senses were tingling. I was beginning to learn to pay more attention to my body, my senses, and what they were telling me. Now, wasn't the time for practice because I needed to hyper-focus on one thing, not try to spread my focus on several.

We reached the wall. Herschel and Otto looked toward me as if I was supposed to do something. I stared blankly in return, trying to put as much sarcasm into the look as I possibly could. I didn't know what the hell I was doing. Rolling my shoulders, I looked back toward the direction of the wall. I noticed that the locket around my neck was warmer than my own body temperature. Not so that it was burning, but more as if a ray of sunlight had found my chest and was warming it.

I spoke the phrase from the back of the photo in choppy German. When nothing happened, I repeated it again and again until it was no longer choppy. But still, nothing. I tried it in English... nothing.

Frustrated, I balled my fist and aimed to slam it into the wall. When my fist should have hit the wall, it shimmered and I fell straight through it. I looked around me shocked as hell and jumped up in the air. "I did it guys!" I whipped around as I stood up to look at Otto and Herschel, and they weren't there.

What the actual fuck?!

I went back through and Otto about had a fit. He grabbed me and inspected me speaking in German the whole time. I pushed back from him, swatting his hands away. "I'm fine, Otto. I just made it through the wall."

Once he was satisfied that I wasn't hurt in any way, I had him try to push through. Herschel wasn't so easily convinced to touch the barrier, considering what had happened the last time. I thought for a few moments, completely ignoring Otto and Hersch talking amongst themselves in the background. Again, my hand went to the locket. I looked down at it, while pondering the heat coming from it. It hadn't begun heating up until we were closer to the wall. Once at the wall, was when it was at its warmest.

I took hold of Otto's hand and pulled him through the wall. This time, he followed. He looked at me in confusion and I laughed. I went back through.

"Hersch, you're going to need to hold my hand to get through."

He grunted in old man. "I guess I'll just have to stay out here."

I narrowed my eyes at him, grabbed his hand in mine, and pulled him through the wall.

∞

Otto was not pleased when Sammy had gone through the wall and he couldn't see her. He had seen the wall itself shimmer and spark around her as she went through, which made him fear that she had been hurt somehow by the wall itself. Their Bond had still functioned, just at a lesser degree. When she came back through, his animal took over and had to be sure she was okay and unharmed. She was, thankfully, but he was beginning to feel a little embarrassed by his horribly protective behavior towards her. She was a woman of the 21st century after all. She would not like him hovering and being overprotective.

Just keep your head, Otto. All will be well.

When Sammy had suddenly pulled him through the barrier, he felt something akin to static electricity surge through his body. It wasn't painful, but it wasn't comfortable either. He really didn't relish the idea of going back through it, but he would have to in order to go home.

- 229 -

Otto was just glad to be through the wall and to see Sammy laughing. He could feel her joy in their success flowing with great strength through the Bond. Smiling, he touched her wrist. "You figured it out, but what is it that you figured out?"

She took the locket she had been wearing off from her neck and held it up for him and Herschel to inspect. "It was my mother's. She never took it off."

She went on to explain how she had thought it was how she kept her magic and kept herself connected to the forest. As they had been growing closer to the barrier, it got warmer and warmer. He reached out tentatively and touched the locket. It was definitely warm. Warmer than body heat would have made it. It felt as if it had been sitting out in the sun all day.

଼ଔ

"Maybe it does both." Otto figured if Sabine had been as powerful as they thought, she could empower an object to both let one through her wall, and keep her connected to the forest through its connection with the wall. "There is one thing to note from this though," Otto began. "When inside the wall, you cannot see out of it."

"Alright kids," Herschel interrupted their brainstorm of ideas. "Let's not forget our purpose in getting *through* the wall."

Otto looked at Sammy just as she rolled her eyes. "Alright, alright. Let's find my dad."

The look of determination on her face was strong. He didn't want to see her disappointed, or heartbroken, if they couldn't find Alaryk in here. Her determination was catching. Otto made eye contact with Herschel after Sammy began walking. Herschel simply furrowed his brows, nodded his head once, and took off after her. At least they were in agreement about not wanting their Sammy to be disappointed. Otto brought up the rear as they started their search of the property.

This is amazing!

It was all I could think at the time. I didn't care about Lena and her bullshit. I wasn't worried about the Witches coming to find me. We had cracked the code and made it through the wall of my mom's personal home. It felt as if nothing could keep me down. Helping this thought, was the fact that the property was so fucking beautiful! Mom must have chosen the area of the forest that had the most waterfalls for her own, because I heard at least three from where we currently were.

Her small cottage was off in the distance. As we grew nearer, I realized it wasn't as small as I thought. The sound of babbling water was also growing louder. Once the cottage was in plain sight, I could see why.

There was a large stream gushing over and bubbling down rocks to the front of the cottage. Attached to the side of the cottage was a water mill, rotating creakily as the water's strength pushed it on. The base of the cottage was stone. It appeared to be the same type of stone that was in the stream. Atop the stone was white painted wood, and dark timbers. The upper level of the cottage was painted a light yellow between the timbers. The roof was thatched. It was the most adorable home I had seen in Germany yet. I loved it even more than the cottage I rented from Herschel.

The front of the cottage had a lovely sprawling deck made of stone matching the house and stream. It was two tiered. Steps from down by the stream led up to the first tier. I could picture Mom sitting down here in the sun in the old chaise lounge chairs that remained, oddly enough, in good condition. Three more steps led you up to the tier that was level with the house. It was partially covered. Under the covered portion was wicker furniture that also remained in good condition. I was beginning to wonder if she hadn't worked some magic to preserve everything against weather and time. Wicker shouldn't still look like new after all this time.

I was standing at the door, holding my breath. My brain wanted me to make the move and open the door, but I couldn't make my body move. By opening this door, I would drastically change me and my life in one way or another. I could have a father. Alternatively, I could find that I was just crazy, my dad was dead, and all of this had been for nothing.

Otto put his hand on my waist and dragged me back to the present moment. I released the breath I had been holding, pushed down on the thumb press handle, and slid the door open.

I am not sure what I was expecting, but for a Forest Witch, it appeared incredibly mundane until you opened your eyes and truly looked at what she had. All over the home were large stones, crystal clusters, and towers. Above the front door was a besom. Stacks of journals, books, and what appeared to be grimoires were all over. Not in a messy way. In an organized, chaotic kind of way, which was so mom. Everything had a place. You might not understand it, or know why that was its place, but it just was.

In her kitchen were herbs that had long since expired. Some were hanging, as if she had intended to come back and finish the process of prepping and storing them. The hum of electricity was still present. I assumed the water mill was generating her electricity somehow.

"Sammy." I was pulled out of my peering into my mother's home by Otto's soft, deep voice. "Let's find your father. We can come back here another time to look."

I knew he was right, though I didn't want him to be. I nodded and headed for the stairs. I figured if she had put him anywhere, it would be somewhere like a bedroom.

Once at the top of the stairs, we went our separate ways. There were several avenues to explore. I assumed at least one of the doors was a bathroom. Another was a storage closet. My breath caught when I heard Herschel say my name. I spun around slowly and saw him standing in a doorway, not looking at me, but looking in the room. I walked over and stopped before I could see into the room. Otto appeared beside me and reached out for my hand. He gave it a squeeze and led me into the room.

I wasn't really sure how to feel at that moment. It seemed my eyes wanted to avoid the very person we had come here to find. Observing the furniture in the room first, I noticed that it was furnished much like the rest of the house. Antique pieces of furniture that didn't match, but somehow worked out to look good all the same. Different colors of corals and blues were everywhere. Things always came back in style. The wood in the furniture was oak. Pretty much my least favorite color of wood under the sun. There was a door into the master bathroom. It seemed her cottage was another that mirrored mine, which is strange. I wondered to myself when she built this place.

Out of things to look at, I went to the bed and touched the quilt. Just like the rest of the home, everything appeared to be untouched by dust, dirt, or age. I wondered why she didn't do this at Alaryk's cottage as well. Finally, I looked at his face.

He just looked like he was sleeping. You could see the gentle rise and fall of his chest, hear his steady and healthy heartbeat, see the youthful glow of his skin. As if somehow, he hadn't been laying here without food or water for 30 years.

The marvels continued. I touched his hand, and he was warm. The first contact I had ever had with my dad. This moment would forever be imprinted in my mind.

I'd foolishly hoped that just by someone of his bloodline touching him, especially one wearing my mother's locket, he would wake up. When he didn't move, I sighed and looked back at Herschel and Otto. "What do we do?" Both of which were just as clueless as I was.

Otto came to stand beside me and put his hand on my shoulder. The feeling I had of nothing keeping me down that I'd had such a short time ago was replaced with square one vibes. Looking up at Otto, I suddenly had deja vu to replace those vibes. I pondered over it for a moment and thought back to the photo. "I was wrong," I murmured.

Otto drew his brows in.

Looking back down to Alaryk, I very clearly spoke. *"Nicht in meinen wildesten Träumen."*

It felt like something snapped. Something tangible in the air. I looked around nervously. Otto was doing the same, backing up a bit with me behind him. Herschel whipped his hand out and I felt like Otto and I had been encased in see-through steel. I smelled his Fae magic strong in the air.

It could be assumed that he had put a bubble of protection around us. It must have been a knee jerk reaction, or the old Fae really was just that untrusting of everyone. Even someone he had known for centuries. He had never used magic around me like that before.

Alaryk took a deep, choppy breath. I was gripping both of Otto's hands tightly, standing on tiptoe behind the barrier that Hersch had thrown out. I felt it slowly dissipating, so Herschel must have been relaxing a bit. I, however, was not.

My entire body was tensed up. My jaw was clenched so tight I thought my teeth would break. When Alaryk's breathing leveled out and he began to blink his eyes, I went to speak, but couldn't figure out what to call him.

Alaryk? ... Ryk? ... Dad?

I looked to Otto for help. He always knew just what I needed. He nodded and looked back toward my dad.

"Alaryk?" There was silence for a few moments. A human could have heard a pin drop.

Finally, in a gravely, deep voice, we heard, "Kumbölt?" Alaryk blinked and began to lift his head. "Otto Kumbölt?"

Chapter 28

laryk opened his eyes, and they felt dry, unused. He moved his toes and fingers around, and it felt strange. He realized he was looking at the ceiling of Sabine's home, and not the forest in the dream realm that Sabine had placed him in. His emotions surged into him like a tsunami. He could sense people in the room. He smelled Fae. It had been a long time, but he never forgot a scent. He knew Herschel was here. He began to sense two others as if their presence was fading in somehow. Then, he heard his name. It took him a moment to place it, but not long. It had been Otto, the nearby Alpha.

Slowly, Alaryk lifted his head and saw them. Herschel looked skeptical, Otto looked relieved, and there she was. She had said her name was Samantha. He and Sabine had taken a very long time to settle on a name, because they couldn't agree on one. He had initially wanted a traditional German name, like Brigitte, or Greta. Sabine had wanted something more modern. They had settled on Samantha together, but the deal was that he got to choose her middle name. "What is your middle name, Samantha?" he asked as he sat himself up.

She looked dazed, as if she was the one in a dream world... again. "Johanne. Samantha Johanne Rush."

Alaryk smiled sadly to himself, nodding his head. She had stuck with their bargain. They would have to work on her last name. Sabine must have used false names for them. He hated that he had missed her entire life up to now, but at least he would know her. In theory, they would have a very long time to get to know one another.

"We took well into your mother's eighth month of pregnancy to agree upon your name."

She looked conflicted as if she wanted to know everything, but was unsure of just what everything was. Slowly, Alaryk stood up. He still felt strong and capable as ever, just a bit rusty. He walked to Samantha and took one of her hands from Otto. "Thank you."

¡¡

I wanted to jump up and down. I wanted to hug him. I wanted to keep my distance. I wanted to know everything! Where to begin was a conundrum. Then, he spoke to me. I was confused by his question, but answered him anyway. You would think I'd never spoken to the man before with how my body didn't know what to do, or how to think anymore.

My dad is alive, he is in the same room as me. I have a dad.

He stood up and came to stand in front of me and took my hand. When he said thank you, it was as if my brain kicked back in. I grinned up at him because he was significantly taller than me. He smiled back, and it was a smile that I saw any time I looked at a photo of myself.

I released Otto's hand, my dad's hand, and threw my arms around his neck to hug him for the first time. I wished Mom could be here with every fiber of my being. Poor Otto must have felt it all. He cleared his throat and took a small step to the side. When I had pulled back from *my dad*- that wasn't going to get any less fun to say any time soon- I could do nothing but smile. Smiling at Otto, I noticed he felt a bit tense and I lifted an eyebrow at him. I reached out to squeeze his hand and he seemed to feel more awkward.

I wondered if he was feeling weird about our relationship in my father's presence.

The father in question looked from me to Otto, our clasped hands, and took a slow breath in. He was scenting the air, and I'm sure he was looking for the Mate Bond scent. What he found had him narrowing his eyes slightly. I felt a certain irritation coming from him. *I suppose Otto knew him well enough to know he should feel weird.* I sighed and snapped my fingers in the air between them. "Hey, Alpha males!" I snapped again. "I think we have other things to discuss and have feelings about that don't involve my relationship status!"

My dad let out a surprised belly laugh and wiped his face. "Yes. Yes, you are right." He looked at Otto one more time and back at me. "But if you do not sound exactly like your mother, then my name is not Alaryk!" His eyes landed on Otto again with direct eye contact. "If she is half as... *special* as her mother was, you have an interesting life ahead, Boy." Being compared to my mom wasn't the worst thing that he could have done I supposed, so I lifted a shoulder and started to walk out of the room. I walked past Herschel and wiggled my eyebrows at him. He only shook his head at me in his grumpy old man way.

"Herschel," I heard my dad say.

I turned around just enough to see him hold his hand out to shake the old Fae's hand and use his other to pat his shoulder. *If that wasn't a perfect greeting of old people, I don't know what is,* I thought to myself. We all made our way down to the kitchen and sat around the table. I let Hersch and Otto fill my dad in on everything that had been happening with me. I was very glad that no one got their panties in a twist when the Mate Bond being sealed was mentioned. They told him what we had found out so far, and finally the situation with Lena and the Witches that was currently developing.

"What is Laurel's last name?" My dad had looked to me to answer that question.

"Fitz." He looked as if he was searching his memory.

"I believe... There is a branch of *deine Mutter's* family with Fitz as a surname. This Laurel may be a cousin of yours."

My eyebrows shot up. *Plot twist!*" So, the very people who wanted to keep me from existence, are my family?" He lifted a shoulder and I recognized it as something I did quite frequently.

"I am not sure. Fitz is a fairly common last name, but being a witch is significantly less common since the Witch Trials began in the 1600s." It struck me then, that he would have been around for that.

My father is a relic.

Suddenly, Otto's face dropped and I felt a gut-wrenching anger building. "What's wrong, Otto?" I touched his knee and he growled in his throat. I knew it wasn't him growling at me, but it did give me pause purely because of just how vicious he sounded.

"Someone is trying to get through the barrier." I gasped and he stood up.

"I have to go."

I growled and stood up so forcefully I scooted the table back a good bit. "*Not* alone you don't!" Had the power of Command not been rolling off of my body so forcefully, he probably would have argued.

"That's not fair, Samantha." Uh-oh, I must be in trouble. He called me Samantha.

"Tough cookies Mr. Alpha. This isn't just your fight." I gave him my best impersonation of a brick wall because that's exactly how flexible I felt about this matter. He expected me to stay behind when Lena was being a bitch because of me? No, no, that didn't work for me. He held my eyes, and probably only could for so long because we were mated, but I felt the vibration of Command in my entire body. Otto eventually looked away and sighed.

"Fine." His facial expression was so intense, I wasn't sure whoever we were going to catch would ever see the light of day again. "But stay where you can't be seen please. I cannot be worrying about you and focusing on them at the same time."

I nodded, taking the win. "Deal."

ଔ

I wasn't going to let any of this rain on my parade. Yes, I'd only had a father for about an hour at this point, and already we were having to rush off into possible danger, but I *had a father*. I had my friends, and last, but most definitely not least, I had Otto. That would take a while to get used to, but I would.

I had anxiety over this impending confrontation. It would be my luck that I finally found someone great, that I let them in, sealed a fucking Mate Bond, and then something would happen to him. I growled out loud at the thought. We wouldn't let that happen. Me, or my animal.

Otto and I had shifted and sprinted off. My father and Herschel were taking the Jeep back as that would take longer than the way Otto and I were going. They would get close enough to the village that they wouldn't have to walk for too long, park the car, and then Herschel would put up a glamour around them and get them as close as they could without being detected. I hated having to drag my dad into this when he had only been back in this realm for an hour or so. In theory, he was more powerful than me. I didn't know if he had any secret powers that I didn't know about either that could be of use.

We had gotten close enough to the village that we slowed down to roam the perimeter. I let my animal come to the forefront of my mind and almost completely take over. My human side needed to be silenced for now. I needed to become the predator. No human ideologies were going to be getting in the way for me tonight. I stayed at Otto's shoulder, bumping him with mine only once to remind him he wasn't in this alone.

∞

The Witches were to meet Lena at the edge of the forest near where the girl of interest's cottage was located. Adelaide knew the general location of the large village that was nestled deep in the Black Forest – but not one of the Witches would ever be able to make it past the barrier when they had tried all those years ago. It reeked of Fae magic. The Fae was a caste of magic bearers whose magic weavings were practically impenetrable, except by their own species.

Adelaide and her group were not doing this out of the goodness of their hearts. After all, witches and shifters were not exactly the best of friends, but when Lena had approached her about a deal, she was unable to pass it up. Herself and a small group of the Coven were being granted access to the village in exchange to remove the Alpha's new mate from the premises.

It would appear that Lena was having difficulty with the fact that she had been replaced in the Alpha's favor. Little did Lena know, the Alpha was their main target. From what Adelaide had seen, Otto was the strongest point of the pack. His Beta wouldn't stand a chance as Alpha. Nor was he likely to move against the Witches, seeing as he was in love with her niece Laurel.

With Otto out of the way, the Witches would be able to move in and hopefully scatter the rest of the Shifters to the wind. Then, Adelaide and her family would be able to move back into the village of her birth. This could never be achieved with the Shifters still around in such large numbers.

When they came across Lena in her Snow Leopard form, the shifter's lips peeled back, and her eyes flashed. She clearly was not any happier about working with them as they were about working with her, but everyone made sacrifices in life to get what they wanted. Although Lena was unaware that she would have her reward for helping them for a very short time...a short time indeed.

Lena scented the Witches before they arrived. Her sense of smell was her greatest strength. There were six witches in total by what she could gather, which is exactly what Lena had allowed them to have. A group of six could appear to be a small hiking party. Any more of them could draw unnecessary attention.

Watching the group approach, Lena felt a momentary sense of unease. Witches were not her favorite group in the Otherworld. Besides the centuries long feud between Shifters and Witches, the Witches were a power-hungry people. They didn't care who they had to wipe off the map to reign supreme, even if it was an entire species.

Unfortunately, they were the best shot at getting rid of the Lynx girl, and quickly. She had no idea what they were planning to do with her once they got her, but she also didn't care. Her only concern was that if they let her live for too long, Otto would sense their Bond still open and hunt them down before they'd had the chance to finish the job. She made a mental note to reiterate that to them once it was all said and done.

Lena had a plan that would be put into action once she knew Sammy was dead. Otto would be distraught, of course. Upon successfully luring him back into her arms – loneliness should help push the timeline up of this happening – she would suddenly find a clue as to where the Witches who took her and killed her were located. This was information she had due to the return address on the card she had pilfered from Laurel's house. Otto and the rest of the shifters would have no choice but to retaliate and kill the Witches.

It seemed like a fool-proof plan. Once the Coven was dead, there would be no one left to tell her tale of treachery. Lena could live out the rest of her days as contented as her cat after a large kill. She had thought this through over and over again until she could think of it no more, only act.

"Lena," said the eldest female of the group in greeting. "This is Johann, Leon, Emma, Hanna, and Petra." The woman pointed to each individual. Then, she turned her hand to her chest, "I am Adelaide. Coven leader." She pursed her lips with obvious dislike. "If this is a setup, your entire village will pay."

Lena, still in her feline form, sniffed and began her shift back to human. This didn't take her as long as it would some younger shifters. "If I were to set you up, I'm sure you would have noticed the presence of others nearby." She turned to begin walking them toward the village, showing them her back as a power play.

"Where will this Samantha girl be?" Adelaide asked mildly, as if planning the kidnapping and murder of a Shifter was an everyday occurrence...maybe it was. They did live North of the city. Perhaps they picked off lone shifters in their area, but she was sure Otto would have heard of that from other packs if someone was going around murdering lone shifters. She had the urge to drop back into her animal and melt into the barrier, but it receded quickly. She told herself she was just being silly because she felt their animosity toward shifters.

"The girl should be in the home just before you get to the Alpha's. It is roughly one mile into the village. I will show you."

Adelaide's eyes flashed. "You didn't think it was pertinent information for us to be made aware of that the place we would be absconding the girl from was *only one house away from the Alpha's*?!"

Lena's own eyes began to streak through with shimmery gold. It would be a lie to say that she wasn't trying to intimidate them. The non-Shifter community tended to forget, she may look young, but she was over 120 years of age. "Do not presume that you know more than I do, Young One. If it was pertinent information, you would have had it," she said with an heir of casual dominance. "If you do not recall," began Lena, with acid in her voice, "you are obtaining access to the village that I have called home for the majority of my life all for the price of abducting one girl."

Adelaide's lips pursed and her ears went red at being reprimanded. "We should have been made aware so we could properly plan our exit strategy."

Lena rolled her eyes at them, unimpressed. "How long do you need to plan?"

Adelaide looked at the one she'd called Johann, then back to Lena. "We'll need at least 30 minutes to discuss this as a group." With that, she flicked her wrist in the air and Lena could no longer hear what they were saying.

Well, that is an interesting party trick. She had heard of witches being able to shroud objects from the sight, but never from being heard.

Lena waited, not quite patiently, leaning up against a nearby tree. When their time was up, and they gave no sign of ending their chat, she picked up a stone and threw it at their feet. She was beginning to wish that she had just killed Sammy herself and saved herself the headache of having to deal with their certain caste of humanoid; however, she would not have been able to lie when Otto inevitably asked her if she had killed Sammy from spite.

Adelaide looked at Lena from the corner of her eye and went back to talking. Lena was sure this was a weak attempt at a dominance move. When Adelaide had finished, Lena watched her flick her wrist again and she could hear them once more. The young male, Leon, looked agitated, as if they'd had a disagreement. He was probably struggling for power and to find his place in his family group. Such was the way of men, and witches. They always needed more power.

"Did you come up with a useful plan?" she asked it sweetly, as a means to mark her heightening annoyance.

Adelaide's face was dark. "Yes. Yes we have a plan."

Lena stayed silent for a few moments more, trying to indicate that she needed to be let in on the plan, but no one rose to the occasion. She shrugged her shoulders.

Let them screw up and wind up dead then.

᎒

While in her soundproof barrier, Adelaide went on to direct that now only Petra would be going into Otto's home. Initially, the group as a whole would have gone together, but Petra was the most clever and capable of the younger witches with them today. She would be responsible for finding any information on Alaryk and Sabine.

It had been made clear, decades ago, that Sabine was still amongst the living. While there had been no sign of Alaryk, the

Shifter-God hybrid, there had been whispers from Covens in America of a German-born witch who felt as if she had the power of generations of witches. This could only be her, several times, great-aunt Sabine.

As there could only be one Black Forest Witch at a time, and this was a power that was highly coveted in her Coven, she fully intended to destroy Sabine and hoped to have the powers pass onto herself. It only seemed natural that the power of the Black Forest would go to her. As the leader of the Coven, she was the most capable of holding the power.

Lena was leading Adelaide and the group toward the Shifter village. Adelaide could feel the Fae magic getting stronger as she moved deeper into the forest. They eventually came to a clearing. Large tire tracks could be seen going toward what appeared to be a horrible excuse for a forest road. This must be how supplies were brought in and out.

Lena stopped when the Fae magic was so strong you could almost taste it. Their particular brand of magic left a dark, metallic taste in one's mouth. Highly reminiscent of blood. Adelaide and the rest stopped, a few of them wrinkling their noses. "I assume by the stench of Fae magic that we have arrived at the barrier?"

Lena nodded her head and touched it almost lovingly. She opened her lips to speak, "*Ohne die Dunkelheit kann es kein Licht geben.*"

When nothing happened, Lena's brows drew together. She tried to move through it anyway, but was pushed back. She repeated the phrase, more forcefully this time. Once again, she attempted to move through it, to no avail. "*Was ist los?!*"

Lena shifted back into her Leopard form and tried to get through the barrier the typical way of walking through in your animal form. When this didn't work, she let out a high-pitched scream that only a Leopard could manage.

As the echo of her scream subsided, she turned to look over her shoulder at the sound of a soft, commanding voice speaking her name.

Chapter 29

As Otto crept up to the scene in the clearing, Lena was shaking into her cat form. It looked like a painful shift. She was a very emotional creature. During times of high emotion, it was harder and more painful for her to shift from one form to another. At over 120 years of age, she should have conquered this, but she had never tamed her emotions.

At this point, it was he who was having to talk himself down from rage. Lena had attempted accessing the village with their pack phrase. He watched her try to walk through the barrier in her cat form. Little did she know, Herschel had rigged the barrier. Everyone had been contacted to be inside the barrier all at a specific time. Those who were inside the barrier while Herschel worked his Fae magic would be able to come and go as they pleased. This included Laurel, Herschel, and Sammy.

When Lena let out her screech, he'd had enough. Stepping forward from the thicket of bushes he and Sammy had been concealed in, Otto spoke her name. Lena slowly turned her head to look over her shoulder. Her posture hunched, knowing she had been caught. The sudden fear she felt was palpable. He was sure even her accomplices could feel it. Otto softly told Lena to change. His entire body was humming with the power of the Alpha and the need to protect what was his to protect, so she would have no choice but to shift.

As she was shifting back to her human skin, he could feel Sammy getting worked up. She was doing her best to stay well hidden. While she fought her internal battle of emotions, her tail was flicking firmly against the tree that sprung up amidst the bushes she was hidden in. He mentally apologized and quickly shut down the Bond as much as it would allow without causing them physical pain.

He could not feel her emotions and remain calm enough to keep a clear head. The more Sammy became agitated, the more agitated he himself would become. A dominant shifter, especially an Alpha, who became too emotional could be very dangerous, and he was already in a dangerous enough mood. It took a dominant with control to make calculated decisions in situations of high stress. He had always been that man. Now, was not going to be any different.

He felt the remnants of her shock, just as much as would be allowed through the restrictions he had put on the Bond. He could apologize later. His Sammy would understand. He knew this as fact. Focusing on the group, he began to slowly move closer.

As an observant man, it didn't take long for him to notice the small tattoos on each of the witches 'wrists. They had Elemental symbols, likely representing which element each witch could control. The woman who appeared to lead had an upright triangle, with a horizontal bar about a third of the way down. *The symbol for air.* Upon inspection of the rest of them, they each had a symbol to correspond to one of the four elements. At least one witch for each element.

For the most part, Otto already knew what was going on here, but he needed to hear it from Lena and maybe the Witches before he could consider his assumptions to be fact. It was time to get answers.

&

When Otto and I had approached Lena, the traitorous bitch that she was, and the Witches, it took everything I had not to leap out from the bushes. Attack first and ask questions later wasn't the best way to approach things. I had given over to the animal, and she was out for blood. Lena had endangered the lives of everyone in that barrier today. Why? Only because she was jealous and wanted me out of the way, so she could attempt to move back in on *my* Mate. My body was pulsating with anger. I felt like my skin was shimmering just from the feeling of the energy dancing over it.

As Otto shifted and prepared to move out of the bushes, he flicked his fingers out in an indication for me to stay put. I knew I would be too big of a distraction for him when he needed to be focused. While I was not offended, my animal was. It was an immense trial on my self-control to not growl at him, but I stayed quiet, energetically humming in the bushes. It was a miracle that none of them felt me. They may have possibly assumed that it was Otto they were feeling. His anger was a force in and of itself.

As Lena was slowly shifting at Otto's Command, my body was shocked at the sudden restriction on the Bond. I was momentarily frozen by it. When the feeling had passed, I exhaled heavily and tried not to make any other noises. I heard Otto begin to speak. "Who are your friends, Lena?"

When Lena struggled, trying not to respond to her Alpha, I inhaled and noticed her fear. *Good*, I thought. *She should be scared.* I have never wanted to kill someone in my life, but I now knew what the sensation felt like. Otto used Command and asked Lena again who her friends were. Who, by the way, were nowhere near scared enough of the barely restrained Alpha standing before them. They were looking smug, if nothing else.

"These are Laurel's family members." *True.* If I was any more human at that moment, I would have felt sorry for Laurel. Her family was clearly awful.

Even if you didn't know Otto was a feline shifter, you could tell just by his protective stance. "What are they doing here, with you at their lead?" His specific timber made me shiver. He exuded danger from his very pores.

"They..." she began, but stammered her way through the word. She was trying to fight Otto's forceful Command. It was no use though. He repeated the question and you could hear the barely restrained growl ripping itself from his throat with his words. She started to speak again, but the female witch at the front of the group cut her off.

"She wanted to rid the pack of the troublesome little whore you have brought into it." Her voice dripped with loathing. "I'd say, she came to the right people."

For the first time, I took a good hard look at the group of witches. You could tell right away who hated us the most. The younger man, who looked about my age, maybe a little younger, didn't look as though he wanted to be there. He was the weak link in this group. His eyes kept flitting between the people in his group and

Otto. If it came down to it, I thought we could use that to our advantage. Focusing my attention back to the woman who spoke, Otto barely gave her the time of day and continued to drill Lena with his eyes.

Otto said her name, giving her the most hateful look I had ever seen. She exposed her neck in submission, but then straightened and attempted to look him in the eye. Though the witch had already answered for her, Lena defiantly answered, "They're here for your whore." Her usually cloyingly sweet voice was full of venom.

Even through the diminished Bond I could feel Otto's anger flare, but all that he showed outwardly was to flare his nostrils and adjust his shoulders. "She had no business coming into *my* territory and taking *my* mate!" Her voice was shaking.

It would remain mind-boggling to me for a long time after this, just how ugly someone could be on the inside when they were so beautiful on the outside.

"I have never been your mate, Lena."

I watched her repeatedly ball her hands into fists as her face scrunched up in anger. "I should have been your mate! But you cast me aside!"

To be honest, I didn't see why he was wasting time talking to her.

I heard the one who had spoken for Lena muttering something about savages needing extinguished. My eyes remained on their group while Otto remained focused on Lena. Though, I was sure he still noticed their every move and heard every word. I felt power building. I was unsure if it was just to be used as backup or if they intended to use it preemptively. We wouldn't be caught off guard today.

"That little Lynx will never be half of the woman I am. Don't you remember how it was with me?" Lena's face went from fury with the threat of violence, to what I imagined was her most seductive smile she had in her arsenal.

At this, my animal gave me no option. I growled loudly and jumped from the bushes to stand beside Otto in a flash. He twitched slightly, but that was the only indication that I'd taken him by surprise. The older male witch shot his hands out quickly, startled by my sudden appearance. I assumed he put a barrier up in front of them, preventing physical attack.

Lena's mouth dropped and the Witches backed up several feet behind the barrier the man had erected. One of them falling down in the process. I smelled fear in the air, and with good reason. If a pissed off Clouded Leopard had jumped out of the bushes that way when I was unsuspecting, I would have been more than startled. The older man had an Earth symbol on his wrist. That was probably why his magic had felt almost soothing, even though I knew it should feel threatening.

Lena, now aware of my presence, stuck her pretty little nose in the air and scented me. Her eyes widened as she recognized my scent. Her head shook slowly as she spoke, "How is this possible?"

Otto growled in warning. He didn't want the Witches to know I had more than one shape. This information hadn't even been made privy to the pack, yet. With that being known, the Witches would be free to make their assumptions about my parentage and then we would never be free of them.

"Is this the girl?" the woman with the Air element marking asked.

I growled and took a step toward them, swiping my paw in the air in warning. The same woman was gathering power the whole time, and as I stepped back from my threatening swipe, she threw the power out at me.

Otto, seeing the intent in her eyes, waited until the last possible second and moved in front of me. The only thing that kept me from pure panic was feeling the Mate Bond still active. I backed up, never taking my eyes off of the Witches, and stepped over Otto, crouching protectively over his limp form.

I saw Lena beginning to move behind the group of witches, who were beginning to move and form a circle around me and Otto. I gave him a gentle nudge with my nose, attempting to wake him. I didn't want to leave him at their mercy, but I didn't want Lena to make an escape from this situation of her making. I looked down at Otto once more, seeing him barely open the corner of one eye to look at me.

Knowing he was awake and feigning sleep, I knew I was free to get to Lena. Witch magic did not work on me. This was something Laurel and I had experimented with when we found Lena had gone missing. This was likely the reason Otto had jumped in front of me. He wouldn't want the Witches to know this bit of information. I could get to Lena in a matter of seconds, and the Witches would be able to do nothing – barring physical strength – to keep me from her.

I crouched lower over Otto and quickly sprang into action. Lena turned to run as soon as she saw me begin to move. *You'll never be as fast as me, bitch.* I ducked a wave of magic sent by the older man with the Earth symbol and wove through the rest of the witches. Some jumped out of my way, not wanting to get caught in the crossfire.

The Witches definitely had their own agenda, and didn't give a rat's ass about Lena and whether or not she lived. Besides the man throwing his one weak spell at me, no one moved to protect her – so I was on her in seconds. I leapt at her from behind and clamped down hard on her clavicle. I felt bone break and blood gush into my mouth. She grabbed me by the scruff with her good arm and flipped me over her head and onto my back. Hard.

Damn it, she's strong.

This only made sense, given how old she was. After that display of strength, I knew I needed to weaken her first. I circled around her when I got my breath back, but she was obviously aware of my attack at this point and wouldn't turn her back to me. I faked to the right, and when she went to protect it, immediately lunged left and swiped at her Achilles tendon. She went down, bleeding and crippled.

I knew she would begin to heal fast, but I took this opportunity to turn back around and check on Otto and the Witches. The group of witches were completely ignoring the scene put on by me and Lena, and Otto was suspended mid-air by magic. I momentarily panicked, but knew that whatever they were doing to him wouldn't affect me.

Driven by the urge to protect my mate more than by the need to kill Lena, I left her to bleed on the ground. The Air element woman had her hands clawed, held out in front of her. I looked to Otto and saw he was gasping. I unfocused my eyes, and could immediately see a grey film bubble had been erected around him. I needed to take out one of the witches who were holding the bubble before I needed to take out the Air element.

I looked at the older man. The younger witches would likely scatter anyway if something happened to one of the elders. So, I took my chances. I started running toward the older man. He heard my approach, as I wasn't trying to be quiet, and turned. I jumped and swiped at his face. I left two, long, jagged, horrible looking gashes down the left side of his face. Facial wounds bled so much that he was covered in seconds.

As predicted, the commotion distracted the rest of the Witches. The bubble was down, the Air element distracted, and two of the younger witches were running past Lena. All by the time Otto hit the ground, sucking in as much oxygen as was humanly possible. The Air element saw her husbands'...I assumed that's who he was to her...face and ran to be next to him.

The remaining young man looked fearfully between me, Otto, and the injured man trying to decide what to do. He eventually succumbed to his fear and began to back away from the scene. Infuriated, the Air element looked at me and threw power at me. A look of surprised horror crossed her face when she saw that it didn't influence me. She threw power at me again, stronger this time, to no avail. I began to move toward her.

She quickly turned her power to Otto, thinking I would instinctively protect him. She was right, but not in the way she was hoping. Otto began writhing on the ground in pain, as if he was being electrocuted. I growled and started toward the Air element who was actively torturing him. When I jumped, I was surprised to be knocked out of the air with a rather large boulder and hit the ground. I guess since their magic wouldn't knock me down, they decided to find a loophole.

I gasped for breath – the boulder hit me with the most force right in the ribcage – and turned to look at my assailant. It was the middle-aged woman who remained, who also appeared to be an Earth element. After knocking me to the ground, she ignored me, thinking I was going to be incapacitated for longer than I was. The Air element was still torturing Otto, who was sweating profusely from the prolonged period of whatever this spell was.

As my instincts had completely taken over, I hadn't noticed the burning in the pit of my stomach. It was quite similar to the feeling at the barrier around my mother's home. The more power that was thrown around, the stronger it became. The witches ahead of me, the woman in particular, was using power in droves. The burning in my stomach was becoming so overwhelming, it did nothing to improve my mood. In fact, it made my rage stronger.

I quietly stood and began toward the group of three witches. The female Earth element now trying to help the older man to his feet while he kept pressure on his facial wounds. I crept up slowly, as low to the ground as I could, a red film at the edge of my vision. I was seeing spots. Otto was so exhausted he was barely moving. My animal had completely taken over by this point and I could no longer control myself.

A very feline scream ripped from my throat as I came up behind her, much like Lena's own scream as we came upon this scene in the forest. The Air element turned as I was mid-air, jaws dangling open to find a fatal mark. She helped me find the kill spot when she turned. When my jaws wrapped around her neck, and I felt the blood fill my mouth, everything became fuzzy. The burning inside my stomach chose this moment to snap, which made me snap.

I barely registered the massive lightning strike that came out of nowhere. Nor did I notice the other two witches begin to stumble out of the clearing. I barely registered Herschel and my father emerge into the clearing. At this point, I was on top of the woman as she had slunk to the ground, her hands gripping the fur of my neck. I felt her blood rush into my mouth in hot pulses. The animal knew what to do. I held her in my mouth this way, while straddling her to keep her immobile until she was no longer a problem; limp and unthreatening.

Otto's rough, deep inhale behind me let me know that she was gone.

Chapter 30

ven though the Witch was gone, my animal didn't want to let go. She wanted to keep hold of her and ensure that she wasn't a threat to anyone we loved anymore. She wanted to know that she was dead.

Somewhere in the distance of my subconscious, I heard someone say my name. I couldn't even decipher who it was. My animal was refusing to relinquish control over our body. She was completely in the driver's seat now. They kept saying my name, softly, soothing - whoever they were. But this just made me clamp down harder on the once-living being I held in my mouth.

My eyes were wide open, staring straight ahead. Every move I would make led to the dead woman's arm dragging lifelessly along the foliage that, like her, had fallen.

Suddenly, I felt the Mate Bond open back up to its full extent. There was an overflow of emotion coming through at me. Worry, regret, victory, love. So much all at one time. I slowly shook my head in short jerky movements trying to sort through them all, though not enough to release the body I was still clinging to. Someone touched my shoulder and began to cloud my vision with their own shape. Even though they were directly in front of me with their hand touching my shoulder, I couldn't tell who it was, so unfocused were my eyes.

Suddenly the person before me lowered their forehead to mine, even though it meant lowering themselves over a dead woman's body. When they settled in and closed their own eyes, that's when mine truly opened. I felt my pupils dilate and my heart pound, much like the night we had been hit with a Bond even though we were perfect strangers. Otto's face became clear as day in my mind, bringing the animal inside to heel and allowing me to regain control of my emotions and body. I dropped the body and shifted in seconds, throwing myself at him and wrapping my arms around his body.

When he grunted, I backed off and inspected him for any injuries and he held up his hands. "I am fine now, thanks to you. I promise." Since I still couldn't speak, I continued to inspect him until I was satisfied that he was in fact, alright. In the distance I could hear the female witch who had moved to knock me out of the way shouting at the man whose face I had torn to hurry. Which reminded me. Turning from Otto I looked behind us to see my dad and Herschel standing with us.

∞

My dad touched my shoulder. "Are you okay Samantha? I was unsure if any of us would be capable of reaching you to get you to release the witch."

I was glad he had said *the witch* instead of *the body*, because that wasn't something I was ready to face again just yet. I nodded my head slightly, "I think I am okay." Really, I just wanted to turn inward. Hide out from everyone. I could still taste her blood in my mouth and feel it in my belly. My body was covered in it and the smell was making me feel just as sick as the taste. Thinking about it just made it all start bubbling up, so I ran a few paces away and promptly was sick in the bushes.

I didn't come out of the bushes for several minutes. I threw up until I couldn't throw up anymore, and even that didn't feel like enough. One thing in my life always had the ability to make me cry. Whether I wanted to or not, and that was throwing up. Naturally, the few pitiful tears that had come out because of the vomiting, turned into full-on weeping.

I had never killed someone before. This didn't feel like just self-defense. I had *wanted* to kill her because of what she had done to Otto and planned to do to me. But the worst was that once she was dead, my animal didn't want to let go of her.

Before I knew it Otto had picked me up and carried me into the barrier. Laurel was inside, horror-stricken. She looked as if she couldn't decide between grief for the witch outside the barrier, or being horrified for me and what I had just done and been through. She reached out and touched my ankle in passing. It was gentle as if

- 253 -

she meant to let me know that she held no ill will toward me. Otto said something to her that I didn't quite catch since I was doing a pretty good job at shutting most everything out besides my own trauma right now. She turned and followed us back toward Otto's cottage and her own.

Later that evening, I woke up bundled in blankets and wrapped around a few pillows like I preferred to sleep. Based on the quality of the sheets, and the smell of brown sugar and patchouli, I knew I was in Otto's bed. I noticed my hair was damp and everything came flooding back into me.

Otto had made sure that Laurel was safely in her borrowed cottage behind us before bringing me to his, carrying me up all the stairs, and taking me directly to the shower. I had gotten sick again in the shower, and he just held my hair back and washed my face and the rest of my body for me as if it was an everyday occurrence for your mate to throw up blood into your shower.

The memory was still fresh, but I was able to look at it with a certain form of detachment now instead of with whatever the hell that was earlier. I'm not sure if it was completely healthy or not, but as long as I wasn't feeling like I did earlier, I was happy. Realizing that I was being watched, I lifted my head and looked at the doorway into the room.

Otto was leaning up against the door jamb with his arms crossed over his chest, smiling softly. "*Guten Abend meine Liebe.*"

I smiled into the pillow I was hugging. *Good evening my love.* I thought that I could definitely get used to being *his love.*

I pulled my face back off of the pillow and put it under my chin instead. "*Guten Abend... mein Lieber.*" I'd recently been researching German terms of endearment to be able to catch him off guard. I already knew the equivalent of "my love" in male or female terms. His smile broadened as he pushed off the door jamb and came to the other side of the bed.

"How are you feeling now?"

Taking mental stock of my body, I answered simply, "Hungry."

He laughed and kissed my forehead. "Then let's get food into your stomach before you waste away."

CR

After I had eaten, we decided to enjoy the nice weather while we still had it and drank some wine on the tree deck. It was early fall, so the nights were getting cooler. The temperature would rise nicely during the day, but not quite as high as they did when I had first moved in July. Herschel, Laurel, and my father joined us.

When we were all comfortable, and I had called Luna at Otto's request - apparently, he had contacted her while I was sleeping - Otto started relaying the information that had been gathered while I slept.

"I suppose I shall begin with the fact that Alaryk captured the young man who had first run off." Herschel cleared his throat. "With the help of Herschel." I could hear the smile in his voice.

Herschel spoke up at this point. "It was a simple illusion. I made it appear to them all as if they were heading in the correct direction to get out of the woods." He paused to cackle at his mastery of trickery. "Really they were being led farther and farther into the forest."

My father's deep voice commanded our attention next. "From there, it was my turn. All I had to do was track him. Catching up to him was easy." He paused to sip his wine and looked at the glass in appreciation. *I know, my dude. My Otto makes good stuff!* "I left the woman and the injured man to the mercy of the forest." I nodded at this because I didn't feel sorry for them in the slightest.

"The boy is magically kept with Laurel just behind us," Otto told me gently. I bristled at this. I didn't want any of them anywhere near us! Laurel was officially the only witch I trusted. To be fair, Lena had been one of us and look what she had done. Otto squeezed my knee in comfort. "Herschel *and* Laurel have used their magic to ensure he cannot get out to hurt anyone." I grumbled something about just being sure.

Laurel, whose eyes were healing from being red from crying, laughed at my grumbling. "I am not as weak as my family believes me to be." She gave me a sly smirk. I decided she and I were going to have to talk about that later.

"That brings us to Adelaide." Otto looked to Laurel and took her hand. "I am sorry for your loss, if she still meant something to you." My brows drew together in confusion and I looked at Laurel.

"Adelaide, the witch who attacked Otto that you rightfully killed, was *meine Tante*."

My face dropped, and my heart sank. I suddenly remembered Lena saying that they were Laurel's family members as she'd been avoiding Otto's questions.

"I don't know what to say," I began, but then apparently I did because I started babbling quickly about how sorry I was and that I had been completely taken over. How her aunt had been right, I was clearly a savage.

Laurel stopped me by holding up her hand. "I don't want to hear you refer to yourself as a savage again." I started to protest. "No," she said, "no buts. They brought this on themselves by cozying up with that bitch who tried to get you killed." I suppose she did have a point.

Though, it didn't make losing someone you may have cared about any easier. "She hasn't been my true family since I was a girl. I was never good enough for her or the rest of them. I haven't spoken to the majority of my family in many years now."

I sighed and nodded, accepting her answer. It didn't do much to alleviate my guilt over killing another person. Her voice calling us savages would be one I would hear for a long time.

Laurel saying the word family *did* remind me though. "Was Sabine Shulz part of your family?"

At this point in our crazy last couple of days, no one mistrusted Laurel because of what she was anymore, which meant that no one batted an eye at me asking her and outing myself as, well... me.

She snapped her head up to look me in the eye. "As in The Black Forest Witch? That Sabine Shulz?"

I nodded my head. "Yes. She was my mother." Her eyes popped with the realization of what that must have made me. It was fairly obvious who my father was at this point. I knew she would put it together quickly. She was a smart woman.

After the shock wore off, she smiled broadly at me and stood to give me a big hug. "Sabine was my three times great aunt." I hugged her back, extra tight.

"I'm not sure what that makes us," I said, "but I'll just call you cousin."

Herschel broke up the party by telling us that he had removed any evidence of the fight outside the barrier. I thanked him and sat back down.

"So, when did you show up to the fight?"

I was so intent on the urge to kill that I didn't hear or smell them come upon us. My dad was the one who answered, Herschel being a Fae of few words.

"We ran to the scene too late to be of much help. All we were able to do was bring the lightning to make the rest of them scatter."

Judging by the growl in his voice, I could tell he was not happy about this. As his emotions heightened, I could have sworn I heard...maybe felt... thunder, even though the sky was perfectly clear. I shook my head and looked back at him. "Thank the gods you two showed up when you did." I felt Otto's silent agreement as he took a slow breath to find his own calm again.

There was no ignoring it anymore. I needed to know. "When we were still looking for my dad, before we'd gotten into Mom's wall, the closer we would get to the wall the more I felt a heat starting here," I settled my fist right under my diaphragm to emphasize where I was referencing. "Today, while Adelaide was torturing Otto and I lost all control, I noticed it again, except it wasn't just a warming sensation or heat anymore. It was burning. It made me even angrier at the time." I was trying to explain it without going into the horribly gory details in the presence of Laurel. "After I attacked Adelaide, and I felt..." I trailed off and looked at Laurel.

"It's okay," she said. "Keep going. Don't censor yourself for me."

I nodded and continued. "When I felt her blood rush into my mouth, the sensation kind of popped. That's the last I remember of it. When I woke up earlier it wasn't there anymore." I stopped speaking, and after a while when no one spoke said, "This is where someone tells me what the hell that was!"

Otto chuckled and Herschel sighed. Laurel smiled softly, and Luna huffed into the phone. It was my dad who looked me square in the eye and spoke. "That was your grandfather's magic at work, My Girl."

I gave him a blank look. "As in *your* father's magic? The god of whom I don't know the name?" I gave him a pointed look and he answered with a chuckle.

"We will leave it that way, for the time being. My father was able to absorb magic and use it to his own benefit." *How interesting, time to look up the lore of the local gods now that everything has slowed down.*

"So, you think that's what I did? I was absorbing her magic and my mind, body, whatever just took over?" My dad nodded and said nothing more.

Clearly, not getting anything else out of him I carried on. "I have another good question for Herschel." If I hadn't been mentally and physically drained, this would have encouraged my anger to build again. "Is your illusion that you wove into the forest going to keep Lena wandering the forest until she is no longer *able* to wander?"

Herschel shook his head. "It would not, if she were still alive."

He looked me in the eye and informed me that they had found her body not far from the scene of the fight. Apparently, I had ripped through a couple of arteries and she couldn't heal fast enough to save herself. So, my body count was two. Not one.

My dad watched me for a reaction, but the only one he was likely to see was me looking smug and nodding my head. Otto poured me and Laurel another glass of wine. "Be careful with that stuff Laurel. It'll knock you on your ass."

I thought it was only fair to warn her. Witches did not have a shifter's metabolism. Otto smirked and I leaned my head back. He could tell I was over this conversation.

"I think we have spoken enough about this for one evening. Though I would like it if we could all question the boy together tomorrow?"

When everyone had agreed on a time, they all stood to go. I stood and hugged everyone, *including* Herschel, who actually had somewhat hugged me back. My dad was staying in the village tonight, so he'd be close.

I told Luna I loved her, and that I'd call her tomorrow. I could tell she was rattled.

"Laurel?" Otto said her name with great care as if handling something extremely delicate and expensive. "Would you stay for a few minutes more?"

She looked at me with a questioning expression on her face. I just shrugged my shoulders and gave her a "who the hell knows" look. Once he heard the multiple doors shut on the way down to the ground level, he saw her sway lightly while she was standing.

"Would you like to stay up here tonight so you don't have to walk down all the stairs?" She was initially going to be staying on the ground level, so she wouldn't have to be in the house with the male witch, her cousin.

She shook her head. "I'm fine to walk down the stairs, but Sammy is right. This stuff will knock you on your ass." I giggled lightly and covered my mouth with my fist. "That is not what you asked me to stay for though, surely?"

Otto shook his head, "You are correct. I wanted to ask you, if you wanted to stay here in the village... permanently."

Her eyes shot to me, and mine shot to him. "What?" Laurel and I said together.

"You're kidding. Why?"

He told Laurel that he didn't think it was safe for her to go back to her own home just yet and that he didn't know when it would be.

"Plus," he added, "it will be good to keep Karl on his toes and to make him squirm."

At that, she and I both laughed. I could just picture Karl's lightly tanned self constantly being the color of a tomato because of being flustered by her. Now, we would get to mess with him, even though I couldn't torment him with threats of outing him for what he was to her anymore.

"Maybe I should speak with him first? I don't want to seem..." Otto cut her off before she could say desperate.

"He knows I am inviting you to stay. He seemed perfectly fine with it."

Half-truth. I kept that internal and showed no outward signs of sensing the fib. Otto had to have a good reason for it.

"Yes. Yes, I'll stay." She seemed excited about it.

"We will hammer out the remaining details in the coming days. For now, I hope you sleep well, Laurel." She nodded, more light-hearted than she had been during this entire meeting.

"I'm sure I will after drinking your wine." She went in to hug him and then gave him a loud kiss on the cheek. She turned to me; I was grinning moronically at her. "Chivalry isn't dead when you're dealing with... older men." I heard her tinkling laughter as she made her way through the kitchen.

When the doors were shut and me and Otto were alone, I stood up and grabbed his hand. "Come on Old Man. Let's go get some more sleep."

Chapter 31

After interrogating the man my dad and Herschel had captured, who Laurel had informed us was named Leon, the whole fiasco was brought to light. Lena, of course, just wanted me gone. So, the witches had become her unlikely allies. More specifically, Adelaide had become her unlikely ally. The man whose face I had likely permanently disfigured, if he lived through the blood loss and Herschel's trick glamour to see the outside of this forest, was Adelaide's husband Johann. He hadn't been keen on the idea, but had caved into his wife's desires.

The woman who had helped the man get away while I dealt with Adelaide, was named Emma. She was Adelaide's younger sister. Besides probably having a bruised ego, she'd be fine. She had been the easiest of them to convince to take part in this, according to Leon. The other two who had run were Petra and Hanna, Leon's sisters. Petra had been on the fence. She was younger than Leon, only 23. He said she was very much a "love and light" type girl. She didn't think that just because their ancestors hated the shifters that they had to as well. He said that Hanna, however, was very easily manipulated.

Petra had been against it from the start. But Adelaide had been someone you didn't disagree with. Leon didn't want to be there either. Leon, Hanna, and Petra were Adelaide and Johann's children. He grieved for the loss of his mother but not her principals. Leon apologized more times than were countable. We could smell that he was telling the truth. Because he was truthful about all his information, we let him go. Had we kept him hostage in the village, it would have painted us in the same light that Adelaide had viewed us in.

"You have been kind enough to believe me and to release me," began Leon after we told him we'd let him go. "But... I am not sure of the welcome I will receive at home. Hanna is something of a telepath and she would know the thoughts that were going through my head at that time." It wasn't that we didn't want him to stay, even though we really didn't, we just didn't believe it was the best course of action.

"I believe it would be wisest for you to go home to them," Otto said. "If you are gone for too long, that's when they will become suspicious of your allegiance. They may just be glad that you are okay as of now." Leon looked as if he understood, and he went on his way after speaking with Laurel for a little bit.

Once Leon was gone, it felt mostly normal. Except that there was a witch among us. Laurel, being Laurel, had everyone wrapped around her finger within a week. Karl grumbled about people liking her so much. Especially when the people who liked her so much happened to be of the opposite sex as her. Naturally, she flirted shamelessly. Which only proved to annoy Karl further. I loved every second of it. So did the rest of the village who weren't qualified as single. Sure, a few females didn't like how much attention she garnered. But they all knew deep down who she really felt her heart belonged to. Super noses helped them out with that.

The night that Leon left, Otto broached the topic of my cottage. We were laying on the bed rolls on the platform. I had all the pillows I could want, and a space heater in the form of Otto laying next to me. "I do not think it would be wise for us to go back to your cottage now." I looked at him in confusion and he continued. "We have not found any of the witches in the woods who ran away during their failed attack. So, they must have made it out alive, despite Herschel's glamour." I stared blankly at him and I could tell he was getting frustrated. "They will come after you. You..." he stopped there, not wanting to say to me what I had done. "Think about it?"

I lifted a brow. "I don't have to think about it." His chest rumbled with an agitated growl. *Awwww, he really is worried.* He'd never growled *at* me before. So, he must be truly worried. His agitation was also clearly flowing through the Bond at me. I laughed at him and tugged on one of his curls. "I don't have to *because* I didn't think it was an issue. Obviously I'm not going back to Herschel's cottage. It's just a matter of getting all my crap here." I knew I had a huge grin on my face as his went slack with surprise. He obviously thought I was going to be putting up a fight for my freedom.

Truth be told, I probably wouldn't have gone back even if this all hadn't happened. The village had grown on me. Its people would probably take a little more time. I still preferred hiding away. Being out and around the other shifters was something I had only done a couple of times. It was too easy to be a hermit out here. Everything you needed was here, so why leave the home? "Well," Otto finally said, looking more perplexed than anything, "I am glad you agree." He sounded skeptical, as if he was waiting for the other shoe to drop. I guess he did know me after all.

"I do indeed." I snuggled in closer to him, it was pretty chilly out. "I enjoy being here, with you."

I'd spoken relatively softly, without looking at him. Feelings were new to me. Especially feelings for him. We had known each other less than three months after all. His look intensified. "I enjoy you being here with me," he responded, his voice rough. He cleared his throat. "If you are going to stay here with me, which I am very happy you have decided to, then I think we may need to solidify your place in this pack." It was my turn to look at him with suspicion.

"And how exactly do you plan to do that?" He smiled just enough to flash me his dimple, likely knowing it was my weakness.

"With an official Mating ceremony of course. You need to be introduced to the pack somehow." When my jaw dropped he used his finger to shut my mouth. "Are you objecting to this *idea?*" I felt like he was careful to use the word idea instead of proposal. Because it sure as shit felt an awful lot like a very informal proposal.

"What... what exactly does that entail?" I had this horribly indecent image in my head of us having to have sex with an audience, much like they would do in the old days to make sure a marriage was consummated.

"It is basically just an excuse to drink strong wine, bier, and eat good food. We introduce you to the pack on the day of the Full Moon, socialize with said alcohol and food, and then at the time of the Full Moon's apex, we will be the first two to shift. And we will shift together."

It seemed simple enough. But with this crowd of people, you never truly knew until you were ready to get down to it. I knew it was just the human half of me that was objecting to this, trying to slam the brakes as quickly as possible. It definitely made me want to rethink the living arrangements again. But I knew the human mask needed to be pulled off at some point. After all, I wasn't human. I was part shifter, part god, and part witch. There was absolutely nothing *human* about me, except my need to act human. Once I had spoken this, wordlessly to myself, it became much easier for me to accept this. Not only accept it, but to almost want it myself.

I let my animal come to the forefront of my consciousness more than I had since that day in the clearing. It hadn't been long, but she was feeling stifled and as soon as I let her up I took a long, deep inhale and let it out slowly. She allowed me to feel more joy in this moment than I could have without her. Only she could know what this meant for us. "Strong wine you say?" I smiled and he returned it. He kissed me and rested his forehead on mine. The peace that came over me every time he did this was incredible. It didn't take long like this for both of us to find sleep.

◌૨

The next morning, I opened my eyes to see a pretty little moth perching on one of my pretty Otto's pretty curls. It just rested there, occasionally flitting its little wings as if it was drying off the morning dew. I recognized it from my studies of the local wildlife as the Garden Tiger Moth. Otto moved to roll back over toward me, and the little moth flew away. I was glad to have woken up to catch that moment. The sun wasn't high enough in the sky yet for it to shine on him, but there was a gentle glow in the air. The kind of glow that couldn't decide if it was orange yet, or still grey.

As I sat there watching him sleep, feeling like a creep, I realized that regardless of everything that had happened since I moved here, I was no longer feeling any kind of regret about moving to Germany. Yeah, I could have died. But the trade-off was well worth it. I found my dad, Laurel, Otto, and even Herschel. I had a tribe here. I had love here. Sure, I had love back home. With Luna, and my mom. But my mom was gone, and Luna had been all I had left. I missed Luna every day. But it was about time for me to schedule a visit back home anyway. Maybe *after* I got back on track at work and out of probationary periods.

After a few more minutes of quiet contemplation, I saw the corner of Otto's mouth turn up. He slit an eye to peep out at me. I gave him a smile in return. He closed his eye back and maneuvered around all my pillows to get to me. Just to be there, in contact. "*Guten Morgen meine Liebe.*"

Snuggling down, I grinned, "*Guten Morgen, mein Knuddelbär.*" I laughed when he pressed his lips together and opened his eyes to look down at me.

"Who taught you that?" I couldn't help but to laugh even more because of the memory.

"Herschel, of course." He groaned into my pillow.

"I will not live that down if I make it to one thousand years old."

☙

The days went on like this. I formed a solid routine. Work, knit, movies, hang out with Dad, observe. Otto, Karl, and some others helped bring all the rest of my stuff from Herschel's cottage back to Otto's. Or, *ours*. I needed to get used to that. I'd never shared space with someone like that before, so it was going to be an adjustment. I wasn't worried though. Luckily, the home was large enough that I didn't have to get rid of anything. And since I had not brought any furniture, I didn't have to move anything like that, except my TV, blu ray, and soundbar.

I had to watch Otto's movements with the pack. He did more than I realized. He held meetings with the higher-ranking members of the pack. I learned there were also meetings involving other packs in the country, as well as surrounding countries. Twice a year, there was even a meeting with the packs from other continents where a representative from each country was chosen, and they would go to the meeting to represent the whole country. Otto had been chosen incredibly frequently since he had become Alpha, and it was almost annually at this point in time that he was chosen.

The second global meeting for the year was coming up and he was being called on again to be a part of it. He didn't seem terribly thrilled about this, but told me it wasn't that he didn't enjoy it. He just wanted to be home with his Mate. He wanted to keep me hidden from the rest of the shifter world for a while. So, I'd be staying home this go around. Which as much as I wanted to be with him too, I didn't relish the idea of anyone catching on to who I was. I still hadn't even gone out around this pack. Whispers were going around, at least that's what Laurel would tell me. But in a few days, on the Full Moon, they would finally all get to officially meet me. I just hoped what happened with Luna after the Bond was sealed didn't happen to *everyone*.

I wasn't allowed to help prepare for anything, because then I would be around people and ruin the whole thing in his eyes. Because if I helped, they would see me. It was beginning to get annoying. But it was mostly taken care of at this point anyway. I did get to help him at least to replenish much of the wine stores that we would be using up for this. Normally I would say drunken shifters were a bad idea, especially on a Full Moon. They are territorial as hell on the best of days. Especially if there were any who were particularly close in their level of dominance. A challenge could happen when they weren't fully in the right frame of mind to make wise choices.

Hanging out with my dad was full of awkward moments. We were both not the best when it came to expressing ourselves. But he was quick to laugh, even if it was at his own expense. So, we got along just fine. He refused to tell me, for now he said, who his father was. And I was having absolutely *no* luck and figuring out who he was on my own. Not surprisingly, Germanic deities didn't have a plethora of information available to them on the internet. I made it a point to go to some bookstores and buy the *Prose Edda* just to see if it would help me out a bit. But I hadn't started reading it yet. I had time. I was a shifter. Unless something happened again, which I'm sure it would eventually, I had a long time to learn.

It was the day before the Full Moon; the air was crisp. We had dipped to a high temperature of 42°F (I would probably never get the hang of Celsius). My dad and I were sitting on the deck drinking coffee while Otto was going off speaking with Karl and some others about some minor planning for the next day. "There is something I wanted to talk to you about, Samantha."

I set my coffee down, suddenly nervous. We hadn't talked about anything really deep yet so I was not mentally prepared for anything of the sort. "Okay... shoot." He smiled lightly and took a drink of his own coffee before setting it down.

"I am just going to come out and say it, there's no other way to do it," he sighed and tapped his hand on the table. I was really nervous now. I bit my lip and just waited. "I do not... I do not think *deine Mutter* is dead."

If I hadn't sat my coffee down, I would have dropped it at this point, or squeezed it so hard that the cup would have broken in my hands. "What do you mean? That's not funny."

He wiped his hands down his face and looked me directly in the eye. "I would not have brought this up to you if I hadn't thought about it long and hard. Use your senses while I say this, I do *not* think your mother is dead."

Truth. Well, what the fuck! "What makes you think she isn't dead? I buried her back home. I saw them lower her into the ground." My voice went up and octave with each statement.

"Calm down," he told me with authority. "We do not need every pack member feeling your distress and having their own panic attacks." He was right. One of the downsides of being so near the "one Alpha to lead them all" was that my emotions were everyone's emotions if they were strong enough. Which hadn't been much of an issue up to now. I took a deep calming breath, but all I could see was Mom's casket being lowered into the ground.

"If Sabine was no longer with us," I was glad he switched terminology, "then her sleep spell would have died with her and I would have awoken. Her magical wall around her home would have melted. Her anti-grime and deterioration spell in her home would have stopped working, the Black Forest Witch magic would have transferred to someone else." He counted the examples off on his fingers. "You get the idea, I am sure. All of these things lead me to believe that maybe she *was not* killed in a car accident. *Maybe*, just maybe, she did to herself in a fashion, what she did to me."

I didn't want to get my hopes up, and I wasn't sure how I felt about this anyway. Half of the reason I wasn't pissed at Mom for keeping everything from me was *because* she was dead. I had no idea how I'd feel with her if she wasn't.

My dad took my silence as his queue to keep talking. "What if the witches were close to finding the two of you? They knew she was largely pregnant when she disappeared. So, someone would have still been looking for her. Who knows for how long. And if they had gotten close to you, she would have done whatever it took to keep you safe." This all sounded exactly like something Mom would do. Especially after finding out what she had done to Dad.

"Okay," I said finally. "What if... what you say is true, then how do we find her? It's not like I'm having weird dream-walker-like experiences like I did with you, where my soul completely leaves this damn realm."

He sighed and shook his head. "I do not know, *Liebling*." He picked up his coffee again and took a few sips. "You know, coffee has gotten significantly better in the last thirty years." I lifted a brow at the abrupt subject change.

"I am a coffee snob and I order a specific brand." I paused briefly, and realized I wasn't quite ready to stop talking about my mom. "We'll find out. I don't care what we have to do. It doesn't matter the result. At least we will know for sure."

He agreed silently, and we drank the rest of our coffee talking about nothing in particular. Favorite colors and such. Just trying to get to know each other.

Chapter 32

The night of the full moon had finally arrived. It felt like those few days had taken decades. I was having anxiety about going out and meeting everyone officially. Not to mention being shown off and shifting in front of everyone. The inevitable having to get naked in front of everyone prior to shifting, more specifically. There was also the little nugget of information that I didn't know what I was going to shift into.

If I look back, this was my main fear. Outing who I was to the rest of the pack. Look what happened with Lena. That was just because of pure jealousy of Otto being with me - even though she and Otto hadn't been together physically in decades. What if someone took me as a threat to the Shifter way of life? What if someone was prejudiced against any form of anomaly? The witches obviously were if they were still looking for my mom. Otto seemed to trust the pack with my secret. So, I would have to trust his judgment.

What the fuck am I supposed to wear to this?! I was beginning to freak out about the little things. Did I wear a cute, flowy sundress with a cardigan? Did I wear sweats and a sweatshirt for ease of removal when I inevitably had to get naked and shift in front of strangers... and my father? *Good lord Sammy. Pull yourself together.* This is the moment that my apparent surprise walked in the door.

"Hey Bob." I turned around so fast; I wasn't sure if my head would stop spinning. There stood Luna and Laurel together. Both grinning. I stood up from my pile of clothes and had to stop myself from tackling my pregnant best friend.

"You're here!" I said, as I threw my arms around her neck.

"Of course, I am. You think I'm going to miss this? And now that it's relatively safe, Otto and my own Alpha male approved this pregnant lady's visit." I glanced up at Laurel while still hugging Lu to see that she was all misty-eyed.

I laughed at her, "Shouldn't I be the one with tears in her eyes?" Laurel quickly wiped them away.

"Allergies." She sniffed and sobered her face. "Now," began Laurel, "let's get you something to wear so you can stop freaking out all the shifters within a ten-mile radius."

I blushed and went back to my piles. In the end, they chose a pair of black skinny jeans, a cozy cowl-neck sweater, and a pair of flat boots. Laurel muttered something about not being able to wear heels on the forest floor. Forever the woman of fashion.

"Thank you guys. You're seriously the best friends a misfit like me could ever ask for." It was almost my turn to get misty-eyed. But I didn't want to ruin the makeup that Laurel had insisted upon fussing with.

ର

The Apex of the moon was a couple hours away at this point, and I was beginning to feel her call. I sat on the deck with Luna and Laurel for the majority of the day. The two of them were getting along fabulously, and truly getting to know each other. Lu, of course, would tell stories from our younger days. Mainly ones where I wound up falling out of a tree, or getting us caught while trying to spy on the pack back home. Basically, any story that made me look dumb. But I was okay with it. I liked that they were getting along so well, even at my expense.

I heard the door from the stairs open and close, and eventually saw Otto walk through the kitchen and to the back door. He smiled his slow smile and did a little half bow, holding out his hand for me. *Shit.* The man could make any activity look appealing; I was sure of it.

I took his hand and let him pull me to my feet. I heard Luna and Laurel sigh at the same time and shot them a glare over my shoulder. "Everything, and everyone, is ready. The time has come to be introduced to the pack." There was a glint of mischief in his eye.

I narrowed my eyes at him. "What are you not telling me?" His smile widened and he shrugged. Dismissing my question. Once we got down to the main level door, I smelled what I would soon learn that he was hiding. Sitting in the kitchen area, was who I assumed was Otto's family - considering one of the males looked strikingly like Otto. They all turned and smiled warmly at the same time.

"Hallo Samantha! Welcome to the family!" Said one of the women. Being shifters, it was hard to determine who were the grandparents, and who were the parents. My confusion must have been evident. "I am Sylvie, Otto's *Mutter*." I went in for a handshake and wound up being pulled into a hug. *There really is no way to be awkward with these people, is there?* I saw Luna smirking over Sylvie's shoulder, and I knew I was in for at least four more hugs.

I was right. I was introduced to, and hugged by Harlow, Anna, Hans, and Lorelei, after I was initially hugged by Sylvie. Harlow and Sylvie were Otto's parents, Anna and Hans were Otto's grandparents, and Lorelei was Otto's sister. Otto very kindly suggested we move the party outside, now that the introductions were out of the way. Which was somehow less threatening to me than sitting in here with his entire family. I had never met someone's family before. So naturally, I was sweating in my sweater.

ℂѲ

Going outside wasn't so bad. There was no formal entry or anything. Thank the baby jesus. We meandered through the crowd of people, who were either eating, or drinking, or both - stopping to talk to most along our way to the food and drink. There was music playing from somewhere, loud enough to be heard over the voices, but quietly enough that it wasn't obnoxious. I went straight for the wine. That should kill the nerves.

Two glasses in and the nerves were all but gone. I was having fun, talking and laughing with people I barely knew. All of whom were quite open and accepting of me. So many of them verbalized their happiness that Otto had been Mated. I learned that Lorelei was the Alpha of a pack in Northern Germany. Which was surprising, as a female Alpha was still not something that was common amongst the Shifter community.

It must have been a silent agreement to not mention Lena and her craziness. I could feel when someone wanted to mention it, as they'd have a look of sorrow in their eyes for a moment. They never did though. No one marred the occasion with her.

I knew when it was almost time for us to shift. The chatter died down, and some of the younger pack members began to get jittery. My dad, Herschell, and Laurel moved to a tree-top balcony to watch what they said was sure to be a show. I think they were just as curious as me to see if I would take a new form tonight. The pack began to form a ring around us - bodies close together. Smaller children and younger pack members in the front of the ring of bodies. I looked up at Otto and drank the rest of my wine in two large gulps, setting the glass on the ground next to me.

Nerves mostly gone, we all undressed in unison. Even Lu. Her baby bump made me smile. She smiled back at me, as she was in front of me in the circle of Shifters. I took a deep breath, and it seemed like everyone else did too. Otto began his change, and I closed my eyes and willed the change to wash over me. I felt the tingling sensation that had become familiar to me. But no pain. I was changed. Not just in form, but in physiology it would seem.

A new form should have brought a painful change as it had the first couple of times. This time, just a warm tingle. I looked up with incredibly sharp vision at my dad, Laurel, and Herschel. Their mouths gaping open. I did a hop or two, then extended a near 8-foot span of wings from tip to tip. I pulsed them several times before leaping up and landing on the banister next to my father. He reached out and touched the soft feathers of my belly. I looked back down at the ground to see Otto's Jaguar looking up at me with a smile in his eyes.

I let out a screech, and everyone watched in unison, as a Golden Eagle flew through the opening in the trees toward the Moon that called her.

Epilogue

Johann had walked with Emma for so long to get out of that damn forest. He knew most of those woods like the back of his hand. Yet, it had taken them days before they finally stumbled across a road that he knew. As soon as they had gotten out of the trees the illusion had dropped. Emma had done a healing spell on his face to get the bleeding to stop. Though he wanted to tell her to just let him die. His Adelaide had died and now he was left here, alone, with a face that was likely permanently disfigured.

He hadn't wanted to be part of this plan of Adelaide and Lena's initially, but Addy had convinced him that they needed to find Sabine and whatever offspring she had. Since none of them would have any luck trying to get into Alaryk's cottage with the Fae magic surrounding it, this seemed like the only alternative. Sabine had been exceedingly powerful, but away from the forest she should have been weak enough for them to find her. That wasn't the case. They had never even found where her cottage was located in the forest.

Now? Now, not only did he want to find Sabine and her abomination of an offspring, but he wanted to take the Alpha and his mate down in the process just as Addy and Lena had planned to do in the first place. Revenge was not something Johann had ever grown a taste for, but his love was gone. He wasn't sure where their children were and if they were able to get out of the forest. They would not have help with their next plan. Lena's body had been found on the way out. It looked like several major vessels in her neck and clavicle had been severed by the strange Leopard in the forest.

Now, sitting on his couch, covered in his own blood and unwilling to move, he began to plan.

www.ingramcontent.com/pod-product-compliance
Lightning Source LLC
Chambersburg PA
CBHW060529260626
47161CB00003B/828